Praise for the first edition o,

IMAGINING AMERICA: STORIES FROM THE PROMISED LAND

Edited by Wesley Brown & Amy Ling

"It's hard to imagine a more eloquent argument against cultural America-Firstism than this marvelous anthology. The voices telling these 37 short stories about immigration to, and migration within, America are as varied as a United Nations membership list, yet highly personal, too.... A vibrant book about a multiplicity of struggling people forming and re-forming a nation."
—*Washington Post Book World*

"[An] unusual and engaging anthology..." —*The Nation*

"[A] potent short story anthology.... *Imagining America* ... hits with sustaining force." —*American Book Review*

"Rich in diversity of viewpoint and literary style, this collection defines multiculturalism, which, we're slowly recognizing, defines America." —*Booklist* (starred review)

"[T]his book is a *must* for the general reader and should be available in every public library." —*Choice*

"Both celebration and indictment, this eloquent anthology well suits the current interest in multiculturalism. Highly recommended for all collections." —*Library Journal*

"Stories [in *Imagining America*] are arranged thematically and expose much more of a sense of place and past than any similar-sounding anthology could achieve." —*Midwest Book Review*

"An excellent tool for exposing young adults to the multicultural experience." —*School Library Journal*

|||||||||||||||||||||||||||||||||||||||||||| REVISED EDITION ||||||||||||||||||||||||||||||||||||||||||

IMAGINING AMERICA

STORIES FROM THE PROMISED LAND

|||||||||||||||||||||||||||||||||||||||||||||||||||||||||||||||||||||||||||||||||||||||||||||||||||||||||||||

EDITED BY WESLEY BROWN & AMY LING

A Karen & Michael Braziller Book

PERSEA BOOKS / NEW YORK

ACKNOWLEDGMENTS

Many people aided us in the completion of this book. For their encouragement and helpful suggestions we thank Magda Bogin, Mitchell Horowitz, Irving Howe, Betsy McTiernan, Julian Moynahan, Molly Moynahan, Ted Solotaroff, Chuck Wachtel, and Cheryl Wall.

Since this page cannot legibly accommodate all copyright notices, pages 401-404 constitute an extension of the copyright page.

Persea Books, Inc.
853 Broadway, Suite 604
New York, NY 10003

Library of Congress Control Number: 2002116921

ISBN 0-89255-277-8

Second Paperback Printing

CONTENTS

III. CROSSINGS

FOR AMY LING
(1939–1999)

INTRODUCTION

This anthology is a reimagining, through short stories, of emigration to and migration within the United States from the first days of the twentieth century to the present. Encompassing the experiences of the nation's first inhabitants, its oldest immigrants, and its most recent arrivals, these stories explore the manner in which a diverse group of writers has imagined an America mythologized for its promise and indicted for its practice. Reconciling our high-minded rhetoric as a nation with our actual behavior as citizens continues to be the pivotal issue in the more than two-hundred-year-old argument over our national identity and the meaning of democracy. When taken together, the stories collected here show not only the different cultural voicings that shape American life but also the remarkable variety and richness of twentieth-century and more recent American fiction.

Since the first edition of *Imagining America: Stories from the Promised Land* in 1991, there has been a proliferation of fiction examining the emotional landscape of America from formerly uncharted perspectives. Fiction writers such as Jessica Hagedorn, Junot Díaz, Edwidge Danticat, David Wong Louie, Chitra Divakaruni, and Sherman Alexie have enriched the ways we continue to reinvent an America still engaged in the arduous business of fulfilling the unrealized promise of democracy. It is fitting, as we begin a new millennium, to put these and other emergent writers into dialogue with many of the writers of the earlier edition in the hope of discovering whether what they have to tell us about ourselves has changed. And if not, why not? and if so, to what extent?

We have retained the part divisions under which the stories in the first edition appeared—Arriving, Belonging, Crossings, and Remembering—since they are also relevant to the new stories. In our reading, a thematic pattern emerges naturally that is replicated again and again in fictional portrayals of characters who first experience disorientation upon arrival in an alien country or city, then struggle to gain acceptance in an indifferent or hostile environment, then make the effort to negotiate the often antagonis-

tic borders of language and race, and finally use memory as a way to rec-
oncile the life left behind with the acquisition of a new life.

Whether the stories concern the lengths people will go to come to
America (Bernard Malamud's "The German Refugee" and Edwidge
Danticat's "Children of the Sea"), the importance of community for those
who are viewed as permanent outsiders (Grace Paley's "The Loudest Voice"
and Jewelle Gomez's "Don't Explain"), the risks and consequences involved
in seeking a wider world beyond the one we are born into (Paule Marshall's
"To Da-Duh, In Memoriam" and Junot Díaz's "How to Date a Browngirl,
Blackgirl, Whitegirl, or Halfie"), or the indispensability of the past to the
present or an imagined future (Richard Bausch's "Old West" and Sherman
Alexie's "A Drug Called Tradition"), the fictional voices in this anthology
persist in challenging the collective myths we create about ourselves in all
their thrilling dissonance.

Wesley Brown
September 2002

I. ARRIVING

IN THE LAND OF THE FREE

Sui Sin Far

1.

"See, Little One—the hills in the morning sun. There is thy home for years to come. It is very beautiful and thou wilt be very happy there."

The Little One looked up into his mother's face in perfect faith. He was engaged in the pleasant occupation of sucking a sweetmeat; but that did not prevent him from gurgling responsively.

"Yes, my olive bud; there is where thy father is making a fortune for thee. Thy Father! Oh, wilt thou not be glad to behold his dear face. 'Twas for thee I left him."

The Little One ducked his chin sympathetically against his mother's knee. She lifted him on to her lap. He was two years old, a round, dimple-cheeked boy with bright brown eyes and a sturdy little frame.

"Ah! Ah! Ah! Ooh! Ooh! Ooh!" puffed he, mocking a tugboat steaming by.

San Francisco's waterfront was lined with ships and steamers, while other craft, large and small, including a couple of white transports from the Philippines, lay at anchor here and there off shore. It was some time before the *Eastern Queen* could get docked, and even after that was accomplished, a lone Chinaman who had been waiting on the wharf for an hour was detained that much longer by men with the initials U.S.C. on their caps, before he could board the steamer and welcome his wife and child.

"This is thy son," announced the happy Lae Choo.

Hom Hing lifted the child, felt of his little body and limbs, gazed into his face with proud and joyous eyes; then turned inquiringly to a customs officer at his elbow.

"That's a fine boy you have there," said the man. "Where was he born?"

"In China," answered Hom Hing, swinging the Little One on his right shoulder, preparatory to leading his wife off the steamer.

"Ever been to America before?"

"No, not he," answered the father with a happy laugh.

The customs officer beckoned to another.

"This little fellow," said he, "is visiting America for the first time."

The other customs officer stroked his chin reflectively.

"Good day," said Hom Hing.

"Wait!" commanded one of the officers. "You cannot go just yet."

"What more now?" asked Hom Hing.

"I'm afraid," said the customs officer, "that we cannot allow the boy to go ashore. There is nothing in the papers that you have shown us—your wife's papers and your own—having any bearing upon the child."

"There was no child when the papers were made out," returned Hom Hing. He spoke calmly; but there was apprehension in his eyes and in his tightening grip on his son.

"What is it? What is it?" quavered Lee Choo, who understood a little English.

The second customs officer regarded her pityingly.

"I don't like this part of the business," he muttered.

The first officer turned to Hom Hing and in an official tone of voice, said:

"Seeing that the boy has no certificate entitling him to admission to the country you will have to leave him with us."

"Leave my boy!" exclaimed Hom Hing.

"Yes; he will be well taken care of, and just as soon as we can hear from Washington he will be handed over to you."

"But," protested Hom Hing, "he is my son."

"We have no proof," answered the man with a shrug of his shoulders; "and even if so we cannot let him pass without orders from the Government."

"He is my son," reiterated Hom Hing, slowly and solemnly. "I am a Chinese merchant and have been in business in San Francisco for many years. When my wife told to me one morning that she dreamed of a green tree with spreading branches and one beautiful red flower growing thereon, I answered her that I wished my son to be born in our country, and for her to prepare to go to China. My wife complied with my wish. After my son was born my mother fell sick and my wife nursed and cared for her; then my father, too, fell sick, and my wife also nursed and cared for him. For twenty moons my wife care for and nurse the old people, and when they die they bless her and my son, and I send for her to return to me. I had no fear of trouble. I was a Chinese merchant and my son was my son."

"Very good, Hom Hing," replied the first officer. "Nevertheless, we take your son."

"No, you not take him; he my son too."

It was Lae Choo. Snatching the child from his father's arms she held and covered him with her own.

The officers conferred together for a few moments; then one drew Hom Hing aside and spoke in his ear.

Resignedly Hom Hing bowed his head, then approached his wife. "'Tis the law," said he, speaking in Chinese, "and 'twill be but for a little while— until tomorrow's sun arises."

"You, too," reproached Lae Choo in a voice eloquent with pain. But accustomed to obedience she yielded the boy to her husband, who in turn delivered him to the first officer. The Little One protested lustily against the transfer; but his mother covered her face with her sleeve and his father silently led her away. Thus was the law of the land complied with.

2.

Day was breaking. Lae Choo, who had been awake all night, dressed herself, then awoke her husband.

"'Tis the morn," she cried. "Go, bring our son."

The man rubbed his eyes and arose upon his elbow so that he could see out of the window. A pale star was visible in the sky. The petals of a lily in a bowl on the windowsill were unfurled.

"'Tis not yet time," said he, laying his head down again.

"Not yet time. Ah, all the time that I lived before yesterday is not so much as the time that has been since my Little One was taken from me."

The mother threw herself down beside the bed and covered her face.

Hom Hing turned on the light, and touching his wife's bowed head with a sympathetic hand inquired if she had slept.

"Slept!" she echoed, weepingly. "Ah, how could I close my eyes with my arms empty of the little body that has filled them every night for more than twenty moons! You do not know—man—what it is to miss the feel of the little fingers and the little toes and the soft round limbs of your little one. Even in the darkness his darling eyes used to shine up to mine, and often have I fallen into slumber with his pretty babble at my ear. And now, I see him not; I touch him not; I hear him not. My baby, my little fat one!"

"Now! Now! Now!" consoled Hom Hing, patting his wife's shoulder reassuringly; "there is no need to grieve so; he will soon gladden you again. There cannot be any law that would keep a child from its mother!"

Lae Choo dried her tears.

"You are right, my husband," she meekly murmured. She arose and stepped about the apartment, setting things to rights. The box of presents she had brought for her California friends had been opened the evening before; and silks, embroideries, carved ivories, ornamental lacquer-ware, brasses, camphorwood boxes, fans, and chinaware were scattered around in confused heaps. In the midst of unpacking the thought of her child in the hands of strangers had overpowered her, and she had left everything to crawl into bed and weep.

Having arranged her gifts in order she stepped out on to the deep balcony.

The star had faded from view and there were bright streaks in the western sky. Lae Choo looked down the street and around. Beneath the flat occupied by her and her husband were quarters for a number of bachelor Chinamen, and she could hear them from where she stood, taking their early morning breakfast. Below their dining-room was her husband's grocery store. Across the way was a large restaurant. Last night it had been resplendent with gay colored lanterns and the sound of music. The rejoicings over "the completion of the moon," by Quong Sum's firstborn, had been long and loud, and had caused her to tie a handkerchief over her ears. She, a bereaved mother, had it not in her heart to rejoice with other parents. This morning the place was more in accord with her mood. It was still and quiet. The revellers had dispersed or were asleep.

A roly-poly woman in black sateen, with long pendant earrings in her ears, looked up from the street below and waved her a smiling greeting. It was her old neighbor, Kuie Hoe, the wife of the gold embosser, Mark Sing. With her was a little boy in yellow jacket and lavender pantaloons. Lae Choo remembered him as a baby. She used to like to play with him in those days when she had no child of her own. What a long time ago that seemed! She caught her breath in a sigh, and laughed instead.

"Why are you so merry?" called her husband from within.

"Because my Little One is coming home," answered Lae Choo. "I am a happy mother—a happy mother."

She pattered into the room with a smile on her face.

*   *   *

The noon hour had arrived. The rice was steaming in the bowls and a fragrant dish of chicken and bamboo shoots was awaiting Hom Hing. Not for one moment had Lae Choo paused to rest during the morning hours; her activity had been ceaseless. Every now and again, however, she had raised her eyes to the gilded clock on the curiously carved mantelpiece. Once, she had exclaimed:

"Why so long, oh! why so long?" Then, apostrophizing herself: "Lae Choo, be happy. The Little One is coming! The Little One is coming!" Several times she burst into tears, and several times she laughed aloud.

Hom Hing entered the room; his arms hung down by his side.

"The Little One!" shrieked Lae Choo.

"They bid me call tomorrow."

With a moan the mother sank to the floor.

The noon hour passed. The dinner remained on the table.

3.

The winter rains were over; the spring had come to California, flushing the hills with green and causing an ever-changing pageant of flowers to pass over them. But there was no spring in Lae Choo's heart, for the Little One remained away from her arms. He was being kept in a mission. White women were caring for him, and though for one full moon he had pined for his mother and refused to be comforted he was now apparently happy and contented. Five moons or five months had gone by since the day he had passed with Lae Choo through the Golden Gate; but the great Government at Washington still delayed sending the answer which would return him to his parents.

Hom Hing was disconsolately rolling up and down the balls in his abacus box when a keen-faced young man stepped into his store.

"What news?" asked the Chinese merchant.

"This!" The young man brought forth a typewritten letter. Hom Hing read the words:

"Re Chinese child, alleged to be the son of Hom Hing, Chinese merchant, doing business at 425 Clay Street, San Francisco.

"Same will have attention as soon as possible."

Hom Hing returned the letter, and without a word continued his manipulation of the counting machine.

"Have you anything to say?" asked the young man.

"Nothing. They have sent the same letter fifteen times before. Have you not yourself showed it to me?"

"True!" The young man eyed the Chinese merchant furtively. He had a proposition to make and was pondering whether or not the time was opportune.

"How is your wife?" he inquired solicitously—and diplomatically.

Hom Hing shook his head mournfully.

"She seems less every day," he replied. "Her food she takes only when I bid her and her tears fall continually. She finds no pleasure in dress or flowers and cares not to see her friends. Her eyes stare all night. I think before another moon she will pass into the land of spirits."

"No!" exclaimed the young man, genuinely startled.

"If the boy not come home I lose my wife sure," continued Hom Hing with bitter sadness.

"It's not right," cried the young man indignantly. Then he made his proposition.

The Chinese father's eyes brightened exceedingly.

"Will I like you to go to Washington and make them give you the paper to restore my son?" cried he. "How can you ask when you know my heart's desire?"

"Then," said the young fellow, "I will start next week. I am anxious to see this thing through if only for the sake of your wife's peace of mind."

"I will call her. To hear what you think to do will make her glad," said Hom Hing.

He called a message to Lae Choo upstairs through a tube in the wall.

In a few moments she appeared, listless, wan, and hollow-eyed; but when her husband told her the young lawyer's suggestion she became electrified; her form straightened, her eyes glistened; the color flushed to her cheeks.

"Oh," she cried, turning to James Clancy. "You are a hundred man good!"

The young man felt somewhat felt embarrassed; his eyes shifted a little under the intense gaze of the Chinese mother.

"Well, we must get your boy for you," he responded. "Of course"— turning to Hom Hing—"it will cost a little money. You can't get fellows to hurry the Government for you without gold in your pocket."

Hom Hing stared blankly for a moment. Then: "How much do you want, Mr. Clancy?" he asked quietly.

"Well, I will need at least five hundred to start with."

Hom Hing cleared his throat.

"I think I told to you the time I last paid you for writing letters for me and seeing the Custom boss here that nearly all I had was gone!"

"Oh, well then we won't talk about it, old fellow. It won't harm the boy to stay where he is, and your wife may get over it all right."

"What that you say?" quavered Lae Choo.

James Clancy looked out of the window.

"He says," explained Hom Hing in English, "that to get our boy we have to have much money."

"Money! Oh, yes."

Lae Choo nodded her head.

"I have not got the money to give him."

For a moment Lae Choo gazed wonderingly from one face to the other; then, comprehension dawning upon her, with swift anger, pointing to the lawyer, she cried: "You not one hundred man good; you just common white man."

"Yes, ma'am," returned James Clancy, bowing and smiling ironically.

Hom Hing pushed his wife behind him and addressed the lawyer again: "I might try," said he, "to raise something; but five hundred—it is not possible."

"What about four?"

"I tell you I have next to nothing left and my friends are not rich."

"Very well!"

The lawyer moved leisurely toward the door, pausing on its threshold to light a cigarette.

"Stop, white man; white man, stop!"

Lae Choo, panting and terrified, had started forward and now stood beside him, clutching his sleeve excitedly.

"You say you can go to get paper to bring my Little One to me if Hom Hing give you five hundred dollars?"

The lawyer nodded carelessly; his eyes were intent upon the cigarette which would not take the fire from the match.

"Then you go and get paper. If Hom Hing not can give you five hundred dollars—I give you perhaps what more that much."

She slipped a heavy gold bracelet from her wrist and held it out to the man. Mechanically he took it.

"I go get more!"

She scurried away, disappearing behind the door through which she had come.

"Oh, look here, I can't accept this," said James Clancy, walking back to Hom Hing and laying down the bracelet before him.

"It's all right," said Hom Hing, seriously, "pure China gold. My wife's parent give it to her when we married."

"But I can't take it anyway," protested the young man.

"It is all same as money. And you want money to go to Washington," replied Hom Hing in a matter-of-fact manner.

"See, my jade earrings—my gold buttons—my hairpins—my comb of pearl and my rings—one, two, three, four, five rings; very good—very good—all same much money. I give them all to you. You take and bring me paper for my Little One."

Lae Choo piled up her jewels before the lawyer.

Hom Hing laid a restraining hand upon her shoulder. "Not all, my wife," he said in Chinese. He selected a ring—his gift to Lae Choo when she dreamed of the tree with the red flower. The rest of the jewels he pushed toward the white man.

"Take them and sell them," said he. "They will pay your fare to Washington and bring you back with the paper."

For one moment James Clancy hesitated. He was not a sentimental man; but something arose against accepting such payment for his services.

"They are good, good," pleadingly asserted Lee Choo, seeing his hesitation.

Whereupon he seized the jewels, thrust them into his coat pocket, and walked rapidly away from the store.

4.

Lae Choo followed after the missionary woman through the mission nursery school. Her heart was beating so high with happiness that she could scarcely breathe. The paper had come at last—the precious paper which gave Hom Hing and his wife the right to the possession of their own child. It was ten months now since he had been taken from them—ten months since the sun had ceased to shine for Lae Choo.

The room was filled with children—most of them wee tots, but none so wee as her own. The mission woman talked as she walked. She told Lae Choo that little Kim, as he had been named by the school, was the pet of the place, and that his little tricks and ways amused and delighted every one. He had been rather difficult to manage at first and had cried much for his mother; "but children so soon forget, and after a month he seemed quite at home and played around as bright and happy as a bird."

"Yes," responded Lae Choo. "Oh, yes, yes!"

But she did not hear what was said to her. She was walking in a maze of anticipatory joy.

"Wait here, please," said the mission woman, placing Lae Choo in a chair. "The very youngest ones are having their breakfast."

She withdrew for a moment—it seemed like an hour to the mother— then she reappeared leading by the hand a little boy dressed in blue cotton overalls and white-soled shoes. The little boy's face was round and dimpled and his eyes were very bright.

"Little One, ah, my Little One!" cried Lae Choo.

She fell on her knees and stretched her hungry arms toward her son.

But the Little One shrunk from her and tried to hide himself in the folds of the white woman's skirt.

"Go 'way, go 'way!" he bade his mother.

ca. 1900

THE WHIPPING

Marita Bonner

The matron picked up her coat. It was a good coat made of heavy men's wear wool and lined with fur. She always liked to let her hands trail fondly over it whenever she was going to put it on (the way women do who are used to nothing).

She shook it out and shrugged her shoulders into it.

"I'll be back home again in time for dinner!" She smiled at the warden as she talked. "Helga will have 'peasant-girl' for dessert, too!"

The hard lines that creased around the man's eyes softened a little. "Peasant-girl-with-a veil! Ah, my mother could make that! Real home-made jam, yellow cream!—good! Nothing here ever tastes as good as it did back in the old country, I tell you!"

The woman balanced her weight on the balls of her feet and drew on one of her leather driving gloves. Through the window she saw her car, nicely trimmed and compactly modern, awaiting her. Beyond the car was a November sky, dismal, darkening and melancholy as the walls that bounded the surrounding acres of land which belonged to the Women's Reformatory.

At the end of her drive of thirty-five miles back to the city again, she would go to her apartment that—through warmth of color and all the right uses of the best comforts—seemed to be full of sunshine on the darkest days. She looked down, now, as she stood near the warden and saw her right hand freshly manicured.

Her mother's hands back in the stone kitchen with the open hearth found in every peasant home in Denmark had always been gray and chapped with blackened nails this time of year. No woman who has to carry wood and coal from a frozen yard can have soft clean hands.

The thought made the matron shrug again. "I like things as they are here—but it would be good to go home some day to visit!"

She hurried a little toward the door now. Nobody lingers in the impersonal grayness of an institution whose very air is heavy with fierce anger and anguish and sorrow, buried and dulled under an angry restraint just as fierce and sorrowful.

She had nearly reached the door before she remembered the colored woman sitting alone on the edge of the bench beside the window. The matron had just driven up from the city to bring the woman on the bench to stay at the Reformatory as long as she should live.

She had killed her little boy.

The judge and the social worker said she had killed him.

But she had told the matron over and over again that she did not do it. You could never tell, though. It is best to leave these things alone.

"Good-bye, Lizabeth!" the matron called in a loud voice. She meant to leave a cheerful note but she only spoke overloud. "Be a good girl!"

"Yes'm!" Lizabeth answered softly. "Yas'm!"

And the women separated. One went out to the light. The other looked at the gray walls—dark—and growing darker in the winter sunset.

Everything had been gray around Lizabeth most all of her life. The two-room hut with a ragged lean-to down on Mr. Davey's place in Mississippi where she had lived before she came North—had been gray.

She and Pa and Ma and Bella and John used to get up when the morning was still gray and work the cotton until the grayness of evening stopped them.

"God knows I'm sick of this!" Pa had cursed suddenly one day.

Ma did not say anything. She was glad that they had sugar once in a while from the commissary and not just molasses like they said you got over at McLaren's place.

Pa cursed a lot that day and kept muttering to himself. One morning when they got up to go to work the cotton, Pa was not there.

"He say he goin' North to work!" Ma explained when she could stop her crying.

Mr. Davey said Pa had left a big bill at the commissary and that Ma and the children would have to work twice as hard to pay it up.

There were not any more hours in any one day than those from sun-up to sun-down, no way you could figure it.

The Christmas after Pa left, Mr. Davey said Ma owed three times as much and that she could not have any flannel for John's chest to cover the place where the misery stayed each winter.

That was the day Ma decided to go North and see if she could find Pa.

They had to plan it all carefully. There was no money to go from Mississippi northward on the train.

John had to get an awful attack of the misery first. Then Bella had to stay home to take care of him.

The day Mr. Davey's man came to find out why Bella and John were not in the field, Bella had her hand tied up in a blood-soaked rag and she was crying.

The axe had slipped and cut her hand, she told them.

That meant Ma would have to wait on Bella and John.

Lizabeth worked the cotton by herself and the Saturday after Ma laid off, Mr. Davey would not let them have any fatback.

"Y'all can make it on meal and molasses until you work off your debts!" he told Lizabeth.

Ma had said nothing when Lizabeth had told her about the fatback. She had sat still a long time. Then she got up and mixed up some meal.

"What you makin' so much bread to oncet?" Bella asked Ma.

"'Gainst our gittin' hungry!"

"Can't eat all that bread one time!" John blared forth. "Better save some 'cause you might not git no meal next time! We owe so much!"

"Heish, boy!" Ma screamed so you could hear her half across the field. "I ain't owe nobody nuthin'!"

Lizabeth's jaw dropped. "Mr. Davey, he say—!"

"Heish, gal!" Ma screamed again. "I ain't owe nuthin', I say! Been right here workin' nigh on forty years!"

She turned the last scrap of meal into a pan. Then she stood up and looked around the table at three pairs of wide-stretched eyes.

"I'm fixin' this 'gainst we git hungry! We goin North to find Pa tonight!"

You would not believe that three women and a half-grown boy could get to Federal Street, Chicago, from Mississippi without a cent of money to start with.

They walked—they begged rides—they stopped in towns, worked a little and they rode as far as they could on the train for what they had earned. It took months, but they found Federal Street.

But they never found Pa.

They found colored people who had worked the cotton just like they themselves had done, but these others were from Alabama and Georgia and parts of Mississippi that they had never seen.

They found the houses on Federal Street were just as gray, just as bare of color and comfort as the hut they had left in Mississippi.

But you could get jobs and earn real money and buy all sorts of things for a little down and a little a week! You could eat what you could afford to buy—and if you could not pay cash, the grocer would put you on the book.

Ma was dazed.

John forgot the misery.

Bella and Lizabeth were looping wider and wider in new circles of joy.

Ma could forget Pa, who was lost, and the hard trip up from the South when she screamed and shouted and got happy in robust leather-lunged style in her store-front church run in the "down-home" tempo.

John spent every cent that he could lay a hand on on a swell outfit, thirty dollars from skin out and from shoes to hat!

Bella's circles of joy spread wider and wider until she took to hanging out with girls who lived "out South" in kitchenettes.

She straightened her hair at first.

Then she curled her hair. After that she "sassed" Ma. Said she was going to get a job in a tavern and stay "out South" too!

They heard she was married.

They heard she was not.

Anyway, she did not come back to 31st and Federal.

John's swell outfit wasn't thick enough to keep the lake winds from his misery. He began to have chills and night sweats. The Sunday he coughed blood, Lizabeth got a doctor from State Street.

The doctor made Ma send John to the hospital.

"He be all right soon?" Ma asked after the ambulance had gone.

The doctor looked grim. "I doubt if they can arrest it!"

"Arrest it! Arrest what? John's a good boy! He ain't done nothing to git arrested!"

The doctor looked grimmer. "I mean that maybe they can't stop this blood from coming!"

Ma looked a little afraid. "Well, if they jes' gives him a tablespoon of salt that will stop any bleeding! My mother always—"

The doctor put his hat on and went out. He did not listen to hear any more.

The second fall that they were on Federal Street, Lizabeth met Benny, a soft-voiced boy from Georgia.

Benny said he was lonely for a girl who did not want him to spend all his money on liquor and things for her every time he took her out. That is what these city girls all seemed to want.

They wanted men to buy things for them that no decent girl down home would accept from men.

Lizabeth was glad for just a ten-cent movie and a bottle of pop or a nickel bag of peanuts.

They were married at Christmas. The next year, in October, baby Benny came.

In November John died.

In February of the second year Benny—who had begun to go "out South" in the evening with the boys—suddenly stayed away all night.

Ma had hysterics in the police station and told the police to find him.

"He may be dead and run over somewhere!" she kept crying.

The policeman took their time. Ma went every day to find out if there were any news. Lizabeth went too!

She stopped going after she saw the policeman at the desk wink at another when he told her, "Sure! Sure! We are looking for him every day!"

Mrs. Rhone who kept the corner store asked Lizabeth one morning, "Where's your man? Left you?"

Lizabeth bridled: "He was none of these men! He was my husband!"

The other woman probed deeper: "Who married you? That feller 'round to the store-front church? Say! Hee-hee. They tell me he ain't no reglar preacher! Any feller what'll slip him a couple dollars can get 'married'—even if he's got a wife and ten kids 'out South,' they tell me—!"

Lizabeth shrank back. Benny had been truly married to her!

But after that Lizabeth grew sensitive if she went on the street and saw women standing together in gossiping groups.

"They talkin' about me! They saying I weren't married!" she would tell herself. She and Ma moved away.

The place where they moved was worse than Federal Street. Folks fought and cursed and cut and killed down in the Twenties in those days.

But rent was cheap.

Lizabeth only got twelve dollars a week scrubbing all night in a theater.

Ma kept little Benny and took care of the house.

There was not much money, but Lizabeth would go without enough to eat and to wear so that little Benny could have good clothes and toys that she really could not afford.

"Every time you pass the store you 'bout buy this boy somethin'!" the grandmother complained once.

"Aw I'd a liked pretty clothes and all that stuff when I was a kid!" Lizabeth answered.

"How she buy so much stuff and just *she* workin'!" the neighbors argued among themselves.

"She must be livin' wrong!" declared those who could understand all the fruits of wrong living in all its multiple forms.

Little Benny grew to expect all the best of things for himself. He learned to whine and cry for things and Lizabeth would manage them somehow.

He was six years old in 1929.

That was the year when Lizabeth could find no more theaters to scrub in and there were no more day's work jobs nor factory jobs. Folks said the rich people had tied up all the money so all the poor people had to go to the relief station.

Lizabeth walked fifteen blocks one winter day to a relief station. She told the worker that there was no coal, no food, the water was frozen and the pipes had burst.

"We'll send an investigator," the worker promised.

"When'll that come?" Lizabeth demanded vaguely.

"*She* will come shortly! In a few days, I hope!"

"I got nothin' for Ma and Benny to eat today!" Lizabeth began to explain all over again.

"I'm sorry! That is all we can do now!" the woman behind the desk began to get red as she spoke this time.

"But Benny ain't had no dinner and—"

"Next!" The woman was crimson as she called the next client.

The client—a stout colored woman—elbowed Lizabeth out of the way.

Already dazed with hunger and bone-weary from her freezing walk, Lizabeth stumbled.

"She's drunk!" the client muttered apologetically to the woman behind the desk.

Lizabeth had had enough. She bought her left hand up in a good old-fashioned back-hand wallop.

Everybody screamed. "They're fighting!"

"Look out for a knife!" yelled the woman behind the desk.

Her books had all told her that colored women carried knives.

A policeman came and took Lizabeth away.

They kept Lizabeth all night that night. The next day they said she could go home but it was the third day that they finally set her on the sidewalk and told her to go home.

Home was thirty blocks away this time.

"Where you been, gal!" Ma screamed as soon as the door opened. "You the las' chile I got and now you start actin' like that Bella! Ain't no food in this house! Ain't a God's bit of fire 'cept one box I busted up—!"

"She busted up my boat! She busted up the box what I play boat in!" Benny added his scream to the confusion. "She make me stay in bed all the time! My stomach hurts me!"

Lizabeth was dizzy. "Ain't nobody been here?" She wanted to wait a little before she told Ma that she had been in the lock-up.

"Nobody been here? For what?"

"Get us some somethin' to eat! That's what the woman said!"

"No, ain't nobody been here!"

Lizabeth put on her hat again.

"Where you going' now?" Ma shouted.

"I got to go back."

"You got to go back where?"

"See 'bout some somethin' to eat, Ma!"

Benny began to scream and jumped out of the bed. "You stay with me!" he cried as he ran to his mother. "I want my dinner! I—"

"Heish!" Lizabeth out-screamed everyone else in the room.

Frightened, Benny cowed away a little. Then he began again. "I want to eat! They lady downstairs, she say my mother ought to get me somethin' 'stead of stayin' out all night with men!"

Lizabeth stared wildly at her mother.

Hostile accusation bristled in her eyes, too.

"That's what the lady say. She say—" Benny repeated.

And Lizabeth, who had never struck Benny in her life, stood up and slapped him to the floor.

As he fell, the child's head struck the iron bedstead.

His grandmother picked him up, still whimpering.

Lizabeth went out without looking back.

Fifteen blocks put a stitch in her left side. Anger made her eyes red.

The woman behind the desk at the relief station paled when she saw Lizabeth this time. "You will have to wait!" she chattered nervously before Lizabeth had even spoken.

"Wait for what? Been waitin'! Nobody been there!"

"We are over-crowded now! It will take ten days to two weeks before our relief workers can get there!"

"What's Ma and little Benny going to do all that time? They gotta eat!"

The other woman grew eloquent. "There are hundreds and hundreds of people like you waiting—!"

"Well I stop waitin'! Benny got to eat!"

Fifteen blocks had put a stitch in her side. Worry and hunger made her head swim. Lizabeth put one hand to her side and wavered against the desk.

This time the woman behind the desk *knew* that Lizabeth had a knife—for her alone! Her chair turned over as she shot up from the desk. Her cries brought the policeman from the next corner.

"We better keep you for thirty days," the police court told Lizabeth when they saw her again.

"But little Benny—!" Lizabeth began crying aloud.

There was a bustle and commotion. A thin pale woman pushed her way up to the desk.

Lizabeth had to draw back. She stood panting, glaring at the judge.

He had been looking at her at first in tolerant amusement. But while this pale woman talked to him across the desk, cold, dreadful anger surged into his eyes.

"What's that you're saying about little Benny?" he demanded suddenly of Lizabeth. "He's dead!"

Lizabeth could not speak nor move at first. Then she cried out. "What happen to him? What happen to my baby?"

"You killed him." The judge was harsh.

A bailiff had to pick Lizabeth up off the floor and stand her up again so the judge could finish. "You whipped him to death!"

"I ain't never whip him! I ain't never whip little Benny!" Lizabeth cried over and over.

They took her away and kept her.

They kept her all the time that they were burying Benny, even. Said she was not fit to see him again.

Later—in court—Ma said that Lizabeth had "whipped Benny's head" the last time she was at home.

"I ain't hit him but once!" Lizabeth tried to cry it to the judge's ears. "He didn't have nuthin' to eat for a long time! That was the trouble."

"There was a deep gash on his head," testified the relief worker. "She was brutal!"

"She brought knives to the relief station and tried to start a fight every time she came there!"

"She's been arrested twice!"

"Bad character! Keep her!" the court decided.

That was why the matron had had to drive Lizabeth to the Women's Reformatory.

She had gone out now to her car. Lizabeth watched her climb into it and whirl around once before she drove away.

"Won't see her no more! She's kinder nice, too," Lizabeth thought.

"It is time for supper! Come this way!" the warden spoke suddenly.

Lizabeth stumbled to her feet and followed him down a long narrow hall lit with one small light.

That relief worker had said she would see that Ma got something to eat.

That seemed to settle itself as soon as they had decided they would send her to this place.

"You will work from dawn to sun-down," the matron had said as they were driving up from the city.

She had always done that in Mississippi.

It did not matter here. But she asked one question. "They got a commissary there?"

"A commissary!" The matron was struck breathless when Lizabeth asked this. She had decided that Lizabeth was not normal. She had seemed too stupid to defend herself in court. "She must be interested in food!" the matron had decided to herself.

A slight sneer was on her face when she answered. "Of course they have a commissary! You get your food there!"

Lizabeth had drawn back into her corner and said nothing more.

A commissary. She understood a commissary. The same gray hopeless drudge—the same long unending row to hoe—lay before her.

The same debt, year in, year out.

How long had they said she had to stay?

As long as she lived. And she was only thirty now.

But she understood a commissary and a debt that grew and grew while you worked to pay it off. And she would never be able to pay for little Benny.

1939

THE ENGLISH LESSON

Nicholasa Mohr

"Remember our assignment for today, everybody! I'm so confident that you will all do exceptionally well!" Mrs. Susan Hamma smiled enthusiastically at her students. "Everyone is to get up and make a brief statement as to why he or she is taking this course in Basic English. You must state your name, where you originally came from, how long you have been here, and . . . uh . . . a little something about yourself, if you wish. Keep it brief, not too long; remember, there are twenty-eight of us. We have a full class, and everyone must have a chance." Mrs. Hamma waved a forefinger at her students. "This is, after all, a democracy, and we have a democratic class; fairness for all!"

Lali grinned and looked at William, who sat directly next to her. He winked and rolled his eyes toward Mrs. Hamma. This was the third class they had attended together. It had not been easy to persuade Rudi that Lali should learn better English.

"Why is it necessary, eh?" Rudi had protested. "She works here in the store with me. She don't have to talk to nobody. Besides, everybody that comes in speaks Spanish—practically everybody, anyway."

But once William had put the idea to Lali and explained how much easier things would be for her, she kept insisting until Rudi finally agreed. "Go on, you're both driving me nuts. But it can't interfere with business or work—I'm warning you!"

Adult Education offered Basic English, Tuesday evenings from 6:30 to 8:00, at a local public school. Night customers did not usually come into Rudi's Luncheonette until after eight. William and Lali promised that they would leave everything prepared and make up for any inconvenience by working harder and longer than usual, if necessary.

The class admitted twenty-eight students, and because there were only twenty-seven registered, Lali was allowed to take the course even after missing the first two classes. William had assured Mrs. Hamma that he would help Lali catch up; she was glad to have another student to make up the full registration.

Most of the students were Spanish-speaking. The majority were American citizens—Puerto Ricans who had migrated to New York and spoke very little English. The rest were immigrants admitted to the United States as legal aliens. There were several Chinese, two Dominicans, one Sicilian, and one Pole.

Every Tuesday Mrs. Hamma traveled to the Lower East Side from Bayside, Queens, where she lived and was employed as a history teacher in the local junior high school. She was convinced that this small group of people desperately needed her services. Mrs. Hamma reiterated her feelings frequently to just about anyone who would listen. "Why, if these people can make it to class after working all day at those miserable, dreary, uninteresting, and often revolting jobs, well, the least I can do is be there to serve them, making every lesson count toward improving their conditions! My grandparents came here from Germany as poor immigrants, working their way up. I'm not one to forget a thing like that!"

By the time class started most of the students were quite tired. And after the lesson was over, many had to go on to part-time jobs, some even without time for supper. As a result there was always sluggishness and yawning among the students. This never discouraged Mrs. Hamma, whose drive and enthusiasm not only amused the class but often kept everyone awake.

"Now this is the moment we have all been preparing for." Mrs. Hamma stood up, nodded, and blinked knowingly at her students. "Five lessons, I think, are enough to prepare us for our oral statements. You may read from prepared notes, as I said before, but please try not to read every word. We want to hear you speak; conversation is what we're after. When someone asks you about yourself, you cannot take a piece of paper and start reading the answers, now can you? That would be foolish. So . . ."

Standing in front of her desk, she put her hands on her hips and spread her feet, giving the impression that she was going to demonstrate calisthenics.

"Shall we begin?"

Mrs. Hamma was a very tall, angular woman with large extremities. She was the tallest person in the room. Her eyes roamed from student to student until they met William's.

"Mr. Colón, will you please begin?"

Nervously William looked around him, hesitating.

"Come on now, we must get the ball rolling. All right now... did you hear what I said? Listen, 'getting the ball rolling' means getting started. Getting things going, such as—" Mrs. Hamma swiftly lifted her right hand over her head, making a fist, then swung her arm around like a pitcher and, with an underhand curve, forcefully threw an imaginary ball out at her students. Trying to maintain her balance, Mrs. Hamma hopped from one leg to the other. Startled, the students looked at one another. In spite of their efforts to restrain themselves, several people in back began to giggle. Lali and William looked away, avoiding each other's eyes and trying not to laugh out loud. With assured countenance, Mrs. Hamma continued.

"An idiom!" she exclaimed, pleased. "You have just seen me demonstrate the meaning of an idiom. Now I want everyone to jot down this information in his notebook." Going to the blackboard, Mrs. Hamma explained, "It's something which literally says one thing, but actually means another. Idiom... idiomatic." Quickly and obediently, everyone began to copy what she wrote. "Has everyone got it? OK, let's *get the ball rolling*, Mr. Colón!"

Uneasily William stood up; he was almost the same height standing as sitting. When speaking to others, especially in a new situation, he always preferred to sit alongside those listening; it gave him a sense of equality with other people. He looked around and cleared his throat; at least everyone else was sitting. Taking a deep breath, William felt better.

"My name is William Horacio Colón," he read from a prepared statement. "I have been here in New York City for five months. I coming from Puerto Rico. My town is located in the mountains in the central part of the island. The name of my town is Aibonito, which means in Spanish 'oh how pretty.' It is name like this because when the Spaniards first seen that place they was very impressed with the beauty of the section and—"

"Make it brief, Mr. Colón," Mrs. Hamma interrupted, "there are others, you know."

William looked at her, unable to continue.

"Go on, go on, Mr. Colón, please!"

"I am working here now, living with my mother and family in Lower East Side of New York City," William spoke rapidly. "I study Basic English por que . . . because my ambition is to learn to speak and read English very good. To get a better job. Y—y también, to help my mother y familia." He shrugged. "Y do better, that's all."

"That's all? Why, that's wonderful! Wonderful! Didn't he do well, class?" Mrs. Hamma bowed slightly toward William and applauded him. The students watched her and slowly each one began to imitate her. Pleased, Mrs. Hamma looked around her; all together they gave William a healthy round of applause.

Next, Mrs. Hamma turned to a Chinese man seated at the other side of the room.

"Mr. Fong, you may go next."

Mr. Fong stood up; he was a man in his late thirties, of medium height and slight build. Cautiously he looked at Mrs. Hamma, and waited.

"Go on, Mr. Fong. Get the ball rolling, remember?"

"All right. Get a ball rolling . . . is idiot!" Mr. Fong smiled.

"No, Mr. Fong, idio*mmmmmm!*" Mrs. Hamma hummed her *m*'s, shaking her head. "Not an—It's idiomatic!"

"What I said!" Mr. Fong responded with self-assurance, looking directly at Mrs. Hamma. "Get a ball rolling, idiomit."

"Never mind." She cleared her throat. "Just go on."

"I said OK?" Mr. Fong waited for an answer.

"Go on, please."

Mr. Fong sighed, "My name is Joseph Fong. I been here in this country United States New York City for most one year." He too read from a prepared statement. "I come from Hong Kong but original born in city of Canton, China. I working delivery food business and live with my brother and his family in Chinatown. I taking the course in Basic English to speak good and improve my position better in this country. Also to be eligible to become American citizen."

Mrs. Hamma selected each student who was to speak from a different part of the room, rather than in the more conventional orderly fashion of row by row, or front to back, or even alphabetical order. This way, she reasoned, no one will know who's next; it will be more spontaneous. Mrs. Hamma enjoyed catching the uncertain looks on the faces of her students. A feeling of control over the situation gave her a pleasing thrill, and she made the most of these moments by looking at several people more than once before making her final choice.

There were more men than women, and Mrs. Hamma called two or three men for each woman. It was her way of maintaining a balance. To her distress, most read from prepared notes, despite her efforts to discourage this. She would interrupt them when she felt they went on too long, then praise them when they finished. Each statement was followed by applause from everyone.

All had similar statements. They had migrated here in search of a better future, were living with relatives, and worked as unskilled laborers. With the exception of Lali, who was childless, every woman gave the ages and sex of her children; most men referred only to their "family." And, among the legal aliens, there was only one who did not want to become an American citizen, Diego Torres, a young man from the Dominican Republic, and he gave his reasons.

". . . and to improve my economic situation." Diego Torres hesitated, looking around the room. "But is one thing I no want, and is to become American citizen"—he pointed to an older man with a dark complexion, seated a few seats away—"like my fellow countryman over there!" The man shook his head disapprovingly at Diego Torres, trying to hide his annoyance. "I no give up my country, Santo Domingo, for nothing," he went on, "nothing in the whole world. OK, man? I come here, pero I cannot help. I got no work at home. There, is political. The United States control most the industry which is sugar and tourismo. Y—you have to know somebody. I tell you, is political to get a job, man! You don't know nobody and you no work, eh? So I come here from necessity, pero this no my country—"

"Mr. Torres," Mrs. Hamma interrupted, "we must be brief, please, there are—"

"I no finish lady!" he snapped. "You wait a minute when I finish!"

There was complete silence as Diego Torres glared at Susan Hamma. No one had ever spoken to her like that, and her confusion was greater than her embarrassment. Without speaking, she lowered her eyes and nodded.

"OK, I prefer live feeling happy in my country, man. Even I don't got too much. I live simple but in my own country I be contento. Pero this is no possible in the situation of Santo Domingo now. Someday we gonna run our own country and be jobs for everybody. My reasons to be here is to make money, man, and go back home buy my house and property. I no be American citizen, no way. I'm Dominican and proud! That's all I got to say." Abruptly, Diego Torres sat down.

"All right." Mrs. Hamma had composed herself. "Very good; you can come here and state your views. That is what America is all about! We may not agree with you, but we defend your right to an opinion. And as long as you are in this classroom, Mr. Torres, you are in America. Now, everyone, let us give Mr. Torres the same courtesy as everyone else in this class." Mrs. Hamma applauded with a polite light clap, then turned to find the next speaker.

"Bullshit," whispered Diego Torres.

Practically everyone had spoken. Lali and the two European immigrants were the only ones left. Mrs. Hamma called upon Lali.

"My name is Rogelia Dolores Padillo. I come from Canovanas in Puerto Rico. Is a small village in the mountains near El Yunque Rain Forest. My family is still living there. I marry and live here with my husband working in his business of restaurant. Call Rudi's Luncheonette. I been here New York City Lower East Side since I marry, which is now about one year. I study Basic English to improve my vocabulario and learn more about here. This way I help my husband in his business and I do more also for myself, including to be able to read better in English. Thank you."

Aldo Fabrizi, the Sicilian, spoke next. He was a very short man, barely five feet tall. Usually he was self-conscious about his height, but William's presence relieved him of these feelings. Looking at William, he thought being short was no big thing: he was, after all, normal. He told the class that he was originally from Palermo, the capital of Sicily, and had gone to Milano, in the north of Italy, looking for work. After three years in Milano, he immigrated here six months ago and now lived with his sister. He had a good steady job, he said, working in a copper wire factory with his brother-in-law in Brooklyn. Aldo Fabrizi wanted to become an American citizen and spoke passionately about it, without reading from his notes.

"I be proud to be American citizen. I no come here find work live good and no have responsibility or no be grateful." He turned and looked threateningly at Diego Torres. "Hey? I tell you all one thing, I got my nephew right now fighting in Vietnam for this country!" Diego Torres stretched his hands over his head, yawning, folded his hands, and lowered his eyelids. "I wish I could be citizen to fight for this country. My whole family is citizens—we all Americans and we love America!" His voice was quite loud. "That's how I feel."

"Very good," Mrs. Hamma called, distracting Aldo Fabrizi. "That was well stated. I'm sure you will not only become a citizen, but you will also be a credit to this country."

The last person to be called on was the Pole. He was always neatly dressed in a business suit, with a shirt and tie, and carried a briefcase. His manner was reserved but friendly.

"Good evening fellow students and Madame Teacher." He nodded politely to Mrs. Hamma. "My name is Stephan Paczkowski. I am originally from Poland about four months ago. My background is I was born in capital city of Poland, Warsaw. Being educated in capital and also graduating from the University with degree of professor of music with specialty in the history of music."

Stephan Paczkowski read from his notes carefully, articulating every word. "I was given appointment of professor of history of music at University of Krakow. I work there for ten years until about year and half ago. At this time the political situation in Poland was so that all Jewish people were requested by the government to leave Poland. My wife who also is being a professor of economics at University of Krakow is of Jewish parents. My wife was told she could not remain in position at University or remain over there. We made arrangements for my wife and daughter who is seven years of age and myself to come here with my wife's cousin who is to be helping us.

"Since four months I am working in large hospital as position of porter in maintenance department. The thing of it is, I wish to take Basic English to improve my knowledge of English language, and be able to return to my position of professor of history of music. Finally, I wish to become a citizen of United States. That is my reasons. I thank you all."

After Stephan Paczkowski sat down, there was a long awkward silence and everyone turned to look at Mrs. Hamma. Even after the confrontation with Diego Torres, she had applauded without hesitation. Now she seemed unable to move.

"Well," she said, almost breathless, "that's admirable! I'm sure, sir, that you will do very well . . . a person of your . . . like yourself, I mean . . . a professor, after all, it's really just admirable." Everyone was listening intently to what she said. "That was well done, class. Now, we have to get to next week's assignment." Mrs. Hamma realized that no one had applauded Stephan Paczkowski. With a slightly pained expression, she began to applaud. "Mustn't forget Mr. Paczkowski; everybody here must be treated equally. This is America!" The class joined her in a round of applause.

As Mrs. Hamma began to write the next week's assignment on the board, some students looked anxiously at their watches and others asked about the time. Then they all quickly copied the information into their notebooks. It was almost eight o'clock. Those who had to get to second jobs did not want to be late; some even hoped to have time for a bite to eat first. Others were just tired and wanted to get home.

Lali looked at William, sighing impatiently. They both hoped Mrs. Hamma would finish quickly. There would be hell to pay with Rudi if the night customers were already at the luncheonette.

"There, that's next week's work, which is very important, by the way. We will be looking at the history of New York City and the different ethnic groups that lived here as far back as the Dutch. I can't tell you how proud I am of the way you all spoke. All of you—I have no favorites, you know."

Mrs. Hamma was interrupted by the long, loud buzzing sound, bringing the lesson to an end. Quickly everyone began to exit.

"Good night, see you all next Tuesday!" Mrs. Hamma called out. "By the way, if any of you here wants extra help, I have a few minutes this evening." Several people bolted past her, excusing themselves. In less than thirty seconds, Mrs. Hamma was standing in an empty classroom.

William and Lali hurried along, struggling against the cold, sharp March wind that whipped across Houston Street, stinging their faces and making their eyes tear.

In a few minutes they would be at Rudi's. So far, they had not been late once.

"You read very well—better than anybody in class. I told you there was nothing to worry about. You caught up in no time."

"Go on. I was so nervous, honestly! But, I'm glad she left me for one of the last. If I had to go first, like you, I don't think I could open my mouth. You were so calm. You started the thing off very well."

"You go on now, I was nervous myself!" He laughed, pleased.

"Mira, Chiquitín," Lali giggled, "I didn't know your name was Horacio, William Horacio. Ave María, so imposing!"

"That's right, because you see, my mother was expecting a valiant warrior! Instead, well"—he threw up his hands—"no one warned me either. And a name for a Chiquitín like me."

Lali smiled, saying nothing. At first she had been very aware of William's dwarfishness. Now it no longer mattered. It was only when she saw others reacting to him for the first time that she was once more momentarily struck with William's physical difference.

"We should really try to speak in English, Lali. It would be good practice for us."

"Dios mío . . . I feel so foolish, and my accent is terrible!"

"But look, we all have to start some place. Besides, what about the

Americanos? When they speak Spanish, they sound pretty awful, but we accept it. You know I'm right. And that's how people get ahead, by not being afraid to try."

They walked in silence for a few moments. Since William had begun to work at Rudi's, Lali's life had become less lonely. Lali was shy by nature; making friends was difficult for her. She had grown up in the sheltered environment of a large family living in a tiny mountain village. She was considered quite plain. Until Rudi had asked her parents for permission to court her, she had only gone out with two local boys. She had accepted his marriage proposal expecting great changes in her life. But the age difference between her and Rudi, being in a strange country without friends or relatives, and the long hours of work at the luncheonette confined Lali to a way of life she could not have imagined. Every evening she found herself waiting for William to come in to work, looking forward to his presence.

Lali glanced over at him as they started across the wide busy street. His grip on her elbow was firm but gentle as he led her to the sidewalk.

"There you are, Miss Lali, please to watch your step!" he spoke in English.

His thick golden-blond hair was slightly mussed and fell softly, partially covering his forehead. His wide smile, white teeth, and large shoulders made him appear quite handsome. Lali found herself staring at William. At that moment she wished he could be just like everybody else.

"Lali?" William asked, confused by her silent stare. "Is something wrong?"

"No." Quickly Lali turned her face. She felt herself blushing. "I . . . I was just thinking how to answer in English, that's all."

"But that's it . . . don't think! What I mean is, don't go worrying about what to say. Just talk natural. Get used to simple phrases and the rest will come, you'll see."

"All right," Lali said, glad the strange feeling of involvement had passed, and William had taken no notice of it. "It's an interesting class, don't you think so? I mean—like that man, the professor. Bendito! Imagine, they had to leave because they were Jewish. What a terrible thing!"

"I don't believe he's Jewish; it's his wife who is Jewish. She was a professor too. But I guess they don't wanna be separated . . . and they have a child."

"Tsk, tsk, los pobres! But, can you imagine, then? A professor from a university doing the job of a porter? My goodness!" Lali sighed. "I never heard of such a thing!"

"But you gotta remember, it's like Mrs. Hanna said, this is America, right? So . . . everybody got a chance to clean toilets! Equality, didn't she say that?"

They both laughed loudly, stepping up their pace until they reached Rudi's Luncheonette.

The small luncheonette was almost empty. One customer sat at the counter.

"Just in time," Rudi called out. "Let's get going. People gonna be coming in hungry any minute. I was beginning to worry about you two!"

William ran in the back to change into his workshirt.

Lali slipped into her uniform and soon was busy at the grill.

"Well, did you learn anything tonight?" Rudi asked her.

"Yes."

"What?"

"I don't know," she answered, without interrupting her work. "We just talked a little bit in English."

"A little bit in English—about what?"

Lali busied herself, ignoring him. Rudi waited, then tried once more.

"You remember what you talked about?" He watched her as she moved, working quickly, not looking in his direction.

"No." Her response was barely audible.

Lately Rudi had begun to reflect on his decision to marry such a young woman. Especially a country girl like Lali, who was shy and timid. He had never had children with his first wife and wondered if he lacked the patience needed for the young. They had little in common and certainly seldom spoke about anything but business. Certainly he could not fault her for being lazy; she was always working without being asked. People would accuse him in jest of over-working his young wife. He assured them there was no need, because she had the endurance of a country mule. After almost one year of marriage, he felt he hardly knew Lali or what he might do to please her.

William began to stack clean glasses behind the counter.

"Chiquitín! How about you and Lali having something to eat? We gotta few minutes yet. There's some fresh rice pudding."

"Later. . . I'll have mine a little later, thanks."

"Ask her if she wants some," Rudi whispered, gesturing toward Lali.

William moved close to Lali and spoke softly to her.

"She said no." William continued his work.

"Listen, Chiquitín, I already spoke to Raquel Martinez who lives next door. You know, she's got all them kids? In case you people are late, she can cover for you and Lali. She said it was OK."

"Thanks, Rudi, I appreciate it. But we'll get back on time."

"She's good, you know. She helps me out during the day whenever I need extra help. Off the books, I give her a few bucks. But, mira, I cannot pay you and Raquel both. So if she comes in, you don't get paid. You know that then, OK?"

"Of course. Thanks, Rudi."

"Sure, well, it's a good thing after all. You and Lali improving yourselves. Not that she really needs it, you know. I provide for her. As I said, she's my wife, so she don't gotta worry. If she wants something, I'll buy it for her. I made it clear she didn't have to bother with none of that, but"—Rudi shrugged—"if that's what she wants, I'm not one to interfere."

The door opened. Several men walked in.

"Here they come, kids!"

Orders were taken and quickly filled. Customers came and went steadily until about eleven o'clock, when Rudi announced that it was closing time.

The weeks passed, then the months, and this evening, William and Lali sat with the other students listening to Mrs. Hamma as she taught the last lesson of the Basic English course.

"It's been fifteen long hard weeks for all of you. And I want you to know how proud I am of each and every one here."

William glanced at Lali; he knew she was upset. He felt it too, wishing that this was not the end of the course. It was the only time he and Lali had free to themselves together. Tuesday had become their evening.

Lali had been especially irritable that week, dreading this last session. For her, Tuesday meant leaving the world of Rudi, the luncheonette, that street, everything that she felt imprisoned her. She was accomplishing something all by herself, and without the help of the man she was dependent upon.

Mrs. Hamma finally felt that she had spent enough time assuring her students of her sincere appreciation.

"I hope some of you will stay and have a cup of coffee or tea, and cookies. There's plenty over there." She pointed to a side table where a large electric coffeepot filled with hot water was steaming. The table was set for instant coffee and tea, complete with several boxes of assorted cookies. "I do this every semester for my classes. I think it's nice to have a little informal chat with one another; perhaps discuss our plans for the future and so on. But it must be in English! Especially those of you who are Spanish-speaking. Just because you outnumber the rest of us, don't think you can get away with it!" Mrs. Hamma lifted her forefinger threateningly but smiled. "Now, it's still early, so there's plenty of time left. Please turn in your books."

Some of the people said good-bye quickly and left, but the majority waited, helping themselves to coffee or tea and cookies. Small clusters formed as people began to chat with one another.

Diego Torres and Aldo Fabrizi were engaged in a friendly but heated debate on the merits of citizenship.

"Hey, you come here a minute, please," Aldo Fabrizi called out to William, who was standing with a few people by the table, helping himself to coffee. William walked over to the two men.

"What's the matter?"

"What do you think of your paisano. He don't wanna be citizen. I say—my opinion—he don't appreciate what he got in this country. This a great country! You the same like him, what do you think?"

"Mira, please tell him we no the same," Diego Torres said with exasperation. "You a citizen, pero not me. Este tipo no comprende, man!"

"Listen, you comprendo . . . yo capito! I know what you say. He be born in Puerto Rico. But you see, we got the same thing. I be born in Sicily—that is another part of the country, separate. But I still Italiano, capito?"

"Dios mío!" Diego Torres smacked his forehead with an open palm. "Mira"—he turned to William—"explain to him, por favor."

William swallowed a mouthful of cookies. "He's right. Puerto Rico is part of the United States. And Sicily is part of Italy. But not the Dominican Republic where he been born. There it is not the United States. I was born a citizen, do you see?"

"Sure!" Aldo Fabrizi nodded. "Capito. Hey, but you still no can vote, right?"

"Sure I can vote; I got all the rights. I am a citizen, just like anybody else," William assured him.

"You some lucky guy then. You got it made! You don't gotta worry like the rest of—"

"Bullshit," Diego Torres interrupted. "Why he got it made, man? He force to leave his country. Pendejo, you no capito nothing, man . . ."

As the two men continued to argue, William waited for the right moment to slip away and join Lali.

She was with some of the women, who were discussing how sincere and devoted Mrs. Hamma was.

"She's hardworking . . ."

"And she's good people . . ." an older woman agreed.

Mr. Fong joined them, and they spoke about the weather and how nice and warm the days were.

Slowly people began to leave, shaking hands with their fellow students and Mrs. Hamma, wishing each other luck.

Mrs. Hamma had been hoping to speak to Stephan Paczkowski privately this evening, but he was always with a group. Now he offered his hand.

"I thank you very much for your good teaching. It was a fine semester."

"Oh, do you think so? Oh, I'm so glad to hear you say that. You don't know how much it means. Especially coming from a person of your caliber. I am confident, yes, indeed, that you will soon be back in your profession, which, after all, is your true calling. If there is anything I can do, please . . ."

"Thank you, miss. This time I am registering in Hunter College, which is in Manhattan on Sixty-eighth Street in Lexington Avenue, with a course of English Literature for beginners." After a slight bow, he left.

"Good-bye." Mrs. Hamma sighed after him.

Lali, William, and several of the women picked up the paper cups and napkins and tossed them into the trash basket.

"Thank you so much, that's just fine. Luis the porter will do the rest. He takes care of these things. He's a lovely person and very helpful. Thank you."

William shook hands with Mrs. Hamma, then waited for Lali to say good-bye. They were the last ones to leave.

"Both of you have been such good students. What are your plans? I hope you will continue with your English."

"Next term, we're taking another course," Lali said, looking at William.

"Yes," William responded, "it's more advance. Over at the Washington Irving High School around Fourteenth Street."

"Wonderful." Mrs. Hamma hesitated. "May I ask you a question before you leave? It's only that I'm a little curious about something."

"Sure, of course." They both nodded.

"Are you two related? I mean, you are always together and yet have different last names, so I was just . . . wondering."

"Oh, we are just friends," Lali answered, blushing.

"I work over in the luncheonette at night, part-time."

"Of course." Mrs. Hamma looked at Lali. "Mrs. Padillo, your husband's place of business. My, that's wonderful, just wonderful! You are all just so ambitious. Very good . . . "

They exchanged farewells.

Outside, the warm June night was sprinkled with the sweetness of the new buds sprouting on the scrawny trees and hedges planted along the sidewalks and in the housing project grounds. A brisk breeze swept over the East River on to Houston Street, providing a freshness in the air.

This time they were early, and Lali and William strolled at a relaxed pace.

"Well," Lali shrugged, "That's that. It's over!"

"Only for a couple of months. In September we'll be taking a more advanced course at a high school."

"I'll probably forget everything I learned by then."

"Come on, Lali, the summer will be over before you know it. Just you wait and see. Besides, we can practice so we don't forget what Mrs. Hamma taught us."

"Sure, what do you like to speak about?" Lali said in English.

William smiled and, clasping his hands, said, "I would like to say to you how wonderful you are, and how you gonna have the most fabulous future . . . after all, you so ambitious!"

When she realized he sounded just like Mrs. Hamma, Lali began to laugh.

"Are you"—Lali tried to keep from giggling, tried to pretend to speak in earnest—"sure there is some hope for me?"

"Oh, heavens, yes! You have shown such ability this"—William was beginning to lose control, laughing loudly—"semester!"

"But I want"—Lali was holding her sides with laughter—"some guarantee of this. I got to know."

"Please, Miss Lali." William was laughing so hard tears were coming to his eyes. "After . . . after all, you now a member in good standing . . . of the promised future!"

William and Lali broke into uncontrollable laughter, swaying and limping, oblivious to the scene they created for the people who stared and pointed at them as they continued on their way to Rudi's.

1986

THE GERMAN REFUGEE

Bernard Malamud

Oskar Gassner sits in his cotton-mesh undershirt and summer bathrobe at the window of his stuffy, hot, dark hotel room on West Tenth Street as I cautiously knock. Outside, across the sky, a late-June green twilight fades in darkness. The refugee fumbles for the light and stares at me, hiding despair but not pain.

I was in those days a poor student and would brashly attempt to teach anybody anything for a buck an hour, although I have since learned better. Mostly I gave English lessons to recently arrived refugees. The college sent me, I had acquired a little experience. Already a few of my students were trying their broken English, theirs and mine, in the American marketplace. I was then just twenty, on my way into my senior year in college, a skinny, life-hungry kid, eating himself waiting for the next world war to start. It was a miserable cheat. Here I was panting to get going, and across the ocean Adolf Hitler, in black boots and a square mustache, was tearing up and spitting at all the flowers. Will I ever forget what went on with Danzig that summer?

Times were still hard from the Depression but I made a little living from the poor refugees. They were all over uptown Broadway in 1939. I had four I tutored—Karl Otto Alp, the former film star; Wolfgang Novak, once a brilliant economist; Friedrich Wilhelm Wolff, who had taught medieval history at Heidelberg; and after the night I met him in his disordered cheap hotel room, Oskar Gassner, the Berlin critic and journalist, at one time on the *Acht Uhr Abendblatt*. They were accomplished men. I had my nerve associating with them, but that's what a world crisis does for people, they get educated.

Oskar was maybe fifty, his thick hair turning gray. He had a big face and heavy hands. His shoulders sagged. His eyes, too, were heavy, a clouded blue; and as he stared at me after I had identified myself, doubt spread in them like underwater currents. It was as if, on seeing me, he had again been defeated. I had to wait until he came to. I stayed at the door in silence. In such cases I would rather be elsewhere, but I had to make a living. Finally he opened the door and I entered. Rather, he released it and I was in. "Bitte"—he offered me a seat and didn't know where to sit himself. He would attempt to say something and then stop, as though it could not possibly be said. The room was cluttered with clothing, boxes of books he had managed to get out of Germany, and some paintings. Oskar sat on a box and attempted to fan himself with his meaty hand. "Zis heat," he muttered, forcing his mind to the deed. "Impozzible. I do not know such heat." It was bad enough for me but terrible for him. He had difficulty breathing. He tried to speak, lifted a hand, and let it drop. He breathed as though he was fighting a war; and maybe he won because after ten minutes we sat and slowly talked.

Like most educated Germans Oskar had at one time studied English. Although he was certain he couldn't say a word he managed to put together a fairly decent, if sometimes comical English sentence. He misplaced consonants, mixed up nouns and verbs, and mangled idioms, yet we were able at once to communicate. We conversed in English, with an occasional assist by me in pidgin-German or Yiddish, what he called "Jiddish." He had been to America before, last year for a short visit. He had come a month before Kristallnacht, when the Nazis shattered the Jewish store windows and burnt all the synagogues, to see if he could find a job for himself; he had no relatives in America and getting a job would permit him quickly to enter the country. He had been promised something, not in journalism, but with the help of a foundation, as a lecturer. Then he returned to Berlin, and after a frightening delay of six months was permitted to emigrate. He had sold whatever he could, managed to get some paintings, gifts of Bauhaus friends, and some boxes of books out by bribing two Dutch border guards; he had said goodbye to his wife and left the accursed country. He gazed at me with cloudy eyes. "We parted amicably," he said in German, "my wife was gentile. Her mother was an appalling anti-Semite. They returned to live in Stettin." I asked no questions. Gentile is gentile, Germany is Germany.

His new job was in the Institute for Public Studies, in New York. He was to give a lecture a week in the fall term and during next spring, a course, in

English translation, in "The Literature of the Weimar Republic." He had never taught before and was afraid to. He was in that way to be introduced to the public, but the thought of giving the lecture in English just about paralyzed him. He didn't see how he could do it. "How is it pozzible? I cannot say two words. I cannot pronounziate. I will make a fool of myself." His melancholy deepened. Already in the two months since his arrival, and a round of diminishingly expensive hotel rooms, he had had two English tutors, and I was the third. The others had given him up, he said, because his progress was so poor, and he thought he also depressed them. He asked whether I felt I could do something for him, or should he go to a speech specialist, someone, say, who charged five dollars an hour, and beg his assistance? "You could try him," I said, "and then come back to me." In those days I figured what I knew, I knew. At that he managed a smile. Still, I wanted him to make up his mind or it would be no confidence down the line. He said, after a while, he would stay with me. If he went to the five-dollar professor it might help his tongue but not his appetite. He would have no money left to eat with. The Institute had paid him in advance for the summer, but it was only three hundred dollars and all he had.

He looked at me dully. "Ich weiss nicht, wie ich weiter machen soll."

I figured it was time to move past the first step. Either we did that quickly or it would be like drilling rock for a long time.

"Let's stand at the mirror," I said.

He rose with a sigh and stood there beside me, I thin, elongated, redheaded, praying for success, his and mine; Oskar uneasy, fearful, finding it hard to face either of us in the faded round glass above his dresser.

"Please," I said to him, "could you say 'right?'"

"Ghight," he gargled.

"No—right. You put your tongue here." I showed him where as he tensely watched the mirror. I tensely watched him. "The tip of it curls behind the ridge on top, like this."

He placed his tongue where I showed him.

"Please," I said, "now say right."

Oskar's tongue fluttered. "Rright."

"That's good. Now say 'treasure'—that's harder."

"Tgheasure."

"The tongue goes up in front, not in the back of the mouth. Look."

He tried, his brow wet, eyes straining. "Trreasure."

"That's it."

"A miracle," Oskar murmured.

I said if he had done that he could do the rest.

We went for a bus ride up Fifth Avenue and then walked for a while around Central Park Lake. He had put on his German hat, with its hatband bow at the back, a broad-lapeled wool suit, a necktie twice as wide as the one I was wearing, and walked with a small-footed waddle. The night wasn't bad, it had got a bit cooler. There were a few large stars in the sky and they made me sad.

"Do you sink I will succezz?"

"Why not?" I asked.

Later he bought me a bottle of beer.

To many of these people, articulate as they were, the great loss was the loss of language—that they could not say what was in them to say. You have some subtle thought and it comes out like a piece of broken bottle. They could, of course, manage to communicate, but just to communicate was frustrating. As Karl Otto Alp, the ex-film star who became a buyer for Macy's, put it years later, "I felt like a child, or worse, often like a moron. I am left with myself unexpressed. What I know, indeed, what I am, becomes to me a burden. My tongue hangs useless." The same with Oskar it figures. There was a terrible sense of useless tongue, and I think the reason for his trouble with his other tutors was that to keep from drowning in things unsaid he wanted to swallow the ocean in a gulp: today he would learn English and tomorrow wow them with an impeccable Fourth of July speech, followed by a successful lecture at the Institute for Public Studies.

We performed our lessons slowly, step by step, everything in its place. After Oskar moved to a two-room apartment in a house on West Eighty-fifth Street, near the Drive, we met three times a week at four-thirty, worked an hour and a half, then, since it was too hot to cook, had supper at the Seventy-second Street Automat and conversed on my time. The lessons we divided into three parts: diction exercises and reading aloud; then grammar, because Oskar felt the necessity of it, and composition correction; with conversation, as I said, thrown in at supper. So far as I could see he was coming along. None of these exercises was giving him as much trouble as they apparently had in the past. He seemed to be learning and his mood lightened. There were moments of elation as he heard his accent flying off. For instance when sink became think. He stopped calling himself "hopelezz," and I became his "bezt teacher," a little joke I liked.

Neither of us said much about the lecture he had to give early in October, and I kept my fingers crossed. It was somehow to come out of what we were doing daily, I think I felt, but exactly how, I had no idea; and to tell the truth, though I didn't say so to Oskar, the lecture frightened me. That and the ten more to follow during the fall term. Later, when I learned that he had been attempting, with the help of the dictionary, to write in English and had produced "a complete disahster," I suggested maybe he ought to stick to German and we could afterwards both try to put it into passable English. I was cheating when I said that because my German is meager, enough to read simple stuff but certainly not good enough for serious translation; anyway, the idea was to get Oskar into production and worry about translating later. He sweated with it, from enervating morning to exhausted night, but no matter what language he tried, though he had been a professional writer for a generation and knew his subject cold, the lecture refused to move past page one.

It was a sticky, hot July, and the heat didn't help at all.

I had met Oskar at the end of June, and by the seventeenth of July we were no longer doing lessons. They had foundered on the "impozzible" lecture. He had worked on it each day in frenzy and growing despair. After writing more than a hundred opening pages he furiously flung his pen against the wall, shouting he could not longer write in that filthy tongue. He cursed the German language. He hated the damned country and the damned people. After that, what was bad became worse. When he gave up attempting to write the lecture, he stopped making progress in English. He seemed to forget what he already knew. His tongue thickened and the accent returned in all its fruitiness. The little he had to say was in handcuffed and tortured English. The only German I heard him speak was in a whisper to himself. I doubt he knew he was talking it. That ended our formal work together, though I did drop in every other day or so to sit with him. For hours he sat motionless in a large green velour armchair, hot enough to broil in, and through tall windows stared at the colorless sky above Eighty-fifth Street with a wet depressed eye.

Then once he said to me, "If I do not this legture prepare, I will take my life."

"Let's begin, Oskar," I said. "You dictate and I'll write. The ideas count, not the spelling."

He didn't answer so I stopped talking.

He had plunged into an involved melancholy. We sat for hours, often in profound silence. This was alarming to me, though I had already had some experience with such depression. Wolfgang Novak, the economist, though English came more easily to him, was another. His problems arose mainly, I think, from physical illness. And he felt a greater sense of the lost country than Oskar. Sometimes in the early evening I persuaded Oskar to come with me for a short walk on the Drive. The tail end of sunsets over the Palisades seemed to appeal to him. At least he looked. He would put on full regalia—hat, suit coat, tie, no matter how hot or what I suggested—and we went slowly down the stairs, I wondering whether he would make it to the bottom.

We walked slowly uptown, stopping to sit on a bench and watch night rise above the Hudson. When we returned to his room, if I sensed he had loosened up a bit, we listened to music on the radio; but if I tried to sneak in a news broadcast, he said to me. "Please, I cannot more stand of world misery." I shut off the radio. He was right, it was a time of no good news. I squeezed my brain. What could I tell him? Was it good news to be alive? Who could argue the point? Sometimes I read aloud to him—I remember he liked the first part of *Life on the Mississippi*. We still went to the Automat once or twice a week, he perhaps out of habit, because he didn't feel like going anywhere—I to get him out of his room. Oskar ate little, he toyed with a spoon. His eyes looked as though they had been squirted with dark dye.

Once after a momentary cooling rainstorm we sat on newspapers on a wet bench overlooking the river and Oskar at last began to talk. In tormented English he conveyed his intense and everlasting hatred of the Nazis for destroying his career, uprooting his life, and flinging him like a piece of bleeding meat to the hawks. He cursed them thickly, the German nation, an inhuman, conscienceless, merciless people. "They are pigs mazquerading as peacogs," he said. "I feel certain that my wife, in her heart, was a Jew hater." It was a terrible bitterness, and eloquence beyond the words he spoke. He became silent again. I wanted to hear more about his wife but decided not to ask.

Afterwards in the dark, Oskar confessed that he had attempted suicide during his first week in America. He was living, at the end of May, in a small hotel, and had one night filled himself with barbiturates; but his phone had fallen off the table and the hotel operator had sent up the elevator boy, who found him unconscious and called the police. He was revived in the hospital.

"I did not mean to do it," he said, "it was a mistage."

"Don't ever think of it," I said, "it's total defeat."

"I don't," he said wearily, "because it is so arduouz to come bag to life."

"Please, for any reason whatever."

Afterwards when we were walking, he surprised me by saying, "Maybe we ought to try now the legture onze more."

We trudged back to the house and he sat at his hot desk, I trying to read as he slowly began to reconstruct the first page of his lecture. He wrote, of course, in German.

He got nowhere. We were back to sitting in silence in the heat. Sometimes, after a few minutes, I had to take off before his mood overcame mine. One afternoon I came unwillingly up the stairs—there were times I felt momentary surges of irritation with him—and was frightened to find Oskar's door ajar. When I knocked no one answered. As I stood there, chilled down the spine, I realized I was thinking about the possibility of his attempting suicide again. "Oskar?" I went into the apartment, looked into both rooms and the bathroom, but he wasn't there. I thought he might have drifted out to get something from a store and took the opportunity to look quickly around. There was nothing startling in the medicine chest, no pills but aspirin, no iodine. Thinking, for some reason, of a gun, I searched his desk drawer. In it I found a thin-paper airmail letter from Germany. Even if I had wanted to, I couldn't read the handwriting, but as I held it in my hand I did make out a sentence: "Ich bin dir siebenundzwanzig Jahre treu gewesen." There was no gun in the drawer. I shut it and stopped looking. It had occurred to me if you want to kill yourself all you need is a straight pin. When Oskar returned he said he had been sitting in the public library, unable to read.

Now we are once more enacting the changeless scene, curtain rising on two speechless characters in a furnished apartment, I in a straight-back chair, Oskar in the velour armchair that smothered rather than supported him, his flesh gray, the big gray face unfocused, sagging. I reached over to switch on the radio but he barely looked at me in a way that begged no. I then got up to leave but Oskar, clearing his throat, thickly asked me to stay. I stayed, thinking, was there more to this than I could see into? His problems, God knows, were real enough, but could there be something more than a refugee's displacement, alienation, financial insecurity, being in a strange land without friends or a speakable tongue? My speculation was the old one: not all drown in this ocean, why does he? After a while I shaped the thought and asked him was there something below the surface, invisible? I was full of this thing from college, and wondered if there mightn't be some unknown quantity in his depression that a psychiatrist maybe might help him with, enough to get him started on his lecture.

He meditated on this and after a few minutes haltingly said he had been psychoanalyzed in Vienna as a young man. "Just the jusual drek," he said, "fears and fantazies that afterwaards no longer bothered me."

"They don't now?"

"Not."

"You've written many articles and lectures before," I said. "What I can't understand, though I know how hard the situation is, is why you can never get past page one."

He half lifted his hand. "It is a paralyzis of my will. The whole legture is clear in my mind, but the minute I write down a single work—or in English or in German—I have a terrible fear I will not be able to write the negst. As though someone has thrown a stone at a window and the whole house—the whole idea zmashes. This repeats, until I am dezperate."

He said the fear grew as he worked that he would die before he completed the lecture, or if not that, he would write it so disgracefully he would wish for death. The fear immobilized him.

"I have lozt faith. I do not—not longer possezz my former value of myself. In my life there has been too much illusion."

I tried to believe what I was saying: "Have confidence, the feeling will pass."

"Confidenze I have not. For this and alzo whatever elze I have lozt I thank the Nazis."

It was by then mid-August and things were growing steadily worse wherever one looked. The Poles were mobilizing for war. Oskar hardly moved. I was full of worries though I pretended calm weather.

He sat in his massive armchair, breathing like a wounded animal.

"Who can write aboud Walt Whitman in such terrible times?"

"Why don't you change the subject?"

"It makes no differenze what is the subject. It is all uzelezz."

I came every day, as a friend, neglecting my other students and therefore my livelihood. I had a panicky feeling that if things went on as they were going they would end in Oskar's suicide; and I felt a frenzied desire to prevent that. What's more, I was sometimes afraid I was myself becoming melancholy, a new talent, call it, of taking less pleasure in my little pleasures. And that heat continued, oppressive, relentless. We thought of escape into the country, but neither of us had the money. One day I bought Oskar a secondhand electric fan—wondering why we hadn't thought of that before—and he sat in the breeze for hours each day, until after a week, shortly after the Soviet-Nazi non-aggression pact was signed, the motor gave out. He could not sleep at night and sat at his desk with a wet towel on his head, still attempting to write the lecture. He wrote reams on a treadmill, it came out nothing. When he slept in exhaustion he had fantastic frightening dreams of the Nazis inflicting torture, sometimes forcing him to look upon the corpses of those they had slain. In one dream he told me about he had gone back to Germany to visit his wife. She wasn't home and he had been directed to a cemetery. There, though the tombstone read another name, her blood seeped out of the earth above her shallow grave. He groaned aloud at the memory.

Afterwards he told me something about her. They had met as students, lived together, and were married at twenty-three. It wasn't a very happy marriage. She had turned into a sickly woman, unable to have children. "Something was wrong with her interior strugture."

Though I asked no questions, Oskar said, "I offered her to come with me here, but she refused this."

"For what reason?"

"She did not think I wished her to come."

"Did you?" I asked.

"Not," he said.

He explained he had lived with her for almost twenty-seven years under difficult circumstances. She had been ambivalent about their Jewish friends and his relatives, though outwardly she seemed not a prejudiced person. But her mother was always a dreadful anti-Semite.

"I have nothing to blame myzelf," Oskar said.

He took to his bed. I took to the New York Public Library. I read some of the German poets he was trying to write about, in English translation. Then I read *Leaves of Grass* and wrote down what I thought one or two of them had got from Whitman. One day, toward the end of August, I brought Oskar what I had written. It was in good part guessing, but my idea wasn't to do the lecture for him. He lay on his back, motionless, and listened sadly to what I had written. Then he said, no, it wasn't the love of death they had got from Whitman—that ran through German poetry—but it was most of all his feeling for Brudermensch, his humanity.

"But this does not grow long on German earth," he said, "and is soon deztroyed."

I said I was sorry I had got it wrong, but he thanked me anyway.

I left, defeated, and as I was going down the stairs, heard the sound of sobbing. I will quit this, I thought, it has got to be too much for me. I can't drown with him.

I stayed home the next day, tasting a new kind of private misery too old for somebody my age, but that same night Oskar called me on the phone, blessing me wildly for having read those notes to him. He had got up to write me a letter to say what I had missed, and it ended in his having written half the lecture. He had slept all day and tonight intended to finish it up.

"I thank you," he said, "for much, alzo including your faith in me."

"Thank God," I said, not telling him I had just about lost it.

Oskar completed his lecture—wrote and rewrote it—during the first week in September. The Nazis invaded Poland, and though we were greatly troubled, there was some sense of release; maybe the brave Poles would beat them. It took another week to translate the lecture, but here we had the assistance of Friedrich Wilhelm Wolff, the historian, a gentle, erudite man, who liked translating and promised his help with future lectures. We then had about two weeks to work on Oskar's delivery. The weather had changed, and so, slowly, had he. He had awakened from defeat, battered, after a weary battle. He had lost close to twenty pounds. His complexion was still gray; when I looked at his face I expected to see scars, but it had lost its flabby unfocused quality. His blue eyes had returned to life and he walked with quick steps, as though to pick up a few for all the steps he hadn't taken during those long hot days he had lain in his room.

We went back to our former routine, meeting three late afternoons a week for diction, grammar, and the other exercises. I taught him the phonetic alphabet and transcribed lists of words he was mispronouncing. He worked many hours trying to fit each sound in place, holding a matchstick between his teeth to keep his jaws apart as he exercised his tongue. All this can be a dreadfully boring business unless you think you have a future. Looking at him, I realized what's meant when somebody is called "another man."

The lecture, which I now knew by heart, went off well. The director of the Institute had invited a number of prominent people. Oskar was the first refugee they had employed, and there was a move to make the public cognizant of what was then a new ingredient in American life. Two reporters had come with a lady photographer. The auditorium of the Institute was crowded. I sat in the last row, promising to put up my hand if he couldn't be heard, but it wasn't necessary. Oskar, in a blue suit, his hair cut, was of course nervous, but you couldn't see it unless you studied him. When he stepped up to the lectern, spread out his manuscript, and spoke his first English sentence in public, my heart hesitated; only he and I, of everybody there, had any idea of the anguish he had been through. His enunciation wasn't at all bad—a few s's for th's, and he once said bag for back, but otherwise he did all right. He read poetry well—in both languages—and though Walt Whitman, in his mouth, sounded a little as though he had come to the shores of Long Island as a German immigrant, still the poetry read as poetry:

> And I know the Spirit of God is the brother of my own,
> And that all the men ever born are also my brothers,
>   and the women my sisters and lovers,
> And that the kelson of creation is love . . .

Oskar read it as though he believed it. Warsaw had fallen, but the verses were somehow protective. I sat back conscious of two things: how easy it is to hide the deepest wounds; and the pride I felt in the job I had done.

Two days later I came up the stairs into Oskar's apartment to find a crowd there. The refugee, his face beet-red, lips bluish, a trace of froth in the corners of his mouth, lay on the floor in his limp pajamas, two firemen on their knees working over him with an inhalator. The windows were open and the air stank.

A policeman asked me who I was and I couldn't answer.

"No, oh no."

I said no but it was unchangingly yes. He had taken his life—gas—I hadn't even thought of the stove in the kitchen.

"Why?" I asked myself. "Why did he do it?" Maybe it was the fate of Poland on top of everything else, but the only answer anyone could come up with was Oskar's scribbled note that he wasn't well, and had left Martin Goldberg all his possessions. I am Martin Goldberg.

I was sick for a week, had no desire either to inherit or investigate, but I thought I ought to look through his things before the court impounded them, so I spent a morning sitting in the depths of Oskar's armchair, trying to read his correspondence. I had found in the top drawer a thin packet of letters from his wife and an airmail letter of recent date from his mother-in-law.

She writes in a tight script it takes me hours to decipher, that her daughter, after Oskar abandons her, against her own mother's fervent pleas and anguish, is converted to Judaism by a vengeful rabbi. One night the Brown Shirts appear, and though the mother wildly waves her bronze crucifix in their faces, they drag Frau Gassner, together with the other Jews, out of the apartment house, and transport them in lorries to a small border town in conquered Poland. There, it is rumored, she is shot in the head and topples into an open ditch with the naked Jewish men, their wives and children, some Polish soldiers, and a handful of gypsies.

1963

THEY WON'T CRACK IT OPEN

Kim Yong Ik

Dick was not at the bus station. I turned my Oriental face in every direction, hoping to be recognized by someone. Perhaps Dick had sent another to meet me since he was apparently unable to come himself.

"Cho," he had said when he was leaving Korea, "just wire me if you ever come to America, so I can meet you anywhere you say." His remark rang again in my ears between the calls of the cab drivers around me.

No one at the station gave me even a curious stare that might invite a foreigner to ask a question, and I felt even more strange.

A taxi driver asked me a second time, "Where ya goin', fella?"

I explained haltingly, "I met a kind American soldier in Korea. I sometimes interpreted for him. I sent him a long telegram. I am waiting for his automobile."

"Better not count on anybody getting up this early, fella," was his only comment. He turned away to seek other faces.

I walked back into the bus station to see what time the huge clock registered. I hadn't wired Dick any exact time, just that I would arrive early Saturday morning. It was a few minutes past four. Dick would come.

The bewildered faces of the children at the school for the blind came back to me. As I was leaving, hadn't they moved toward me to say, "Teacher, go well!" Puffing white vapor in the cold morning air, hadn't they made small bows and big bows only after I had said that I would visit their "Crown Dick" and write to them about him?

Picking up my suitcase at the baggage room, I ran for a taxi just as it was about to leave. Seated in the car, I wanted to be assured, so I said to the driver, "This is Sara-Sota?"

He nodded. I gave him one of my copies of Dick's address, for I had made several in case I should lose one, and I asked further, "This town has the greatest show on earth?"

Pulling his car into the city street sharply, the driver answered, "Sure does. It's here now for the winter."

I was driven along beneath hanging decorations of colorful lights. A breeze rushed in, cool, as if from the sea. Wondering if this street was the very one the greatest show on earth marched, I lifted my chin high. I was going to see "Crown Dick."

With the increasing breeze, I let my mind turn to the big pages of the magazine, *Life*, the circus issue that Dick had brought one day to show the children the colorful pages like an endless scroll. I watched each page closely as though I were about to describe the pictures to the children who could not see well enough: the elephant dancing, the lions obeying their trainer, some odd-looking animals with stripes, and then the circus parade. I saw again the children nearest Dick and me stand up, trying to touch the pictures, making the white parts of their eyes as large as possible.

The taxi rolled on under a long pine arch with lights at each intersection. Feeling as if I were myself in one of those magazine pictures, I clenched my fingers together like tense fists of a delighted child. The dimming, large signs blurred as the taxi sped on past FLAMINGO, DRIFTWOOD, and FOUR WINDS. I had no time to think what these signs meant, for I was already composing a letter to the school children. "I am in 'Hello' country and visiting Crown," I was saying; and at the word "Crown" I smiled. A happy moment was repeated in my mind.

It was the moment when Dick had first visited the blind children's school near Pusan. I had been teaching them for a short time. Our school was in a bleak building that had once been a warehouse. Everything at the home for the blind children of refugees was bleak, but that day I had heard for the first time their laughing shouts. Again I saw Dick's big, long nose that had almost touched the picture of a pink, laughing clown in the magazine as he described it for the children who could not see it and explained, "Clown!"

The cold, flat faces of the children rounded into happiness as they moved forward in the direction of Dick's voice, some saying "Crown!"

Although I repeated "Clown," "Clown," time and again, they had no ear for an "l," and the word "Crown" kept coming from their mouths, echoing with wonder. As I could not think of a Korean equivalent, I explained,

"You see, a 'clown' has a big nose, twice as large as yours, and he can fill his great big mouth with laughter, and fill yours too with laughter."

Right in front of me a child with some vision, though dim, had stretched his hand up to touch Dick's big nose that reached from his narrow forehead almost to his laughing mouth.

"You, Crown," the boy cried out, pointing. "You, Crown. You Hello Crown!" and the children kept repeating after him, "Crown! Crown!" even those who could not see at all. Always after that day, when the children would hear his voice, they would shout, "Crown!" Some with slight vision would pile out over the windowsills while those completely blind would follow, calling, "Crown! Crown!" to their friends. I would become excited, too. If Dick did not come for a day or two, they would ask me over and over, "Where is Crown?"

I was interrupted in my reverie by the taxi turning noiselessly, then speeding up again as it darted by shell-white houses that were still asleep in the dim early morning. I expected the driver to stop at one of these homes whose large glass windows seemed to hold an underwater richness. For when Dick had been telling the children about the circus pictures, some had asked, "Where is Crown home?" Dick, finding out from me what they meant, had answered vaguely, "Not in this picture." Then pointing to the margin of the page and beyond, he had added definitely, "Very near though."

Now my mind again chatted with Dick, recalling how he and I had prolonged our farewell in the coastal market, slowly sipping rice wine together. I pulled my necktie tighter to my throat and straightened out my socks, preparing to hop out any time now. The beautiful homes with shiny cars in the driveways had televisions inside, I knew. Dick had told me and the children about them.

Instead of slowing down, the taxi picked up speed. Now we were at the end of the residential section, and no lights were in view. Through the window a patch of opening sky appeared like the enlarged whiteness of a blind eye. Before I could gather my thoughts, which had been tipped over by the unexpected speed, the car began to kick sand along a bumpy road through an orange grove.

For a brief interval, I feared the driver might have deliberately chosen a long way in order to empty my billfold. As we bumped along he began to scan mailboxes for a name, slowing down, then speeding on. The flat land was marked with tall grasses, sedge, and water in narrow ditches. Still I wondered why Dick had not come to meet me, and I tried to talk myself into believing that he was ill. I could not understand, however, why he had not written to me, since I had told him that I had received a scholarship for my education in America and would visit him on my way to the university. I had also mentioned that the children would be happy to hear about their Crown. But no reply had come. Now I was more puzzled. There had not even been a picture postcard like those he had been sending the children after he returned to his home. Hadn't he said to the children, "When I go home, I'll buy candies, clothes, and shoes and send them to you. You'll have many things from the 'Hello' country." I could remember his words vividly and even now tried to interpret Dick's words for the children.

The taxi jolted, turned, and wiggled down close to a mailbox, whose number was faded but still recognizable, then passed under an oak tree trailing long strings of Spanish moss. It stopped beside a battered old car parked by a worn clapboard shed. An electric light through a curtained window assured me that the house was not abandoned. Across a patch of cattails near the porch, a woman was pumping water. She did not turn to look, as though she knew the car was only driving in to turn around.

A tall man, dressed in army pants only, came slowly down the porch. It was Dick. There was his big nose just above the thin lips.

Quickly I handed a five-dollar bill to the driver, not knowing how much to pay him, and turned to Dick to reach his hand in an American clasp, at the same time bowing slightly in my habitual manner. His smile did not spread beyond his rather sunken cheek, and his manner was restrained as though he were meeting me for the first time. For a moment I wondered. Could this be his brother?

The taxi driver handed me back only one dollar, and recalling that Dick had said it was a Western practice to give a tip, I said, "Keep it, please."

Dick led me through a door that squeaked. The light bulb cast a tired yellow on the sooty wooden ceiling and a dull glow on the uneven floor and the few chairs. Dick hastily picked up a blanket and a pillow from the couch under the window and invited, "Sit down."

Carrying a bucket of water in each hand, the woman came in, her back bent, her gaze turned slightly upward. Dick announced, "Cho is here, Ma."

The woman without turning to me said, "Pardon me for a minute." Before I could step forward to help her, she parted a half-open white curtain by a door I had not noticed. She went through, and I got the glimpse of a pile of wood near a stove.

Coming back to the couch, I wondered where the television box was, the one he was always telling the children about.

"Cho, the taxi is on me." I turned to see Dick holding out five dollars in his hand.

"Oh, no." I refused, covering my pocket with my hand.

Dick insisted. "Oh, tourists are thick this year. I'm doing all right. You'll need it at the university."

Then I heard an unsteady voice short of breath from behind the curtain. "Dick!" He shoved the money into my pocket and went into the kitchen. I overheard, "Dick, don't! How're we goin' to manage? I have asked Mary and Olga to spend Christmas with us."

"It's nothing, Ma. You don't know what you're talking about."

Angrily she retorted, "You are always saying it's nothing. My eyesight is poor but I can hear. I can tell, too, how you smell from your drinking."

Dick stepped out of the kitchen and, pushing the curtain aside, said, "You haven't met Cho yet."

She came out, wiping her hands on her shabby, long skirt. She dragged herself toward me, her shoes too large for her feet. "I'm glad you could come, Cho," she said.

As I returned her nod, he pushed her gently toward the kitchen. "You go fix some breakfast," he suggested.

Now and then I heard a woeful expression, "Oh, God," and then, "Oh, my God."

Dick stretched himself to his full height and put out the light by unscrewing the bulb. The room became shadowy and cooler. Pointing to the couch, he said, "Cho, you rest awhile there. I'll be back soon." He hurried out.

After the car left I still could hear Dick's mother's voice from the kitchen, "There he goes to borrow money again. He's been talking about Christmas presents. Such expensive things at that."

Before I walked out of the room into the morning air, I placed Dick's money on the chair by the door. Then I walked behind the house to view the scenes that were now emerging with the full daylight. Amid tall grass, a few hibiscus were blooming along the barbed-wire fence. On the other side of the fence, a few brown cows were huddled together, each a tail's distance from the other.

Watching the silent cows and wondering about the coldness of Dick's greeting and other things, I was startled by a voice that said, "Cho, thank you for the money." I turned to see Dick's mother coming closer to me. She was humbly grateful as if she had received alms. "Forgive Dick for not going to meet you. He got your telegram. He just didn't think you'd ever really come here.

Our home's not much, but I am not ashamed of it," she added hesitatingly. "He always says you will get a wrong impression of America if you come to visit us."

She was talking directly into my face and standing very close to see me better. I didn't have anything to say. She opened her mouth very wide as she talked and squinted so hard I could hardly see her eyes.

"We came to this country from Rumania and after Dick's father died moved down here from Iowa. Dick was always ashamed of me, always ashamed of my secondhand clothes and my speaking broken English.

"Once he was playing with some neighbor kids on the street when a cow passed by, dropping dung. I went to the front of the house with a basket and called to him. You understand, Cho, using cow dung for fuel when it is dried is an old practice in my country—I think in your country, too. When I told him, 'Pick them up,' he pretended not to hear and ran away. Then I started to gather up the refuse. His friends' eyes bulged and they asked me, 'What's that for?'

"I answered why I was doing this. Later Dick came home angry and wouldn't speak to me for several days. That happened a long time ago, but even now he mentions it whenever he gets angry with me.

"You see, Cho, when a guest comes to our house, Dick takes him out to buy him dinner and drink. He doesn't entertain his guest at our house. I was afraid a while ago he'd spend all he has whistling you back to town to restaurants, movies, and the circus quarters," she explained with a stifled sob. Apologetically, she continued. "Dick is a good boy, but he always wants to show off. His friends want to give him jobs, but he's been trying to find a big job by himself—that would impress his friends who want to help him. A man who was in our church often asked Dick to come down to Fort Myers to work in an orange grove, but he's been fooling around with getting magazine subscriptions and driving old tourist couples around. When he was away, he was so good to me, writing to me every week. Now at home he never talks to me and gets cross with me easy. Last night—no, this morning—he came home drunk again. I asked him for some money, but he just shouted at me that he had promised the Korean children Christmas presents."

For a while I couldn't believe I was listening to an American woman. When she walked away to the house, her bent figure in the unsteady step reminded me of a tired Korean woman on the road.

I walked from one fence post to another and then still farther. Always I had thought of Dick as being gay, certainly not quiet. To entertain the blind children he would try to describe an escalator by leapfrogging, circus animals by imitating their noises, and a television set by letting the children almost touch one in the picture.

Before he left Korea, he had brought a jeepful of blankets and canned goods to the refugee house. Later an army investigator had come a few times inquiring about some missing army goods.

Even in those summer days he would cheerfully announce, "I'll perform the greatest show on earth." He would climb up on an electric light pole near the shoreline and leap into the sea in beautiful diving form. As he rose, he would whistle to imitate the breathing of the women who dive for abalone shells. The children would stretch their hands toward him in glee. When the villagers gathered to watch, he would say, "Tell them, Cho, that the diving chased out my evil spirit."

For a brief moment I heard again the sound of his jeep on the road, then at a rumbling sound, I turned to see Dick's car returning. I noticed the cows, staring at me now, unblinking, but hastened to the home that Dick had described as being "very near the circus, though."

As I approached the kitchen window, I heard my name spoken, followed by, "I didn't ask him to return the money, Dick."

I hesitated, not wishing to hear. Dick's angry voice blurted out, "What will Cho think of us? You told him your damn story of how poor we are, didn't you?"

"Dick, hush!" The mother's voice broke.

Coughing, I stepped up onto the porch. Dick, forcing a smile, opened the door for me. I said, "Dick, I must leave now so I can see the dean at the college before the holidays." I avoided the hurt look in his eyes. Turning toward the mother, I nodded. "Good-bye."

Dick followed me outside, and we got into his old battered car. Thin piles of magazines lay on the floor. He sat, not starting the engine, then asked, "Cho, can't you stay over till Sunday afternoon? You can see a performance at the circus quarters then. That would give me time to get a package ready for you to address to the children for me. I want it in Korean to be sure they get it."

"Dick, I had better go." I insisted. Realizing I sounded abrupt, I explained, "I left my baggage at the station and did not plan to stay over."

As he was backing slowly out, the Spanish moss swept the top of the car. His mother called, "Dick! Wait!" She wobbled out, waving a paper sack. "This is your breakfast, Cho. It's too expensive to buy food outside." As I took the sack, she offered me a crumpled dollar bill and a quarter, "Cho, buy some Christmas gifts for those children."

Dick let me out an embarrassed laugh which was close to a hoarse cry and shook his head. "Ma, we can't send them a stingy gift."

I quickly took the money from her hand and raised my voice high over the now angry fit of the motor. "Thank you very much. The children will be so happy."

Neither of us spoke as Dick drove toward the city. When I thought the car must be nearing the station, I tried to think of something cheerful to say. Through the cracked glass window, I saw jagged hunks of tall buildings. "This is the street down which the greatest show on earth parades," I said half aloud. Then I cleared my voice and asked, "Isn't it?" When no word came from Dick, I regretted my remark. "In winter"—I went on to ask another question—"can you swim in the sea here in winter?"

Then he broke the silence. "Would you like to drive along the beach before you go to the bus?" Steering the car with one hand, he reached to open the glove compartment, took out a bottle of whiskey. He invited me to drink, "Have American *sake*, Cho." I bent my face back, refusing it. He poured much of the contents into his mouth.

As soon as I said, "I want to see the surf, the sandy shore, and the palm trees you talked about," the old car swerved at the next corner and ran at full speed for some distance. It was soon puffing over a long, white bridge, and then down a street shaded completely with tall pines. The foliage of a tall, straight tree danced in the light breeze under the morning sky that was yet too young for me to foretell the weather. Dick slowed down and announced, "There is a palm tree."

I no longer wanted to see a palm tree, a television, an escalator, or an electric eye. I was homesick; homesick to see a dimly lit thatched house with shadows of those blind children on the paper windows, those shadows growing closer and brighter.

Beyond a floating line of surf suds, I saw wheeling sea gulls over the water and in the distance the skeleton of a building that apparently had been begun and never finished. On it was the framework of a tall tower, and immediately I said out loud, "You used to dive into the sea back in Korea from an electric light pole. Don't you remember?"

He drove on without answering till he suddenly stopped in front of a clump of tall sea oats. Then he spoke as if he had just heard my question, "I have been thinking about that, too." He asked, "How are my children?"

"They are fine. I'd better write to them today."

"Do they still call me Clown?" Correcting himself, he repeated, "Crown;

Crown." He smiled, but it did not quite remove the furrows from his forehead. He hunched over the wheel and asked timidly, "What are you going to write?"

"Write?" I merely replied, "I hadn't thought about that yet."

He was gazing beyond the gulf below a red-crested cloud and speaking as if talking with himself. "It is strange that I seem to feel more concerned about what they should think about me, those children I shall never see again, than about what people here think."

"The children will never forget you, Dick. You were the most delightful hello soldier."

"Cho," Dick for the first time looked at me straight in the eye, "I am sorry for the things that happened a while ago. "Before I could tell him anything, he went on. "My mother is OK. I often get cross with her.

"When the war broke our and I went to your country, she was very upset. She had already begun to complain of her eyes and written our officers asking them to send me home. I was sorry for having been rude to my mother and worried about her. I visited your school for the blind the first time to see what somebody with weak eyes would look like. When I saw those children, I wanted to talk and act. But I don't have the grace of your people who can still tell beautiful, human stories in spite of hard poverty and war. I just told fairy stories of what I would do when I got back home. Cho, I hope you don't tell them anything to disillusion them, those kids, because I love them now more than ever."

Many of the sea gulls had lighted on the sands and some crowded in before us, screeching. As though Dick and I had previously agreed upon giving the gulls the breakfast I had been given, we stepped out of the car and tossed pieces of toast, boiled egg bits, and bacon strips up as high as we could. The gulls piled one upon another and whirled away in wild, shrieking delight. Dick blew his breath into the empty sack and hit it against his other palm, bursting it with a bang. I told Dick loud, "I'll tell those children what a beautiful time we had right here."

Dick ran back to the car, took the flask of whiskey again from the glove compartment, and emptied its contents down his throat, throwing the empty bottle into the sea oats. He sang "Alyran Alyran Alaryo" while a radiant glow suffused his face, a face as radiant as an actor's. As he started to dance, his knees gave way and fell to the sands. He rolled over to lie on his side and resumed "Alyran" brokenly.

I rested for a brief space near the uprooted pine at the high-water mark, waiting for him to rouse himself. I saw his chest rising and falling slowly but evenly.

When I called his name, he mumbled without waking, "What, Mom? Oh, I'll go down to work in a grove."

The tide gradually receded. There was nothing for me to do but to doodle in the sand, "Merry Christmas, Dick." I became impatient, realizing I must catch the bus. I went over again to him and called him. Not being able to wake him, I shook him hard from his shoulder. He was snoring, occasionally puffing out his mouth as he tried to moisten his lips. When I gave him quite a tug and called him louder, he mumbled angrily, "Cut it out, son of a bitch. I can't help snoring."

Automatically, I pulled back my hands. I realized that I could not rouse him and he must lie there till the incoming tide would no doubt wake him. When I left him, he was not snoring at all. Sleeping it off, I thought, as I remembered what other soldiers had sometimes called it.

Walking back to the foot of a long, white bridge, I came upon a pile of coconuts with tags on them and a placard above, reading, "Send one home—only 25 cents." I purchased one, imagining the owner I didn't see.

With the strange fruit under my arm, I made my way back to the city, finally turning into the street where Dick had said the greatest show on earth marched. A block farther on I entered a post office and addressed a tag to the children's home in Korea. From "Crown," I put on it, "Sarasota, Florida, U.S.A." and handed it in at a window.

The clerk said in surprise. "A coconut for Korea? What do you do a thing like that for?" He set it on the scales and added, "Why, the people are starving over there, aren't they?"

I did not talk back to him but said to myself, "I like the idea of sending a coconut across a continent, across the Pacific, then to a tiny Korean village on the seacoast." I could plainly see those blind children putting their round heads together, touching and hugging the strange fruit and even its shadow while they laughed about their Crown. "No, no!" they would say. "We will not crack it open to see what is inside. We want to keep it whole." My own lips moved faintly to form the words. "No, they won't crack the image of Crown."

"Come on!" I heard the clerk say, tapping his pencil at the window, "Eighty-eight cents, please."

A line of people was pressing behind me. I threw down the dollar bill and ran out, hearing, "Hey, don't you want your change?"

But I kept on, making my way toward the bus station and that college campus.

1969

A WIFE'S STORY

Bharati Mukherjee

Imre says forget it, but I'm going to write David Mamet. So Patels are hard to sell real estate to. You buy them a beer, whisper Glengary Glen Ross, and they smell swamp instead of sun and surf. The work hard, eat cheap, live ten to a room, stash their savings under futons in Queens, and before you know it they own half of Hoboken. You say, where's the sweet gullibility that made this nation great?

Polish jokes, Patel jokes: that's not why I want to write Mamet.

Seen their women?

Everybody laughs. Imre laughs. The dozing fat man with the Barnes & Noble sack between his legs, the woman next to him, the usher, everybody. The theater isn't so dark that they can't see me. In my red silk sari I'm conspicuous. Plump, gold paisleys sparkle on my chest.

The actor is just warming up. *Seen their women?* He plays a salesman, he's had a bad day and now he's in a Chinese restaurant trying to loosen up. His face is pink. His wool-blend slacks are creased at the crotch. We bought our tickets at half-price, we're sitting in the front row, but at the edge, and we see things we shouldn't be seeing. At least I do, or think I do. Spittle, actors goosing each other, little winks, streaks of makeup.

Maybe they're improvising dialogue too. Maybe Mamet's provided them with insult kits, Thursdays for Chinese, Wednesdays for Hispanics, today for Indians. Maybe they get together before curtain time, see an Indian woman settling in the front row off to the side, and say to each other: "Hey, forget Friday. Let's get *her* today. See if she cries. See if she walks out." Maybe, like the salesmen they play, they have a little bet on.

Maybe I shouldn't feel betrayed.

Their women, he goes again. They look like they've just been fucked by a dead cat.

The fat man hoots so hard he nudges my elbow off our shared armrest.

"Imre. I'm going home." But Imre's hunched so far forward he doesn't hear. English isn't his best language. A refugee from Budapest, he has to listen hard. "I didn't pay eighteen dollars to be insulted."

I don't hate Mamet. It's the tyranny of the American dream that scares me. First, you don't exist. Then you're invisible. Then you're funny. Then you're disgusting. Insult, my American friends will tell me, is a kind of acceptance. No instant dignity here. A play like this, back home, would cause riots. Communal, racist, and antisocial. The actors wouldn't make it off stage. This play, and all these awful feelings, would be safely locked up.

I long, at times, for clear-cut answers. Offer me instant dignity, today, and I'll take it.

"What?" Imre moves toward me without taking his eyes off the actor. "Come again?"

Tears come. I want to stand, scream, make an awful scene. I long for ugly, nasty rage.

The actor is ranting, flinging spittle. *Give me a chance. I'm not finished, I can get back on the board. I tell that asshole, give me a real lead. And what does that asshole give me? Patels. Nothing but Patels.*

This time Imre works an arm around my shoulders. "Panna, what is Patel? Why are you taking it all so personally?"

I shrink from his touch, but I don't walk out. Expensive girls' schools in Lausanne and Bombay have trained me to behave well. My manners are exquisite, my feelings are delicate, my gestures refined, my moods undetectable. They have seen me through riots, uprootings, separation, my son's death.

"I'm not taking it personally."

The fat man looks at us. The woman looks too, and shushes.

I stare back at the two of them. Then I stare, mean and cool, at the man's elbow. Under the bright blue polyester Hawaiian shirt sleeve, the elbow looks soft and runny. "Excuse me," I say. My voice has the effortless meanness of well-bred displaced Third World women, though my rhetoric has been learned elsewhere. "You're exploiting my space."

Startled, the man snatches his arm away from me. He cradles it against his breast. By the time he's ready with comebacks, I've turned my back on him. I've probably ruined the first act for him. I know I've ruined it for Imre.

It's not my fault; it's the *situation*. Old colonies wear down. Patels—the new pioneers—have to be suspicious. Idi Amin's lesson is permanent. AT&T wires move good advice from continent to continent. Keep all assets liquid. Get into 7-11s, get out of condos and motels. I know how both sides feel, that's the trouble. The Patel sniffing out scams, the sad salesmen on the stage: postcolonialism has made me their referee. It's hate I long for; simple, brutish, partisan hate.

After the show Imre and I make our way toward Broadway. Sometimes he holds my hand; it doesn't mean anything more than that crazies and drunks are crouched in doorways. Imre's been here over two years, but he's stayed very old-world, very courtly, openly protective of women. I met him in a seminar on special ed. last semester. His wife is a nurse somewhere in the Hungarian countryside. There are two sons, and miles of petitions for their emigration. My husband manages a mill two hundred miles north of Bombay. There are no children.

"You make things tough on yourself," Imre says. He assumed Patel was a Jewish name or maybe Hispanic; everything makes equal sense to him. He found the play tasteless, he worried about the effect of vulgar language on my sensitive ears. "You have to let go a bit." And as though to show me how to let go, he breaks away from me, bounds ahead with his head ducked tight, then dances on amazingly jerky legs. He's a Magyar, he often tells me, and deep down, he's an Asian too. I catch glimpses of it, knife-blade Attila cheekbones, despite the blondish hair. In his faded jeans and leather jacket, he's a rock video star. I watch MTV for hours in the apartment when Charity's working the evening shift at Macy's. I listen to WPLJ on Charity's earphones. Why should I be ashamed? Television in India is so uplifting.

Imre stops as suddenly as he'd started. People walk around us. The summer sidewalk is full of theatergoers in seersucker suits; Imre's year-round jacket is out of place. European. Cops in twos and threes huddle, lightly tap their thighs with night sticks and smile at me with benevolence. I want to wink at them, get us all in trouble, tell them the crazy dancing man is from the Warsaw Pact. I'm too shy to break into dance on Broadway. So I hug Imre instead.

The hug takes him by surprise. He wants me to let go, but he doesn't really expect me to let go. He staggers, though I weigh no more than 104 pounds, and with him, I pitch forward slightly. Then he catches me, and we walk arm in arm to the bus stop. My husband would never dance or hug a woman on Broadway. Nor would my brothers. They aren't stuffy people, but they went to Anglican boarding schools and they have a well-developed sense of what's silly.

"Imre." I squeeze his big, rough hand. "I'm sorry I ruined the evening for you."

"You did nothing of the kind." He sounds tired. "Let's not wait for the bus. Let's splurge and take a cab instead."

Imre always has unexpected funds. The Network, he calls it, Class of '56.

In the back of the cab, without even trying, I feel light, almost free. Memories of Indian destitutes mix with hordes of New York street people, and they float free, like astronauts, inside my head. I've made it. I'm making something of my life. I've left home, my husband, to get a Ph.D. in special ed. I have a multiple-entry visa and a small scholarship for two years. After that, we'll see. My mother was beaten by her mother-in-law, my grandmother, when she'd registered for French lessons at the Alliance Française. My grandmother, the eldest daughter of a rich zamindar, was illiterate.

Imre and the cabdriver talk away in Russian. I keep my eyes closed. That way I can feel the floaters better. I'll write Mamet tonight. I feel strong, reckless. Maybe I'll write Steven Spielberg too; tell him that Indians don't eat monkey brains.

We've made it. Patels must have made it. Mamet, Spielberg: they're not condescending to us. Maybe they're a little bit afraid.

Charity Chin, my roommate, is sitting on the floor drinking Chablis out of a plastic wineglass. She is five foot six, three inches taller than me, but weighs a kilo and a half less than I do. She is a "hands" model. Orientals are supposed to have a monopoly in the hands-modeling business, she says. She had her eyes fixed eight or nine months ago and out of gratitude sleeps with her plastic surgeon every third Wednesday.

"Oh, good," Charity says. "I'm glad you're back early. I need to talk."

She's been writing checks, MCI, Con Ed, Bonwit Teller, Envelopes, already stamped and sealed, form a pyramid between her shapely, knee-socked legs. The checkbook's cover is brown plastic, grained to look like cowhide. Each time Charity flips back the cover, white geese fly over sky-colored checks. She makes good money, but she's extravagant. The difference adds up to this shared, rent-controlled Chelsea one-bedroom.

"All right. Talk."

When I first moved in, she was seeing an analyst. Now she sees a nutritionist.

"Eric called. From Oregon."

"What did he want?"

"He wants me to pay half the rent on his loft for last spring. He asked me to move back, remember? He *begged* me."

Eric is Charity's estranged husband.

"What does your nutritionist say?" Eric now wears a red jumpsuit and tills the soil in Rajneeshpuram.

"You think Phil's a creep too, don't you? What else can he be when creeps are all I attract?"

Phil is a flutist with thinning hair. He's very touchy on the subject of *flautists* versus *flutists*. He's touchy on every subject, from music to books to foods to clothes. He teaches at a small college upstate, and Charity bought a used blue Datsun ("Nissan," Phil insists) last month so she could spend weekends with him. She returns every Sunday night, exhausted and exasperated. Phil and I don't have much to say to each other—he's the only musician I know; the men in my family are lawyers, engineers, or in business—but I like him. Around me, he loosens up. When he visits, he bakes us loaves of pumpernickel bread. He waxes our kitchen floor. Like many men in this country, he seems to me a displaced child, or even a woman, looking for something that passed him by, or for something that he can never have. If he thinks I'm not looking, he sneaks his hands under Charity's sweater, but there isn't too much there. Here, she's a model with high ambitions. In India, she'd be a flat-chested old maid.

I'm shy in front of the lovers. A darkness comes over me when I see them horsing around.

"It isn't the money," Charity says. Oh? I think. "He says he still loves me. Then he turns around and asks me for five hundred."

What's so strange about that, I want to ask. She still loves Eric, and Eric, red jumpsuit and all, is smart enough to know it. Love is a commodity, hoarded like any other. Mamet knows. But I say, "I'm not the person to ask about love." Charity knows that mine was a traditional Hindu marriage. My parents, with the help of a marriage broker, who was my mother's cousin, picked out a groom. All I had to do was get to know his taste in food.

It'll be a long evening, I'm afraid. Charity likes to confess. I unpleat my silk sari—it no longer looks too showy—wrap it in muslin cloth and put it away in a dresser drawer. Saris are hard to have laundered in Manhattan, though there's a good man in Jackson Heights. My next step will be to brew us a pot of chrysanthemum tea. It's a very special tea from the mainland. Charity's uncle gave it to us. I like him. He's a humpbacked, awkward, terrified man. He runs a gift store on Mott Street, and though he doesn't speak much English, he seems to have done well. Once upon a time he worked for the railways in Chengdu, Szechwan Province, and during the Wuchang Uprising, he was shot at. When I'm down, when I'm lonely for my husband, when I think of our son, or when I need to be held, I think of Charity's uncle. If I hadn't left home, I'd never have heard of the Wuchang Uprising. I've broadened my horizons.

Very late that night my husband calls me from Ahmadabad, a town of textile mills north of Bombay. My husband is a vice president at Lakshmi Cotton Mills. Lakshmi is the goddess of wealth, but LCM (Priv.), Ltd., is doing poorly. Lockouts, strikes, rock-throwings. My husband lives on digitalis, which he calls the food for our *yuga* of discontent.

"We had a bad mishap at the mill today." Then he says nothing for seconds.

The operator comes on. "Do you have the right party, sir? We're trying to reach Mrs. Butt."

"Bhatt," I insist. "*B* for Bombay, *H* for Haryana, *A* for Ahmadabad, double *T* for Tamil Naddu." It's a litany. "This is she."

"One of our lorries was firebombed today. Resulting in three deaths. The driver, old Karamchand, and his two children."

I know how my husband's eyes look this minute, how the eye rims sag and the yellow corneas shine and bulge with pain. He is not an emotional man—the Ahmadabad Institute of Management has trained him to cut losses, to look on the bright side of economic catastrophes—but tonight he's feeling low. I try to remember a driver named Karamchand, but can't. That part of my life is over, the way *trucks* have replaced *lorries* in my vocabulary, the way Charity Chin and her lurid love life have replaced inherited notions of marital duty. Tomorrow he'll come out of it. Soon he'll be eating again. He'll sleep like a baby. He's been trained to believe in turnovers. Every morning he rubs his scalp with cantharidine oil so his hair will grow back again.

"It could be your car next." Affection, love. Who can tell the difference in a traditional marriage in which a wife still doesn't call her husband by his first name?

"No. They know I'm a flunky, just like them. Well paid, maybe. No need for undue anxiety, please."

Then his voice breaks. He says he needs me, he misses me, he wants me to come to him damp from my evening shower, smiling of sandalwood soap, my braid decorated with jasmines.

"I need you too."

"Not to worry, please," he says. "I am coming in a fortnight's time. I have already made arrangements."

Outside my window, fire trucks whine, up Eighth Avenue. I wonder if he can hear them, what he thinks of a life like mine, led amid disorder.

"I am thinking it'll be like a honeymoon. More or less."

When I was in college, waiting to be married, I imagined honeymoons were only for the more fashionable girls, the girls who came from slightly racy families, smoked Sobranies in the dorm lavatories and put up posters of Kabir Bedi, who was supposed to have made it as a big star in the West. My husband wants us to go to Niagara. I'm not to worry about foreign exchange. He's arranged for extra dollars through the Gujarati Network, with a cousin in San Jose. And he's bought four hundred more on the black market. "Tell me you need me. Panna, please tell me again."

I change out of the cotton pants and shirt I've been wearing all day and put on a sari to meet my husband at JFK. I don't forget jewelry; the marriage necklace of *mangalsutra*, gold drop earrings, heavy gold bangles. I don't wear them every day. In this borough of vice and greed, who knows when, or whom, desire will overwhelm.

My husband spots me in the crowd and waves. He has lost weight, and changed his glasses. The arm, uplifted in a cheery wave, is bony, frail, almost opalescent.

In the Carey Coach, we hold hands. He strokes my fingers one by one. "How come you aren't wearing my mother's ring?"

"Because muggers know about Indian women," I say. They know with us it's 24-karat. His mother's ring is showy, in ghastly taste anywhere but India: a blood-red Burma ruby set in a gold frame of floral sprays. My mother-in-law got her guru to bless the ring before I left for the States.

He looks disconcerted. He's used to a different role. He's the knowing, suspicious one in the family. He seems to be sulking, and finally he comes out with it. "You've said nothing about my new glasses." I compliment him on the glasses, how chic and Western-executive they make him look. But I can't help the other things, necessities until he learns the ropes. I handle the money, buy the tickets. I don't know if this makes me unhappy.

✻   ✻   ✻

Charity drives her Nissan upstate, so for two weeks we are to have the apartment to ourselves. This is more privacy than we ever had in India. No parents, no servants, to keep us modest. We play at housekeeping. Imre has lent us a hibachi, and I grill saffron chicken breasts. My husband marvels at the size of the Perdue hens. "They're big like peacocks, no? These Americans, they're really something!" He tries out pizzas, burgers, McNuggets. He chews. He explores. He judges. He loves it all, fears nothing, feels at home in the summer odors, the clutter of Manhattan streets. Since he thinks that the American palate is bland, he carries a bottle of red peppers in his pocket. I wheel a shopping cart down the aisles of the neighborhood Grand Union, and he follows, swiftly, greedily. He picks up hair rinses and high-protein diet powders. There's so much I already take for granted.

One night, Imre stops by. He wants us to go with him to a movie. In his work shirt and red leather tie, he looks arty or strung out. It's only been a week, but I feel as though I am really seeing him for the first time. The yellow hair worn very short at the sides, the wide, narrow lips. He's a good-looking man, but very self-conscious, almost arrogant. He's picked the movie we should see. He always tells me what to see, what to read. He buys the *Voice*. He's a natural avant-gardist. For tonight, he's chosen *Numéro Deux*.

"Is it a musical?" my husband asks. The Radio City Music Hall is on his list of sights to see. He's read up on the history of the Rockettes. He doesn't catch Imre's sympathetic wink.

Guilt, shame, loyalty. I long to be ungracious, not ingratiate myself with both men.

That night my husband calculates in rupees the money we've wasted on Godard. "That refugee fellow, Nagy, must have a screw loose in his head. I paid very steep price for dollars on the black market."

Some afternoons we go shopping. Back home we hated shopping, but now it is a lovers' project. My husband's shopping list startles me. I feel I am just getting to know him. Maybe, like Imre, freed from the dignities of old-world culture, he too could get drunk and squirt Cheez Whiz on a guest. I watch him dart into stores in his gleaming leather shoes. Jockey shorts on sale in outdoor bins on Broadway entrance him. White tube socks with different bands of color delight him. He looks for microcassettes, for anything small and electronic and smuggleable. He needs a garment bag. He calls it a "wardrobe," and I have to translate.

"All of New York is having sales, no?"

My heart speeds watching him this happy. It's the third week in August, almost the end of summer, and the city smells ripe, it cannot bear more heat, more money, more energy.

"This is so smashing! The prices are so excellent!" Recklessly, my prudent husband signs away traveler's checks. How he intends to smuggle it all back I don't dare ask. With a microwave, he calculates, we could get rid of our cook.

This has to be love, I think. Charity, Eric, Phil: they may be experts on sex. My husband doesn't chase me around the sofa, but he pushes me down on Charity's battered cushions, and the man who has never entered the kitchen of our Ahmadabad house now comes toward me with a dish tub of steamy water to massage away the pavement heat.

Ten days into his vacation my husband checks out brochures for sightseeing tours. Shortline, Grayline, Crossroads: his new vinyl briefcase is full of schedules and pamphlets. While I make pancakes out of a mix, he comparison-shops. Tour number one costs $10.95 and will give us the World Trade Center, Chinatown, and the United Nations. Tour number three would take us both uptown *and* downtown for $14.95, but my husband is absolutely sure he doesn't want to see Harlem. We settle for tour number four: Downtown and the Dame. It's offered by a new tour company with a small, dirty office at Eighth and Forty-eighth.

The sidewalk outside the office is colorful with tourists. My husband sends me in to buy the tickets because he has come to feel Americans don't understand his accent.

The dark man, Lebanese probably, behind the counter comes on too friendly. "Come on, doll, make my day!" He won't say which tour is his. "Number four? Honey, no! Look, you've wrecked me! Say you'll change your mind." He takes two twenties and gives back change. He holds the tickets, forcing me to pull. He leans closer. "I'm off after lunch."

My husband must have been watching me from the sidewalk. "What was the chap saying?" he demands. "I told you not to wear pants. He thinks you are Puerto Rican. He thinks he can treat you with disrespect."

The bus is crowded and we have to sit across the aisle from each other. The tour guide begins his patter on Forty-sixth. He looks like an actor, his hair bleached and blow-dried. Up close he must look middle-aged, but from where I sit his skin is smooth and his cheeks faintly red.

"Welcome to the Big Apple, folks." The guide uses a microphone. "Big Apple. That's what we native Manhattan degenerates call our city. Today we have guests from fifteen foreign countries and six states from the U. S. of A. That makes the Tourist Bureau real happy. And let me assure you that while we may be the richest city in the richest country in the world, it's okay to tip your charming and talented attendant." He laughs. Then he swings his hip out into the aisle and sings a song.

"And it's mighty fancy on old Delancey Street, you know. . . . "

My husband looks irritable. The guide is, as expected, a good singer. "The bloody man should be giving us histories of buildings we are passing, no?" I pat his hand, the mood passes. He cranes his neck. Our window seats have both gone to Japanese. It's the tour of his life. Next to this, the quick business trips to Manchester and Glasgow pale.

"And tell me what street compares to Mott Street, in July. . . . "

The guide wants applause. He manages a derisive laugh from the American up front. He's working the aisles now. "I coulda been somebody, right? I coulda been a star!" Two or three of us smile, those of us who recognize the parody. He catches my smile. The sun is on his harsh, bleached hair. "Right, your highness? Look, we gotta maharani with us! Couldn't I have been a star?"

"Right!" I say, my voice coming out a squeal. I've been trained to adapt; what else can I say?

We drive through traffic past landmark office buildings and churches. The guide flips his hands. "Art Deco," he keeps saying. I hear him confide to one of the Americans: "Beats me. I went to a cheap guide's school." My husband wants to know more about this Art Deco, but the guide sings another song.

"We made a foolish choice," my husband grumbles. "We are sitting in the bus only. We're not going into famous buildings." He scrutinizes the pamphlets in his jacket pocket. I think, at least it's air-conditioned in here. I could sit here in the cool shadows of the city forever.

Only five of us appear to have opted for the "Downtown and the Dame" tour. The others will ride back uptown past the United Nations after we've been dropped off at the pier for the ferry to the Statue of Liberty.

An elderly European pulls a camera out of his wife's designer tote bag. He takes pictures of the boats in the harbor, the Japanese in kimonos eating popcorn, scavenging pigeons, me. Then, pushing his wife ahead of him, he climbs back on the bus and waves at us. For a second I feel terribly lost. I wish we were on the bus going back to the apartment. I know I'll not be able to describe any of this to Charity, or to Imre. I'm too proud to admit I went on a guided tour.

The view of the city from the Circle Line ferry is seductive, unreal. The skyline wavers out of reach, but never quite vanishes. The summer sun pushes through fluffy clouds and dapples the glass of office towers. My husband looks thrilled, even more than he had on the shopping trips down Broadway. Tourists and dreamers, we have spent our life's savings to see this skyline, this statue.

"Quick, take a picture of me!" my husband yells as he moves toward a gap of railings. A Japanese matron has given up her position in order to change film. "Before the Twin Towers disappear!"

I focus, I wait for a large Oriental family to walk out of my range. My husband holds his pose tight against the railing. He wants to look more relaxed, an international businessman at home in all the financial markets.

A bearded man slides across the bench toward me. "Like this," he says and helps me get my husband in focus. "You want me to take the photo for you?" His name, he says, is Goran. He is Goran from Yugoslavia, as though that were enough for tracking him down. Imre from Hungary. Panna from India. He pulls the old Leica out of my hand, signaling the Orientals to beat it, and clicks away. "I'm a photographer," he says. He could have been a camera thief. That's what my husband would have assumed. Somehow, I trusted. "Get you a beer?" he asks.

"I don't. Drink, I mean. Thank you very much." I say those last words very loud, for everyone's benefit. The odd bottles of Soave with Imre don't count.

"Too bad." Goran gives back the camera.

"Take one more!" my husband shouts from the railing. "Just to be sure!"

The island itself disappoints. The Lady has brutal scaffolding holding her in. The museum is closed. The snack bar is dirty and expensive. My husband reads out the prices to me. He orders two french fries and two Cokes. We sit at picnic tables and wait for the ferry to take us back.

"What was that hippie chap saying?"

As if I could say. A day-care center has brought its kids, at least forty of them, to the island for the day. The kids, all wearing name tags, run around us. I can't help noticing how many are Indian. Even a Patel, probably a Bhatt if I looked hard enough. They toss hamburger bits at pigeons. They kick styrofoam cups. The pigeons are slow, greedy, persistent. I have to shoo one off the table top. I don't think my husband thinks about our son.

"What hippie?"

"The one on the boat. With the beard and the hair."

My husband doesn't look at me. He shakes out his paper napkin and tries to protect his french fries from pigeon feathers.

"Oh, him. He said he was from Dubrovnik." It isn't true, but I don't want trouble.

"What did he say about Dubrovnik?"

I know enough about Dubrovnik to get by. Imre's told me about it. And about Mostar and Zagreb. In Mostar white Muslims sing the call to prayer. I would like to see that before I die: white Muslims. Whole peoples have moved before me; they've adapted. The night Imre told me about Mostar was also the night I saw my first snow in Manhattan. We'd walked down to Chelsea from Columbia. We'd walked and talked and I hadn't felt tired at all.

"You're too innocent," my husband says. He reaches for my hand. "Panna," he cries with pain in his voice, and I am brought back from perfect, floating memories of snow, "I've come to take you back. I have seen how men watch you."

"What?"

"Come back, now. I have tickets. We have all the things we will ever need. I can't live without you."

A little girl with wiry braids kicks a bottle cap at his shoes. The pigeons wheel and scuttle around us. My husband covers his fries with spread-out fingers. "No kicking," he tells the girl. Her name, Beulah, is printed in green ink on a heart-shaped name tag. He forces a smile, and Beulah smiles back. Then she starts to flap her arms. She flaps, she hops. The pigeons go crazy for fries and scraps.

"Special ed. course is two years," I remind him. "I can't go back."

My husband picks up our trays and throws them into the garbage before I can stop him. He's carried disposability a little too far. "We've been taken," he says, moving toward the dock, though the ferry will not arrive for another twenty minutes. "The ferry costs only two dollars round-trip per person. We should have chosen tour number one for $10.95 instead of tour number four for $14.95."

With my Lebanese friend, I think. "But this way we don't have to worry about cabs. The bus will pick us up at the pier and take us back to midtown. Then we can walk home."

"New York is full of cheats and whatnot. Just like Bombay." He is not accusing me of infidelity. I feel dread all the same.

That night, after we've gone to bed, the phone rings. My husband listens, then hands the phone to me. "What is this woman saying?" He turns on the pink Macy's lamp by the bed. "I am not understanding these Negro people's accents."

The operator repeats the message. It's a cable from one of the directors of Lakshmi Cotton Mills. "Massive violent labor confrontation anticipated. Stop. Return posthaste. Stop. Cable flight details. Signed Kantilal Shah."

"It's not your factory," I say. "You're supposed to be on vacation."

"So, you are worrying about me? Yes? You reject my heartfelt wishes but you worry about me?" He pulls me close, slips the straps of my night-dress off my shoulder. "Wait a minute."

I wait, unclothed, for my husband to come back to me. The water is running in the bathroom. In the ten days he has been here he has learned American rites: deodorants, fragrances. Tomorrow morning he'll call Air India; tomorrow evening he'll be on his way back to Bombay. Tonight I should make up to him for my years away, the gutted trucks, the degree I'll never use in India. I want to pretend with him that nothing has changed.

In the mirror that hangs on the bathroom door, I watch my naked body turn, the breasts, the thighs glow. The body's beauty amazes. I stand here shameless, in ways he has never seen me. I am free, afloat, watching somebody else.

1988

SILVER PAVEMENTS, GOLDEN ROOFS

Chitra Divakaruni

I've looked forward to this day for so long that when I finally board the plane I can hardly breathe. In my hurry I bump into the air hostess who is at the door welcoming us, her brilliant pink smile an exact match for her brilliant pink nails.

"Sorry," I say, "so very very sorry," like the nuns had taught me to in those old, high-ceilinged classrooms cooled by the breeze from the convent *neem* trees. And I am. She is so blond, so American.

"No problem," she replies her smile as golden as the wavy hair that falls in perfect curls to her shoulder. I have never heard the expression before. *No problem,* I whisper to myself as I make my way down the aisle, in love with the exotic syllables. *No problem.* I finger my long hair, imprisoned in the customary tight braid that reaches below my waist. It feels coarse and oily. As soon as I get to Chicago, I promise myself, I will have it cut and styled.

The air inside the plane smells different from the air I've known all my life in Calcutta, moist and weighted with smell of mango blossoms and bus fumes and human sweat. This air is dry and cool and leaves a slight metallic aftertaste on my lips. I lick at them, wanting to capture that taste, make it part of me forever.

The little tray of food is so pretty, so sanitary. The knife and fork sealed in their own plastic packet, the monogrammed paper napkin. I want to save the shiny tinfoil that covers the steaming dish. I feel sadness for my friends—Prema, Vaswati, Sabitri—who will never see any of this. I picture them standing outside Ramu's *pakora* stall, munching on the spicy batter-dipped onion rings that our parents have expressly forbidden us to eat, look-ing up for a moment, eyes squinched against the sun, at the tiny silver plane. I pick up the candy in its crackly pink wrap from the dessert dish. *Almond Roca*, I read, and run my fingers over its nubby surface. I slip it into my purse, then take it out, laughing at my silliness. I am going to the land of Almond Rocas, I remind myself. The American chocolate melts in my mouth, just as sweet as I thought it would be.

But then the worries come.

I hardly know Aunt Pratima, my mother's younger sister with whom I am to stay while I attend college. And her husband, whom I am to call Bikram-uncle—I don't know him at all. They left India a week after their wedding (I was eight then) and have not been back since. Aunt is not much of a letter writer; every year at Bijoya she sends us a card stating how much she misses us, and that's all. In response to my letter asking for permission to stay with her, she wrote back only, *yes of course, but we live very simply.*

I wasn't quite sure what to make of it. All the women I know—my mother, her friends, my other aunts—are avid talkers, filling up lazy heat-hazed afternoons with long, gossipy tales while they drink tea and chew on betel leaves and laugh loud enough to scare away the *ghu-ghu* birds sleep-ing under the eaves. I couldn't ask my mother—she'd been against my com-ing to America and would surely use that letter to strengthen her arsenal. So I told myself that was how Americans (Aunt Pratima had lived there long enough to qualify as one) expressed themselves. Economically. And that second part, about living simply—she was just being modest. We all knew that Bikram-uncle owned his own auto business.

Now I look down on the dazzle-bright clouds packed tight as snow cones, deceptively solid. (But I know they are only mist and gauze, unable to save us should an engine fail and the plane plummet downward.) I pull my blue silk sari, which I bought for this trip, close around me. The air feels suddenly stale, heavy with other people's exhalations. I think, *What if Uncle and Aunt don't like me? What if I don't like them?* I remember the only pic-ture I've seen of them, the faded sepia marriage photo where they gazed into the camera, stoic and unsmiling, their heavy garlands pulling at their necks. (Why had they never sent any other pictures?) What if they hadn't really wanted me to come and were only being polite? (Americans, I'd heard, like their privacy. They liked their lives to be smooth and uninter-rupted by the claims of relatives.) What if they're not even at the airport? What if they're there but I don't recognize them? I imagine myself stranded, my suitcases strewn around me, the only one left in a large, echo-ing building after all the happily reunited families have gone home. Maybe I should have listened to Mother after all, I say to myself. Should have let her arrange that marriage for me with Aunt Sarita's neighbor's nephew. Saying it makes the fear something I can see and breathe, like the gray fog that hangs above the smoking section of the aircraft, where someone has placed me by mistake.

Later, of course, I will laugh at my foolishness. Aunt and Uncle are there, just as Aunt had promised, and I pick them out right away (how can I not?) from among the swirl of smart business suits and shiny leather briefcases, the elegant skirts that swing above stiletto-thin high heels.

Bikram-uncle is a short, stocky man dressed in greasy mechanic's over-alls that surprise me. He has a belligerent mustache and very dark skin and a scar that runs up the side of his neck. (Had it been hidden in the wedding photo under the garlands?) I am struck at once by how ugly he is—the gar-lands had hidden that as well—how unlike Aunt, who stoops a bit to match her husband's height, her fine, nervous hands worrying the edge of her shawl as she scans the travelers emerging from Immigration.

I touch their feet like a good Indian girl should, though I am some-what embarrassed. Everyone in the airport is watching us, I'm sure of it. Aunt is embarrassed too, and shifts her weight from leg to leg. Then she kisses me on both cheeks, but a little hesitantly—I get the feeling she hasn't done something like this in a long time.

"O Jayanti!" she says. "I am having no idea you are growing so beauti-ful. And so fair-skinned. And you such a thin thin girl with scabby knees when I left India. It is making me very happy." Her voice is soft and uncer-tain, as though she rarely speaks above a whisper, but her eyes are warm, flecked with bits of light.

I don't know what Uncle thinks. This makes me smile too widely and speak too fast and thank them too effusively for taking me in. I start to take out letters and packets from my carry-on bag.

"This is from Mother," I tell Aunt. "This fat one wrapped in twine is from Grandfather. And here's a jar of the lemon-mango pickle you used to like so much—Great-aunt Rama made it herself when she heard—"

Bikram-uncle interrupts. Unlike Aunt, who speaks refined Bengali, he uses a staccato American English. His accent jars my ears. I have trouble understanding it.

"Can we get going? I got to be back at work. You women can chat all day once you get home."

His voice isn't unkind. Still I feel reprimanded, as though I am a little girl again, and spitefully I wonder how a marriage could ever have been arranged between a man like Bikram-uncle and my aunt, who comes from an old and wealthy landowning family.

The overalls are part of the problem. They make him seem so—I hesitate to use the word, but only briefly—low-class. Why, even Mr. Bhalani, who owned the Lakshmi Motor Works near the Mint, always wore a starched white linen suit and a diamond on his little finger. Now as I stare from the back of the car at the fold of neck that overlaps the grimy collar of Uncle's overalls, I feel that something is very wrong.

But only for a moment. Outside, America is whizzing by the fogged-up car window, blurry silhouettes of brick and stone and tall black glass that glint in the sun, making me dizzy. I wipe the moisture from the pane with the edge of my sari.

"What's this?" I ask. "And this?"

"The central post office," Aunt replies, laughing a little at my excitement. "The Sears Tower." But a lot of the time she says, "I am not knowing this one." Uncle busies himself with swerving in and out of traffic, humming along with the song on the radio.

The apartment is another disappointment, not at all what an American home should be like. I've seen the pictures in *Good Housekeeping* and *Sunset* at the USIS library, and once our neighbor Aditi brought over the photos her *chachaji* had sent from Akron, Ohio. I remember clearly the neat red brick house with matching flowery drapes, the huge, perfectly mowed lawn green like it had been painted, the shiny concrete driveway on which sat two shiny motorcars. And Akron isn't even as big as Chicago. And Aditi's *chachaji* only works in an office, selling insurance.

This apartment smells of stale curry. It is crowded with faded, overstuffed sofas and rickety end tables that look like they've come from a larger place. A wadded newspaper is wedged under one of the legs of the dining table. Uncle and Aunt are watching me, his eyes defiant, hers anxious. I shift my gaze to the dingy walls hung with prints of landscapes, cattle standing under droopy weeping willows looking vaguely bored (surely they are not Aunt's choice?) and try to keep my face polite. My monogrammed leather cases are an embarrassment in this household. I push them under the bed in the tiny room I am to occupy—it is the same size as my bath-room at home. I remember that cool green mosaic floor, the claw-footed marble bathtub from colonial days, the large window that looks out on my mother's crimson and gold dahlias, and want to cry. But I tell Aunt that I will be very comfortable here, and I thank her for the rose she has put in a jelly jar and placed on the windowsill.

Aunt cooks happily all afternoon. Whenever I offer help she says, "No, no, you just sit and rest your feet and tell me what-all's going on at home."

Dinner turns out to be an elaborate affair—a spicy almond-chicken curry arranged over hot rice, a spinach-lentil *dal*, a yogurt cucumber *raita*, fried potato *pakoras*, crisp golden *papads*, and sweet white *kheer*—which has taken hours to prepare—for dessert. I have a guilty feeling that Aunt and Uncle don't usually eat this way, and as we sit down I glance at Uncle for confirmation. But he has already started on the food. He eats quickly and with concentration, without raising his head. When he wants more he points silently, and Aunt hurries to serve him. He has taken a shower and put on the muslin *kurta-pajama* I brought him as a gift from India. With his hair brushed back wetly and *chappals* on his feet, he could be any Indian man sitting down to his dinner after a hard day's work. As I watch Aunt ladle more *dal* onto his plate, I have a strange sense of disorientation, and for a moment I wonder whether I've left Calcutta at all.

"I think he is liking you," whispers Aunt Pratima when we are alone in the kitchen. She stops spooning dessert into bowls to touch me lightly on the wrist, her face bright. "See how he is wearing the clothes you brought for him? Most nights he does not even change out of his overalls, let alone take a shower."

I am dubious. Uncle's attitude toward me, as far as I can tell, is one of testy tolerance. But I give Aunt a hug and hope, for her sake, that she is right. And as I help her pour tea into chipped cups of fine bone china that look like they might have once been part of her dowry, I make a special effort. I offer Uncle my most charming smile.

"I can't believe I'm finally here in the U.S.," I tell him. "I've heard so much about Chicago—Lake Michigan, which is surely big as an ocean, the Egyptian museum with mummies three thousand years old, and is it true that the big downtown stores have real silver mannequins in their windows?"

Uncle grunts uncommittally, regarding the teacups with disfavor. He stomps into the kitchen where I hear him rummage in the refrigerator.

"I can't wait to see it all!" I call after him. "I'm so glad I have the summer, though of course I'm looking forward to starting at the university in September!"

"You will do well, I know." Aunt nods encouragingly. "You are such a smart girl to be getting into this university where people from all over the world are trying to become students. Soon you will have many many American friends, and—"

"Don't be too sure of that," Bikram-uncle breaks in, startling me. His voice is harsh, raspy. He stands in the kitchen doorway, drinking from a can which glints in his fist. "Things here aren't as perfect as people at home like to think. We all thought we'd become millionaires. But it's not easy."

"Please." Aunt says, but he seems not to hear her. He tips his head back to swallow, and the scar on his neck glistens pinkly like a live thing. *Budweiser,* I read as he sets the can down, and am shocked to realize he's drinking beer. At home in Calcutta none of the family members touches alcohol, not even cousin Ramesh, who attends St. Xavier's College and sports a navy-blue blazer and a British accent. Mother has always told me what a disgusting habit it is, and she's right. I remember Grandfather's village at harvesttime, the farmhands lying in ditches, drunk on palm-toddy, flies buzzing around their faces. I try not to let my distaste show on my face.

Now Uncle's tone is dark and raw. The bitterness in it coats my mouth like the *karela* juice Mother used to give me to cool my liver.

"The Americans hate us. They're always putting us down because we're dark-skinned foreigners, *kala admi.* Blaming us for the damn economy, for taking away their jobs. You'll see it for yourself soon enough."

What has made him detest this country so much?

I look beyond Uncle's head at the window. All I can see is a dark rectangle. But I know the sky outside is filled with strange and beautiful stars, and I am suddenly angry with him for trying to ruin it for me. I take a deep breath. I tell myself, I'll wait to make up my own mind.

At night I lie in my lumpy bed under a coarse green blanket. I try to sleep, but the night noises that still seem unfamiliar after a week—the desperate *whee-whee* of a siren, the wind sighing as it coils about the house—keep me awake. Small sounds filter, too, through the walls from Aunt's bedroom. And though they are quite innocent—the bedsprings creaking as someone turns over in sleep, footsteps and then the hum of the exhaust as the bathroom light is switched on—each time I stiffen with embarrassment. I cannot stop thinking of Uncle and Aunt. I would rather think only of Aunt, but like the shawls of the bride and groom at an Indian wedding ceremony, their lives are inextricably knotted together. I try to imagine her arriving in this country, speaking only a little English, red-veiled, wearing the heavy, elaborate jewelry I've seen in the wedding photo. (What happened to it all? Now Aunt only wears a thin gold chain and the tiniest of pearls in her ears.) Her shock at discovering that her husband was not the owner of an automobile empire (as the matchmaker had assured her family) but only a mechanic who had a dingy garage in an undesirable part of town.

I haven't seen Uncle's shop yet. Of course I haven't seen anything else either, but as soon as the weather—which has been a bone-chilling gray—improves, I plan to. I've already called the people at Midwest Bus Tours, which picks up passengers from their homes for an extra five dollars. But I have a feeling I'll never get to see the shop, and so—again spitefully—I make it, in my head, a cheerless place that smells of sweat and grease, where the hiss of hydraulics and the clanging of tools mix with the curses of mechanics who are all as surly as Bikram-uncle.

But soon, with the self-absorption of the young. I move on the wings of imagination to more exciting matters. In my Modern Novel class at the university, I sit dressed in a plaid skirt and a matching sweater. My legs, elegant in knee-high boots like the ones I have seen on one of the afternoon TV shows that Aunt likes, are casually crossed. My bobbed hair swings around my face as I spiritedly argue against the handsome professor's interpretation of Dreiser's philosophy. I discourse brilliantly on the character of Sister Carrie until he is convinced, and later we go out for dinner to a quiet little French restaurant. Candlelight shines on the professor's reddish hair, on his gold spectacle frames. On the rims of our wineglasses. Chopin plays in the background as he confesses his admiration, his love for me. He slips onto my finger a ring with stones that sparkle like his eyes and tells me of the trips we will go on around the world, the books we will coauthor when I am his wife. (No arranged marriage like Aunt's for me!) After dinner he takes me to his apartment overlooking the lake, where fairy lights twinkle and shiver on the water. He pulls me down, respectfully but ardently, on the couch. His lips are hot against my throat, his . . .

But here my imagination, conditioned by a lifetime of maternal censorship, shuts itself down.

*   *   *

After lunch the next day I walk out onto the narrow balcony. It is still cold, but the sun is finally out. The sky stretches over me, a sheet of polished metal. The skyscrapers of downtown Chicago float glimmering in the distance, enchanted towers out of an old storybook. The air is so new and crisp that it makes me suddenly happy, full of hope.

As a child in India, sometimes I used to sing a song. *Will I marry a prince from a far-off magic land, where the pavements are silver and the roofs are all gold?* My girlfriends and I would play skipping games to its rhythm, laughing carelessly, thoughtlessly. And now here I am. *America*, I think, and the word opens inside me like a folded paper flower placed in water, filling me until there is no room to breathe.

The apartment with its faded cushions and its crookedly hung pictures seems newly oppressive when I go back inside. Aunt is in the kitchen — where I have noticed she spends most of her time — chopping vegetables.

"Can we go for a walk?" I ask. "Please?"

Aunt looks doubtful. "It is being very cold outside," she tells me.

"Oh no," I assure her. "I was just out on the balcony and it's lovely, it really it."

"Your uncle does not like me to go out. He is telling me it is dangerous."

"How can it be dangerous?" I say. It's just a ploy of his to keep her shut up in the house and under his control. He would like to do the same with me, only I won't let him. I pull her by the hand to the window. "Look," I say. The streets are clean and empty and very wide. A gleaming blue car speeds by. A bus belches to a stop and two laughing girls get down.

I can feel Aunt weakening. But she says, "Better to wait. This weekend he is taking us to the mall. So many big big shops there, you'll like it. He says he will buy pizza for dinner. Do you know pizza? Is it coming to India yet?"

I want to tell her that the walls are closing in on me. My brain is dying. Soon I will turn into one of those mournful-eyed cows in the painting behind the sofa.

"Just a short walk for some exercise," I say. "We'll be back long before Uncle. He need not even know."

Maybe Aunt Pratima hears the longing in my voice. Maybe it makes her feel guilty. She lifts her thin face. When she smiles, she seems not that much older than me.

"In the village before marriage I was always walking everywhere — it was so nice, the fresh air, the sky, the ponds with lotus flowers, the dogs and goats and chickens all around. Of course, here we cannot be expecting such country things. . . ."

I wait.

"No harm in it, I am thinking," she finally says. "As long as we are staying close to the house. As long as we are coming back in time to fix a nice dinner for your uncle."

"Just a half-hour walk," I assure her. "We'll be back in plenty of time."

As we walk down the dim corridor that smells, just like the apartment, of stale curry (do the neighbors mind?), she adds, a bit apologetically. "Please do not be saying anything to Uncle. It will make him angry." She shakes her head. "He worries too much since . . ."

I want to ask her since what, but I sense she doesn't want to talk about it. I give her a bright smile. "I won't say a word to Uncle. It'll be our secret."

In coats and saris we walk down the street. A few pedestrians stare at us silently as they sidle past. I miss the bustle of the Calcutta streets a little, the hawkers with their bright wares, the honking buses loaded with people, the rickshaw-wallahs calling out *make way*, but I say, "It's so neat and quiet, isn't it?"

"Every Wednesday the cleaning truck is coming with big brushes to sweep the streets," Aunt tells me proudly.

The sun has ducked behind a cloud, and it is colder than I had thought. When I look up the April light is a muted glare that hurts my eyes.

"It is probably snowing later today." Aunt says.

"That's wonderful! You know, I've only seen snow in movies! It always looked so pretty and delicate. I didn't think I'd get to see any this late in the year. . . ."

Aunt pulls her shapeless coat tighter around her. "It is not that great," she says. Her tone is regretful, as though she is sorry to disillusion me. "It melts inside the collar of your jacket and drips down your back. Cars are skidding when it turns to ice. And see how it looks like afterward. . . ." She kicks at the brown slush on the side of the road with a force that surprises me.

I like my aunt though, the endearing way in which her eyes widen like a little girl's when she asks a question, the small frown line between her eyebrows when she listens, the sudden, liquid shift of her features when she smiles. I remember that she'd been considered a beauty back home, someone who deserved the good luck of having a marriage arranged with a man who lived in America.

As we walk, the brisk, invigorating air seems to loosen something inside of Aunt. She talks and talks. She asks about the design on my sari, deep rose-embroidered peacocks dancing against a cream background. Is this being the latest fashion in India? (She uses the word *desh*, country, to refer to India, as though it were the only one in the world.) "I am always loving Calcutta, visiting your mother in that beautiful old house with marble fountains and lions." She wants to know what movies are showing at the Roxy. Do children still fly the moon-shaped kites at the Maidan and do the street vendors still sell puffed rice spiced with green chilies? How about Victoria Memorial with the black angel on top of the white marble dome, is it still the same? Is it true that New Market with all those charming little clothing stores has burnt down? Have I been on the new subway she has read about in *India Abroad?* The words pour from her in a rush. "Imagine all those tunnels under the city, you could be getting lost in there and nobody will be finding you if you do not want them to." I hear the hunger in her voice. And so I hold back my own eagerness to learn about America and answer her the best I can.

The street has narrowed now and the apartment buildings look run-down, even to me, with peeling walls and patchy yellow spots on lawns where the snow has melted. There are chain-link fences and garbage on the pavement. Broken-down cars, their rusted hoods gaping, sit in several front yards. The sweet stench of rot rises from the drains. I am disconnected. I thought I had left all such smells behind in Calcutta.

"Shouldn't we be going back, Aunt?" I ask, suddenly nervous.

"Yes, yes, my goodness, is it that late already? Look at that black sky. It is so nice to be talking to someone about home that I am forgetting the time completely."

We start back, lifting up our saris to walk faster, our steps echoing aloong the empty sidewalk, and when we go back a bit Aunt stops and looks up and down the street without recognition, her head pivoting loosely like a lost animal's.

Then we see the boys. Four of them, playing in the middle of the street with cans and sticks. They hadn't been there before, or maybe it is a different street we are on now. The boys look up and I see that their sallow faces are grime-streaked. Their blond hair hangs limply over their foreheads, and their eyes are pale and slippery, like pebbles left under water for a long time. They may be anywhere from eight to fourteen—I can't tell their ages as I would with the boys back home. They scare me on this deserted street although surely there's no reason for fear. They're just boys after all, with thin wrists that stick out from the sleeves of too-small jackets, standing under a tree on which the first leaves of spring are opening a pale and delicate green. I glance at Aunt Pratima for reassurance, but the skin on her face stretches tightly across her sharp, fragile cheekbones.

The boys bend their heads together, consulting, then the tallest one takes a step toward us and says, "Nigger." He says it softly, his upper lip curling away from his teeth. The word arcs through the empty street like a rock, an impossible word which belongs to another place and time. In the mouth of a red-faced gin-and-tonic drinking British official, perhaps, in his colonial bungalow, or a sneering overseer out of *Uncle Tom's Cabin* as he plies his whip in the cotton fields. But here is this boy, younger than my cousin Anup, saying it as easily as one might say *thank you* or *please*. Or *no problem*.

Now the others take up the word, chanting it in high singsong voices that have not broken yet, *nigger, nigger,* until I want to scream, or weep. Or laugh, because can't they see that I'm not black at all but an Indian girl of good family? When our chauffeur Gurbans Singh drives me down Calcutta streets in our silver-colored Fiat, people stop to whisper, *Isn't that Jayanti Ganguli, daughter of the Bhavanipur Gangulis?*

I don't see which boy first picks up the fistful of slush, but now they're all throwing it at us. It splatters on our coats and runs down our saris, leaving long streaks. I take a step toward the boys. I'm not sure what I'll do when I get to them—shake them? explain the mistake they've made? smash their faces into the pavement?—but Aunt holds tight to my arm.

"No, Jayanti, no."

I try to pull free but she is surprisingly strong, or perhaps I'm not trying hard enough. Perhaps I'm secretly thankful that she's begging me—*Let's go home, Jayanti*—so that I don't have to confront those boys with more hate in their eyes than boys should ever have. There is slush on Aunt's face; her trembling lips are ash-colored. She's sobbing, and when I put out my hand to comfort her I realize that I too am sobbing.

Half running, tripping on the wet saris which slap at our legs, we retreat down the street. The voices follow us for a long time. *Nigger, nigger.* Slush-voices, trickling into us even when we've finally found the right road back to our building, which had been only one street away all the time. Even when in the creaking elevator we tidy each other as best we can, wiping at faces, brushing off coats, holding each other's shivering hands, looking away from each other's eyes.

The light has burned out in the passage outside the door. Aunt Pratima fumbles in her purse for the key, saying "It was here, I am keeping it right here, where can it go?"

In their thin Indian shoes, my feet are colder that I have ever imagined possible. My teeth chatter as I say, "It's all right, calm down, Auntie, we'll find it."

But Aunt's voice quavers higher and higher, a bucking, runaway voice. She turns her purse upside down and shakes it, coins and wrappers and pens and safety pins tumbling out and skittering to the edges of the passage. Then she gets down on all fours on the mangy brown carpet to grope through them.

That is when Bikram-uncle opens the door. He is still wearing his grease-stained overalls. "What the hell is going on?" he says, looking down at Aunt. Standing across from him, I look down too, and see what he must be seeing, the parting in Aunt Pratima's tightly pulled-back hair, the stretched line of the scalp pointing grayly at her lowered forehead like an accusation.

"Where the hell have you been?" Bikram-uncle asks, more loudly this time. "Get in here right now."

I kneel and help Aunt gather up some of her things, leaving the rest behind.

Inside, Bikram-uncle yells, "Haven't I *told* you not to walk around this trashy neighborhood? Haven't I *told* you it wasn't safe? Don't you remember what happened to my shop last year, how they smashed everything? And still you had to go out, had to give them the chance to do *this* to you?" He draws in a ragged breath, like a sob. "My God, look at you."

I try not to stare at Aunt's mud-splotched cheek, her ruined coat, her red-rimmed, pleading glance. But I can't drag my eyes away. Once when I was little, I'd looked down into an old well behind Grandfather's house and seen my face, pale and distorted, reflected in the brackish water. I have that same dizzying sensation now. *Is this what my life too will be like?*

"It was my fault," I say. "Aunt didn't want to go."

But no one hears me.

Aunt takes a hesitant, sideways step toward Uncle. It is a small movement, something an injured animal might make toward its keeper. "They were only children," she says in a wondering tone.

"Bastards," cries Uncle, his voice choking, his accent suddenly thick and Indian. "Bloody bastards. I want to kill them, all of them." His entire face wavers, as though it will collapse in on itself. He raises his arm.

"No," I shout. I run toward them. But my body moves slowly, as though underwater. Perhaps it cannot believe that he will really do it.

When the back of his hand catches Aunt Pratima across the mouth, I flinch as if his knuckles had made that thwacking bone sound against my own flesh. My mouth fills with an ominous salt taste.

Will I marry a prince from a far-off magic land?

I put out my hand to shield Aunt, but Uncle is quicker. He has her already tight in his grasp. I look about wildly for something—perhaps a chair to bring crashing down on his head. Then I hear him.

"Pratima," he cries in a broken voice, "Pratima, Pratima." He touches her face, his fingers groping uncertainly like a blind man's, his whole body shaking.

"Hush, Ram," says my aunt. "Hush." She strokes his hair as though he were a child, and perhaps he is.

"Pratima, how could I. . . ."

"Shhh, I am understanding."

"Something exploded in my head . . . it was like that time at the shop . . . remember . . . how the fire they started took everything. . . ."

"Don't be thinking of it now, Ram," says Aunt Pratima. She pulls his head down to her breast and lays her cheek on his hair. Her fingers caress the scar on his neck. Her face is calm, almost happy. She—they—have forgotten me.

I feel like an intruder, a fool. How little I've understood. As I turn to tip-toe away to my room, I hear my uncle say, "I tried so hard, Pratima. I wanted to give you so many things—but even your jewelry is gone." Grief scrapes at his voice. "This damn country, like a *dain*, a witch—it pretends to give and then snatches everything back."

And Aunt's voice, pure and musical with the lilt of a smile in it, "O Ram, I am having all I need."

Now it is night but no one has thought to turn on the family-room lights. Bikram-uncle sits in front of the TV, his feet up on the rickety coffee table. He is finishing his third beer. The can gleams faintly as it catches the uneven blue flickers from the tube. I feel I should say something to him, but he is not looking at me, and I don't know what to say. Aunt Pratima is in the kitchen preparing dinner as though this were an evening like all the others. I should go and help her. But I remain in my chair in the corner of the room. I am not sure how to face her either, how to start talking about what has happened. (In my head I am trying to make sense of it still.) Am I to ignore it all (*can* I?)—the hate-suffused faces of the boys, the swelling spreading its dark blotch across Aunt's jaw, the memory of Uncle's head pressed trembling to her breast? *Home*, I whisper desperately, *homehome-home*, and suddenly, intensely, I want my room in Calcutta, where things were so much simpler. I want the high mahogany bed in which I've slept as long as I can remember, the comforting smell of sun-dried cotton sheets to pull around my head. I want my childhood again. But I am too far away for the spell to work, for the words to take me back, even in my head.

Then out of the corner of my eye I catch a white movement. It is snowing. I step outside onto the balcony, drawing my breath in at the silver marvel of it, the fat flakes cool and wet against my face as in a half-forgotten movie. It is cold, so cold that I can feel the insides of my nostrils stiffening. The air—there is no smell to it at all—carves a freezing path all the way into my chest. But I don't go back inside. The snow has covered the dirty cement pavements, the sad warped shingles of the rooftops, has softened, forgivingly, the rough noisy edges of things. I hold out my hands to it, palms down, shivering a little.

The snow falls on them, chill, stinging all the way to the bone. But after a while the excruciating pain fades. I am thinking of hands. The pink-tipped blond hand of the air hostess as she offers me a warm towelette that smells like unknown flowers. They boy's grimy one pushing back his limp hair, then tightening into a fist to throw a lump of slush. Uncle's with its black nails, its oddly defenseless scraped knuckles, arcing though the air to knock Aunt's head sideways. And Aunt's hand, stroking the angry pink scar. Threading her long elegant fingers (the fingers, still, of a Bengali aristocrat's daughter) through his graying hair to pull him to her. All these American hands that I know will keep coming back in my dreams.

> Will I marry a prince from a far-off magic land
> Where the pavements are silver and the roofs all gold?

When I finally look down, I notice that the snow has covered my own hands so they are no longer brown but white, white, white. And now it makes sense that the beauty and the pain should be part of each other. I continue holding them out in front of me, gazing at them, until they're completely covered. Until they do not hurt at all.

1995

THE BLOSSOMING OF BONGBONG

Jessica Hagedorn

Antonio Gargazulio-Duarte, also fondly known as Bongbong to family and friends, had been in America for less than two years and was going mad. He didn't know it, of course, having left the country of his birth, the Philippines, for the very reason that his sanity was at stake. As he often told his friend, the painter Frisquito, "I can no longer tolerate contradiction. This country is full of contradiction. I have to leave before I go crazy."

His friend Frisquito would only laugh. His laugh was eerie because it was soundless. When he laughed, his body would shake—and his face, which was already grotesque, would distort—but no sound would emit from him.

People were afraid of Frisquito. They bought his paintings, but they stayed away from him. Especially when he was high. Frisquito loved to get high. He had taken acid more than fifty times, and he was only twenty-six years old. He had once lived in New York, where people were used to his grotesque face, and ignored him. Frisquito had a face that resembled a retarded child: eyes slanted, huge forehead, droopy mouth, and pale, luminous skin. Bongbong once said to him, "You have skin like the surface of the moon." Frisquito's skull was also unusually large, which put people off, especially women. Frisquito soon learned to do without women or men. "My paintings are masturbatory," he once said to the wife of the president of the Philippines. She never blinked an eye, later commissioning three obscene murals. She was often referred to as a "trendsetter."

Frisquito told Bongbong, "There's nothing wrong with being crazy. The thing to do is to get comfortable with it."

Not only had Frisquito taken acid more than fifty times, he had also taken peyote and cocaine and heroin at a rate that doctors often said would normally kill a man. "But I'm like a bull," he would say. "Nothing can really hurt me, except the creator of the universe."

At which point he would smile.

Bongbong finally left Manila on a plane for San Francisco. He was deathly afraid. He wore an olive-green velvet jacket, and dark velvet pants, with a long scarf thrown casually around his scrawny neck. Frisquito saw him off to the airport. "You look like a faggot," he said to Bongbong, who was once named best-dressed young VIP in Manila. Bongbong felt ridiculously out of place and took two downers so he could sleep during the long ride to America. He arrived, constipated and haggard, and was met by his sister and brother-in-law, Carmen and Pochoy Guevara. "You look terrible," his sister said. She was embarrassed to be seen with him. Secretly she feared he was homosexual, especially since he was such good friends with Frisquito.

Bongbong had moved in with his sister and brother-in-law, who lived in a plush apartment on Twin Peaks. His brother-in-law Pochoy, who had graduated as a computer programmer from Heald's Business College, worked for the Bank of America. His sister Carmen, who was rather beautiful in a bland, colorless kind of way, had enrolled in an Elizabeth Arden beauty course, and had hopes of being a fashion model.

"Or maybe I could go into merchandising," she would say, in the afternoons when she wouldn't go to class. She would sit in her stainless-steel, carpeted electric kitchen. She drank cup after cup of instant Yuban coffee, and changed her nail polish every three days.

"You should wear navy blue on your nails," Bongbong said to her one of those afternoons, when she was removing her polish with Cutex lemon-scented remover. "It would look wonderful with your sallow complexion." "Sallow" was a word Bongbong had learned from Frisquito.

"Sallow? What does that mean?" Carmen never knew if her brother was insulting or complimenting her.

"It means pale and unhealthy," Bongbong said. "Anyway, it's in style now. I've seen lots of girls wearing it."

He wrote Frisquito a letter:

Dear Frisquito,
Everyone is a liar. My sister is the biggest one of them all. I am a liar.
I lie to myself every second of the day. I look in the mirror and I don't

know what's there. My sister hates me. I hate her. She is inhuman. But then, she doesn't know how to be human. She thinks I'm inhuman. I am surrounded by androids. Do you know what that is? I'm glad I never took acid.

I wish I was a movie star.

Love,
Bongbong

The apartment had two bedrooms. Pochoy had bought a leather couch and a Magnavox record player on credit. He owned the largest and most complete collection of Johnny Mathis records. At night Bongbong would lie awake and listen to their silent fucking in the next room, and wonder if Carmen was enjoying herself. Sometimes they would fuck to "Misty."

Carmen didn't cook too often, and Pochoy had a gluttonous appetite. Since he didn't believe in men cooking, they would often order Chinese food or pizzas to be delivered. Once in a while Bongbong would try to fix a meal, but he was never talented in that direction. Frisquito had taught him how to cook two dishes: fried chicken & spaghetti.

Dear Frisquito,
I can't seem to find a job. I have no skills, and no college degree. Carmen thinks I should apply at Heald's Business College and go into computer programming. The idea makes me sick. I am twenty-six years old and no good at anything. Yesterday I considered getting a job as a busboy in a restaurant, but Carmen was horrified. She was certain everyone in Manila would hear about it (which they will), and she swears she'll kill herself out of shame. Not a bad idea, but I am not a murderer. If I went back to Manila I could be a movie star.

Love,
Bongbong

Bongbong stood in the middle of a Market Street intersection, slowly going mad. He imagined streetcars melting and running him over, grinding his flesh and bones into one hideous, bloody mess. He saw the scurrying Chinese women, no more than four feet tall, run amok and beat him to death with their shopping bags, which were filled to the brim with slippery, silver-scaled fish.

He watched a lot of television. His eyes became bloodshot. He began to read—anything from best-sellers to plays to political science to poetry. A lot of it he didn't quite understand, but the names and events fascinated him. He would often visit bookshops just to get out of the apartment. He chose books at random, sometimes for their titles or the color of their book jackets. His favorite before he went crazy was *Vibration Cooking* by Verta Mae Grosvenor. He even tried out some of Verta Mae's recipes, when he was in better moods on the days when Carmen and Pochoy were away. He had found Verta Mae's book for seventy-five cents in a used-book store he frequented.

"What is this?" Carmen asked, staring at the book cover, which featured Verta Mae in her colorful African motif outfit.

"That, my dear, is a cookbook," Bongbong answered, snatching the book out of her hands, now decorated in Max Factor's "Regency Red."

On the bus going home there was a young girl sitting behind Bongbong wearing a Catholic school uniform and carrying several books in her pale, luminous arms, which reminded him of the surface of the moon. When the bus came to a stop, she walked quietly in the front and before getting off she turned, very slowly and deliberately, and stared deeply into Bongbong's eyes. "You will get what you deserve," she said.

One time when Bongbong was feeling particularly lonely, he went to a bar on Union Street where young men and women stand around and drink weak Irish coffees. The bar was sometimes jokingly known as a "meat factory." The young men were usually executives, or trying to look like executives. They wore their hair slightly long, with rather tacky muttonchop whiskers, and they all smoked dope. They women were usually chic or terribly hip. Either way they eyed each other coolly and all wore platform shoes.

A drink was sent to Bongbong from the other end of the bar by a twenty-eight-year-old sometime actress and boutique salesgirl named Charmaine. She was from Nicaragua, and quite stunning, with frizzy brown hair and the biggest ass Bongbong had ever seen.

"What're you having?" she asked, grinning. Her lips were moist and glossy, and the Fertile Crescent was tattooed in miniature on her left cheek.

Bongbong, needless to say, was silent for a moment. Ladies like Charmaine were uncommon in Manila. "Gimlet," he murmured, embarrassed because he disliked the idea of being hustled.

Charmaine had a habit of tossing her head back, so that her frizzy curls bounced, as if she were always secretly dancing. "Awright," she said, turning to the bartender, "bring the gentleman a gimlet." She giggled, turning to look fully at Bongbong. "I'm Charmaine. Wha's your name?"

Bongbong blushed. "Antonio," he said, "But I go by my nickname." He dreaded her next question, but braced himself for it, feeling the familiar nausea rising within him. Once Frisquito had told him that witches and other types of human beings only had power over you if they knew your name. Since that time Bongbong always hesitated when anyone asked him for his name, especially women. "Women are more prone to occult powers than men," Frisquito warned. "It comes natural to them."

Charmaine was smiling now. "Oh yeah? Whatisit?"

"Bongbong."

The bartender handed him the gimlet, and Charmaine shrugged. "Tha's a funky name, man. You Chicano?"

Bongbong was offended. He wanted to say No, I'm Ethiopian, or Moroccan, or Nepalese, what the fuck do you care . . . Silently he drank his gimlet. Then he decided, the nausea subsiding, that Charmaine wasn't malicious, and left the bar with her shortly after.

Charmaine showed him the boutique where she worked, which was next door to the bar. Bongbong stared at the platform shoes in the display window as if he were seeing them for the first time. Their glittering colors and whimsical designs intrigued him. Charmaine watched his face curiously as he stood with his face pressed against the glass like a small child; then she took his arm and led him to her VW.

She lived in a large flat in the Fillmore district with another sometime actress and boutique salesgirl named Colelia. They had six cats, and the place smelled like a combination of cat piss and incense.

Colelia thought she was from Honey Patch, South Carolina, but she wasn't sure. "I'm all mixed up," she said. Sometimes she thought she was a geechee. She was the only person Bongbong knew who had ever read *Vibration Cooking*. She had even met Verta Mae at a party in New York.

Bongbong spent the night in Charmaine's bed, but he couldn't bring himself to even touch her. She was amused, and asked him if he was gay. At first he didn't understand the term. English sometimes escaped him, and certain colloquialisms, like "gay," never made sense. He finally shook his head and mumbled no. Charmaine told him she didn't really mind. Then she asked him to go down on her.

Dear Frisquito:
I enrolled at Heald's College today so that Carmen would shut up.
I plan on leaving the house every morning and pretending I'm going
to school. That way no one will bother me.

I think I may come back to Manila soon, but somehow I feel I'm
being trapped into staying here. I don't understand anything. Everyone
is an artist, but I don't see them doing anything. Which is what I don't
understand . . . but one good thing is I am becoming a good cook.

Enclosed is a copy of Vibration Cooking *by Verta Mae.*

Love,
B.

Sometimes Bongbong would open the refrigerator door and oranges would fly out at him. He was fascinated by eggs, and would often say to his sister, "We're eating the sunset," or "We're eating embryos." Or he would frown and say, "I never did like chicken."

He began riding streetcars and buses from one end of the city to the other, often going into trances and reliving the nightmare of the streetcar melting and running him over. Always the Chinese women would appear, beating him to death with silver-scaled fish, or eggs.

Bongbong saw Charmaine almost every day for a month. His parents sent him an allowance, thinking he was in school. This allowance he spent lavishly on her. He bought her all the dazzling shoes her heart desired. He took her to fancy nightclubs so she could dance and wiggle her magnificent ass to his delight. She loved Sly Stone and Willie Colon, so he bought her all their records. They ate curry and spice cake every night of the week (sometimes alternating with yogurt pie and gumbo) and Charmaine put on ten pounds.

He never fucked her. Sometimes he went down on her, which she liked even better. She had replaced books and television in his life. He thought he was saved.

One afternoon while he was waiting for Charmaine in the bar where they had met, Bongbong had a vision. A young woman entered the bar, wearing a turban on her head made of torn rags. Her hair was braided and stood out from her scalp like branches on a young tree. Her skin was so black she was almost blue.

Around her extremely firm breasts she wore an old yellow crocheted doily, tied loosely. Her long black skirt was slit up the front all the way to her crotch, and underneath she wore torn black lace tights, and shocking pink suede boots, laced all the way up to her knees. She carried a small basket as a handbag, and she was smoking Eve cigarettes elegantly, as if she were a dowager empress.

She sat next to Bongbong and gazed at him coolly and deliberately. People in the bar turned their heads and stared at her, some of them laughing. She asked Bongbong for a match. He lit her cigarette. His hands were trembling. She smiled, and he saw that some of her teeth were missing. After she smoked her cigarette, she left the bar.

Another day while Bongbong was walking in the Tenderloin, he had another vision. A young woman offered to fuck him for a mere twenty-five dollars. He hesitated, looking at her. She had shoulder-length, greasy blond hair. She had several teeth missing too, and what other teeth she had left were rotten. Her eyes, which were a dull brown, were heavily painted with midnight-blue mascara. She wore a short red skirt, a tight little sweater, and her black sheer tights had runs and snags all over them. Bongbong noticed that she had on expensive silver platform shoes that were sold in Charmaine's boutique.

He asked her name.

Her voice was dull as her eyes. "Sandra," she replied.

He suddenly felt bold in her presence. "How old are you?"

"Nineteen. How old are you honey?" She leered at him, then saw the blank look on his face, and all the contempt washed out of her. He took her to a restaurant where they served watery hamburgers and watery coffee. He asked her if she had a pimp.

"Yup. And I been busted ten times. I been a hooker since I was thirteen, and my parents are more dead than alive. Anything else you wanna know?"

Her full name was Sandra Broussard. He told her she was beautiful. She laughed. She said her pimp would kill her if she ever left the business. She showed him her scars. "He cut my face once, with a razor," she said.

He felt useless. He went back to the apartment and Carmen was waiting for him. "We've decided you should move out of this place as soon as possible," she said. "I'm pregnant, and I want to redecorate your room for the baby. I'm going to paint your room pink."

He went into the bathroom and stared at the bottles of perfume near the sink, the underarm deodorant, the foot deodorant, the cinnamon-flavored mouthwash, and the vaginal spray. They used Colgate brand toothpaste. Dove soap. Zee toilet paper. A Snoopy poster hung behind the toilet. It filled him with despair.

Bongbong moved into Charmaine's flat shortly after. He brought his velvet suit and his books. Colelia reacted strangely at first. She had been Charmaine's lover for some time, and felt Bongbong would be an intrusion. But all he did was read his books and watch television. He slept on a mattress in the living room. He hardly even spoke to Charmaine anymore. Sometimes they would come home from work in the evenings and find Bongbong in the kitchen, preparing Verta Mae's Kalalou Noisy Le Sec or her Codfish with Green Sauce for all of them. Colelia realized he wasn't a threat to her love life at all. Life became peaceful for her and Charmaine.

During the long afternoons when Colelia and Charmaine were gone and the cats were gone and the smell of piss from the catbox lingered in the chilly air, Bongbong would put on his velvety suit and take long walks in the Tenderloin, trying to find Sandra Broussard. He thought he saw her once, inside a bar, but when he went in, he found it was a mistake. The woman turned out to be much older, and when she turned to smile at him, he noticed she wore the hand of Fatima on a silver chain around her neck.

When he really thought about it, in his more lucid moments, he realized he didn't even remember what Sandra looked like anymore. Dullness was all he could conjure of her presence. Her fatigue and resignation.

Charmaine, on the other hand, was bright, beautiful, and selfish. She was queen of the house, and most activity revolved around her. Colelia always came home from work with a gift for Charmaine, which they both referred to as "prizes." Sometimes they were valuable, like jade rings or amethyst stones for Charmaine's pierced nose, or silly—like an old Walt Disney cup with Donald Duck painted on it.

Bongbong found the two women charming and often said so when he was in a talkative mood. "You are full of charm and your lives will be full of success," he would say to them, as they sat in their antique Chinese robes, painting each other's faces.

"You sound like a fortune cookie," Charmaine would say, glaring at him.

He would be silent at her outbursts, which naturally made her more furious. "I wish you'd tell me how much you want me," she would demand, ignoring her female lover's presence in the room.

Sometimes Charmaine would watch Bongbong as he read his books, and she would get evil with him out of boredom. She was easily distracted and therefore easily bored, especially when she wasn't the center of attention. This was often the case when Colelia was at work and it was Charmaine's day off.

Bongbong said to her, "Once you were a witch, but you misused your powers. Now you resent me because I remind you of those past days."

Charmaine circled Bongbong as he sat in the living room immersed in *Green Mansions* by W. H. Hudson. He had found the hardback novel for one dollar in another secondhand-book shop, called Memory Lane.

"I'm going to take my clothes off, Bongbong," Charmaine would tease. "What're you going to do about it?" Bongbong would look up at her, puzzled. Then she would put her hands on her enormous hips. "Men like me most of all because of my ass, Bongbong . . . but they can't really get next to me. Most of them have no style . . . but you have a sort of style—" By this time she often removed her skirt. "I don't wear panties," she said, "so whenever I want, Colelia can feel me up." Bongbong tried to ignore her. He was getting skilled in self-hypnosis, and whenever external disturbances would occur, he would stare off into the distance and block them slowly from his mind.

The more skilled he became in his powers, the more furious Charmaine would get with him. One time she actually wrenched the book from his hands and threw it out the window. Then she lay on the couch in front of him and spread her legs. "You know what I've got, Bongbong? Uterina Furor . . . That's what my mother used to say . . . Nuns get it all the time. Like a fire in the womb."

To make her smile, Bongbong would kiss her between the legs, and then Colelia would come home and pay more attention to Charmaine and Bongbong would cook more of Verta Mae's recipes, such as Stuffed Heart Honky Style (one of Charmaine's favorites), and everything would be all right.

Charmaine's destructive moods focused on Bongbong twice a month, and got worse when the moon was full. "You're in a time of perennial menstruation," Bongbong told her solemnly after one of her fits.

Once morning while they were having breakfast together, Colelia accused Charmaine of being in love with Bongbong. "Why, I don't know—" Colelia said. "He's so funny-looking and weird. You're just into such an ego trip you want what you can't have."

Charmaine giggled. "Forever analyzing me! Don't I love you enough?"

"It's not that."

"Well, then—why bring him up? You never undersood him from the very beginning," Charmaine said. "Or why I even brought him here in the first place. I must confess—I don't quite know why I brought him home myself. Somehow, I knew he wasn't going to fuck me . . . I really didn't want a fuck though. It was more like I wanted him around to teach me something about myself . . . Something like that, anyway."

Colelia looked away. "That's vague enough."

"Are you really jealous of him?" Charmaine asked.

Colelia finally shook her head. "Not in that way . . . but maybe because I don't understand him, or the two of you together—I am jealous. I guess because I feel left out of his mystique."

Charmaine embraced her, and the two of them wept.

Bongbong's visions and revelations were becoming more frequent. A Chinese woman with a blond wig and a map of the world on her legs. A black man with three breasts. A cat turning doorknobs. A tortoise crawling out of a sewer on the sidewalk, and junkies making soup out of him. Frisquito assassinating the president of the Philippines who happens to be his wife in drag who happens to be a concert pianist's mother . . . The visions were endless, circular, and always moving.

Dear Frisquito:

Yesterday a friend of Charmaine's named Ra brought a record over by a man named John Coltrane. Ra tells me that Mr. Coltrane died not too long ago, I believe when we were just out of high school. Ra decided that I could keep the record, which is called "Meditations." I believe it is the title of one of your paintings.

Every morning I plan on waking up to this man's music. It keeps my face from disintegrating. You once said your whole being had disintegrated long ago, and that you had the power to pick up the pieces from time to time, when it was necessary—such as the time you gave an exhibit of your works, for the benefit of the First Lady. I think there may be some hope left for me.

Yesterday, I cooked Verta Mae's Uptight Ragout in your honor.

Love,

B.

Bongbong now referred to himself as "B." He could not stand to speak in long sentences, and tried to live and speak as minimally as possible. Charmaine worried about him, especially when he would go on one of his rampages and cook delicious gumbo dinners for herself and Colelia, and not eat with them.

"But B," she protested, "I never see you eat anymore."

One time he said, "Maybe I eat a saxophone."

He loved the word "saxophone."

His parents stopped sending money, since Carmen wrote them that he had never attended one day of school at Heald's Business College. His father wrote him and warned him never to set foot in the Philippines again, or he would have him executed for the crime of deception and subversion to one's parents, a new law put into practice in the current dictator's regime.

Bongbong decided to visit Carmen. She was almost six months pregnant, and very ugly. Her face had broken out in rashes and pimples, and her whole body was swollen. Her once shimmering black hair was now dry and brittle, and she had cut it short. Her nails were painted a pale pink, like the bedroom that had once been his. He stared at her for a long time as they sat in the kitchen in silence. She finally suggested that he see the baby's room.

She had decorated the room with more Snoopy posters, and mobiles with wooden angels hung from the ceiling. A pink baby bed stood in the center of the room, which was heavily scented with floral spray.

"It's awful," Bongbong said.

"Oh, you're always insulting everything!" his sister screamed, shoving him out the door. She shut the door behind her, as if guarding a sacred temple, and looked at him, shaking with rage. "You make everything evil. Are you on drugs? I think you're insane," she said. "Leave this house before I call the police." She hated him because he made her feel ashamed in his presence, but she couldn't understand why.

Frisquito, who never answered any of his letters, sent him a check for a considerable amount of money. A postcard later arrived with "Don't Worry" scratched across it, and Frisquito's signature below the message. Bongbong, who now wore his velvet suit every day, went to a pawnshop and bought a soprano saxophone.

In the mornings he would study with Ra, who taught him circular breathing. He never did not understand chords and scales, but he could hear what Ra was trying to teach him and he surprised everyone in the house with the eerie sounds he was making out of his new instrument. Charmaine told Colelia that she thought Bongbong was going to be all right, because Bongbong had at last found his "thing."

Which was wrong, because Bongbong's music only increased his natural visionary powers. He confessed to Ra that he could actually see the notes in the air, much as he could see the wind. Ra would smile, not saying anything.

Bongbong watched Charmaine at the kitchen table eating breakfast, and when she looked up at him, she would suddenly turn into his mother, with Minnie Mouse ears and long, exaggerated Minnie Mouse eyelashes, which glittered and threw off sparks when she blinked. This frightened him sometimes because he would forget who Charmaine was. As long as he could remember who everyone was, he felt a surge of relief. But these moments were becoming more and more confusing, and it was getting harder and harder for him to remember everyone's name, including his own.

Colelia decided that Bongbong was a "paranoid schizophrenic" and that she and Charmaine should move out, for their own safety. "One of these days we'll come home from work and find all our kitty cats with their throats slit," she said. She refused to eat any more of Bongbong's cooking, for fear he would poison her. "He doesn't like women basically. That's the root of this problem," she told Charmaine. "I mean, the guy doesn't even jack off! How unnatural can he be? Remember Emil Kemper!"

"Remember Emil Kemper" became the motto of the household. Emil Kemper was a young madman in Santa Cruz, California, who murdered his grandmother when he was something like thirteen years old, murdered his mother later on after he was released from the looney bin—cut her head off—and murdered about a million other female hitchhikers.

Charmaine sympathized with Bongbong, but she wasn't sure about him either. Only Ra vouched for his sanity. "Sure the cat is crazy," he said, "but he'll never hurt any of you."

Bongbong practiced the saxophone everyday, and seemed to survive on a diet of water and air. Charmaine came home from the boutique one night and brought him two pairs of jeans and two T-shirts. One T-shirt had glittery blue and silver thread woven into it, and Bongbong saw the shirt become a cloud floating above his narrow bed. "Well," Charmaine said, trying to sound casual as she watched Bongbong drift off dreamily, "aren't you going to try it on? Do you like it? I seriously think you should have your velvet suit dry-cleaned, before it falls apart."

Bongbong touched the cloud. "Oh, how beautiful," he said.

He never wore the shirt. He hung it above his head like a canopy, where he could study it at night. His ceiling became a galaxy. To appease Charmaine (he was very sensitive to her feelings, and loved her in his own way), he wore the other shirt and sent his velvet suit to the cleaners.

Frisquito sent him more money the next month, and Bongbong bought a telescope.

Dear Frisquito,

Do you know I am only five feet and two inches tall? Without my platform shoes, of course. Whey do people like to look like cripples? Yesterday I saw a fat woman wearing platform shoes that made her feet look like boats. Her dress was too short on her fat body and you could see her cellulite wobbling in her forest-green panythose. Cellulite is the new fad in America. Some Frenchwoman discovered it and is urging everyone to feel for it in their skin. It's sort of like crepe-paper tissue that happens when you put on too much weight. I told the fat young woman she was beautiful, and she told me to fuck off. She was very angry, and I realized there are a lot of angry people around me. Except in the house I live in, which is why I've stayed so long.

The Coltrane record is warped from having been left in the sun. I am writing a song about it in my head.

With my telescope I can see
everyone, and they don't have to
see me.
Love,
B.

Bongbong often brought the telescope up to the roof of their building and watched the people on the streets below. Then at night he would watch the stars in the sky and try and figure out different constellations. Charmaine took him to the planetarium for his birthday, and they watched a show on Chinese astronomy called "The Emperor of the Heavens," narrated by a man called Alvin. Bongbong was moved to tears. "I love you," he told Charmaine, as they lay back in their seats and watched the heavens.

But he had forgotten that she was Charmaine Lopez, and that she lived with him. He thought she was Sandra Broussard, or the blue lady with the rag turban on her head. When the show was over, he asked her to marry him.

He didn't say another word until they reached the flat. He cooked Verta Mae's Jamaican Curried Goat for birthday dinner and Colelia baked him a cake decorated with a sugar-coated model airplane. Bongbong removed the airplane and hung it next to the canopy above his bed.

After dinner he asked Charmaine if she would sleep with him. She didn't have the heart to refuse, and kissing Colelia on her forehead, followed

Bongbong into his room. The next morning Charmaine told Colelia they should both move out.

"Was he a freak? I mean, did he hurt you?" Colelia asked.

Charmaine shook her head. "No. But I don't want to live around him anymore. It may be best if we left today."

They packed their clothes and rounded up their cats and drove away in Charmaine's VW, leaving Bongbong with a note on the kitchen table: "We'll send for the rest of our things. Forgive us. C & C."

Bongbong awoke from a beautiful dream, in which he had learned how to fly. Everything in the dream had an airy quality. He floated and glided through the atmosphere, and went swimming in the clouds, which turned out to be his glittery blue sweater. Charmaine Lopez and her dancing girls did the rhumba in the heavens, which were guarded by smiling Chinese deities. Alvin from the planetarium sang "Stardust" for him as he flew by. He was happy. He could play his saxophone forever. Then he saw Frisquito flying far away, waving to him. He tried and tried, but he couldn't get any closer to him. Frisquito became smaller and smaller, then vanished, and when Bongbong opened his eyes, he found Charmaine gone.

He decided to stay in the flat, and left the other rooms just as they were. Even Ra stopped coming to visit, so Bongbong had to teach himself about the saxophone. There were brief moments when he found that the powers of levitation were within him, so while he practiced the saxophone he would also practice levitating.

Frisquito,
Just two things. The power of light has been in me all along. All I needed was to want it bad enough.

Another is something someone once said to me. Never is forever, she said.

Love

He didn't sign his name or his initial, because he had finally forgotten who he was.

2002

CHILDREN OF THE SEA

Edwidge Danticat

They say behind the mountains are more mountains. Now I know it's true. I also know there are timeless waters, endless seas, and lots of people in this world whose names don't matter to anyone but themselves. I look up at the sky and I see you there. I see you crying like a crushed snail, they way you cried when I helped you pull out your first loose tooth. Yes, I did love you then. Somehow when I looked at you, I thought of fiery red ants. I wanted you to dig your fingernails into my skin and drain out all my blood.

I don't know how long we'll be at sea. There are thirty-six other deserting souls on this little boat with me. White sheets with bright red spots float as our sail.

When I got on board I thought I could still smell the semen and the innocence lost to those sheets. I look up there and I think of you and all those times you resisted. Sometimes I felt like you wanted to, but I knew you wanted me to respect you. You thought I was testing your will, but all I wanted was to be near you. Maybe it's like you've always said. I imagine too much. I am afraid I am going to start having nightmares once we get deep at sea. I really hate having the sun in my face all day long. If you see me again, I'll be so dark.

Your father will probably marry you off now, since I am gone. Whatever you do, please don't marry a soldier. They're almost not human.

haiti est comme tu l'as laissé. yes, just the way you left it. bullets day and night. same hole. same everything. i'm tired of the whole mess. i get so cross and irritable. i pass the time by chasing roaches around

*the house. i pound my heel on their heads. they make me so mad.
everything makes me mad. i am cramped inside all day. they've
closed the schools since the army took over. no one is mentioning the
old president's name. papa burnt all his campaign posters and old
buttons. manman buried her buttons in a hole behind the house. she
thinks he might come back. she says she will unearth them when he
does. no one comes out of their house. not a single person. papa
wants me to throw out those tapes of your radio shows. i destroyed
some music tapes, but i still have your voice. i thank god you got out
when you did. all the other youth federation members have disappeared. no one has heard from them. i think they might all be in
prison. maybe they're all dead. papa worries a little about you. he
doesn't hate you as much as you think. the other day i heard him asking manman, do you think the boy is dead? manman said she didn't
know. i think he regrets being so mean to you. i don't sketch my butterflies anymore because i don't even like seeing the sun. besides,
manman says that butterflies can bring news. the bright ones bring
happy news and the black ones warn us of deaths. we have our whole
lives ahead of us. you used to say that, remember? but then again
things were so very different then.*

There is a pregnant girl on board. She looks like she might be our age.
Nineteen or twenty. Her face is covered with scars that look like razor
marks. She is short and speaks in a singsong that reminds me of the villagers
in the north. Most of the other people on the boat are much older than I
am. I have heard that a lot of these boats have young children on board. I
am glad this one does not. I think it would break my heart watching some
little boy or girl every single day on this sea, looking into their empty faces
to remind me of the hopelessness of the future in our country. It's hard
enough with the adults. It's hard enough with me.

I used to read a lot about America before I had to study so much for
the university exams. I am trying to think, to see if I read anything more
about Miami. It is sunny. It doesn't snow there like it does in other parts
of America. I can't tell exactly how far we are from there. We might be
barely out of our own shores. There are no borderlines on the sea. The
whole thing looks like one. I cannot even tell if we are about to drop off
the face of the earth. Maybe the world is flat and we are going to find out,
like the navigators of old. As you know, I am not very religious. Still I pray

every night that we won't hit a storm. When I do manage to sleep, I dream that we are caught in one hurricane after another. I dream that the winds come out of the sky and claim us for the sea. We go under and no one hears from us again.

I am more comfortable now with the idea of dying. Not that I have completely accepted it, but I know that it might happen. Don't be mistaken. I really do not want to be a martyr. I know I am no good to anybody dead, but if that is what's coming, I know I cannot just scream at it and tell it to go away.

I hope another group of young people can do the radio show. For a long time that radio show was my whole life. It was nice to have radio like that for a while, where we could talk about what we wanted from government, what we wanted for the future of our country.

There are a lot of Protestants on this boat. A lot of them see themselves as Job or the Children of Israel. I think some of them are hoping something will plunge down from the sky and part the sea for us. They say the Lord gives and the Lord takes away. I have never been given very much. What was there to take away?

if only i could kill. if i knew some good wanga magic, i would wipe them off the face of the earth. a group of students got shot in front of fort dimanche prison today. they were demonstrating for the bodies of the radio six. that is what they are calling you all. the radio six. you have a name. you have a reputation. a lot of people think you are dead like the others. they want the bodies turned over to the families. this afternoon, the army finally did give some bodies back. they told the families to go collect them at the rooms for indigents at the morgue. our neighbor madan roger came home with her son's head and not much else. honest to god, it was just his head. at the morgue, they say a car ran over him and took the head off his body. when madan roger went to the morgue, they gave her the head. by the time we saw her, she had been carrying the head all over port-au-prince. just to show what's been done to her son. the macoutes by the house were laughing at her. they asked her if that was her dinner. it took ten people to hold her back from jumping on them. they would have killed her, the dogs. i will never go outside again. not even in the yard to breathe the air. they are always watching you, like vultures. at night i can't sleep. i count the bullets in the dark. i keep wondering if it is true. did you really get out? i wish there was some way i could be sure that you really went away. yes, i will. i will keep writing like we promised to do. i hate it, but i will keep writing. you keep writing too, okay? and when we see each other again, it will seem like we lost no time.

Today was our first real day at sea. Everyone was vomiting with each small rocking of the boat. The faces around me are showing their first charcoal layer of sunburn. "Now we will never be mistaken for Cubans," one man said. Even though some of the Cubans are black too. The man said he was once on a boat with a group of Cubans. His boat had stopped to pick up the Cubans on an island off the Bahamas. When the Coast Guard came for them, they took the Cubans to Miami and sent him back to Haiti. Now he was back on the boat with some papers and documents to show that the police in Haiti were after him. He had a broken leg too, in case there was any doubt.

One old lady fainted from sunstroke. I helped revive her by rubbing some of the salt water on her lips. During the day it can be so hot. At night, it is so cold. Since there are no mirrors, we look at each other's faces to see just how frail and sick we are starting to look.

Some of the women sing and tell stories to each other to appease the vomiting. Still, I watch the sea. At night, the sky and the sea are one. The starts look so huge and so close. They make for very bright reflections in the sea. At times I feel like I can just reach out and pull a star down from the sky as though it is a breadfruit or a calabash or something that could be of use to us on this journey.

When we sing, *Beloved Haiti, there is no place like you. I had to leave you before I could understand you,* some of the women start crying. At times, I just want to stop in the middle of the song and cry myself. To hide my tears, I pretend like I am getting another attack of nausea, from the sea smell. I no longer join in the singing.

You probably do not know much about this, because you have always been so closely watched by your father in that well-guarded house with your genteel mother. No, I am not making fun of you for this. If anything, I am jealous. If I was a girl, maybe I would have been at home and not out politicking and getting myself into something like this. Once you have been at sea for a couple of days, it smells like every fish you have ever eaten, every crab you have ever caught, every jellyfish that has ever bitten your leg. I am so tired of the smell. I am also tired of the way the people on this boat are starting to stink. The pregnant girl, Célianne, I don't know how she takes it. She stares into space all the time and rubs her stomach.

I have never seen her eat. Sometimes the other women offer her a piece of bread and she takes it, but she has no food of her own. I cannot help feeling like she will have this child as soon as she gets hungry enough.

She woke up screaming the other night. I thought she had a stomach ache. Some water started coming into the boat in the spot where she was sleeping. There is a crack at the bottom of the boat that looks as though, if it gets any bigger, it will split the boat in two. The captain cleared us aside and used some tar to clog up the hole. Everyone started asking him if it was okay, if they were going to be okay. He said he hoped the Coast Guard would find us soon.

You can't really go to sleep after that. So we all stared at the tar by the moonlight. We did this until dawn. I cannot help but wonder how long this tar will hold out.

> *papa found your tapes. he started yelling at me, asking if i was crazy keeping them. he is just waiting for the gasoline ban to be lifted so we can get out of the city. he is always pestering me these days because he cannot go out driving his van. all the american factories are closed. he kept yelling at me about the tapes. he called me selfish, and he asked if I hadn't seen or heard what was happening to man-crazy whores like me. i shouted that i wasn't a whore. he had no business calling me that. he pushed me against the wall for disrespecting him. he spat in my face. i wish those macoutes would kill him. i wish he would catch a bullet so we could see how scared he really is. he said to me, i didn't send your stupid trouble maker away. i started yelling at him. yes, you did. yes, you did. yes, you did, you pig peasant. i don't know why i said that. he slapped me and kept slapping me really hard until manman came and grabbed me away from him. i wish one of those bullets would hit me.*

The tar is holding up so far. Two days and no more leaks. Yes, I am finally an African. I am even darker than your father. I wanted to buy a straw hat from one of the ladies, but she would not sell it to me for the last two gourdes I have left in change. Do you think your money is worth anything to me here? she asked me. Sometimes, I forget where I am. If I keep daydreaming like I have been doing, I will walk off the boat to go for a stroll.

The other night I dreamt that I died and went to heaven. This heaven was nothing like I expected. It was at the bottom of the sea. There were starfishes and mermaids all around me. The mermaids were dancing and singing in Latin like the priests do at the cathedral during Mass. You were there with me too, at the bottom of the sea. You were with your family, off to the side. Your father was acting like he was better than everyone else and he was standing in front of a sea cave blocking you from my view. I tried to talk to you, but every time I opened my mouth, water bubbles came out. No sounds.

they have this thing now that they do. if they come into a house and there is a son and mother there, they hold a gun to their heads. they make the son sleep with his mother. if it is a daughter and father, they do the same thing. some nights papa sleeps at his brother's, uncle pressoir's house. uncle pressoir sleeps at our house, just in case they come. that way papa will never be forced to lie down in bed with me. instead, uncle pressoir would be forced to, but that would not be so bad. we know a girl who had a child by her father that way. that is what papa does not want to happen, even if he is killed. there is no gasoline to buy. otherwise we would be in ville rose already. papa has a friend who is going to get him some gasoline from a soldier. as soon as we get the gasoline, we are going to drive quick and fast until we find civilization. that's how papa puts it, civilization. he says things are not as bad in the provinces. i am still not talking to him. i don't think i ever will. manman says it is not his fault. he is trying to protect us. he cannot protect us. only god can protect us. the soldiers can come and do with us what they want. that makes papa feel weak, she says. he gets angry when he feels weak. why should he be angry with me? i am not one of the pigs with the machine guns. she asked me what really happened to you. she said she saw your parents before they left for the provinces. they did not want to tell her anything. i told her you took a boat after they raided the radio station. you escaped and took a boat to heaven knows where. she said, he was going to make a good man, that boy. sharp, like a needle point, that boy, he took the university exams a year before everyone else in this area. manman has respect for people with ambitions. she said papa did not want you for me because it did not seem as though you were going to do any better for me than he and manman could. he wants me to find a man who will do me some good. someone who will make sure that i have more than i have now. it is not enough for a girl to be just pretty anymore. we are not that well connected in society. the kind of man that papa wants for me would never have anything to do with me. all anyone can hope for is just a tiny bit of love, man-man says, like a drop in a cup if you can get it, or a waterfall, a flood, if you can get that too. we do not have all that many high-up con-nections, she says, but you are an educated girl. what she counts for educated is not much to anyone but us anyway. they should be announcing the university exams on the radio next week. then i will know if you passed. i will listen for your name.

We spent most of yesterday telling stories. Someone says, Krik? You answer, Krak! And they say, I have many stories I could tell you, and then they go on and tell these stories to you, but mostly to themselves. Sometimes it feels like we have been at sea longer than the many years that I have been on this earth. The sun comes up and goes down. That is how you know it has been a whole day. I feel like we are sailing for Africa. Maybe we will go to Guinin, to live with the spirits, to be with everyone who has come and has died before us. They would probably turn us away from there too. Someone has a transistor and sometimes we listen to radio from the Bahamas. They treat Haitians like dogs in the Bahamas, a woman says. To them, we are not human. Even though their music sounds like ours. Their people look like ours. Even though we had the same African fathers who probably crossed these same seas together.

Do you want to know how people go to the bathroom on the boat? Probably the same way they did on those slaves ships years ago. They set aside a little corner for that. When I have to pee, I just pull it, lean over the rail, and do it very quickly. When I have to do the other thing, I rip a piece of something, squat down and do it, and throw the waste in the sea. I am always embarrassed by the smell. It is so demeaning having to squat in front of so many people. People turn away, but not always. At times I wonder if there is really land on the other side of the sea. Maybe the sea is endless. Like my love for you.

last night they came to madan roger's house. papa hurried inside as soon as madan roger's screaming started. the soldiers were looking for her son. madan roger was screaming, you killed him already. we buried his head. you can't kill him twice. they were shouting at her, do you belong to the youth federation with those vagabonds who were on the radio? she was yelling, do i look like a youth to you? can you identify your son's other associates? they asked her. papa had us tiptoe from the house into the latrine out back. we could hear it all from there. i thought i was going to choke on the smell of rotting poupou. they kept shouting at madan roger, did your son belong to the youth federation? wasn't he on the radio talking about the police? did he say, down with tonton macoutes? did he say, down with the army? he said that the military had to go; didn't he write slogans? he had meetings, didn't he? he demonstrated on the streets. you should have advised him better. she cursed on their mothers' graves. she just came out and shouted it, i hope your mothers will never rest in their cursed graves! she was just shouting it out, you killed him once already! you want to kill me too? go ahead. i don't care anymore. i'm dead already. you have already done the worst to me that you can do. you have killed my soul. they kept at it, asking her questions at the top of their voices: was your son a traitor? tell me all the names of his friends who were traitors just like him. madan roger finally shouts, yes, he was one! he belonged to that group. he was on the radio. he was on the streets at these demonstrations. he hated you like i hate you criminals. you killed him. they start to pound at her. you can hear it. you can hear the guns coming down on her head. it sounds like they are cracking all the bones in her body. manman whispers to papa, you can't just let them kill her. go and give them some money like you gave them for your daughter. papa says, the only money i have left is to get us out of here tomorrow. manman whispers, we cannot just stay here and let them kill her. manman starts moving like she is going out the door. papa grabs her neck and pins her to the latrine wall. tomorrow we are going to ville rose, he says. you will not spoil that for the family. you will not put us in that situation. you will not get us killed. going out there will be like trying to raise the dead. she is not dead yet, manman says, maybe we can help her. i will make you stay if i have to, he says to her. my mother buries her face in the latrine wall. she starts to cry. you can hear madan roger screaming. they are beating her, pounding on her until you don't hear anything else. manman tells papa, you cannot let them kill somebody just because you are afraid. papa

says, oh yes, you can let them kill somebody because you are afraid.
they are the law. it is their right. we are just being good citizens, fol-
lowing the law of the land. it has happened before all over this coun-
try and tonight it will happen again and there is nothing we can do.

Célianne spent the night groaning. She looks like she has been ready for a
while, but maybe the child is being stubborn. She just screamed that she
is bleeding. There is an older woman here who looks like she has had a lot
of children herself. She says Célianne is not bleeding at all. He water sack
has broken.

The only babies I have ever seen right after birth are baby mice. Their
skin looks veil thin. You can see all the blood vessels and all their organs. I
have always wanted to poke them to see if my finger would go all the way
through the skin.

I have moved to the other side of the boat so I will not have to look
inside Célianne. People are just watching. The captain asks the midwife to
keep Célianne steady so she will not rock any more holes into the boat.
Now we have three cracks covered with tar. I am scared to think of what
would happen if we had to choose among ourselves who would stay on the
boat and who should die. Given the choice to make a decision like that, we
would all act like vultures, including me.

The sun will set soon. Someone says that this child will be just another
pair of hungry lips. At least it will have its mother's breasts, says an old man.
Everyone will eat their last scraps of food today.

there is a rumor that the old president is coming back. there is a
whole bunch of people going to the airport to meet him. papa says
we are not going to stay in port-au-prince to find out if this is true
or if it is a lie. they are selling gasoline at the market again. the car-
nival groups have taken to the streets. we are heading the other way,
to ville rose. maybe there i will be able to sleep at night. it is not
going to turn out well with the old president coming back, manman
now says. people are just too hopeful, and sometimes hope is the
biggest weapon of all to use against us. people will believe any-
thing. they will claim to see the christ return and march on the cross
backwards if there is enough hope. manman told papa that you
took the boat. papa told me before we left this morning that he
thought himself a bad father for everything that happened. he says

a father should be able to speak to his children like a civilized man. all the craziness here has made him feel like he cannot do that anymore. all he wants to do is live. he and manman have not said a word to one another since we left the latrine. i know that papa does not hate us, not in the way that i hate those soldiers, those macoutes, and all those people here who shoot guns. on our way to ville rose, we saw dogs licking two dead faces. one of them was a little boy who was lying on the side of the road with the sun in his dead open eyes. we saw a soldier shoving a woman out of a hut, calling her a witch. he was shaving the woman's head, but of course we never stopped. papa didn't want to go in madan roger's house and check on her before we left. he thought the soldiers might still be there. papa was driving the van real fast. i thought he was going to kill us. we stopped at an open market on the way. manman got some black cloth for herself and for me. she cut the cloth in two pieces and we wrapped them around our heads to mourn madan roger. when i am used to ville rose, maybe i will sketch you some butterflies, depending on the news that they bring me.

Célianne had a girl baby. The woman acting as a midwife is holding the baby to the moon and whispering prayers. . . . *God, this child You bring into the world, please guide her as You please through all her days on this earth.* The baby has not cried.

We had to throw our extra things in the sea because the water is beginning to creep in slowly. The boat needs to be lighter. My two gourdes in change had to be thrown overboard as an offering to Agwé, the spirit of the water. I heard the captain whisper to someone yesterday that they might have to do *something* with some of the people who never recovered from seasickness. I am afraid that soon they may ask me to throw out this notebook. We might all have to strip down to the way we were born, to keep ourselves from drowning.

Célianne's child is a beautiful child. They are calling her Swiss, because the word *Swiss* was written on the small knife they used to cut her umbilical cord. If she was my daughter, I would call her soleil, sun, moon, or star, after the elements. She still hasn't cried. There is gossip circulating about how Célianne became pregnant. Some people are saying that she had an affair with a married man and her parents threw her out. Gossip spreads here like everywhere else.

Do you remember our silly dreams? Passing the university exams and then studying hard to go until the end, that farthest of all that we can go in school. I know your father might never approve of me. I was going to try to win him over. He would have to cut out my heart to keep me from loving you. I hope you are writing like you promised. Jésus, Marie, Joseph! Everyone smells so bad. They get into arguments and they say to one another, "It is only my misfortune that would lump me together with an indigent like you." Think of it. They are fighting about being superior when we all might drown like straw.

There is an old toothless man leaning over to see what I am writing. He is sucking on the end of an old wooden pipe that has not seen any fire for a very long time now. He looks like a painting. Seeing things simply, you could fill a museum with the sights you have here. I still feel like such a coward for running away. Have you heard anything about my parents? Last time I saw them on the beach, my mother had a *kriz*. She just fainted on the sand. I saw her coming to as we started sailing away. But of course I don't know if she is doing all right.

The water is really piling into the boat. We take turns pouring bowls of it out. I don't know what is keeping the boat from splitting in two. Swiss isn't crying. They keep slapping her behind, but she is not crying.

of course the old president didn't come. they arrested a lot of people at the airport, shot a whole bunch of them down. i heard it on the radio. while we were eating tonight, i told papa that i love you. i don't know if it will make a difference. i just want him to know that i have loved somebody in my life. in case something happens to one of us, i think he should know this about me, that i have loved some-one besides only my mother and father in my life. i know you would understand. you are the one for large noble gestures. i just wanted him to know that i was capable of loving somebody. he looked me straight in the eye and said nothing to me. i love you until my hair shivers at the thought of anything happening to you. papa just turned his face away like he was rejecting my very birth. i am writing you from under the banyan tree in the yard in our new house. there are only two rooms and a tin roof that makes music when it rains, especially when there is hail, which falls like angry tears from heaven. there is a stream down the hill from the house, a stream that is too shallow for me to drown myself. manman and i spend a lot of

time talking under the banyan tree. she told me today that some-
times you have to choose between your father and the man you love.
her whole family did not want her to marry papa because he was a
gardener from ville rose and her family was from the city and some of
them had even gone to university. she whispered everything under
the banyan tree in the yard so as not to hurt his feelings. i saw him
looking at us hard from the house. i heard him clearing his throat
like he heard us anyway, like we hurt him very deeply somehow just
by being together.

Célianne is lying with her head against the side of the boat. The baby still
will not cry. The both look very peaceful in all this chaos. Célianne is holding her baby tight against her chest. She just cannot seem to let herself
throw it in the ocean. I asked her about the baby's father. She keeps repeating the story now with her eyes closed, her lips barely moving.

She was home one night with her mother and brother Lionel when
some ten or twelve soldiers burst into the house. The soldiers held a gun
to Lionel's head and ordered him to lie down and become intimate with
his mother. Lionel refused. Their mother told him to go ahead and obey
the soldiers because she was afraid that they would kill Lionel on the spot
if he put up more of a fight. Lionel did as his mother told him, crying as
the soldiers laughed at him, pressing the gun barrels farther and farther
into his neck.

Afterwards, the soldiers tied up Lionel and their mother, then they each
took turns raping Célianne. When they were done, they arrested Lionel,
accusing him of moral crimes. After that night, Célianne never heard from
Lionel again.

The same night, Célianne cut her face with a razor so that no one
would know who she was. Then as facial scars were healing, she started
throwing up and getting rashes. Next thing she knew, she was getting big.
She found out about the boat and got on. She is fifteen.

manman told me the whole story today under the banyan tree. the
bastards were coming to get me. they were going to arrest me. they
were going to peg me as a member of the youth federation and then
take me away. papa heard about it. he went to the post and paid
them money, all the money he had. our house in port-au-prince and
all the land his father had left him, he gave it all away to save my

life. this is why he was so mad. tonight manman told me this under the banyan tree. i have no words to thank him for this. i don't know how. you must love him for this, manman says, you must. it is something you can never forget, the sacrifice he has made. i cannot bring myself to say thank you. now he is more than my father. he is a man who gave everything he had to save my life. on the radio tonight, they read the list of names of people who passed the university exams. you passed.

We got some relief from the seawater coming in. The captain used the last of his tar, and most of the water is staying out for a while. Many people have volunteered to throw Célianne's baby overboard for her. She will not let them. They are waiting for her to go to sleep so they can do it, but she will not sleep. I never knew before that dead children looked purple. The lips are the most purple because the baby is so dark. Purple like the sea after the sun has set.

Célianne is slowly drifting off to sleep. She is very tired from the labor. I do not want to touch the child. If anybody is going to throw it in the ocean, I think it should be her. I keep thinking, they have thrown every piece of flesh that followed the child out of her body into the water. They are going to throw the dead baby in the water. Won't these things attract sharks?

Célianne's fingernails are buried deep in the child's naked back. The old man with the pipe just asked, "Kompè, what are you writing?" I told him, "My will."

i am getting used to ville rose. there are butterflies here, tons of butterflies. so far none has landed on my hand, which means they have no news for me. i cannot always bathe in the stream near the house because the water is freezing cold. the only time it feels just right is at noon, and then there are a dozen eyes who might see me bathing. i solved that by getting a bucket of water in the morning and leaving it in the sun and then bathing myself once it is night under the banyan tree. the banyan now is my most trusted friend. they say banyans can last hundreds of years. even the branches that lean down from them become like trees themselves. a banyan could become a forest, manman says, if it were given a chance. from the spot where i stand under the banyan, i see the mountains, and

behind those are more mountains still. so many mountains that are
bare like rocks. i feel like all those mountains are pushing me farther
and farther away from you.

She threw it overboard. I watched her face knot up like a thread, and then
she let go. It fell in a splash, floated for a while, and then sank. And quickly
after that she jumped in too. And just as the baby's head sank, so did hers.
They went together like two bottles beneath a waterfall. The shock lasts only
so long. There was no time to even try and save her. There was no question
of it. The sea in that spot is like the sharks that live there. It has no mercy.

They say I have to throw my notebook out. The old man has to throw
out his hat and his pipe. The water is rising again and they are scooping it
out. I asked for a few seconds to write this last page and then promised that
I would let it go. I know you will probably never see this, but it was nice
imagining that I had you here to talk to.

I hope my parents are alive. I asked the old man to tell them what happened to me, if he makes it anywhere. He asked me to write his name in
"my book." I asked him for his full name. It is Justin Moïse André Nozius
Joseph Frank Osnac Maximilien. He says it all with such an air that you
would think him a king. The old man says, "I know a Coast Guard ship is
coming. It came to me in my dream." He points to a spot far into the distance. I look where he is pointing. I see nothing. From here, ships must be
like a mirage in the desert.

I must throw my book out now. It goes down to them, Célianne and her
daughter and all those children of the sea who might soon be claiming me.

I go to them now as though it was always meant to be, as though the
very day that my mother birthed me, she had chosen me to live life eternal,
among the children of the deep blue sea, those who have escaped the
chains of slavery to form a world beneath the heavens and the blood-
drenched earth where you live.

Perhaps I was chosen from the beginning of time to live there with
Agwé at the bottom of the sea. Maybe this is why I dreamed of the starfish
and the mermaids having the Catholic Mass under the sea. Maybe this was
my invitation to go. In any case, I know that my memory of you will live
even there as I too become a child of the sea.

today i said thank you. i said thank you, papa, because you saved
my life. he groaned and just touched my shoulder, moving his hand

*quickly away like a butterfly. and then there it was, the black butter-
fly floating around us. i began to run and run so it wouldn't land on
me, but it had already carried its news. i know what must have happened. tonight i listened to manman's transistor under the banyan
tree. all i hear from the radio is more killing in port-au-prince. the
pigs are refusing to let up. i don't know what's going to happen, but
i cannot see staying here forever. i am writing to you from the bottom
of the banyan tree. manman says that banyan trees are holy and
sometimes if we call the gods from beneath them, they will hear our
voices clearer. now there are always butterflies around me, black ones
that i refuse to let find my hand. i throw big rocks at them, but they
are always too fast. last night on the radio, i heard that another boat
sank off the coast of the bahamas. i can't think about you being in
there in the waves. my hair shivers. from here, i cannot even see the
sea. behind these mountains are more mountains and more black
butterflies still and a sea that is endless like my love for you.*

1995

II. BELONGING

HIS GRACE

Mikhail Naimy

I was having supper at a Syrian restaurant in New York with a friend of mine. It was after nine and the place had emptied of customers; the owner came over and sat with us, adding his own interesting anecdotes to help us consume and digest his fare. He was a convival fellow, who took a liking to us and went out of his way to please us because we were regulars. Indicating his watch, my friend said to him: "We're late tonight, Abu 'Assaf; I imagine you're ready to shut up shop and go home, so don't delay on account of us."

Abu 'Assaf shook his head and swore he counted it an honor to sit with us and would stay open on our account until midnight; and that both he and his restaurant were at our disposal. He added that he seldom locked his door before ten o'clock, because "the Bey" never came before half-past nine.

We both asked him the same question at once: "Who's 'the Bey,' Abu 'Assaf?"

You would have thought we had blasphemed against the prophets and saints, whom Abu 'Assaf worshipped more than his Lord, or had denied the existence of the Almighty, or at least found a beetle in our soup. Abu 'Assaf's eyes widened and he said, as if he could not believe his ears, "Are you joking, or do you really not know the Bey? How can you not know him?"

And before Abu 'Assaf could get over his amazement at our utter ignorance, the door opened, and in came a man tall and erect, narrow-shouldered and pot-bellied, with long hands and fingers. In his right hand he carried a stick, crooked as a dog's hind leg, and in his left an Arabic newspaper. He wore a suit consisting of gray trousers and a brown jacket, all worn and frayed at the edges, from which dangled threads of varying lengths. All I could see of his face at first was a pair of bushy whiskers that reached right up to his ears, a bulbous nose and leathery brown skin.

The newcomer strode slowly to the back of the restaurant, laid his stick and his hat on one side of the table, sat down and began to read his paper. Intrigued by his curious costume and demeanor, I studied his features more closely. What struck me as most odd about him was the shape of his head, like a pinecone, the size of his ears, flat and stuck to the side of his head like two pieces of dough, and his short hair, which began little more than an inch above his eyebrows.

"Abu 'Assaf, bring me a zucchini with stuffed vineleaves, tripe with *hummus, hummus* and sesame oil, and a bit of watermelon," said our visitor, without raising his eyes from his newspaper, and in a voice accustomed to giving orders since early youth without risk of refusal. The moment he saw him come in, Abu 'Assaf had scurried to the kitchen; he prepared his order in a trice and brought it to him with every sign of awe and reverence, and without uttering a word, as if his client were some redoubtable potentate. Abu 'Assaf bustled back and forth with plates and dishes until the visitor finished his meal, put on his hat, picked up his stick in one hand and his newspaper in the other, and left as he had arrived—with a slow, steady pace, looking neither left nor right, and without paying Abu 'Assaf a solitary cent.

A moment later, Abu 'Assaf came back to us, apologizing for having neglected us while this third customer was in the restaurant, but in strangely subdued tones, as if tongue-tied. Before we could reply at all, he told us: "That was the Bey. Did you see him?"

We asked him "the Bey's" name and what he did, and he told us.

"His name is As'ad al-Da'waq, and he is from my own village in Lebanon—the last of the sheikhs of the house of Da'waq, who have ruled our village for a long time. Their power was absolute: the local people were like their slaves, they did not own so much as a clod of the land they tilled. Then after a while, fortune turned against them, as it has against so many other emirs and sheikhs. One of their former tenants emigrated to America, came back rich and bought a large part of the land that had belonged to the Da'waq estate. And so the house of Da'waq steadily declined generation after generation, until the only one left was Sheikh As'ad, and all *he* had left was the title and astronomical debts.

"Then it so happened that one of the villagers, and a former servant of Sheikh As'ad's at that, amassed a great deal of money in America, then returned home, built a splendid mansion and bought himself the title of 'Bey.' You know how such titles are bought and sold in our part of the world.

"Up to that time Sheikh As'ad had been happy enough, content with his lot, satisfied still to be the local sheikh, the accepted and unrivaled celebrity. But once there was a Bey in the community, there was no longer any place for a mere sheikh. And how could a Da'waq possibly accept that there should be someone in the community of higher status than himself?

"Worse than anything was the fact that this Bey was a former servant of the Sheikh. This was a disgrace not to be endured! And all of a sudden the Sheikh changed completely, as if an unseen hand had whisked him away and substituted someone else. He no longer went to church, though he never used to miss a single Sunday or holiday; he forbade his wife to set foot outside the house; he took his sons away from school; he locked his doors to all comers and never received a single visitor.

"When he walked through the streets he would not look to left or right. When passers-by greeted him, he never returned the greeting. And if he happened to run across the Bey, he would turn up his nose, twirl his moustache, swing his stick, clear his throat loudly and spit on the ground with full force.

"The villagers were baffled by the Sheikh's behavior, and many and varied were the interpretations put on it. Some said that all the sins and crimes of the house of Da'waq had been hung like a millstone round his neck, and as a result the Sheikh had lost his wits. Some said he had simply become chronically unsociable ever since the glory of his ancestors had dwindled and disappeared. Others thought the Sheikh was too embarrassed to face people because of his many debts, and that he would not receive visitors because he had nothing to offer them in the way of hospitality.

"So the talk went on in the village, till the news went around that the Sheikh had been snatched away by a jinni—for nobody had seen hide nor hair of him for nearly a week. The community was most alarmed, and the elders assembled, headed by the priest, to look into this serious matter and see how they might save the Sheikh from the clutches of the jinni, or else get rid of the rest of the Sheikh's family in order to ward off from the village the danger of evil spirits. And while they were gabbling prayers and charms in utter consternation, and the priest was explaining how they would have to break into the Sheikh's house to sprinkle it with holy water, and send his wife and children away from the village for fear that by means of them the jinn might extend their power over the whole community—lo and behold, the Sheikh suddenly reappeared. For a moment they all sat rooted to the spot; then they rose to their feet as one man. They remained standing like statues for several minutes, without a one opening his mouth, totally numbed by fear. Finally the priest plucked up courage and, first crossing himself, quavered: 'Welcome back, Sheikh As'ad!'

"With a twirl of his moustache, the Sheikh broke in, 'His Grace As'ad Bey Da'waq, Father, His Grace As'ad Bey, if you please. Sheikh As'ad is dead, and as from now is succeeded by His Grace As'ad Bey!'"

"That night the church bell pealed for almost an hour, announcing to the populace the glad tidings that their Sheikh had become a Bey. The news spread through the village like wildfire that the reason Sheikh As'ad had been absent so long was that the Ottoman governor had summoned him to tell him of his elevation to the beylik. The villagers used up all their dry straw and petroleum for bonfires, danced the *dabka*, cheered 'their Bey' to the echo; and for the last time in the history of the Da'waq family their house was once more packed with throngs of people, once again the lights shone from its balconies, again it was surrounded by young men and girls cheering and singing and ululating, and all convinced that the glory of the house of Da'waq was on the way to being fully restored and might well surpass that of the previous generations.

"The first thing Sheikh As'ad did on becoming 'His Grace' was to set his wife at liberty and send his children back to school (admonishing the teacher to seat them at the head of the class since they were sons of *'the Bey,'* and not to take it into his head ever to place the sons of the other bey above them), and to call a truce with God and resume his visits to church.

"So proud was he of his new title that he refused to accept a letter that came addressed merely to 'His Excellency As'ad Bey Da'waq,' and notified the village postmaster that henceforth he would not accept any mail unless correctly addressed to 'His Grace As'ad Bey.' He no longer referred to his wife by her name, or even her maiden name, in front of other people, but by the title of 'Begum.' 'The Begum is at home,' he would say, or 'The Begum is not at home to visitors today,' and resented anyone's mentioning her in his presence without using her title.

"And here I must take you back to the first bey, the one who was a servant of Sheikh As'ad's and emigrated, came back wealthy and bought himself the title before the Sheikh obtained his. This man, whose name was Roukus Nusour, harbored a grudge against the Sheikh: he had asked the hand of the Sheikh's daughter in marriage, at which the Sheikh had flown into a rage and driven him from the house with the injunction never again to set foot on his threshold and not to forget he was a servant, and how dare a servant ask the hand of a gentleman's daughter? Roukus Nusour left the Sheikh's house with a burning resentment. He resolved to deal him a crushing blow in his most sensitive spot—his pride in his ancestry, and in still being the foremost in the whole community in rank and station. So he went and bought himself the title of Bey, and thought he had floored his adversary for good. All too soon, however, word spread of the Sheikh's journey to the provincial capital and his return with the beylik. What was to be done now?

"Roukus Nusour racked his brains for a way to revenge himself on his rival, till one day a novel thought occurred to him. Where had the Sheikh got the money to buy himself a beylik, when Roukus Nusour knew that he was up to his ears in debt and had long since pawned all but what he stood up in?

"This thought led him to the provincial capital, where he made extensive inquiries only to find no one who knew the Sheikh or had even heard of him; and it became abundantly clear that the Sheikh had not visited the governor's seat and had not obtained any beylik, but had fabricated the whole thing in order to fight his rival with his own weapon. And the trick had taken in the villagers because they were simple folk, to whom the name of Da'waq meant power and glory.

"No sooner had Roukus Nusour returned with his discovery than the news spread from house to house in record time that 'His Grace As'ad Bey Da'waq' was not His Grace at all, but was still plain Sheikh As'ad. That same day the Sheikh left the village, and no more was heard of him.

"Time went by, and I emigrated to America and opened a restaurant in New York. One night I happened to overhear three of my customers talking about 'His Grace the Bey': one of them said he had seen him in a park a long way from the Syrian neighborhood, polishing shoes. Another mentioned that he sold newspapers in the street. The third said he had found him one night sleeping on a bench in a subway station. I asked them who this 'Bey' was they were talking about, and was told he was a Syrian who called himself As'ad Bey Da'waq, and defied anyone to call him by name without using his title. Now I was certain that Sheikh As'ad was in New York, and became keen to meet him. And only a few days later, I saw him come in of his own accord.

"It was on a night when I had no other customers, about half-past nine. I recognized him at once, and knew that he recognized me, and I rushed up to shake his hand and welcome him. He didn't give me his hand or ask how I was keeping or anything. And when I made the inevitable slip of the tongue and greeted him as 'Sheikh As'ad,' he glared at me enough to wither me on the spot said: 'As'ad *Bey*, Bu 'Assaf! As'ad Bey!' Then he went straight to a table, sat down, and ordered a meal. I brought him all he ordered and more, and tried several times to talk to him, but he wouldn't speak to me. When he had eaten his fill he stood up, said: 'Put it on my bill, Abu 'Assaf,' and left.

"Almost seven years have passed since that happened, and ever since, every night without fail, he visits me at the same time and in the very same way as he first did. He comes as you saw him tonight: with a walking-stick, and a newspaper he pretends to read, though I know he can't read or write much. Then he eats, and leaves without paying a cent, and I wish him goodnight and thank him for coming.

"I just can't bring myself to disillusion him. It wouldn't be right. He's nothing if not a Da'waq. I've offered him money more than once, but he won't accept a penny. Poor fellow!"

And our host heaved a deep sigh that came from the very depths of his heart.

ca. 1925

—*Translated from the Arabic by J. R. Perry*

JAPANESE HAMLET

Toshio Mori

He used to come to the house and ask me to hear him recite. Each time he handed me a volume of *The Complete Works of William Shakespeare*. He never forgot to do that. He wanted me to sit in front of him, open the book, and follow him as he recited his lines. I did willingly. There was little for me to do in the evenings so when Tom Fukunaga came over I was ready to help out almost any time. And as his love for Shakespeare's plays grew with the years he did not want anything else in the world but to be a Shakespearean actor.

Tom Fukunaga was a schoolboy in a Piedmont home. He had been one since his freshman days in high school. When he was thirty-one he was still a schoolboy. Nobody knew his age but he and the relatives. Every time his relatives came to the city they put up a roar and said he was a good-for-nothing loafer and ought to be ashamed of himself for being a schoolboy at this age.

"I am not loafing," he told his relatives. "I am studying very hard."

One of his uncles came often to the city to see him. He tried a number of times to persuade Tom to quit stage hopes and schoolboy attitude. "Your parents have already disowned you. Come to your senses," he said. "You should go out and earn a man's salary. You are alone now. Pretty soon even your relatives will drop you."

"That's all right," Tom Fukunaga said. He kept shaking his head until his uncle went away.

When Tom Fukunaga came over to the house he used to tell me about his parents and relatives in the country. He told me in particular about the uncle who kept coming back to warn and persuade him. Tom said he really was sorry for Uncle Bill to take the trouble to see him.

"Why don't you work for someone in the daytime and study at night?" I said to Tom.

"I cannot be bothered with such a change at this time," he said. "Besides, I get five dollars a week plus room and board. That is enough for me. If I should go out and work for someone I would have to pay for room and board besides carfare so I would not be richer. And even if I should save a little more it would not help me become a better Shakespearean actor."

When we came down to the business of recitation there was no recess. Tom Fukunaga wanted none of it. He would place a cup of water before him and never touch it. "Tonight we'll begin with Hamlet," he said many times during the years. *Hamlet* was his favorite play. When he talked about Shakespeare to anyone he began by mentioning Hamlet. He played parts in other plays but always he came back to Hamlet. This was his special role, the role which would establish him in Shakespearean history.

There were moments when I was afraid that Tom's energy and time were wasted and I helped along to waste it. We were miles away from the stage world. Tom Fukunaga had not seen a backstage. He was just as far from the stagedoor in his thirties as he was in his high school days. Sometimes as I sat holding Shakespeare's book and listening to Tom I must have looked worried and discouraged.

"Come on, come on!" he said. "Have you got the blues?"

One day I told him the truth: I was afraid we were not getting anywhere, that perhaps we were attempting the impossible. "If you could contact the stage people it might help," I said. "Otherwise we are wasting our lives."

"I don't think so," Tom said. "I am improving every day. That is what counts. Our time will come later."

That night we took up Macbeth. He went through his parts smoothly. This made him feel good. "Some day I'll be the ranking Shakespearean actor," he said.

Sometimes I told him I liked best to hear him recite the sonnets. I thought he was better with the sonnets than in the parts of Macbeth or Hamlet.

"I'd much rather hear you recite his sonnets, Tom," I said.

"Perhaps you like his sonnets best of all," he said. "Hamlet is my forte. I know I am at my best playing Hamlet."

For a year Tom Fukunaga did not miss a week coming to the house. Each time he brought a copy of Shakespeare's complete works and asked me to hear him say the lines. For better or worse he was not a bit down-hearted. He still had no contact with the stage people. He did not talk about his uncle who kept coming back urging him to quit. I found out later that his uncle did not come to see him any more.

In the meantime Tom stayed at the Piedmont home as a schoolboy. He accepted his five dollars a week just as he had done years ago when he was a freshman at Piedmont High. This fact did not bother Tom at all when I mentioned it to him. "What are you worrying for?" he said. "I know I am taking chances. I went into this with my eyes open, so don't worry."

But I could not get over worrying about Tom Fukunaga's chances. Every time he came over I felt bad for he was wasting his life and for the fact that I was mixed in it. Several times I told him to go somewhere and find a job. He laughed. He kept coming to the house and asked me to sit and hear him recite Hamlet.

The longer I came to know Tom the more I wished to see him well off in business or with a job. I got so I could not stand his coming to the house and asking me to sit while he recited. I began to dread his presence in the house as if his figure reminded me of my part in the mock play that his life was, and the prominence that my house and attention played.

One night I became desperate. "That book is destroying you, Tom. Why don't you give this up for a while?"

He looked at me curiously without a word. He recited several pages and left early that evening.

Tom did not come to the house again. I guess it got so that Tom could not stand me any more than his uncle and parents. When he quit coming I felt bad. I knew he would never abandon his ambition. I was equally sure that Tom would never rank with the great Shakespearean actors, but I could not forget his simple persistence.

One day, years later, I saw him on the Piedmont car at Fourteenth and Broadway. He was sitting with his head buried in a book and I was sure it was a copy of Shakespeare's. For a moment he looked up and stared at me as if I were a stranger. Then his face broke into a smile and he raised his hand. I waved back eagerly.

"How are you, Tom" I shouted.

He waved his hand politely again but did not get off, and the car started up Broadway.

1939

NEW YEAR FOR FONG WING

Monfoon Leong

"Come, Wing. We go to the House of Ten-Thousand Delights. Good?" The Chung Shan accents of Lee Mun, the chef, rumbled up from deep in his round belly. He grinned at Fong Wing, a grin that put crinkles in the shiny smoothness of his face.

Fong Wing did not reply. He picked up his pay from the cashier's counter and followed Lee Mun out the door. With the back of a gnarled hand, reddened from years of dishwashing, he brushed back a few wisps of gray hair that hung over his eyes.

Lee Mun spoke again. "Tired, eh, Wing? When New Year comes, everybody comes to Chinatown."

They stepped out of the restaurant into a gray world of fog. In it, the diffused yellow gleam from the windows made a semi-circular island of light in which they stood for a moment. As if at a signal, they both shivered with a spasm from the sudden damp cold.

"If I lose all my money again in fan tan game, old woman will nag me without rest," Fong Wing finally answered. Although he had come from the Hoy Ping district, he adapted his reedy voice to the tones of the more generally known Sam Yup dialect so that Lee Mun could understand him.

The chef chuckled. "You can blame only yourself for taking wife who thinks gambling not good."

"Wife is good woman," Fong Wing snapped.

They hesitated in the light as if afraid to venture into the early-morning darkness of the fog.

"May be good woman, but she nags you for gambling. Makes you feel guilty about one of joys of living."

Fong Wing nodded slowly. "When I have no money left for foodstuffs, she scolds night and day."

"I will go with you to buy things for New Year's feast," said the rotund Lee Mun. "Not want you to start year with wifely din. Store of Chun Bock is only one open all night. We will go there."

Relieved that his friend did not tempt him further, Fong Wing did not answer, but shrugged his coat tighter around his narrow shoulders and started up the street toward Chun Bock's. Lee Mun waddled along beside him.

Through the thick screen of fog, the few cars still parked on the street looked like so many shapeless monsters. Porcelain Buddhas squatted placidly in the dimness behind the plate glass of modernistic shop fronts. The steps of the two men, as they shuffled along, kicked up small clouds of shattered red paper, the remains of thousands of firecrackers exploded during the night in celebration of the coming of the New Year. What a din there must have been! The street was still now. Still and empty, mused Fong Wing, empty as was his life. He cast a sidelong glance at Lee Mun and marveled at the vigor of his step after the long night of work.

"Why you not marry, Mun?" he asked suddenly. "You are now over forty years of age and still no family to carry on name."

The chef's body quivered with his barely audible laughter. He could have been a reincarnation of the Laughing Buddha. "I like fan tan. And I do not like chatter of woman." His laughter slowly subsided as they walked a few steps in silence. Then he added, "Who carry on your name? You have only one daughter left." He recognized too late the effect that his words would have, for a contrite wrinkling of his brow obliterated the twinkle of his expression almost before the words had left his lips.

Fong Wing knew that his friend had not meant to hurt him, his own words had planted the thought, but his jaw muscles tightened convulsively. He quickened his stride. Lee Mun had difficulty keeping up with him.

They had not reached the corner when Fong Wing felt the chef's hand on his arm. "Wing! Wing! To be angry is of no use." He slowed his steps. Lee Mun took his hand away. As they continued at a slower pace, the chef asked, "How old is your daughter now?"

Fong Wing looked sharply at him. "Too young for you," he said.

Lee Mun's laughter shook him so violently that he had to stop walking. Fong Wing waited for him. "No need to worry," Lee Mun said between gasps. "I not want child for bride."

"She is seventeen. Why do you ask?"

"Is old enough for young husband." They started walking again. "Why do you not get husband for her?" Lee Mun hesitated, then added, "Husband of daughter would be son for you."

Fong Wing snapped, "Why worry about son for me? I do not worry."

"Do not tell me you do not worry—" Lee Mun began. He looked at his friend and became silent.

Chun Bock's was empty but for a clerk drowsing on a stool behind the counter that occupied one side of the narrow store. The opposite wall was lined with shelves of canned goods labeled in English and Chinese. On the floor beneath the shelves was a row of lug boxes full of vegetables. From one of them, Fong Wing picked up a bunch of foot-long string beans and plunked it on the counter to arouse the clerk. He awoke with a start and rubbed his eyes.

Lee Mun picked up a warty, bright-green bitter-melon and examined it with the eye of a connoisseur while Fong Wing asked the clerk, "You have good salted duck eggs?"

The clerk had no chance to answer. Lee Mun erupted, 'Salted duck eggs! Such food is for every day! For New Year's dinner should have more fancy dishes. Fish bellies make excellent soup." He pointed to a jar on the counter. In it were puffed-up, airy-looking pieces of golden yellow the size of a man's fist.

"No. No. No fish bellies." A lump rose in Fong Wing's throat and he turned his face from Lee Mun.

"Why not? You like fish bellies, I know."

"Was third son's favorite dish." Fong Wing whispered the words, bending down to a jar as if to examine the contents more closely so that the moisture in his eyes would not be noticed.

Lee Mun burst out brusquely, "Wing, skin of your face is wrinkled, hair on your head is turning white, but you do not have wisdom of age. Yearning for sons will not bring them back."

"Two first-born killed in France in Big War. Was that not enough?" Fong Wing could contain himself no longer. The coming of the New Year had brought sharply to his mind and to his heart the realization that he could hope for no new beginning, for no grandchildren of his own name.

Without that hope, the future was empty as a hollow gourd, there was left only the shell of the past. "Why did third son have to go?" Months of anguish were poured into the question.

Lee Mun soothed, "He returned from War on Fourth of July heroes' ship. Received hero's burial."

Lee Mun spoke of heroes. He had never had sons, had never poured his life into young bodies and spirits.

"No sons, no grandson will tell of his heroism," muttered Fong Wing.

The clerk was becoming restive as he waited for them to buy, but the two ignored him. Lee Mun moved his hand as if to put it on Fong Wing's shoulder. Before completing the gesture, he drew back his hand and said instead, very slowly and hesitantly, "For long time I have wanted to ask you, Wing. How did boy feel about fighting Asian brothers?"

The question was not an unexpected one for Fong Wing, but he gazed at Lee Mun for a long moment before replying. He felt a bit ashamed as he answered, "Before son went to war, I asked him same question. He said he was not going to fight brothers; he was American fighting for his country against enemy." He shook his head sadly. "Mun, young men are not like us. Old country, old brotherhood of blood means very little to them. They are too much American, too little Chinese." Then he added, as if to himself, "Maybe—maybe it is good thing."

Lee Mun nodded slowly. "Your sons were born here, Wing. Home-land is heart-land."

"What does it matter now. They are beyond ties of blood or home." Fong Wing's words were almost inaudible.

Gently, very gently, Lee Mun said, "What is past cannot be helped. Is it not better to accept what is done? There is still tomorrow."

"How many tomorrows has old man without sons?"

Lee Mun shook his head as he said, "You have wisdom of old fool." Then he shrugged his massive shoulders and showed his teeth in a grin. "Enjoy today then. Flavor of fine birds' nest soup will drown bitter taste of melancholy. Today is New Year, Wing!"

Fong Wing could not resist the chef's cheerfulness. He had to admit to himself that his black thoughts could bring nothing but pain. He smiled wanly and shrugged. "Cannot afford good birds' nest."

"Money! Of what use is money?" Lee Mun exploded. "I buy you box of finest for New Year present." Brushing aside Fong Wing's protests, he ordered a box of the most expensive, snow-white birds' nest. Soon Fong

Wing had filled a large bag with all manner of delicacies. For New Year's Day, at least, there would be no nagging from his wife.

He cradled the bag in his arm and followed Lee Mun out into the grayness. The fog chilled somewhat the warmth that was returning to Fong Wing's spirits and he was silent as they walked to the corner and turned up the steep street toward the two-room apartment that was his home.

Even the exuberance of Lee Mun was dampened. He respected his companion's silence. He stopped when they reached the entrance to an alley that was little more than a narrow passageway between the buildings. "I will go see if have good luck in New Year," he said. "You truly do not want to come?"

Fong Wing hesitated a long moment, but finally muttered, "Wife will chop off my head. Besides, what you do on New Year's Day, you will do all rest of year."

Lee Mun chuckled, "I say that will be fine. Nothing I like better than gamble all year. I will show you my winnings at work tonight." He turned and started off up the alley.

Fong Wing watched the waddling figure as it thrust its way through the fog. The chef was hardly a dozen paces away, but was already almost hidden. Fong Wing started to call to him, but remembered the hour and instead, broke into a shuffling trot to catch the receding back. He hugged the bag of groceries with one arm, holding the top with his free hand so that nothing would be shaken out. "Wait. I will go," he said when he drew abreast of Lee Mun. He was puffing from the exertion. Lee Mun said nothing, but his teeth gleamed in a broad grin.

They stopped before a store, dark as all the others. In the light of the street lamps that barely filtered its way through the fog, a weathered wooden sign was visible over the doorway. It contained two Chinese characters, "Ten-Thousand Delights." They opened the unlocked door and entered. In a back corner of the dark and empty cubicle that was the shop, a dim light glimmered through a hole at eye level. Lee Mun led the way to the door and knocked sharply upon it. An eye appeared at the hole. "Lee Mun," he said, and the door opened. They entered and proceeded down the dimly lit corridor toward another door. After a second scrutiny, they passed through into a large, oblong room in which the smoke was almost as heavy as the fog outdoors.

At the back was a washroom, a broom closet, and a door that Fong Wing knew opened on a corridor that led to the back entrance. Round tables were ranged along each bare wall, tables around which crowded Filipinos, Negroes, Mexicans, Japanese, whites, Chinese, all men, all intent upon their games of poker, black jack, craps, pai gow, or fan tan. The clothes of most of them were worn and frayed as Fong Wing's. They all looked so worn and tired that Fong Wing wondered why they stayed. "You play pai gow?" he asked Lee Mun, nodding toward a group of men, all Chinese, playing dominoes.

"I will watch beans with you tonight," Lee Mun said, moving to the fan tan table. Fong Wing took a place beside him. He watched the operator for a few minutes before he started to bet. The operator was young, he could not have been over twenty-five, but the skin over his gaunt cheeks and high forehead looked old and sallow. If he had not known that this generation no longer used the pipe, Fong Wing would have judged him to be an opium addict. He handled the ivory wand dexterously with the tips of his bony fingers.

With his left hand, he would scoop a handful of the white soybeans out of the box at his elbow and pour them into a pile in front of him. Checking the bets with a quick glance, he would spread out the pile with a sweep of his wand, a chopstick-like instrument with a curved, flattened end. With deft flicks of the wand, he would sort out the beans, four by four, and scoop them back into a pile. After the last group of four was taken out, he would intone in an emotionless voice the number remaining, rake in the money of the losers, and pay the winners.

Fong Wing, watching the boy, was disturbed. In his own youth working in a gambling house was understandable. A Chinese in America could find work only in restaurants, laundries, or gambling houses. Today there was opportunity almost without limit. Fong Wing came in the hope of winning enough to ease the emptiness, the barrenness of his existence. But this boy had all of life before him, and he did not even have the chance to win for himself, as had the men whose money he raked in. "Young fool," Fong Wing mumbled under his breath. "Young fool."

He set his bag of groceries under the table.

"You are speaking to me?" It was Lee Mun, who had already begun to play and was gleefully sweeping in his winnings. Folds of flesh formed under his jaw as he cocked his head toward Fong Wing.

"That boy," Fong Wing nodded in the dealer's direction. "My boy died so he can waste life running bean game."

Before Lee Mun could say anything, a voice intruded. "You are playing?" The young operator was polite, but there was a tinge of impatience in his voice.

Fong Wing shot him a look of resentment, but pulled out his old, leather purse. Without a word, he began to play. He started betting on the four individual numbers. His weariness and resentment began to drop from him as he won again and again. He thought he would buy a nice dress for his woman. It had been a long time — . But his luck did not last. As his stack of coins dwindled, he switched to playing the odds and evens. They paid less when he won, but there was more chance of winning. He watched the dealer raking in his money. Once their eyes met and Fong Wing thought he saw a look almost of regret. He shook off the thought. Soon his stack of coins was gone.

His hand was trembling when he pulled the worn purse from his pocket. The five dollar bill was all that remained in it. He looked at Lee Mun. The rotund chef was beaming happily, one arm wrapped around a large pile of coins while his gleaming black eyes followed the darting movement of the ivory wand. What need had he for money? No wife, no family — .

Fong Wing looked at the bill in his hand. There was handwriting scrawled across it. The signatures of generals, he had been told. A short-snorter bill they called it, sent home with the rest of his third son's personal belongings. He looked up and found the young dealer watching him expectantly. He was about to place the entire five dollars on number three when a heavy thumping and the splintering of wood broke through the subdued hum of the room. He looked toward the door. The first doorkeeper was scurrying through it, piping "Police!" to the room in general. The second doorkeeper slammed the door shut and placed a wooden bar across it. No one in the room said a word, but almost all hurried toward the back door. The dealers were scooping their money into canvas bags. The thumping and splintering noise continued.

Fong Wing stuffed the bill back into his pocket. He looked for Lee Mun and found him still sitting, smiling imperturbably. Noticing Fong Wing's look, he said with a shrug of his shoulders, "I wait for police. They always wait at back door anyway—and I am too fat for closet door." He nodded toward the broom closet to which the dealers were hurrying. "You better hurry."

The young fan tan operator had already filled his bag with the money on the table. Noticing that he had not moved from his seat, Fong Wing started to urge him to hurry, but the youth spoke first. Very quietly, but with a note of desperate urgency in his voice, he said in Sam Yup dialect with a touch of Fong Wing's Hoy Ping accent, "Can you carry me to closet?"

"I carry you?"

"I do not weigh much. You see—" He looked downward. Fong Wing moved around the table to see. "I am only half a man." Fong Wing saw that the young man's trousers legs were indeed folded and pinned up almost to his hips. Anticipating his question, the youth added, "Army doctors said not enough left to fit man-made legs." A loud crash that shook the room announced the breaching of the first door. "Can you carry?" He asked again. Fong Wing picked him up and shuffled toward the closet. Even without legs, the youth was a heavy load for the old man, but the strong arm about his neck lent him added strength.

"War?" Fong Wing asked.

The lines about the young man's mouth sharpened and he nodded. Fong Wing felt a tensing of the body in his arms.

"My third son died there," he said.

"I should have." The arm tightened about his neck.

They were almost to the closet. Fong Wing shook him as if chiding a naughty boy. "Do not say that." He fumbled in his mind for words of reassurance and came across a happy thought. "My woman and I—," he hesitated, then continued, "we need son." He felt the youth relax somewhat in his arms and then become tense again almost at once. He was shaking his head.

"You would not—," the youth started, but he was interrupted by one of the other dealers who hurried out of the closet door calling, "We forgot you."

Reaching them in a few strides, the man said, "Here, old man. I will take him," lifted the youth easily from Fong Wing's reluctant arms, and turned back to the closet. Fong Wing's effort to clutch the young body to him had been futile.

Over the dealer's shoulder, the youth smiled and said, "Half a son is worse than none. But many thanks, uncle."

Fong Wing's heart warmed at the respectful title. They squeezed through the narrow opening at the back of the closet. The last one through, Fong Wing closed the panel behind him. He followed the others silently through door after door until they stopped in a shop that he knew faced the same alley which he had entered earlier. The other dealers were there, huddled in a group, some of them swearing softly in the darkness.

Fong Wing suddenly remembered with a deep groan of anguish that he had left the bag of delicacies in the gambling room. He thought of going back after it when the police had left, but remembered that they would probably leave someone to watch the place. Better to go home empty-handed than to chance the disgrace of a night in jail. That would indeed be good cause for endless harangues from his woman.

He looked for the legless youth, but could no longer distinguish him from the others in the darkness. Soon the fading sound of the patrol wagon in the distance emboldened them to steal quietly out of the shop. Fong Wing strained to catch a glimpse of the youth again in the crowd at the door. Too many were pushing through. He thought to ask someone and realized that he did not know the young man's name. By the time he had slipped into the alley most of the group was gone. The legless one was nowhere in sight. At the end of the alley, he watched the others melt into the wall of fog. It occurred to him that he could have asked for "the man without legs." Now it was too late. Even half a son—.

He took the five dollar bill out of his pocket and stuffed it carefully back into the purse. The thought came into his mind to spend the night at Lee Mun's lodgings, but he pushed it away almost as soon as it came and headed homeward, shrugging his thin coat closer around his spare form. He shuffled heavily along, feeling the thick fog like an enormous weight on his shoulders, pushing him down.

1949

SEVENTEEN SYLLABLES

Hisaye Yamamoto

The first Rosie knew that her mother had taken to writing poems was one evening when she finished one and read it aloud for her daughter's approval. It was about cats, and Rosie pretended to understand it thoroughly and appreciate it no end, partly because she hesitated to disillusion her mother about the quantity and quality of Japanese she had learned in all the years now that she had been going to Japanese school every Saturday (and Wednesday, too, in the summer). Even so, her mother must have been skeptical about the depth of Rosie's understanding, because she explained afterwards about the kind of poem she was trying to write.

See, Rosie, she said, it was a *haiku*, a poem in which she must pack all her meaning into seventeen syllables only, which were divided into three lines of five, seven, and five syllables. In the one she had just read, she had tried to capture the charm of a kitten, as well as comment on the superstition that owning a cat of three colors meant good luck.

"Yes, yes, I understand. How utterly lovely," Rosie said, and her mother, either satisfied or seeing through the deception and resigned, went back to composing.

The truth was that Rosie was lazy; English lay ready on the tongue but Japanese had to be searched for and examined, and even then put forth tentatively (probably to meet with laughter). It was so much easier to say yes, yes, even when one meant no, no. Besides, this was what was in her mind to say: I was looking through one of your magazines from Japan last night, Mother, and towards the back I found some *haiku* in English that delighted me. There was one that made me giggle off and on until I fell asleep —

> *It is morning, and lo!*
> *I lie awake, comme il faut,*
> *sighing for some dough.*

Now, how to reach her mother, how to communicate the melancholy song? Rosie knew formal Japanese by fits and starts, her mother had even less English, no French. It was much more possible to say yes, yes.

It developed that her mother was writing the *haiku* for a daily newspaper, the *Mainichi Shimbun,* that was published in San Francisco. Los Angeles, to be sure, was closer to the farming community in which the Hayashi family lived and several Japanese vernaculars were printed there, but Rosie's parents said they preferred the tone of the northern paper. Once a week, the *Mainichi* would have a section devoted to *haiku,* and her mother became an extravagant contributor, taking for herself the blossoming pen name, Ume Hanazono.

So Rosie and her father lived for a while with two women, her mother and Ume Hanazono. Her mother (Tome Hayashi by name) kept house, cooked, washed, and, along with her husband and the Carrascos, the Mexican family hired for the harvest, did her ample share of picking tomatoes out in the sweltering fields and boxing them in tidy strata in the cool packing shed. Ume Hanazono, who came to life after the dinner dishes were done, was an earnest, muttering stranger who often neglected speaking when spoken to and stayed busy at the parlor table as late as midnight scribbling with pencil on scratch paper or carefully copying characters on good paper with her fat, pale green Parker.

The new interest had some repercussions on the household routine. Before, Rosie had been accustomed to her parents and herself taking their hot baths early and going to bed almost immediately afterwards, unless her parents challenged each other to a game of flower cards or unless company dropped in. Now if her father wanted to play cards, he had to resort to solitaire (at which he always cheated fearlessly), and if a group of friends came over, it was bound to contain someone who was also writing *haiku,* and the small assemblage would be split in two, her father entertaining the non-literary members and her mother comparing ecstatic notes with the visiting poet.

If they went out, it was more of the same thing. But Ume Hanazono's life span, even for a poet's, was very brief—perhaps three months at most.

One night they went over to see the Hayano family in the neighboring town to the west, an adventure both painful and attractive to Rosie. It was attractive because there were four Hayano girls, all lovely and each one named after a season of the year (Haru, Natsu, Aki, Fuyu), painful because something had been wrong with Mrs. Hayano ever since the birth of her first child. Rosie would sometimes watch Mrs. Hayano, reputed to have been the belle of her native village, making her way about a room, stooped, slowly shuffling, violently trembling (*always* trembling), and she would be reminded that this woman, in this same condition, had carried and given issue to three babies. She would look wonderingly at Mr. Hayano, handsome, tall, and strong, and she would look at her four pretty friends. But it was not a matter she could come to any decision about.

On this visit, however, Mrs. Hayano sat all evening in the rocker, as motionless and unobtrusive as it was possible for her to be, and Rosie found the greater part of the evening practically anaesthetic. Too, Rosie spent most of it in the girls' room, because Haru, the garrulous one, said almost as soon as the bows and other greetings were over, "Oh, you must see my new coat!"

It was a pale plaid of gray, sand, and blue, with an enormous collar, and Rosie, seeing nothing special in it, said, "Gee, how nice."

"Nice?" said Haru, indignantly. "Is that all you can say about it? It's gorgeous! And so cheap, too. Only seventeen-ninety-eight, because it was a sale. The saleslady said it was twenty-five dollars regular."

"Gee," said Rosie. Natsu, who never said much and when she said anything said it shyly, fingered the coat covetously and Haru pulled it away.

"Mine," she said, putting it on. She minced in the aisle between the two large beds and smiled happily. "Let's see how your mother likes it."

She broke into the front room and the adult conversation and went to stand in front of Rosie's mother, while the rest watched from the door. Rosie's mother was properly envious. "May I inherit it when you're through with it?"

Haru, pleased, giggled and said yes, she could, but Natsu reminded gravely from the door, "You promised me, Haru."

Everyone laughed but Natsu, who shamefacedly retreated into the bedroom. Haru came in laughing, taking off the coat. "We were only kidding, Natsu," she said. "Here, you try it on now."

After Natsu buttoned herself into the coat, inspected herself solemnly in the bureau mirror, and reluctantly shed it, Rosie, Aki, and Fuyu got their turns, and Fuyu, who was eight, drowned in it while her sisters and Rosie doubled up in amusement. They all went into the front room later, because Haru's mother quaveringly called to her to fix the tea and rice cakes and open a can of sliced peaches for everybody. Rosie noticed that her mother and Mr. Hayano were talking together at the little table—they were discussing a *haiku* that Mr. Hayano was planning to send to *Mainichi*, while her father was sitting at one end of the sofa looking through a copy of *Life*, the new picture magazine. Occasionally, her father would comment on a photograph, holding it toward Mrs. Hayano and speaking to her as he always did—loudly, as though he thought someone such as she must surely be at least a trifle deaf also.

The five girls had their refreshment at the kitchen table, and it was while Rosie was showing the sisters her trick of swallowing peach slices without chewing (she chased each slippery crescent down with a swig of tea) that her father brought his empty teacup and untouched saucer to the sink and said, "Come on, Rosie, we're going home now."

"Already?" asked Rosie.

"Work tomorrow," he said.

He sounded irritated, and Rosie, puzzled, gulped one last yellow slice and stood up to go, while the sisters began protesting, as was their wont.

"We have to get up at five-thirty," he told them, going into the front room quickly, so that they did not have their usual chance to hang onto his hands and plead for an extension of time.

Rosie, following, saw that her mother and Mr. Hayano were sipping tea and still talking together, while Mrs. Hayano concentrated, quivering, on raising the handleless Japanese cup to her lips with both her hands and lowering it back to her lap. Her father, saying nothing, went out the door, onto the bright porch, and down the steps. Her mother looked up and asked, "Where is he going?"

"Where is he going?" Rosie said. "He said we were going home now."

"Going home?" Her mother looked with embarrassment at Mr. Hayano and his absorbed wife and then forced a smile. "He must be tired," she said.

Haru was not giving up yet. "May Rosie stay overnight?" she asked, and Natsu, Aki, and Fuyu came to reinforce their sister's plea by helping her make a circle around Rosie's mother. Rosie, for once having no desire to stay, was relieved when her mother, apologizing to the perturbed Mr. and Mrs. Hayano for her father's abruptness, at the same time managed to shake her head no at the quartet, kindly but adamant, so that they broke their circle and let her go.

Rosie's father looked up ahead into the windshield as the two joined him. "I'm sorry," her mother said. "You must be tired." Her father, stepping on the starter, said nothing. "You know how I get when it's *haiku*," she continued, "I forget what time it is." He only grunted.

As they rode homeward silently, Rosie, sitting between, felt a rush of hate for both—for her mother for begging, for her father for denying her mother. I wish this old Ford would crash, right now, she thought, then immediately, no, no, I wish my father would laugh, but it was too late: already the vision had passed through her mind of the green pickup crumpled in the dark against one of the mighty eucalyptus trees they were just riding past, of the three contorted, bleeding bodies, one of them hers.

Rosie ran between two patches of tomatoes, her heart working more rambunctiously than she had ever known it to. How lucky it was that Aunt Taka and Uncle Gimpachi had come tonight, though, how very lucky. Otherwise she might not have really kept her half-promise to meet Jesus Carrasco. Jesus was going to be a senior in September at the same school she went to, and his parents were the ones helping with the tomatoes this year. She and Jesus, who hardly remembered seeing each other at Cleveland High where there were so many other people and two whole grades between them, had become great friends this summer—he always had a joke for her when he periodically drove the loaded pickup from the fields to the shed where she was usually sorting while her mother and father did the packing, and they laughed a great deal together over infinitesimal repartee during the afternoon break for chilled watermelon or ice cream in the shade of the shed.

What she enjoyed most was racing him to see which could finish picking a double row first. He, who could work faster, would tease her by slowing down until she thought she would surely pass him this time, then speeding up furiously to leave her several sprawling vines behind. Once he had made her screech hideously by crossing over, while her back was turned, to place atop the tomatoes in her green-stained bucket a truly monstrous, pale green worm (it had looked more like an infant snake). And it was when they had

finished a contest this morning, after she had pantingly pointed a green finger at the immature tomatoes evident in the lugs at the end of his row and
he had returned the accusation (with justice), that he had startlingly
brought up the matter of their possibly meeting outside the range of both
their parents' dubious eyes.

"What for?" she had asked.

"I've got a secret I want to tell you," he said.

"Tell me now," she demanded.

"It won't be ready till tonight," he said.

She laughed. "Tell me tomorrow then."

"It'll be gone tomorrow," he threatened.

"Well, for seven hakes, what is it?" she had asked, more than twice, and
when he had suggested that the packing shed would be an appropriate
place to find out, she had cautiously answered maybe. She had not been
certain she was going to keep the appointment until the arrival of mother's
sister and her husband. Their coming seemed a sort of signal of permission,
of grace, and she had definitely made up her mind to lie and leave as she
was bowing them welcome.

So as soon as everyone appeared settled back for the evening, she
announced loudly that she was going to the privy outside, "I'm going to the
benjo!" and slipped out the door. And now that she was actually on her way,
her heart pumped in such an undisciplined way that she could hear it with
her ears. It's because I'm running, she told herself, slowing to a walk. The
shed was up ahead, one more patch away, in the middle of the fields. Its
bulk, looming in the dimness, took on a sinisterness that was funny when
Rosie reminded herself that it was only a wooden frame with a canvas roof
and three canvas walls that made a slapping noise on breezy days.

Jesus was sitting on the narrow plank that was the sorting platform and she
went around to the other side and jumped backwards to seat herself on the
rim of a packing stand. "Well, tell me," she said without greeting, thinking
her voice sounded reassuringly familiar.

"I saw you coming out the door," Jesus said. "I heard you running part
of the way, too."

"Uh-huh," Rosie said. "Now tell me the secret."

"I was afraid you wouldn't come," he said.

Rosie delved around on the chicken-wire bottom of the stall for number two tomatoes, ripe, which she was sitting beside, and came up with a

left-over that felt edible. She bit into it and began sucking out the pulp and seeds. "I'm here," she pointed out.

"Rosie, are you sorry you came?"

"Sorry? What for?" she said. "You said you were going to tell me something."

"I will, I will," Jesus said, but his voice contained disappointment, and Rosie fleetingly felt the older of the two, realizing a brand-new power which vanished without category under her recognition.

"I have to go back in a minute," she said. "My aunt and uncle are here from Wintersburg. I told them I was going to the privy."

Jesus laughed. "You funny thing," he said. "You slay me!"

"Just because you have a bathroom *inside*," Rosie said. "Come on, tell me."

Chuckling, Jesus came around to lean on the stand facing her. They still could not see each other very clearly, but Rosie noticed that Jesus became very sober again as he took the hollow tomato from her hand and dropped it back into the stall. When he took hold of her empty hand, she could find no words to protest; her vocabulary had become distressingly constricted and she thought desperately that all that remained intact now was yes and no and oh, and even these few sounds would not easily out. Thus, kissed by Jesus, Rosie fell for the first time entirely victim to a helplessness delectable beyond speech. But the terrible, beautiful sensation lasted no more than a second, and the reality of Jesus' lips and tongue and teeth and hands made her pull away with such strength that she nearly tumbled.

Rosie stopped running as she approached the lights from the windows of home. How long since she had left? She could not guess, but gasping yet, she went to the privy in back and locked herself in. Her own breathing deafened her in the dark, close space, and she sat and waited until she could hear at last the nightly calling of the frogs and crickets. Even then, all she could think to say was oh, my, and the pressure of Jesus' face against her face would not leave.

No one missed her in the parlor, however, and Rosie walked in and through quickly, announcing that she was next going to take a bath. "Your father's in the bathhouse," her mother said, and Rosie, in her room, recalled that she had not seen him when she entered. There had been only Aunt Taka and Uncle Gimpachi with her mother at the table, drinking tea. She got her robe and straw sandals and crossed the parlor again to go outside. Her mother was telling them about the *haiku* competition in the *Mainichi* and the poem she had entered.

Rosie met her father coming out of the bathhouse. "Are you through, Father?" she asked. "I was going to ask you to scrub my back."

"Scrub your own back," he said shortly, going toward the main house.

"What have I done now?" she yelled after him. She suddenly felt like doing a lot of yelling. But he did not answer, and she went into the bathhouse. Turning on the dangling light, she removed her denims and T-shirt and threw them in the big carton for dirty clothes standing next to the washing machine. Her other things she took with her into the bath compartment to wash after her bath. After she had scooped a basin of hot water from the square wooden tub, she sat on the gray cement of the floor and soaped herself at exaggerated leisure, singing "Red Sails in the Sunset" at the top of her voice and using da-da-da where she suspected her words. Then, standing up, still singing, for she was possessed by the notion that any attempt now to analyze would result in spoilage and she believed that the larger her volume the less she would be able to hear herself think, she obtained more hot water and poured it on until she was free of lather. Only then did she allow herself to step into the steaming vat, one leg first, then the remainder of her body inch until the water no longer stung and she could move around at will.

She took a long time soaking, afterwards remembering to go around outside to stoke the embers of the tin-lined fireplace beneath the tub and to throw on a few more sticks so that the water might keep its heat for her mother, and when she finally returned to the parlor, she found her mother still talking *haiku* with her aunt and uncle, the three of them on another round of tea. Her father was nowhere in sight.

At Japanese school the next day (Wednesday, it was), Rosie was grave and giddy by turns. Preoccupied at her desk in the row for students on Book Eight, she made up for it at recess by performing wild mimicry for the benefit of her friend Chizuko. She held her nose and whined a witticism or two in what she considered was the manner of Fred Allen; she assumed intoxication and a British accent to go over the climax of the Rudy Vallee recording of the pub conversation about William Ewart Gladstone; she was the child Shirley Temple piping, "On the Good Ship Lollipop"; she was the gentleman soprano of the Four Inkspots trilling, "If I Didn't Care." And she felt reasonably satisfied when Chizuko wept and gasped, "Oh, Rosie, you ought to be in the movies!"

Her father came after her at noon, bringing her sandwiches of minced ham and two nectarines to eat while she rode, so that she could pitch right into the sorting when they got home. The lugs were piling up, he said, and the ripe tomatoes in them would probably have to be taken to the cannery tomorrow if they were not ready for the produce haulers tonight. "This heat's not doing them any good. And we've got no time for a break today."

It *was* hot, probably the hottest day of the year, and Rosie's blouse stuck damply to her back even under the protection of the canvas. But she worked as efficiently as a flawless machine and kept the stalls heaped, with one part of her mind listening in to the parental mumuring about the heat and the tomatoes and with another part planning the exact words she would say to Jesus when he drove up with the first load of the afternoon. But when at last she saw that the pickup was coming, her hands went berserk and the tomatoes started falling in the wrong stalls, and her father said, "Hey, hey! Rosie, watch what you're doing!"

"Well, I have to go to the *benjo*," she said, hiding panic.

"Go in the weeds over there," he said, only half-joking.

"Oh, Father!" she protested.

"Oh, go home," her mother said. "We'll make out for a while."

In the privy Rosie peered through a knothole toward the fields, watching as much as she could of Jesus. Happily she thought she saw him look in the direction of the house from time to time before he finished unloading and went back toward the patch where his mother and father worked. As she was heading for the shed, a very presentable black car purred up the dirt driveway to the house and its driver motioned to her. Was this the Hayashi home, he wanted to know. She nodded. Was she a Hayashi? Yes, she said, thinking that he was a good-looking man. He got out of the car with a huge, flat package and she saw that he warmly wore a business suit. "I have something here for your mother then," he said, in a more elegant Japanese than she was used to.

She told him where her mother was and he came along with her, patting his face with an immaculate white handkerchief and saying something about the coolness of San Francisco. To her surprised mother and father, he bowed and introduced himself as, among other things, this *haiku* editor of the *Mainichi Shimbun*, saying that since he had been coming as far as Los Angeles anyway, he had decided to bring her the first prize she had won in the recent contest.

"First prize?" her mother echoed, believing and not believing, pleased and overwhelmed. Handed the package with a bow, she bobbed her head up and down numerous times to express her utter gratitude.

"It is nothing much," he added, "but I hope it will serve as a token of our great appreciation for your contributions and our great admiration of your considerable talent."

"I am not worthy," she said, falling easily into his style. "It is I who should make some sign of my humble thanks for being permitted to contribute."

"No, no, to the contrary," he said, bowing again.

But Rosie's mother insisted, and then saying that she knew she was being unorthodox, she asked if she might open the package because her curiosity was so great. Certainly she might. In fact, he would like her reaction to it, for personally, it was one of his favorite Hiroshiges.

Rosie thought it was a pleasant picture, which looked to have been sketched with delicate quickness. There were pink clouds, containing some graceful calligraphy, and a sea that was a pale blue except at the edges, containing four sampans with indications of people in them. Pines edged the water and on the far-off beach there was a cluster of thatched huts towered over by pine-dotted mountains of gray and blue. The frame was scalloped and gilt.

After Rosie's mother pronounced it without peer and somewhat prodded her father into nodding agreement, she said Mr. Kuroda must at least have a cup of tea after coming all this way, and although Mr. Kuroda did not want to impose, he soon agreed that a cup of tea would be refreshing and went along with her to the house, carrying the picture for her.

"Ha, your mother's crazy!" Rosie's father said, and Rosie laughed uneasily as she resumed judgment on the tomatoes. She had emptied six lugs when he broke into an imaginary conversation with Jesus to tell her to go and remind her mother of the tomatoes, and she went slowly.

Mr. Kuroda was in his shirtsleeves expounding some *haiku* theory as he munched a rice cake, and her mother was rapt. Abashed in the great man's presence, Rosie stood next to her mother's chair until her mother looked up inquiringly, and then she started to whisper the message, but her mother pushed her gently away and reproached, "You are not being very polite to our guest."

"Father says the tomatoes . . ." Rosie said aloud, smiling foolishly.

"Tell him I shall only be a minute," her mother said, speaking the language of Mr. Kuroda.

When Rosie carried the reply to her father, he did not seem to hear and she said again, "Mother says she'll be back in a minute."

"All right, all right," he nodded, and they worked again in silence. But suddenly, her father uttered an incredible noise, exactly like a cork of a bottle popping, and the next Rosie knew, he was stalking angrily toward the house, almost running in fact, and she chased after him crying, "Father! Father! What are you going to do?"

He stopped long enough to order her back to the shed. "Never mind!" he shouted. "Get on with the sorting!"

And from the place in the fields where she stood, frightened and vacillating, Rosie saw her father enter the house. Soon Mr. Kuroda came out alone, putting on his coat. Mr. Kuroda got into his car and backed out down the driveway onto the highway. Next her father emerged, also alone, something in his arms (it was the picture, she realized), and, going over to the bathhouse woodpile, he threw the picture on the ground and picked up the axe. Smashing the picture, glass and all (she heard the explosion faintly), he reached over for the kerosene that was used to encourage the bath fire and poured it over the wreckage. I am dreaming, Rosie said to herself, I am dreaming, but her father, having made sure that his act of cremation was irrevocable, was even then returning to the fields.

Rosie ran past him and toward the house. What had become of her mother? She burst into the parlor and found her mother at the back window watching the dying fire. They watched together until there remained only a feeble smoke under the blazing sun. Her mother was very calm.

"Do you know why I married your father?" she said without turning.

"No," said Rosie. It was the most frightening question she had ever been called upon to answer. Don't tell me now, she wanted to say, tell me tomorrow, tell me next week, don't tell me today. But she knew she would be told now, that the telling would combine with the other violence of the hot afternoon to level her life, her world to the very ground.

It was like a story out of the magazines illustrated in sepia, which she had consumed so greedily for a period until the information had somehow reached her that those wretchedly unhappy autobiographies, offered to her as the testimonials of living men and women, were largely inventions: Her mother, at nineteen, had come to America and married her father as an alternative to suicide.

At eighteen she had been in love with the first son of one of the well-to-do families in her village. The two had met whenever and wherever they could, secretly, because it would not have done for his family to see him favor her—her father had no money; he was a drunkard and a gambler besides. She had learned she was with child; an excellent match had already been arranged for her lover. Despised by her family, she had given premature birth to a stillborn son, who would be seventeen now. Her family did not turn her out, but she could no longer project herself in any direction without refreshing in them the memory of her indiscretion. She wrote to Aunt Taka, her favorite sister in America, threatening to kill herself if Aunt Taka would not send for her. Aunt Taka hastily arranged a marriage with a young man of whom she knew, but lately arrived from Japan, a young man of simple mind, it was said, but of kindly heart. The young man was never told why his unseen betrothed was so eager to hasten the day of meeting.

The story was told perfectly, with neither groping for words nor untoward passion. It was as though her mother had memorized it by heart, reciting it to herself so many times over that its nagging vileness had long since gone.

"I had a brother then?" Rosie asked, for this was what seemed to matter now; she would think about the other later, she assured herself, pushing the illumination which threatened all the darkness that had hitherto been merely mysterious or even glamorous. "A half-brother?"

"Yes."

"I would have liked a brother," she said.

Suddenly, her mother knelt on the floor and took her by the wrists. "Rosie," she said urgently, "Promise me you will never marry!" Shocked more by the request than the revelation, Rosie stared at her mother's face. Jesus, Jesus, she called silently, not certain whether she was invoking the help of the son of the Carrascos or of God, until there returned sweetly the memory of Jesus' hand, how it had touched her and where. Still her mother waited for an answer, holding her wrists so tightly that her hands were going numb. She tried to pull free. Promise, her mother whispered fiercely, promise. Yes, yes, I promise, Rosie said. But for an instant she turned away, and her mother, hearing the familiar glib agreement, released her. Oh, you, you, you, her eyes and twisted mouth said, you fool. Rosie, covering her face, began at last to cry, and the embrace and consoling hand came much later than she expected.

1949

THE LESSON

Toni Cade Bambara

Back in the days when everyone was old and stupid or young and foolish and me and Sugar were the only ones just right, this lady moved on our block with nappy hair and proper speech and no makeup. And quite naturally we laughed at her, laughed the way we did at the junk man who went about his business like he was some big-time president and his sorry-ass horse his secretary. And we kinda hated her too, hated the way we did the winos who cluttered up our parks and pissed on our handball walls and stank up our hallways and stairs so you couldn't halfway play hide-and-seek without a goddamn gas mask. Miss Moore was her name. The only woman on the block with no first name. And she was black as hell, cept for her feet, which were fish-white and spooky. And she was always planning these bor-ing-ass things for us to do, us being my cousin, mostly, who lived on the block cause we all moved North the same time and to the same apartment then spread out gradual to breathe. And our parents would yank our heads into some kinda shape and crisp up our clothes so we'd be presentable for travel with Miss Moore, who always looked like she was going to church, though she never did. Which is just one of the things the grown-ups talked about when they talked behind her back like a dog. But when she came calling with some sachet she'd sewed up or some gingerbread she'd made or some book, why then they'd all be too embarrassed to turn her down and we'd get handed over all spruced up. She'd been to college and said it was only right that she should take responsibility for the young ones' education, and she not even related by marriage or blood. So they'd go for it. Specially Aunt Gretchen. She was the main gofer in the family. You got some ole dumb shit foolishness you want somebody to go for, you send for Aunt Gretchen. She been screwed into the go-along for so long, it's a blood-deep natural thing with her. Which is how she got saddled with me and Sugar and Junior in the first place while our mothers were in a la-de-da apartment up the block having a good ole time.

So this one day Miss Moore rounds us all up at the mailbox and it's puredee hot and she's knockin herself out about arithmetic. And school suppose to let up in summer I heard, but she don't never let up. And the starch in my pinafore scratching the shit outta me and I'm really hating this nappy-head bitch and her goddamn college degree. I'd much rather go to the pool or to the show where it's cool. So me and Sugar leaning on the mailbox being surly, which is a Miss Moore word. And Flyboy checking out what everybody brought for lunch. And Fat Butt already wasting his peanut-butter-and-jelly sandwich like the pig he is. And Junebug punchin on Q.T.'s arm for potato chips. And Rosie Giraffe shifting from one hip to the other waiting for somebody to step on her foot or ask her if she from Georgia so she can kick ass, preferably Mercedes'. And Miss Moore asking us do we know what money is, like we a bunch of retards. I mean real money, she say, like it's only poker chips or monopoly papers we lay on the grocer. So right away I'm tired of this and say so. And would much rather snatch Sugar and go to the Sunset and terrorize the West Indian kids and take their hair ribbons and their money too. And Miss Moore files that remark away for next week's lesson on brotherhood, I can tell. And finally I say we oughta get to the subway cause it's cooler and besides we might meet some cute boys. Sugar done swiped her mama's lipstick, so we ready.

So we heading down the street and she's boring us silly about what things cost and what our parents make and how much goes for rent and how money ain't divided up right in this country. And then she gets to the part about we all poor and live in the slums, which I don't feature. And I'm ready to speak on that, but she steps out in the street and hails two cabs just like that. Then she hustles half the crew in with her and hands me a five-dollar bill and tells me to calculate ten percent tip for the driver. And we're off. Me and Sugar and Junebug and Flyboy hangin out the window and hollering to everybody, putting lipstick on each other cause Flyboy a faggot anyway, and making farts with our sweaty armpits. But I'm mostly trying to figure how to spend this money. But they all fascinated with the meter ticking and Junebug starts laying bets as to how much it'll read when Flyboy can't hold his breath no more. Then Sugar lays bets as to how much it'll be when we get there. So I'm stuck. Don't nobody want to go for my plan, which is to jump out at the next light and run off to the first bar-b-que we can find. Then the driver tells us to get the hell out cause we there already. And the meter reads eighty-five cents. And I'm stalling to figure out the tip and Sugar say give him a dime. And I decide he don't need it bad as I do, so later for him. But then he tried to take off with Junebug foot still in the door so we talk about his mama something ferocious. Then we check out that we on Fifth Avenue and everybody dressed up in stockings. One lady in a fur coat, hot as it is. White folks crazy.

"This is the place," Miss Moore say, presenting it to us in the voice she uses at the museum. "Let's look in the windows before we go in."

"Can we steal?" Sugar asks very serious like she's getting the ground rules squared away before she plays. "I beg your pardon," say Miss Moore, and we fall out. So she leads us around the windows of the toy store and me and Sugar screamin, "This is mine, that's mine, I gotta have that, that was made for me, I was born for that," till Big Butt drowns us out.

"Hey, I'm goin to buy that there."

"That there? You don't even know what it is, stupid."

"I do so," he say punchin on Rosie Giraffe. "It's a microscope."

"Whatcha gonna do with a microscope, fool?"

"Look at things."

"Like what, Ronald?" ask Miss Moore. And Big Butt ain't got the first notion. So here go Miss Moore gabbing about the thousands of bacteria in a drop of water and the somethinorother in a speck of blood and the million and one living things in the air around us is invisible to the naked eye. And what she say that for? Junebug go to town on that "naked" and we rolling. Then Miss Moore ask what it cost. So we all jam into the window smudgin it up and the price tag say $300. So then she ask how long'd take for Big Butt and Junebug to save up their allowances. "Too long," I say. "Yeh," adds Sugar, "outgrown it by that time." And Miss Moore say no, you never outgrow learning instruments. "Why, even medical students and interns and," blah, blah, blah. And we ready to choke Big Butt for bringing it up in the first damn place.

"This here costs four hundred eighty dollars," say Rosie Giraffe. So we pile up all over her to see what she pointin out. My eyes tell me it's a chunk of glass cracked with something heavy, and different-color inks dripped into the splits, then the whole thing put into a oven or something. But for $480 it don't make sense.

"That's a paperweight made of semi-precious stones fused together under tremendous pressure," she explains slowly, with her hands doing the mining and all the factory work.

"So what's a paperweight?" asks Rosie Giraffe.

"To weigh paper with, dumbbell," say Flyboy, the wise man from the East.

"Not exactly," say Miss Moore, which is what she say when you warm or way off too. "It's to weigh paper down so it won't scatter and make your desk untidy." So right away me and Sugar curtsy to each other and then to Mercedes who is more the tidy type.

"We don't keep paper on top of the desk in my class," say Junebug, figuring Miss Moore crazy or lying one.

"At home, then," she say. "Don't you have a calendar and a pencil case and a blotter and a letter-opener on your desk at home where you do your homework?" And she know damn well what our homes look like cause she nosys around in them every chance gets.

"I don't even have a desk," say Junebug. "Do we?"

"No. And I don't get no homework neither," say Big Butt.

"And I don't even have a home," say Flyboy like he do at school to keep the white folks off his back and sorry for him. Send this poor kid to camp posters, is his specialty.

"I do," says Mercedes. "I have a box of stationery on my desk and a picture of my cat. My godmother bought the stationery and the desk. There's a big rose on each sheet and the envelopes smell like roses."

"Who wants to know about your smelly-ass stationery," say Rosie Giraffe fore I can get my two cents in.

"It's important to have a work area all your own so that . . ."

"Will you look at this sailboat, please," say Flyboy, cutting her off and pointin to the thing like it was his. So once again we tumble all over each other to gaze at this magnificent thing in the toy store which is just big enough to maybe sail two kittens across the pond if you strap them to the posts tight. We all start reciting the price tag like we in assembly. "Handcrafted sailboat of fiberglass at one thousand one hundred ninety-five dollars."

"Unbelievable," I hear myself say and am really stunned. I read it again for myself just in case the group recitation put me in a trance. Same thing. For some reason this pisses me off. We look at Miss Moore and she lookin at us, waiting for I dunno what.

Who'd pay all that when you can buy a sailboat set for a quarter at Pop's, a tube of glue for a dime, and a ball of string for eight cents? "It must have a motor and a whole lot else besides," I say. "My sailboat cost me about fifty cents."

"But will it take water?" say Mercedes with her smart ass.

"Took mine to Alley Pond once," say Flyboy. "String broke. Lost it. Pity."

"Sailed mine in Central Park and it keeled over and sank. Had to ask my father for another dollar."

"And you got the strap," laugh Big Butt. "The jerk didn't even have a string on it. My old man wailed on his behind."

Little Q.T. was staring hard at the sailboat and you could see he wanted it bad. But he too little and somebody'd just take it from him. So what the hell. "This boat for kids, Miss Moore?"

"Parents silly to buy something like that just to get all broke up," say Rosie Giraffe.

"That much money it should last forever," I figure.

"My father'd buy it for me if I wanted it."

"Your father, my ass," say Rosie Giraffe getting a chance to finally push Mercedes.

"Must be rich people shop here," say Q.T.

"You are a very bright boy," say Flyboy. "What was your first clue?" And he rap him on the head with the back of his knuckles, since Q.T. the only one he could get away with. Though Q.T. liable to come up behind you years later and get his licks in when you half expect it.

"What I want to know is," I says to Miss Moore though I never talk to her, I wouldn't give the bitch that satisfaction, "is how much a real boat costs? I figure a thousand'd get you a yacht any day."

"Why don't you check that out," she says, "and report back to the group?" Which really pains my ass. If you gonna mess up a perfectly good swim day least you could do is have some answers. "Let's go in," she say like she got something up her sleeve. Only she don't lead the way. So me and Sugar turn the corner to where the entrance is, but when we get there I kinda hang back. Not that I'm scared, what's there to be afraid of, just a toy store. But I feel funny, shame. But what I got to be shamed about? Got as much right to go in as anybody. But somehow I can't seem to get hold of the door, so I step away for Sugar to lead. But she hangs back too. And I look at her and she looks at me and this is ridiculous. I mean, damn, I have never

ever been shy about doing nothing or going nowhere. But then Mercedes steps up and then Rosie Giraffe and Big Butt crowd in behind and shove, and next thing we all stuffed into the doorway with only Mercedes squeezing past us, smoothing out her jumper and walking right down the aisle. Then the rest of us tumble in like a glued-together jigsaw done all wrong. And people lookin at us. And it's like the time me and Sugar crashed into the Catholic church on a dare. But once we got in there and everything so hushed and holy and the candles and the bowin and the handkerchiefs on all the drooping heads, I just couldn't go through with the plan. Which was for me to run up to the altar and do a tap dance while Sugar played the nose flute and messed around in the holy water. And Sugar kept givin me the elbow. Then later teased me so bad I tied her up in the shower and turned it on and locked her in. And she'd be there till this day if Aunt Gretchen hadn't finally figured I was lyin about the boarder takin a shower.

Same thing in the store. We all walkin on tiptoe and hardly touchin the games and puzzles and things. And I watched Miss Moore who is steady watchin us like she waitin for a sign. Like Mama Drewery watches the sky and sniffs the air and takes note of just how much slant is in the bird formation. Then me and Sugar bump smack into each other, so busy gazing at the toys, specially the sailboat. But we don't laugh and go into our fat-lady bump-stomach routine. We just stare at that price tag. Then Sugar run a finger over the whole boat. And I'm jealous and want to hit her. Maybe not her, but I sure want to punch somebody in the mouth.

"Watcha bring us here for, Miss Moore?"

"You sound angry, Sylvia. Are you mad about something?" Givin me one of them grins like she telling a grown-up joke that never turns out to be funny. And she's lookin very closely at me like maybe she plannin to do my portrait from memory. I'm mad, but I won't give her that satisfaction. So I slouch around the store bein very bored and say, "Let's go."

Me and Sugar at the back of the train watchin the tracks whizzin by large then small then getting gobbled up in the dark. I'm thinkin about this tricky toy I saw in the store. A clown that somersaults on a bar then does chin-ups just cause you yank lightly at his leg. Cost $35. I could see me askin my mother for a $35 birthday clown. "You wanna who that costs what?" she'd say, cocking her head to the side to get a better view of the hole in my head. Thirty-five dollars could buy new bunk beds for Junior and Gretchen's boy. Thirty-five dollars and the whole household could go to visit Granddaddy Nelson in the country. Thirty-five dollars would pay for the rent and the piano bill too. Who are these people that spend that much for performing clowns and $1,000 for toy sailboats? What kinda work do they do and how they live and how come we ain't in on it? Where we are is who we are, Miss Moore always pointin out. But it don't necessarily have to be that way, she always adds then waits for somebody to say that poor people have to wake up and demand their share of the pie and don't none of us know what kind of pie she talkin about in the first damn place. But she ain't so smart cause I still got her four dollars from the taxi and she ain't getting it. Messin up my day with this shit. Sugar nudges me in my pocket and winks.

Miss Moore lines up in front of the mailbox where we started from, seem like years ago, and I got a headache for thinkin so hard. And we lean all over each other so we can hold up under the draggy-ass lecture she always finishes us off with at the end before we thank her for borin us to tears. But she just looks at us like she readin tea leaves. Finally she say, "Well, what did you think of F.A.O. Schwarz?"

Rosie Giraffe mumbles, "White folks crazy."

"I'd like to go there again when I get my birthday money," says Mercedes, and we shove her out the pack so she has to lean on the mailbox by herself.

"I'd like a shower. Tiring day," say Flyboy.

Then Sugar surprises me by sayin, "You know, Miss Moore, I don't think all of us here put together eat in a year what that sailboat costs." And Miss Moore lights up like somebody goosed her. "And?" she say, urging Sugar on. Only I'm standin on her foot so she don't continue.

"Imagine for a minute what kind of society it is in which some people can spend on a toy what it would cost to feed a family of six or seven. What do you think?"

"I think," say Sugar pushing me off her feet like she never done before, cause I whip her ass in a minute, "that this is not much of a democracy if you ask me. Equal chance to pursue happiness means an equal crack at the dough, don't it?" Miss Moore is besides herself and I am disgusted with Sugar's treachery. So I stand on her foot one more time to see if she'll shove me. She shuts up, and Miss Moore looks at me, sorrowfully I'm thinkin. And somethin weird is goin on, I can feel it in my chest.

"Anybody else learn anything today?" lookin dead at me. I walk away and Sugar has to run to catch up and don't even seem to notice when I shrug her arm off my shoulder.

"Well, we got four dollars anyway," she says.

"Uh hunh."

"We could go to Hascombs and get half a chocolate layer and then go to the Sunset and still have plenty of money for potato chips and ice-cream sodas."

"Uh hunh."

"Race you to Hascombs," she say.

We start down the block and she gets ahead which is OK by me cause I'm goin to the West End and then over to the Drive to think this day through. She can run if she want to and even run faster. But ain't nobody gonna beat me at nuthin.

1972

THE DEATH OF HORATIO ALGER

LeRoi Jones / Amiri Baraka

The cold red building burned my eyes. The bricks hung together, like the city, the nation, under the dubious cement of rationalism and need. A need so controlled, it only erupted out of the used-car lots, or sat parked, Saturdays, in front of our orange house, for Orlando, or Algernon, or Danny, or J.D. to polish. There was silence, or summers, noise. But this was a few days after Christmas, and the ice melted from the roofs and the almost frozen water knocked lethargically against windows, tar roofs and slow dogs moping through the yards. The building was Central Avenue School. And its tired red sat on the corner of Central Avenue and Dey (pronounced *die* by the natives, *day* by the teachers, or any non-resident whites) Street. Then, on Dey, halfway up the block, the playground took over. A tarred-over yard, though once there had been gravel, surrounded by cement and a wire metal fence.

The snow was dirty as it sat dull and melting near the Greek restaurants, and the dimly lit "grocery" stores of the Negroes. The rich boys had metal wagons, the poor rode in. The poor made up games, the rich played them. The poor won the games, or as an emergency measure, the fights. No one thought of the snow except Mr. Feld, the playground director, who was in charge of it, or Miss Martin, the husky gym teacher Matthew Stodges had pushed into the cloakroom, who had no chains on her car. Gray slush ran over the curbs, and our dogs drank it out of boredom, shaking their heads and snorting.

I had said something about J.D.'s father, as to who he was, or had he ever been. And J., usually a confederate, and private strong arm, broke bad because Augie, Norman, and white Johnny were there, and laughed, misunderstanding simple "dozens" with ugly insult, in that curious scholarship the white man affects when he suspects a stronger link than sociology, or the tired cultural lies of Harcourt, Brace sixth-grade histories. And under their naïveté he grabbed my shirt and pushed me in the snow. I got up, brushing dead ice from my ears, and he pushed me down again, this time dumping a couple pounds of cold dirty slush down my neck, calmly hysterical at his act.

J. moved away and stood on an icy garbage hamper, sullenly throwing wet snow at the trucks on Central Avenue. I pushed myself into a sitting position, shaking my head. Tears full in my eyes, and the cold slicing minutes from my life. I wasn't making a sound. I wasn't thinking any thought I could make someone else understand. Just the rush of young fear and anger and disgust. I could have murdered God, in that simple practical way we kick dogs off the bottom step.

Augie (my best friend), fat Norman, whose hook shots usually hit the rim, and were good for easy tip-ins by our big men, and useless white Johnny who had some weird disease that made him stare, even in the middle of a game, he'd freeze, and sometimes line drives almost knocked his head off while he shuddered slightly, cracking and recracking his huge knuckles. They were howling and hopping, they thought it was so funny that J. and I had come to blows. And especially, I guess, that I had got my lumps. "Hey, wiseass, somebody's gonna break your nose!" fat Norman would say over and over whenever I did something to him. Hold his pants when he tried his jump shot; spike him sliding into home (he was a lousy catcher); talk about his brother who hung out under the El and got naked in the alleyways.

(The clucks of Autumn could have, right at that moment, easily seduced me. Away, and into school. To masquerade as a half-rich nigra with shiny feet. Back through the clean station, and up the street. Stopping to talk on the way. One beer gets you drunk and you stand in an empty corridor, lined with Italian paintings, talking about the glamours of sodomy.)

Rise and Slay.

I hurt so bad, and inside without bleeding I realized the filthy gray scratches my blood would carry to my heart. John walked off staring, and Augie and Norman disappeared, so easily there in the snow. And J.D. too, my first love, drifted against the easy sky. Weeping at what he'd done. No one there but me. THE SHORT SKINNY BOY WITH THE BUBBLE EYES.

Could leap up and slay them. Could hammer my fist and misery through their faces. Could strangle and bake them in the crude jungle of my feeling. Could stuff them in the sewie hole with the collected garbage of children's guilt. Could elevate them into heroic images of my own despair. A righteous messenger from the wrong side of the tracks. Gym teachers, cutthroats, aging pickets, ease by in the cold. The same lyric chart, exchange of particulars, that held me in my minutes, the time "Brownie" rammed the glass door down and ate up my suit. Even my mother, in a desperate fit of rhythm, was not equal to the task. Which was simple economics. I.e., a white man's dog cannot bite your son if he has been taught that something very ugly will happen to him if he does. He might pace stupidly in his ugly fur, but he will never bite.

But what really stays to be found completely out, except stupid enterprises like art? The word on the page, the paint on the canvas (Marzette dragging used-up canvases to revive their hopeless correspondence with the times), stone clinging to air, as it it were real. Or something a Deacon would admit was beautiful. The conscience rules against ideas. The point was to be where you wanted to, and do what you wanted to. After all is "said and done," what is left but those sheepish constructions. "I've got to go to the toilet" is no less pressing than the Puritans taking off for Massachusetts, and dragging their devils with them. (There is in those parts, even now, the peculiar smell of roasted sex organs. And when a good New Englander leaves his house in the earnestly moral sub-towns to go into the smoking hells of soon to be destroyed Yankee Gomorrahs, you watch him pull very firmly at his tie, or strapping on very tightly his evil watch.) The penitence there. The masochism. So complete and conscious a phenomenon. Like a standard of beauty; for instance, the bespectacled soft-breasted, gently pigeon-toed maidens of America. Neither rich nor poor, with intelligent smiles and straight lovely noses. No one would think of them as beautiful but these mysterious scions of the puritans. They value health and devotion, and their good women, the lefty power of all our nation, are unpresuming subtle beauties, who could even live with poets (if they are from the right stock), if pushed to that. But mostly they are where they should be, reading good books and opening windows to air out their bedrooms. And it is a useful memory here, because such things as these were the vague images that had even so early, helped shape me. Light freckles, sandy hair, narrow clean bodies. Though none lived where I lived then. And I don't remember a direct look at them even, with clear knowledge of my desire, until one afternoon I gave a speech at East Orange High, as sports editor of our high school paper, which should have been printed in Italian, and I saw there, in the auditorium, young American girls for the first time. And have loved them as flesh things emanating from real life, that is, in contrast to my own, a scraping and floating through the last three red and blue stripes of the flag, that settles the hash of the lower middle class. So that even sprawled there in the snow, with my blood and pompous isolation, I vaguely knew of a glamorous world and was mistaken into thinking it could be gotten from books. Negroes and Italians beat and shaped me, and my allegiance is there. But the triumph of romanticism was parquet floors, yellow dresses, gardens and sandy hair. I must have felt the loss and could not rise against a cardboard world of dark hair and linoleum. Reality was something I was convinced was something I could not have.

And thus to be flogged or put to the rack. For all our secret energies. The first leap over the barrier: when the victim finds he can no longer stomach his own "group." Politics whinnies, but is still correct, and asleep in a windy barn. The beautiful statue of victory, whose arms were called duty. And they curdle in her snatch thrust there by angry minorities, along with their own consciences. Poets climb, briefly, off their motorcycles, to find out who owns their words. We are named by all things we will never understand. Whether we can fight or not, or even at the moment of our hugest triumph we stare off into space remembering the snow melting in our cuts, and all the pimps of reason who've ever conquered us. It is the harshest form of love.

I could not see when I "chased" Norman and Augie. Chased in quotes because, they really did not have to run. They could have turned, and myth aside, calmly whipped my ass. But they ran, laughing and keeping warm. And J.D. kicked snow from around a fire hydrant flatly into the gutter. Smiling and broken, with his head hung just slanted towards the yellow dog ice running down a hole. I took six or seven long running steps and tripped. I couldn't have been less interested, but the whole project had gotten out of hand. I was crying, and my hands were freezing, and the two white boys leaned against the pointed metal fence and laughed and slapped their knees. I threw snow stupidly in their direction. It fell short and was not even noticed as it dropped.

(All of it rings in your ears for a long time. But the pay-back . . . in simple terms against such actual sin as supposing quite confidently that the big sweating purple whore staring from her peed up hall very casually at your whipping has *never* been loved . . . is hard. We used to say.)

Then I pushed to my knees and could only see J. leaning there against the hydrant looking just over my head. I called to him, for help really. But the words rang full of dead venom. I screamed his mother a purple nigger with alligator titties. His father a bilious white man with sores on his jowls. I was screaming for help in my hatred and loss, and only the hatred would show. And he came over shouting for me to shut up. Shut Up skinny bastard. I'll break your ass if you don't. Norman had both hands on his stomach, his laugh was getting so violent, and he danced awkwardly toward us howling to agitate J. to beat me some more. But J. whirled on him perfectly and rapped him hard under his second chin. Norman was going to say, "Hey me-an," in that hated twist of our speech, and J. hit him again, between his shoulder and chest, and almost dropped him to his knees. Augie cooled his howl to a giggle of concern and backed up until Norman turned and they both went shouting up the street.

I got to my feet, wiping my freezing hands on my jacket. J. was looking at me hard, like country boys do, when their language, or the new tone they need to take on once they come to this cold climate (1940's New Jersey) fails, and they are left with only the old Southern tongue, which cruel farts like me used to deride their lack of interest in America. I turned to walk away. Both my eyes were nothing but water, though it held at their rims, stoically refusing to blink and thus begin to sob uncontrollably. And to keep from breaking down I wheeled and hid the weeping by screaming at the boy. You nigger without a father. You eat your mother's pussy. And he wheeled me around and started to hit me again.

Someone called my house and my mother and father and grandmother and sister were strung along Dey Street, in some odd order. (They couldn't have come out of the house "together.") And I was conscious first of my father saying, "Go on Mickey, hit him. Fight back." And for a few seconds, under the weight of that plea for my dignity, I tried. I feinted and danced, but I couldn't even roll up my fists. The whole street was blurred and hot as my eyes. I swung and swung, but J.D. bashed me when he wanted to.

My mother stopped the fight finally, shuddering at the thing she'd made. "His hands are frozen, Michael. His hands are frozen." And my father looks at me even now, wondering if they'll ever thaw.

1967

IN THE AMERICAN SOCIETY

Gish Jen

1. HIS OWN SOCIETY

When my father took over the pancake house, it was to send my little sister Mona and me to college. We were only in junior high at the time, but my father believed in getting a jump on things. "Those Americans always saying it," he told us. "Smart guys thinking in advance." My mother elaborated, explaining that businesses took bringing up, like children. They could take years to get going, she said, years.

In this case, though, we got rich right away. At two months we were breaking even, and at four, those same hotcakes that could barely withstand the weight of butter and syrup were supporting our family with ease. My mother bought a station wagon with air conditioning, my father an oversized, red vinyl recliner for the back room; and as time went on and the business continued to thrive, my father started to talk about his grandfather and the village he had reigned over in China—things my father had never talked about when he worked for other people. He told us about the bags of rice his family would give out to the poor at New Year's, and about the people who came to beg, on their hands and knees, for his grandfather to intercede for the more wayward of their relatives. "Like that Godfather in the movie," he would tell us as, his feet up, he distributed paychecks. Sometimes an employee would get two green envelopes instead of one, which meant that Jimmy needed a tooth pulled, say, or that Tiffany's husband was in the clinker again.

"It's nothing, nothing," he would insist, sinking back into his chair. "Who else is going to take care of you people?"

My mother would mostly just sigh about it. "Your father thinks this is China," she would say, and then she would go back to her mending. Once in a while, though, when my father had given away a particularly large sum, she would exclaim, outraged, "But this here is the U-S-of-A!"—this apparently having been what she used to tell immigrant stock boys when they came in late.

She didn't work at the supermarket anymore; but she had made it to the rank of manager before she left, and this had given her not only new words and phrases, but new ideas about herself, and about America, and about what was what in general. She had opinions, now, on how downtown should be zoned; she could pump her own gas and check her own oil; and for all she used to chide Mona and me for being "copycats," she herself was now interested in espadrilles, and wallpaper, and most recently, the town country club.

"So join already," said Mona, flicking a fly off her knee.

My mother enumerated the problems as she sliced up a quarter round of watermelon: there was the cost. There was the waiting list. There was the fact that no one in our family played either tennis or golf.

"So what?" said Mona.

"It would be waste," said my mother.

"Me and Callie can swim in the pool."

"Plus you need that recommendation letter from a member."

"Come *on*," said Mona. "Annie's mom'd write you a letter in a *sec*."

My mother's knife glinted in the early summer sun. I spread some more newspaper on the picnic table.

"*Plus* you have to eat there twice a month. You know what that means." My mother cut another, enormous slice of fruit.

"No, I *don't* know what that means," said Mona.

"It means dad would have to wear a jacket, dummy," I said.

"Oh! Oh! Oh!" said Mona, clasping her hand to her hand to her breast. "Oh! Oh! Oh! Oh! Oh!"

We all laughed: my father had no use for nice clothes, and would wear only ten-year-old shirts, with grease-spotted pants, to show how little he cared what anyone thought.

"Your father doesn't believe in joining the American society," said my mother. "He wants to have his own society."

"So go to dinner without him." Mona shot her seeds out in long arcs over the lawn. "Who cares what he thinks?"

But of course we all did care, and knew my mother could not simply up and do as she pleased. For in my father's mind, a family owed its head a degree of loyalty that left no room for dissent. To embrace what he embraced was to love; and to embrace something else was to betray him.

He demanded a similar sort of loyalty of his workers, whom he treated more like servants than employees. Not in the beginning, of course. In the beginning all he wanted was for them to keep on doing what they used to do, and to that end he concentrated mostly on leaving them alone. As the months passed, though, he expected more and more of them, with the result that for all his largesse, he began to have trouble keeping help. The cooks and busboys complained that he asked them to fix radiators and trim hedges, not only at the restaurant, but at our house; the waitresses that he sent them on errands and made them chauffeur him around. Our head waitress, Gertrude, claimed that he once even asked her to scratch his back.

"It's not just the blacks don't believe in slavery," she said when she quit.

My father never quite registered her complaint, though, nor those of the others who left. Even after Eleanor quit, then Tiffany, then Gerald, and Jimmy, and even his best cook, Eureka Andy, for whom he had bought new glasses, he remained mostly convinced that the fault lay with them.

"All they understand is that assembly line," he lamented. "Robots, they are. They want to be robots."

There *were* occasions when the clear running truth seemed to eddy, when he would pinch they vinyl of his chair up into little peaks and wonder if he were doing things right. But with time he would always smooth the peaks back down; and when business started to slide in the spring, he kept on like a horse in his ways.

By the summer our dishboy was overwhelmed with scraping. It was no longer just the hashbrowns that people were leaving for trash, and the service was as bad as the food. The waitresses served up French pancakes instead of German, apple juice instead of orange, spilt things on laps, on coats. On the Fourth of July some greenhorn sent an entire side of fries slaloming down a lady's *massif centrale*. Meanwhile in the back room, my father labored through articles on the economy.

"What is housing starts?" he puzzled. "What is GNP?"

Mona and I did what we could, filling in as busgirls and bookkeepers and, one afternoon, stuffing the comments box that hung by the cashier's desk. That was Mona's idea. We rustled up a variety of pens and pencils, checked boxes for an hour, smeared the cards up with coffee and grease, and waited. It took a few days for my father to notice that the box was full, and he didn't say anything about it for a few days more. Finally, though, he started to complain of fatigue; and then he began to complain that the staff was not what it could be. We encouraged him in this—pointing out, for instance, how many dishes got chipped—but in the end all that happened was that, for the first time since we took over the restaurant, my father got it into his head to fire someone. Skip, a skinny busboy who was saving up for a sports car, said nothing as my father mumbled on about the price of dishes. My father's hands shook as he wrote out the severance check; and he spent the rest of the day napping in his chair once it was over.

As it was going on midsummer, Skip wasn't easy to replace. We hung a sign in the window and advertised in the paper, but no one called the first week, and the person who called the second didn't show up for his interview. The third week, my father phoned Skip to see if he would come back, but a friend of his had already sold him a Corvette for cheap.

Finally a Chinese guy named Booker turned up. He couldn't have been more than thirty, and was wearing a lighthearted seersucker suit, but he looked as though life had him pinned: his eyes were bloodshot and his chest sunken, and the muscles of his neck seemed to strain with the effort of holding his head up. In a single dry breath he told us that he had never bussed tables but was willing to learn, and that he was on the lam from the deportation authorities.

"I do not want to lie to you," he kept saying. He had come to the United States on a student visa, had run out of money, and was now in a bind. He was loath to go back to Taiwan, as it happened—he looked up at this point, to be sure my father wasn't pro-KMT—but all he had was a phony social security card and a willingness to absorb all the blame, should anything untoward come to pass.

"I do not think, anyway, that it is against law to hire me, only to be me," he said, smiling faintly.

Anyone else would have examined him on this, but my father conceived of laws as speed bumps rather than curbs. He wiped the counter with his sleeve, and told Booker to report the next morning.

"I will be good worker," said Booker.

"Good," said my father.

"Anything you want me to do, I will do."

My father nodded.

Booker seemed to sink into himself for a moment. "Thank you," he said finally. "I am appreciate your help. I am very, very, very appreciate for everything." He reached out to shake my father's hand.

My father looked at him. "Did you eat today?" he asked in Mandarin. Booker pulled at the hem of his jacket.

"Sit down," said my father. "Please, have a seat."

My father didn't tell my mother about Booker, and my mother didn't tell my father about the country club. She would never have applied except that Mona, while over at Annie's, had let it drop that our mother wanted to join. Mrs. Lardner came by the very next day.

"Why, I'd be honored and delighted to write you people a letter," she said. Her skirt billowed around her.

"Thank you so much," said my mother. "But it's too much trouble for you, and also my husband is . . ."

"Oh, it's no trouble at all, no trouble at all. I tell you." She leaned forward so that her chest freckles showed. "I know just how it is. It's a secret of course, but you know, my natural father was Jewish. Can you see it? Just look at my skin."

"My husband," said my mother.

"I'd be honored and delighted," said Mrs. Lardner with a little wave of her hands. "Just honored and delighted."

Mona was triumphant. "See, Mom," she said, waltzing around the kitchen when Mrs. Lardner left. "What did I tell you? 'I'm just honored and delighted, just honored and delighted.'" She waved her hands in the air.

"You know, the Chinese have a saying," said my mother. "To do nothing is better than to overdo. You mean well, but you tell me now what will happen."

"I'll talk Dad into it," said Mona, still waltzing. "Or I bet Callie can. He'll do anything Callie says."

"I can try, anyway," I said.

"Did you hear what I said?" said my mother. Mona bumped into the broom closet door. "You're not going to talk anything; you've already made enough trouble." She started on the dishes with a clatter.

Mona poked diffidently at a mop.

I sponged off the counter. "Anyway," I ventured. "I bet our name'll never even come up."

"That's if we're lucky," said my mother.

"There's all these people waiting," I said.

"Good," she said. She started on a pot.

I looked over at Mona, who was still cowering in the broom closet. "In fact, there's some black family's been waiting so long, they're going to sue," I said.

My mother turned off the water. "Where'd you hear that?"

"Patty told me."

She turned the water back on, started to wash a dish, then put it back down and shut the faucet.

"I'm sorry," said Mona.

"Forget it," said my mother. "Just forget it."

Booker turned out to be a model worker, whose boundless gratitude translated into a willingness to do anything. As he also learned quickly, he soon knew not only how to bus, but how to cook, and how to wait table, and how to keep the books. He fixed the walk-in door so that it stayed shut, reupholstered the torn seats in the dining room, and devised a system for tracking inventory. The only stone in the rice was that he tended to be sickly; but, reliable even in illness, he would always send a friend to take his place. In this way we got to know Ronald, Lynn, Dirk, and Cedric, all of whom, like Booker, had problems with their legal status and were anxious to please. They weren't all as capable as Booker, though, with the exception of Cedric, whom my father often hired even when Booker was well. A round wag of a man who called Mona and me *shou hou* —skinny monkeys—he was professed nonsmoker who was nevertheless always begging drags off of other people's cigarettes. This last habit drove our head cook, Fernando, crazy, especially since, when refused a hit, Cedric would occasionally snitch one. Winking impishly at Mona and me, he would steal up to an ashtray, take a quick puff, and then break out laughing so that the smoke came rolling out of his mouth in a great incriminatory cloud. Fernando accused him of stealing fresh cigarettes too, even whole packs.

"Why else do you think he's weaseling around in the back of the store all the time," he said. His face was blotchy with anger. "The man is a frigging thief."

Other members of the staff supported him in this contention and joined in on an "Operation Identification," which involved numbering and initialing their cigarettes—even though what they seemed to fear for wasn't so much their cigarettes as their jobs. Then one of the cooks quit; and rather than promote someone, my father hired Cedric for the position. Rumors flew that he was taking only half the normal salary, that Alex had been pressured to resign, and that my father was looking for a position with which to placate Booker, who had been bypassed because of his health.

The result was that Fernando categorically refused to work with Cedric.

"The only way I'll cook with that piece of slime," he said, shaking his huge tattooed fist, "is if it's his ass frying on the grill."

My father cajoled and cajoled, to no avail, and in the end was simply forced to put them on different schedules.

The next week Fernando got caught stealing a carton of minute steaks. My father would not tell even Mona and me how he knew to be standing by the back door when Fernando was on his way out, but everyone suspected Booker. Everyone but Fernando, that is, who was sure Cedric had been the tip-off. My father held a staff meeting in which he tried to reassure everyone that Alex had left on his own, and that he had no intention of firing anyone. But though he was careful not to mention Fernando, everyone was so amazed that he was being allowed to stay that Fernando was incensed nonetheless.

"Don't you all be putting your bug eyes on me," he said. "*He's* the frigging crook." He grabbed Cedric by the collar.

Cedric raised an eyebrow. "Cook, you mean," he said.

At this Fernando punched Cedric in the mouth; and the words he had just uttered notwithstanding, my father fired him on the spot.

With everything that was happening, Mona and I were ready to be getting out of the restaurant. It was almost time: the days were still stuffy with summer, but our window shade had started flapping in the evening as if gearing up to go out. That year the breezes were full of salt, as they sometimes were when they came in from the East, and they blew anchors and docks through my mind like so many tumbleweeds, filling my dreams with wherries and lobsters and grainy-faced men who squinted, day in and day out, at the sky.

It was time for a change, you could feel it; and yet the pancake house was the same as ever. The day before school started my father came home with bad news.

"Fernando called police," he said, wiping his hand on his pant leg.

My mother naturally wanted to know what police; and so with much coughing and hawing, the long story began, the latest installment of which had the police calling immigration, and immigration sending an investigator. My mother sat stiff as whalebone as my father described how the man summarily refused lunch on the house and how my father had admitted, under pressure, that he knew there were "things" about his workers.

"So now what happens?"

My father didn't know. "Booker and Cedric went with him to the jail," he said. "But me, here I am." He laughed uncomfortably.

The next day my father posted bail for "his boys" and waited apprehensively for something to happen. The day after that he waited again, and the day after that he called our neighbor's law student son, who suggested my father call the immigration department under an alias. My father took his advice; and it was thus that he discovered that Booker was right: it was illegal for aliens to work, but it wasn't to hire them.

In the happy interval that ensued, my father apologized to my mother, who in turn confessed about the country club, for which my father had no choice but to forgive her. Then he turned his attention back to "his boys."

My mother didn't see that there was anything to do.

"I like to talking to the judge," said my father.

"This is not China," said my mother.

"I'm only talking to him. I'm not give him money unless he wants it."

"You're going to land up in jail."

"So what else I should do?" My father threw up his hands. "Those are my boys."

"Your boys!" exploded my mother. "What about your family? What about your wife?"

My father took a long sip of tea. "You know," he said finally. "In the war my father sent our cook to the soldiers to use. He always said it—the province comes before the town, the town comes before the family."

"A restaurant is not a town," said my mother.

My father sipped at his tea again. "You know, when I first come to the United States, I also had to hide-and-seek with those deportation guys. If people did not helping me, I'm not here today."

My mother scrutinized her hem.

After a minute I volunteered that before seeing a judge, he might try a lawyer.

He turned. "Since when did you become so afraid like your mother?"

I started to say that it wasn't a matter of fear, but he cut me off.

"What I need today," he said, "is a son."

My father and I spent the better part of the next day standing in lines at the immigration office. He did not get to speak to a judge, but with much persistence he managed to speak to a judge's clerk, who tried to persuade him that it was not her place to extend him advice. My father, though, shamelessly plied her with compliments and offers of free pancakes until she finally conceded that she personally doubted anything would happen to either Cedric or Booker.

"Especially if they're 'needed workers,'" she said, rubbing at the red marks her glasses left on her nose. She yawned. "Have you thought about sponsoring them to become permanent residents?"

Could he do that? My father was overjoyed. And what if he saw to it right away? Would she perhaps put in a good word with the judge?

She yawned again, her nostrils flaring. "Don't worry," she said. "They'll get a fair hearing."

My father returned jubilant. Booker and Cedric hailed him as their savior, their Buddha incarnate. He was like a father to them, they said; and laughing and clapping, they made him tell the story over and over, sorting over the details like jewels. And how old was the assistant judge? And what did she say?

That evening my father tipped the paperboy a dollar and bought a pot of mums for my mother, who suffered them to be placed on the dining room table. The next night he took us all out to dinner. Then on Saturday, Mona found a letter on my father's chair at the restaurant.

Dear Mr. Chang,
You are the grat boss. But, we do not like to trial, so will runing away now. Plese to excus us. People saying the law in America is fears like dragon. Here is only $140. We hope some day we can pay back the rest bale. You will getting interest, as you diserving, so grat a boss you are. Thank you for every thing. In next life you will be burn in rich family, with no more pancaks.

Yours truley,
Booker + Cedric

In the weeks that followed my father went to the pancake house for crises, but otherwise hung around our house, fiddling idly with the sump pump and boiler in an effort, he said, to get ready for winter. It was as though he had gone into retirement, except that instead of moving South, he had moved to the basement. He even took to showering my mother with little attentions, and to calling her "old girl," and when we finally heard that the club had entertained all the applications it could for the year, he was so sympathetic that he seemed more disappointed than my mother.

2. IN THE AMERICAN SOCIETY

Mrs. Lardner tempered the bad news with an invitation to a bon voyage "bash" she was throwing for a friend of hers who was going to Greece for six months.

"Do come," she urged. "You'll meet everyone, and then, you know, if things open up in the spring . . ." She waved her hands.

My mother wondered if it would be appropriate to show up at a party for someone they didn't know, but "the honest truth" was that this was an annual affair. "If it's not Greece, it's Antibes," sighed Mrs. Lardner. "We really just do it because his wife left him and his daughter doesn't speak to him, and poor Jeremy just feels so *unloved*."

She also invited Mona and me to the going on, as "*demi*-guests" to keep Annie out of the champagne. I wasn't too keen on the idea, but before I could say anything, she had already thanked us for so generously agreeing to honor her with our presence.

"A pair of little princesses, you are!" she told us. "A pair of princesses!"

The party was that Sunday. On Saturday, my mother took my father out shopping for a suit. As it was the end of September, she insisted that he buy a worsted rather than a seersucker, even though it was only ten, rather than fifty percent off. My father protested that it was as hot out as ever, which was true—a thick Indian summer had cozied murderously up to us—but to no avail. Summer clothes, said my mother, were not properly worn after Labor Day.

The suit was unfortunately as extravagant in length as it was in price, which posed an additional quandary, since the tailor wouldn't be in until Monday. The salesgirl, though, found a way of tacking it up temporarily.

"Maybe this suit not fit me," fretted my father.

"Just don't take your jacket off," said the salesgirl.

He gave her a tip before they left, but when he got home refused to remove the price tag.

"I like to asking the tailor about the size," he insisted.

"You mean you're going to *wear* it and then return it?" Mona rolled her eyes.

"I didn't say I'm return it," said my father stiffly. "I like to asking the tailor, that's all."

✿   ✿   ✿

The party started off swimmingly, except that most people were wearing bermudas or wrap skirts. Still, my parents carried on, sharing with great feeling the complaints about the heat. Of course my father tried to eat a cracker full of shallots and burnt himself in an attempt to help Mr. Lardner turn the coals of the barbecue; but on the whole he seemed to be doing all right. Not nearly so well as my mother, though, who had accepted an entire cupful of Mrs. Lardner's magic punch and seemed indeed to be under some spell. As Mona and Annie skirmished over whether some boy in their class inhaled when he smoked, I watched my mother take off her shoes, laughing and laughing as a man with a beard regaled her with Navy stories by the pool. Apparently he had been stationed in the Orient and remembered a few words of Chinese, which made my mother laugh still more. My father excused himself to go the men's room then drifted back and weighed anchor at the hors d'oeuvres table, while my mother sailed on to a group of women, who tinkled at length over the clarity of her complexion. I dug out a book I had brought.

Just when I'd cracked the spine, though, Mrs. Lardner came by to bewail her shortage of servers. Her caterers were criminals, I agreed; and the next thing I knew I was handing out bits of marine life, making the rounds as amicably as I could.

"Here you go, Dad," I said when I got to the hors d'oeuvres table.

"Everything is fine," he said.

I hesitated to leave him alone; but then the man with the beard zeroed in on him, and though he talked of nothing but my mother, I thought it would be okay to get back to work. Just that moment, though, Jeremy Brothers lurched our way, an empty, albeit corked, wine bottle in hand. He was a slim, well-proportioned man, with a Roman nose and small eyes and a nice manly jaw that he allowed to hang agape.

"Hello," he said drunkenly. "Pleased to meet you."

"Pleased to meeting you," said my father.

"Right," said Jeremy. "Right. Listen. I have this bottle here, this most recalcitrant bottle. You see that it refuses to do my bidding. I bid it open sesame, please, and it does nothing." He pulled the cork out with his teeth, then turned the bottle upside down.

My father nodded.

"Would you have a word with it, please?" said Jeremy. The man with the beard excused himself. "Would you please have a goddamned word with it?"

My father laughed uncomfortably.

"Ah!" Jeremy bowed a little. "Excuse me, excuse me, excuse me. You are not my man, not my man at all." He bowed again and started to leave, but then circled back. "Viticulture is not your forte, yes I can see that, see that plainly. But may I trouble you on another matter? Forget the damned bottle." He threw it into the pool, and winked at the people he splashed. "I have another matter. Do you speak Chinese?"

My father said he did not, but Jeremy pulled out a handkerchief with some characters on it anyway, saying that his daughter had sent it from Hong Kong and that he thought the characters might be a secret message.

"Long life," said my father.

"But you haven't looked at it yet."

"I know what it says without looking." My father winked at me.

"You do?"

"Yes, I do."

"You're making fun of me, aren't you?"

"No, no, no," said my father, winking again.

"Who are you anyway?" said Jeremy.

His smile fading, my father shrugged.

"*Who are you?*"

My father shrugged again.

Jeremy began to roar. "This is my party, *my party*, and I've never seen you before in my life." My father backed up as Jeremy came toward him. "*Who are you? WHO ARE YOU?*"

Just as my father was going to step back into the pool, Mrs. Lardner came running up. Jeremy informed her that there was a man crashing his party.

"Nonsense," said Mrs. Lardner. "This is Ralph Chang, who I invited extra especially so he could meet you." She straightened the collar of Jeremy's peach-colored polo shirt for him.

"Yes, well we've had a chance to chat," said Jeremy.

She whispered in his ear; he mumbled something; she whispered something more.

"I do apologize," he said finally.

My father didn't say anything.

"I do." Jeremy seemed genuinely contrite. "Doubtless you've seen drunks before, haven't you? You must have them in China."

"Okay," said my father.

As Mrs. Lardner glided off, Jeremy clapped his arm over my father's shoulders. "You know, I really am quite sorry, quite sorry."

My father nodded.

"What can I do, how can I make it up to you?"

"No thank you."

"No, tell me, tell me," wheedled Jeremy. "Tickets to casino night?" My father shook his head. "You don't gamble. Dinner at Bartholomew's?" My father shook his head again. "You don't eat." Jeremy scratched his chin. "You know, my wife was like you. Old Annabelle could never let me make things up—never, never, never, never, never."

My father wriggled out from under his arm.

"How about sport clothes? You are rather overdressed, you know, excuse me for saying so. But here." He took off his polo shirt and folded it up. "You can have this with my most profound apologies." He ruffled his chest hairs with his free hand.

"No thank you," said my father.

"No, take it, take it. Accept my apologies." He thrust the shirt into my father's arms. "I am so very sorry, so very sorry. Please, try it on."

Helplessly holding the shirt, my father searched the crowd for my mother.

"Here, I'll help you off with your coat."

My father froze.

Jeremy reached over and took his jacket off. "Milton's one hundred twenty-five dollars reduced to one hundred twelve-fifty," he read. "What a bargain, what a bargain!"

"Please give it back," pleaded my father. "Please."

"Now for your shirt," ordered Jeremy.

Heads began to turn.

"Take off your shirt."

"I do not take orders like a servant," announced my father.

"Take off your shirt, or I'm going to throw this jacket right into the pool, just right into this little pool here." Jeremy held it over the water.

"Go ahead."

"One hundred twelve-fifty," taunted Jeremy. "One hundred twelve . . ."

My father flung the polo shirt into the water with such force that part of it bounced back up into the air like a fluorescent fountain. Then it settled into a soft heap on top of the water. My mother hurried up.

"You're a sport!" said Jeremy, suddenly breaking into a smile and slapping my father on the back. "You're a sport! I like that. A man with spirit, that's what you are. A man with panache. Allow me to return to you your jacket." He handed it back to my father. "Good value you got on that, good value."

My father hurled the coat into the pool too. "We're leaving," he said grimly. "Leaving!"

"Now, Ralphie," said Mrs. Lardner, bustling up; but my father was already stomping off.

"Get your sister," he told me. To my mother: "Get your shoes."

"That was *great*, Dad," said Mona as we walked down to the car. "You were *stupendous*."

"Way to show 'em," I said.

"What?" said my father offhandedly.

Although it was only just dusk, we were in a gulch, which made it hard to see anything except the gleam of his white shirt moving up the hill ahead of us.

"It was all my fault," began my mother.

"Forget it," said my father grandly. Then he said, "The only trouble is I left those keys in my jacket pocket."

"Oh *no*," said Mona.

"Oh no is right," said my mother.

"So we'll walk home," I said.

"But how're we going to get into the *house*," said Mona.

The noise of the party churned through the silence.

"Someone has to going back," said my father.

"Let's go to the pancake house first," suggested my mother. "We can wait there until the party is finished, and then call Mrs. Lardner."

Having all agreed that that was a good plan, we started walking again.

"God, just think," said Mona. "We're going to have to *dive* for them."

My father stopped a moment. We waited.

"You girls are good swimmers," he said finally. "Not like me."

Then his shirt started moving again, and we trooped up the hill after it, into the dark.

1986

NEAR THE END OF THE WORLD

Bruce Morrow

Sometimes I have visions. Mostly they're about me jumping off a roof, or something. Sometimes they're about me and other people taking the big leap—off a cliff, a diving board. Off the curb, into the gutter. I call them visions because they're not dreams, you know, they're not at night while I'm in bed, trying to sleep. I don't dream—or at least I don't remember my dreams. Each morning when I wake it's like someone presses a button and my eyes just pop open.

But since I've been out here in California (I've decided not to go back to college) and got these tattoos, the visions, the things I envisioned happening to me, don't bother me anymore.

It had gotten worse. Before I came out West I was imagining not only that I was falling but that someone, my father as a little boy, was pushing me. He'd run up behind me, scream, and knock me over; over and over again; his fist, hard as stone, would jab into my diaphragm and force the air out of my lungs, like a hard hiccup. And even though each successive push would be as unexpected as the first, I never fell. These vines would leap out of the ground, grab hold of my ankles and wrist, and twist, binding me till I couldn't move. Scary. I could smell them, too, bitter, pungent green leaves, sweet sickening flowers I couldn't name—but their identities would be so clear to me, stuffed up my nose, sliming my tongue, smothering me.

Although I remember these visions happening in Venice Beach, on an old boardwalk like the one at Coney Island, I know this can't be true. There's no boardwalk in Venice. Only blacktop and sand. But I remember walking on weather-worn wood planks in Venice and carrying my big blue backpack, which contained everything that was important to me. I was checking it all out. The muscle men, the surfers, the tangerine-orange and lime-green bikinis. Bodies. Bodies laid out all in the same direction, neatly in groups of twos and threes, as if a caretaker had placed them there to rest—for good. I was looking at everything: the bikinis and the bodies; the water rocking, slamming itself into white foam, softly sliding onto the sand, then slowly slipping back; the zigzag pattern of the boardwalk (that's the way I remember it) under my feet; the little stores and booths, tucked under the shade of their own roofs. I felt all right, fine, because all I had to do was follow the boardwalk and not think about which direction to go in. No forks. No exit ramps. Then the vines crept up and grabbed my ankles, wrapped around them. I almost tripped, but the strength of the vines held me up as they stretched and took hold of my neck. I felt like I was being pulled down, straight down into the boardwalk, into the zigs of the zags. They wouldn't let me go, wouldn't go away. Some Rollerblade kids streaked by and I heard them call me something I've never heard before or never heard used that way. (What was it? I can't remember.) And more Rollerbladers. And skateboarders. I thought they were trying to run me over—I'm the pin, and they're the bowling balls—but they flew past me, shrinking into neon-colored flames, down the boardwalk.

This woman, dressed all in white, must have seen the whole thing. Her eyes, golden in the brilliant sunlight, focused on me and me only as she ran toward me, shouting, waving her hands and yelling, "Move. The lane, the lane. Get out the lane." Then she touched me, and the vines were gone and I could breathe. She yanked me over. "The lane, that's the skating lane and these kids are likely to run you over nowadays." I rubbed my wrist, and I could see red welts around it. She kept talking a lot, real fast, like she was on speed or something; but she pronounced each word with the utmost care. "They glow in the night, you know. Scares the hell out of me, too." Long strands of brown hair clung to her pale, sweat-dampened face, and her nostrils flared as she spoke. She looked fit but not slender, middle-aged—forty-five, fifty—but not old, beautiful but not pretty.

I offered thanks for the rescue, but she seemed to not hear me, telling me about how all these fluorescent colors everybody wears out here in California are signaling UFOs, and I better get myself some protection before I get picked up for extermination. Insects get exterminated, I tried to tell her, but that was the wrong thing to say. She went off on how the Nazis exterminated tons of Jews: "The measured them by weight, not as individuals." How all kinds of exterminations had occurred. In the Soviet Union. In Cambodia. In America. "Don't see no Aztecs running around, do you?" She went on. And on.

She told me that these skateboard and Rollerblade kids knew something, and that's why they all had at least one neon-colored article on at all times. "Keeps their skates safe, too, with fluorescent wheels," she explained. I noticed she had on those Day-Glo cords around her neck, her wrist, and her ankles, the ones they sell at baseball games and afterward you have to keep in the refrigerator to recharge.

I don't know what made me tell her this, what made me talk to her, but I told her I was having all these visions about being bound and strangled by vines. I had to make myself stop. I didn't tell her then why I'd come here from New York, why I was trying not to think; but thinking about it was all I could do. My father had been sick for two years with AIDS when he died (I dropped out of my first year at Swarthmore to care for him), and some days, close to the end, he couldn't recognize me, or he'd think I was him and he was all young again and have conversations with himself my whole visit: "You've got to set an example for your race. Get married. Get affirmative-actioned, Mel. And stop having that part cut into your hair. You're a respectable accountant, a family man. Not Shaft."

Since we shared the name Melvin, it could get confusing. But I knew he wasn't talking to me; he was talking to his younger self, twenty years old, in college, married, and miserable.

Sometimes he wouldn't talk to me at all. Sometimes he'd ask me to leave his semiprivate hospital room. He'd say I smelled like the rotting earth; or he'd say the smell of my shampoo offended him: "You're no Breck girl; you're a black boy. And ain't no Breck girls black, and no black boys use Breck. We use Prell." Sometimes he'd call the nurse and have the flowers I'd just bought for him removed from the room: "Poinsettias in Puerto Rico can be beautiful and grow as tall as cherry trees. Poinsettias at Christmastime in New York—or Oklahoma—are awful. Nothing could be tackier."

The virus had gotten inside his brain, the doctor told me. His mind had been completely taken over, and he needed constant care. (There was never any time for me to register at City College. Or Hunter. Every time he got a little better I took him home and waited on him until the hospital had to take him back. That's how the insurance worked.)

"Get yourself some fluorescents," said the woman on the beach still talking a mile a minute. "That's what I'd do." And I imagined the many alien particles that had taken over my father's body retreating, shrinking away from fluorescent colors. Running. "Sounds strange," she continued, "but you can die from a trick of the mind. If that is what it is."

I believed her. It made lots of sense to me—at the time.

Turned out she'd just invented this neon tattoo dye that gave permanent protection. She said she was a tattoo artist. Before I met her, I definitely wasn't into tattoos. But then she showed me her book, a black leatherbound notebook filled with color photographs, examples of her work—intricate miniature designs made with needle and dye.

"I would show you mine," she said, pointing to her white linen sarong, "but I don't know you well enough. That is, if you wanted to see the real thing and not reproductions."

I took her at her word. The photos didn't look like they'd been retouched or anything. She asked if she could just paint some colors on my skin. My skin, she kept saying, was such a beautiful color to go with her neons. "Must be a lot of cultures mixed in there. Powerful. Ancient. Thick blood. Like maple syrup. Makes your skin shine. But you don't have much meat on your bones. Put your backpack down."

"I'll forget it," I said in a panic. That bag had everything in it—all I owned, all that was truly mine.

She started painting on my wrist with a thin brush, about five squirrel hairs thick, in small dabs and strokes. It tickled, so I turned and looked out to the bright sky, the domed ceiling of a god's castle. Not that I'm religious or anything—or into crystals—but out here in California, it seems like the sky is the inside of a god's head, the fissures on the brain where thoughts roll by. Or: the sky is the screen of a TV set seen from the inside. But who's watching on the outside? Gods? Aliens? Or viruses? Everything looked so washed out in the sunlight, even brightly colored bikinis looked pastel in the glare. The ocean appeared to be covered in white feathers that floated on the crests of waves. The whole sea ready to fly away. But where?

"You can look now. Hello. My friend, you can look now," she said. "Isn't it beautiful? It's a little rough sketch. I don't know why I painted that design, I'm usually not into flowers. I'll have better control with the needle. Do you like it?"

I didn't know what to say. They didn't look exactly like the ones in my visions, but they were close enough, close enough that I thought they *were* the vines that were always trying to pull me down.

"How'd you know?" I asked.

"I just started."

"But these are like the flowers in my visions. How'd you know? What are they?" I couldn't believe how detailed they were.

"Don't touch them yet. Let them dry. Well, let me see. These are wild daisies, and these are chicory with miniature ivy leaves. Twinflowers, grass-of-parnassus, wild oats and hepatica and sea lavender." Seven different miniature florets in all. "I'm going to break for lunch," she continued. "Would you like to join me? Then I can get started afterward. At least on the wrist. I have to think about the rest."

She stood up and started putting things away. I didn't pay much atten-tion to what was going on, except the way that flowers twisted around my wrist and tied in a loose knot on the inside of my arm. It was a rough sketch, but it had the potential of being as intricate as an engraving.

"Are you coming?" she continued. "You can rest here if you want. Leave your bag here and I'll lock up. I know you've had an unsettling morning. My name's Tasha, by the way. Could you help me with some of this?"

"Melvin. Mel. Where are we going?" I asked. And in my first moment of relative calm in a long time, I set my backpack on the floor, lifted a large lunch basket, and followed Tasha down the boardwalk.

We walked to a less crowded part of the beach, where she set out a big white umbrella and a white blanket. She didn't stop talking the whole time, asking for assistance, describing the lunch she'd prepared—a redleaf let-tuce, tomato, and garbanzo bean salad with tahini vinaigrette dressing, cold brown rice with almonds and raisins, and whole grain pita bread. She told me not to feel obligated to get a tattoo even though she had just saved my life and was sharing her lunch. Good sense of humor. Her yellow eyes flashed in the sun when she laughed, and she flicked her light chestnut hair out of her face at the end of each good chuckle.

She told me about her life. She was a native Californian but had gone to school back East, at Smith, and she hadn't been back in twenty-five years. She had learned how to tattoo in New York, back when New York was the capital of tattooing.

"After college," she said, "like everybody else, I guess I moved to New York to seek my fame and fortune. Instead I worked as a secretary at a few law firms. All my girlfriends said I was lucky. 'How to Marry a Millionaire.' What better way is there to meet one than to work for one?

But I didn't make a good cup of coffee, and I didn't take shorthand. I had a small flat on the Lower East Side, but when I got fired—no lawyer lover/husband for me—I moved out to a cheaper place in Brooklyn. A boardinghouse for twenty-five dollars a month, I think. And I started hanging out there, going out to the beach, the rides, the freak show at Coney Island. Do you have enough salad dressing? It's in that dish. I just made it this morning, so tomorrow it'll be really great. You know, the spices start coming out.

"Anyway, I met this guy Tony, Tony the Pirate, they called him, and he taught me everything I know. He was the best. The best on the boardwalk. The Pirate," she repeated as if she were trying to conjure him up, "but he didn't have any fake appendages. What part of New York are you from?"

"Harlem," I said with difficulty. My mouth was full, and everything was so good, I couldn't stop stuffing myself long enough to talk. I hadn't eaten all morning; I hadn't eaten anything good for me in months. Saving money: the less I spent on food and stuff, the longer I could stay. I think Tasha could tell I didn't want to talk about myself, because she didn't wait for me to elaborate.

"Tony, Tony the Pirate? I don't know where he is now. See, they destroyed the tattoo business in New York in the sixties, said it contributed to the spread of disease—hepatitis, I think it was. They said that all the *crazies* were spreading hepatitis." She wiggled her fingers in the air when she said "crazies." "If they got rid of tattooing, then they'd get rid of all the undesirables, you know. Just like that. Poof.

"Back then New York was the center of everything, tattoos and crazies. We were professional artists—working in the art capital of the world, and now we're illegal there. Everything went underground. Or disappeared. Everything went down except for you-know-what. So I made way back home, to the beach, to a place where you can't go any farther. You know what I mean?"

She finished chewing the last of her salad and placed her dishes to the side. Her skin was warmly tanned, dark in contrast to the fluorescent jewelry she wore, dark against the white umbrella behind her, but light compared to mine, I noticed her fingers now resting in her lap, wrinkled at the knuckles—unadorned, practical fingers with closely trimmed nails and permanently stained cuticles. The pattern of veins on the back of her hands. She held her hands just so, poised, with the tips of index finger and thumb touching, as if they were kissing.

She started talking faster, and her story changed from New York to the West as frontier to outer space. She said that the space and aeronautics industries were concentrated in the West because there were no other places on earth to explore. "I think is was Horace Greeley who told all those young ambitious men, 'Go West!' (It didn't make him president, but unlike all the other losers, he's remembered for something other than losing.) At the same time, I think, mid-nineteenth century, good old Ralph Waldo Emerson told those same robust young men—it's always young men, you see—'Hitch your wagon to a star.' Now he was always so prophetic. Really. You see, the question to ask," she said, laughing at what she'd just said, "is how close is California to the heavens? You could probably just hitch a couple of horses to the space shuttle and go. And the aliens must know the answer to that one. That's why they're always coming here: they've run out of frontiers on their own planets. You must think I'm crazy."

I didn't know what to say; I was following the path of ideas she'd made, and I couldn't believe I was right there beside her. "It's funny," I said after a long pause, "we think alike, you know?" even though I didn't think this was true at all. But I couldn't find any more words. I'm not used to talking. Dad never used to let me get a word in edgewise. He always talked to me as if he were holding court—very royal, indeed. Taking care of him was like taking care of a prince—not a queen—a little prince lost at some edge of the world where his royal lineage wasn't apparent anymore; he lost his crown of silver hair before he lost his scepter of wit and intelligence. He lost a few teeth. His fingernails turned black.

"I want you to know," he said to me, "that I'm leaving you everything, all I have. Take my letters, my journals, all my books, my albums, and remember me. Remember me. I give you all these, my estate, my jewels, my leather chaps, my braided whip. Take it and use it wisely, sparingly. They won't know who you are until you pull out that mighty strap. It takes a masochist to create a sadist. Don't let them cut you to pieces. And don't be afraid to use commas. And exclamation points—I know they're so out of fashion." His hands, with their blackened nails, fluttered around his mouth, an open wound I could peer inside and see, past his swollen tongue, down his throat, to the sickness in his stomach, lungs, intestines, right through to the sphincter muscle he couldn't control anymore.

When Dad stopped talking altogether, I still didn't speak up. I didn't know what to say except, *How could you do this to me? I can't do this by myself, you crazy old man. I still need you. You would've died all alone with-*

out me. Crazy old man. There's no one left. Can't you see? There's nothing but your blackened nails, your stinking body, an open wound, your melting body, hot as wax. You fool. You damn fool, stop holding on. But I didn't say that. Instead I started reading everything he gave me, his journals and books, his bills and business plans. My inheritance.

"You know," I said to Tasha, stumbling on my words, trying to fill in the blanks with anything that came to mind. "You know, that's why I came here. That's why Hollywood's here. The apparatus. You know what I mean? It's like a frontier, new technologies. The apparatus of film. And now there's Silicon Valley."

"Are you into computers?" she asked when I didn't say anything else. "I don't like them. I don't trust them. I did some designs on them once and then they disappeared. I couldn't find them, and I had spent hours on it."

She looked to the ocean and became very quiet. I could see her pulse beating at her temples, and the speediness and slowness of her life. She was alone, like me, aware of the effects of atmospheric pressures and gravity weighing her down. I could tell that hers was a life of wishing to be more, daydreaming but never making it, getting distracted by the details of cutting vegetables and tearing green leaves; her was a life of trusting others because the real enemy, aliens and viruses, could only come from another place. Like out there in the heavens.

I'm saying this now, but I wished I'd known it then. See, the thing is, Dad became more and more innocent as he got sicker, weaker. He smiled a lot. He stopped getting embarrassed when he burped loudly or drooled. He didn't cry out anymore when his diaper leaked and he had to lie there for hours in the mess, in the smell and everything. I know he stopped talking to me before he wasn't able to speak. He stopped looking at me before he went blind. I don't know why. I blamed him. Now I know it makes just as much sense to blame it all on aliens as it does to blame it on him, on his life after he left me and my mother and my sister. But I did. I held him responsible for his own death. Until I read his journals and diaries and letters and little poems he wrote in the margins of books. (I took them with me and read them on the bus ride out here; but before that all I knew was I was going to spread my father's ashes over the Pacific Ocean.)

When I was twelve Dad moved down to the Village while my mother, my sister, and I remained on 147th Street. He became a black queen—no, a prince—happy with his life and his lover, who died four years before him. I got scared when Walter died. I was sixteen, and these visions, which I now know were only panic attacks, would start and the anxiety would take control of my body, seizing me and squeezing me senseless. Like a carnival ride spinning out of control.

It was up to me to take care of everything when Dad got too sick to handle it himself. I paid the bills, closed all the accounts, cleaned up after him, washed him, made sure the hospital kept him there as long as possible. We couldn't afford a private nurse. We couldn't afford the hospital. The insurance kept trying to drop him, but I kept paying for the coverage. I also had my mother's lawyer give them a call. She helped when she could, but it was too hard for her. "I can only do so much," she said. "You might not understand, and I don't expect you to, but I can only do so much." She bought groceries for us once a week. After the second year I couldn't pay the maintenance on Dad's apartment anymore, so I turned it over to the management company, put all his stuff in storage, and moved in with friends. It was his fault, dammit, all of it, I thought when it was happening.

But now I know the reason Dad's fingernails were black and rotting. It was a black fungus, growing out of control. He hadn't painted them that way.

Tasha started gathering our picnic leftovers, and I tried to help, but she insisted on doing it herself. She said I looked emaciated. But she finally gave in and let me carry the basket back to her shop. Her Day-Glo necklace looked like a broken halo come to rest around her neck, her white sarong an apostle's robe. I wanted to be in love with her at that moment, and I could feel the blood rush to my face when she handed me the basket. I realized I didn't have my backpack with me. I thought I'd lost it. His ashes were in there. In a plastic bag. In a cardboard box. Lumpy, grey cinders, smooth to the touch. Unburned shards of teeth and bone. I could feel the thump, thump in my ears, pounding out the sounds of the crashing waves, consuming me. I was on a roller-coaster, in the first car, holding my hands up, screaming and laughing. But I wasn't. I was holding it all in, and I had to tell myself to breathe, let it out, breathe.

They started again. Sea lavender and wild oats, goldenrod and witch hazel, grass-of-parnassus and strong green vines. I knew their names now. Pollen in my eyes and nose, a catch in the back of my throat. So, I kept thinking: I'm like him, every day I'm more and more like him, I want to be like him, I have no other choice. Soft petals. Fibrous, tough stems. If there is such a thing as a gay gene, then I think it was passed on to me. But not the virus. I tried to get that all by myself. Not exactly by myself, but in a selfish, half-crazed, half-I-don't-know-what moment. A one-night stand of unsafe sex back at school, when I hated myself and hated my father. Hated everything gay. They won't go away. Aromatic leaves. Thin prickly thorns. Trickles of blood on my arms, legs, dripping from my eyes, connecting me to him and him to us all.

All I did, all I could do, was wipe the tears away, and catch my breath, and wipe the tears away.

"I know, you don't have to tell me," Tasha said in a very low voice. "Just let it take its time to get out of your stomach and into your bloodstream. You shouldn't go so long without eating. It ain't good," she said, and the panic retreated.

We walked in silence back down the beach, and I thought how I couldn't get enough of California, couldn't take it all in. The endless sky. The sun setting over the ocean. Everything has a reason out here in California. Earthquakes happen because . . . UFOs are seen more often because . . . I met Tasha just in time because, because, because I came to L.A. after my father died. Because there was no place else to go. Because I couldn't go any farther. I came out here to get rid of his ashes, spread them out in the desert or sprinkle them in the ocean. But now I think I'm going to keep them. They keep me anchored, keep me from floating off the edge, away, somewhere.

We walked back to Tasha's booth, and she checked the painting on my wrist. She asked if I was ready, and I said yes. I didn't want to rationalize, give myself time to figure it all out. I sat, and she sat holding my hand and my arm so I couldn't move around, get away from the pain. I didn't look at what she was doing, and after a little while the stinging went away. I missed the hurting. I wanted to know the pain—just like when I was a kid and the dentist did four, five fillings a visit without Novocain, and the only thing that was unpleasant was the smell of burning enamel and the stiff neck afterward from holding my head in one place for so long. That was the first time Dad said I was like him, talking all the pain and holding it all in.

1996

DON'T EXPLAIN

Jewelle Gomez

BOSTON 1959

Letty deposited the hot platters on the table, effortlessly. She slid one deep-fried chicken, a club-steak with boiled potatoes and a fried porgie plat-ter down her thick arm as if removing beaded bracelets. Each plate landed with a solid clink on the shiny Formica, in its appropriate place. The last barely settled before Letty turned back to the kitchen to get Bo John his lemonade and extra biscuits and then to put her feet up. Out of the corner of her eye she saw Tip come in the lounge. His huge shoulders, draped in sharkskin, barely cleared the narrow door frame.

"Damn! He's early tonight!" she thought but kept going. Tip was known for his generosity, that's how he'd gotten his nickname. He always sat at Letty's station because they were both from Virginia, although neither had been back in years. Letty had come up to Boston in 1946 and been wait-ing tables in the 411 Lounge since '52. She liked people: the pimps were limited but flashy; the musicians who hung around were unpredictable in their pursuit of a good time and the "business" girls were generous and always willing to embroider a wild story. After Letty's mother died there'd been no reason to go back to Burkeville.

Letty took her newspaper from the locker behind the kitchen and filled a large glass with the tart grape juice punch for which the cook, Mabel, was famous.

"I'm going on break, Mabel. Delia's takin' my station."

She sat in the back booth nearest the kitchen beneath the large blackboard which displayed the menu. When Delia came out of the bathroom Letty hissed to get her attention. The reddish-brown skin of

Delia's face was shiny with a country freshness that always made Letty feel a little warm.

"What's up, Miss Letty?" Her voice was soft and saucy.

"Take my tables for twenty minutes. Tip just came in."

The girl's already bright smile widened, as she started to thank Letty.

"Go 'head, go 'head. He don't like to wait. You can thank me if he don't run you back and forth fifty times."

Delia hurried away as Letty sank into the coolness of the overstuffed booth and removed her shoes. After a few sips of her punch she rested her head on the back of the seat with her eyes closed. The sounds around her were as familiar as her own breathing: squeaking Red Cross shoes as Delia and Vinnie passed, the click of high heels around the bar, the clatter of dishes in the kitchen and ice clinking in glasses. The din of conversation rose, leveled and rose again over the juke box. Letty had not played her record in days but the words spun around in her head as if they were on the turntable:

> . . . right or wrong don't matter
> when you're with me sweet
> Hush now, don't explain
> You're my joy and pain.

Letty sipped her cool drink; sweat ran down her spine soaking into the nylon uniform. July weather promised to give no breaks and the fans were working overtime like everybody else.

She saw Delia cross to Tip's table again. In spite of the dyed red hair, no matter how you looked at her, Delia was still a country girl: long and self-conscious, shy and bold because she didn't know any better. She'd moved up from Anniston with her cousin a year before and landed the job at the 411 immediately. She worked hard and sometimes Letty and she shared a cab going uptown after work, when Delia's cousin didn't pick them up in her green Pontiac.

Letty caught Tip eyeing Delia as she strode on long, tight-muscled legs back to the kitchen. "That lounge lizard!" Lettty thought to herself. Letty had trained Delia: how to balance plates, how to make tips and how to keep the customer's hands on the table. She was certain Delia would have no problem putting Tip in his place. In the year she'd been working Delia hadn't gone out with any of the bar flies, though plenty had asked. Letty figured that

Delia and her cousin must run with a different crowd. They talked to each other sporadically in the kitchen or during their break but Letty never felt that wire across the chest like Delia was going to ask her something she couldn't answer.

She closed her eyes again for a few remaining minutes. The song was back in her head and Letty had to squeeze her lips together to keep from humming aloud. She pushed her thoughts on to something else. But when she did she always stumbled upon Maxine. Letty opened her eyes. When she'd quit working at Salmagundi's and come to the 411 she'd promised herself never to think about any woman like that again. She didn't know why missing Billie so much brought it all back to her. She'd not thought of that time or those feelings for a while.

She heard Abe shout a greeting at Duke behind the bar as he surveyed his domain. That was Letty's signal. No matter whether it was her break or not she knew white people didn't like to see their employees sitting down, especially with their shoes off. By the time Abe was settled on his stool near the door, Letty was up, her glass in hand and on her way through the kitchen's squeaky swinging door.

"You finished your break already?" Delia asked.

"Abe just come in."

"Uh oh, let me git this steak out there to that man. Boy he sure is nosey!"

"Who, Tip?"

"Yeah, he ask me where I live, who I live with, where I come from like he supposed to know me!"

"Well just don't take nothing he say to heart and you'll be fine. And don't take no rides from him!"

"Yeah, he asked if he could take me home after I get off. I told him me and you had something to do."

Letty was silent as she sliced the fresh bread and stacked it on plates for the next orders.

"My cousin's coming by, so it ain't a lie, really. She can ride us."

"Yeah," Letty said as Delia giggled and turned away with her platter.

Vinnie burst through the door like she always did, looking breathless and bossy. "Abe up there, girl! You better get back on station. You got a customer."

Letty drained her glass with deliberation, wiped her hands on her thickly starched white apron and walked casually past Vinnie as if she'd never spoken. She heard Mabel's soft chuckle float behind her. She went over to Tip, who was digging into the steak like his life depended on devouring it before the plate got dirty.

"Everything alright tonight?" Letty asked, her ample brown body towering over the table.

"Yeah, baby, everything alright. You ain't workin' this side no more?"

"I was on break. My feet can't wait for your stomach, you know."

Tip laughed. "Break! What you need a break for, big and healthy as you is!"

"We all gets old, Tip. But the feet get old first, let me tell you that!"

"Not in my business, baby. Why don't you come on and work for me and you ain't got to worry 'bout your feet."

Letty sucked her teeth loudly, the exaggeration a part of the game they played over the years. "Man, I'm too old for that mess!"

"You ain't too old for me."

"Ain't nobody too old for you! Or too young neither, looks like."

"Where you and that gal goin' tonight?"

"To a funeral," Letty responded dryly.

"Aw woman get on away from my food!" The gold cap on his front tooth gleamed from behind his greasy lips when he laughed. Letty was pleased. Besides giving away money Tip liked to hurt people. It was better when he laughed.

The kitchen closed at 11:00 P.M. Delia and Letty slipped out of their uniforms in the tiny bathroom and were on their way out the door by 11:15. Delia looked even younger in her knife-pleated skirt and white cotton blouse. Letty did feel old tonight in her slacks and long-sleeved shirt. The movement of car headlights played across her face, which was set in exhaustion. The dark green car pulled up and they slipped in quietly, both anticipating tomorrow, Sunday, the last night of their work week.

Delia's cousin was a stocky woman who looked forty, Letty's age. She never spoke much. Not that she wasn't friendly. She always greeted Letty with a smile and laughed at Delia's stories about the customers. "Just close to the chest like me, that's all," Letty often thought. As they pulled up to the corner of Columbus Avenue and Cunard Street, Letty opened the rear door. Delia turned to her and said, "I'm sorry you don't play your record on your break no more, Miss Letty. I know you don't want to, but I'm sorry just the same."

Delia's cousin looked back at them with a puzzled expression but said nothing. Letty slammed the car door shut and turned to climb the short flight of stairs to her apartment. Cunard Street was quiet outside her window and the guy upstairs wasn't blasting his record player for once. Still, Letty lay awake and restless in her single bed. The fan was pointed at the ceiling, bouncing warm air over her, rustling her sheer nightgown.

Inevitably the strains of Billie Holiday's songs brushed against her, much like the breeze that fanned around her. She felt silly when she thought about it, but the melodies gripped her like a solid presence. It was more than the music. Billie had been her hero. Letty saw Billie as big, like herself, with big hungers, and some secret that she couldn't tell anyone. Two weeks ago, when Letty heard that the Lady had died, sorrow enveloped her. A refuge had been closed that she could not consciously identify to herself or to anyone. It embarrassed her to think about. Like it did when she remembered Maxine.

When Letty first started working at the 411 she met Billie when she'd come into the club with several musicians on her way back from the Jazz Festival. There the audience, curious to see what a real, live junkie looked like, had sat back waiting for Billie to fall on her face. Instead she'd killed them dead with her liquid voice and rough urgency. Still, the young, thin horn player kept having to reassure her: "Billie, you were the show, the whole show!"

Once convinced, Billie became the show again, loud and commanding. She demanded her food be served at the bar and sent Mabel, who insisted on waiting on her personally, back to the kitchen fifteen times. Billie laughed at jokes that Letty could barely hear as she hustled back and forth between the abandoned kitchen and her own tables. The sound of that laugh from the bar penetrated her bones. She'd watched and listened, certain she saw something no one else did. When Billie had finished eating and gathered her entourage to get back on the road she left a tip, not just for Mabel but for each of the waitresses and the bartender. "Generous just like the 'business' girls," Letty was happy to note. She still had the two one-dollar bills in an envelope at the back of her lingerie drawer.

After that, Letty felt even closer to Billie. She played one of the few Lady Day records on the juke box every night during her break. Everyone at the 411 had learned not to bother her when her song came on. Letty realized, as she lay waiting for sleep, that she'd always felt that if she had been able to say or do something that night to make friends with Billie, it might all have been different. In half sleep the faces of Billie, Maxine and Delia blended in her mind. Letty slid her hand along the soft nylon of her gown to rest it between her full thighs. She pressed firmly, as if holding desire inside herself. Letty could have loved her enough to make it better. That was Letty's final thought as she dropped off to sleep.

Sunday nights at the 411 were generally mellow. Even the pimps and prostitutes used it as a day of rest. Letty came in early and had a drink at the bar and talked with the bartender before going to the back to change into her uniform. She saw Delia through the window as she stepped out of the green Pontiac, looking as if she'd just come from Concord Baptist Church. "Satin Doll" was on the juke box, wrapping the bar in cool nostalgia.

Abe let Mabel close the kitchen early on Sunday and Letty looked forward to getting done by 10:00 or 10:30, and maybe enjoying some of the evening. When her break time came Letty started for the juke box automatically. She hadn't played anything by Billie in two weeks; now, looking down at the inviting glare, she knew she still couldn't do it. She punched the buttons that would bring up Jackie Wilson's "Lonely Teardrops" and went to the back booth.

She'd almost dropped off to sleep when she heard Delia whisper her name. She opened her eyes and looked up into the girl's smiling face. Her head was haloed in tight, shiny curls.

"Miss Letty, won't you come home with me tonight?"

"What?"

"I'm sorry to bother you, but your break time almost up. I wanted to ask if you'd come over to the house tonight . . . after work. My cousin'll bring you back home after."

Letty didn't speak. Her puzzled look prompted Delia to start again.

"Sometime on Sunday my cousin's friends from work come over to play cards, listen to music, you know. Nothin' special, just some of the girls from the office building down on Winter Street where she work, cleaning. She, I mean we, thought you might want to come over tonight. Have a drink, play some cards . . ."

"I don't play cards much."

"Well not everybody play cards . . . just talk . . . sitting around talking. My cousin said you might like to for a change."

Letty wasn't sure she liked the last part: "for a change," as if they had to entertain an old aunt.

"I really want you to come, Letty. They always her friends but none of them is my own friends. They alright, I don't mean nothin' against them, but it would be fun to have my own personal friend there, you know?"

Delia was a good girl. Those were the perfect words to describe her, Letty thought smiling. "Sure honey, I'd just as soon spend my time with you as lose my money with some fools."

They got off at 10:15 and Delia apologized that they had to take a cab uptown. Her cousin and her friends didn't work on Sunday so they were already at home. Afraid that the snag would give Letty an opportunity to back out, Delia hadn't mentioned it until they were out of their uniforms and on the sidewalk. Letty almost declined, tempted to go home to the safe silence of her room. But she didn't. She stepped into the street and waved down a Red and White cab. All the way uptown Delia apologized that the evening wasn't a big deal and cautioned Letty not to expect much. "Just a few friends, hanging around, drinking and talking." She was jumpy and Letty tried to put her at ease. She had not expected her first visit would make Delia so anxious.

The apartment was located halfway up Blue Hill Avenue in an area where a few blacks had recently been permitted to rent. They entered a long, carpeted hallway and heard the sounds of laughter and music ringing from the rooms at the far end.

Once inside, with the door closed, Delia's personality took on another dimension. This was clearly her home and Letty could not believe she ever really needed an ally to back her up. Delia stepped out of her shoes at the door and walked to the back with her same, long-legged gait. They passed a closed door, which Letty assumed to be one of the bedrooms, then came to a kitchen ablaze wih light. Food and bottles were strewn across the pink and gray Formica-top table. A counter opened from the kitchen into the dining-room, which was the center of activity. Around a large mahogany table sat five women in smoke-filled concentration, playing poker.

Delia's cousin looked up from her cards with the same slight smile as usual. Here it seemed welcoming, not guarded as it did in those brief moments in her car. She wore brown slacks and a matching sweater. The pink, starched points of her shirt collar peeked out at the neck.

Delia crossed to her and kissed her cheek lightly. Letty looked around the table to see if she recognized anyone. The women all seemed familiar in the way that city neighbors can, but Letty was sure she hadn't met any of them before. Delia introduced her to each one: Karen, a short, round woman with West Indian bangles up to her pudgy elbow; Betty, who stared intently at her cards through thick eyeglasses encased in blue cat-eye frames; Irene, a big, dark woman with long black hair and a gold tooth in front. Beside her sat Myrtle, who was wearing army fatigues and a gold Masonic ring on her pinky finger. She said hello in the softest voice Letty had ever heard. Hovering over her was Clara, a large red woman whose hair was bound tightly in a bun at the nape of her neck. She spoke with a delectable southern accent that drawled her "How're you doin" into a full paragraph that was draped around an inquisitive smile.

Delia became ill-at-ease again as she pulled Letty by the arm toward the French doors behind the players. There was a small den with a desk, some books and a television set. Through the next set of glass doors was a living-room. At the record player was an extremely tall, brown-skinned woman. She bent over the wooden cabinet searching for the next selection, oblivious to the rest of the gathering. Two women sat on the divan in deep conversation, which they punctuated with constrained giggles.

"Maryalice, Sheila, Dolores . . . this is Letty."

They looked up at her quickly, smiled, then went back to their preoccupations: two to their gossip, the other returning to the record collection. Delia directed Letty back toward the foyer and the kitchen.

"Come on, let me get you a drink. You know, I don't even know what you drink!"

"Delia?" Her cousin's voice reached them over the counter, just as they stepped into the kitchen. "Bring a couple of beers back when you come, OK?"

"Sure, babe." Delia went to the refrigerator and pulled out two bottles. "Let me just take these in. I'll be right back."

"Go 'head, I can take care of myself in this department, girl." Letty surveyed the array of bottles on the table. Delia went to the dining-room and Letty mixed a Scotch and soda. She poured slowly as the reality settled on her. These women were friends, perhaps lovers, like she and Maxine had been. The name she'd heard for women like these burst inside her head: bulldagger. Letty flinched, angry she had let it in, angry that it frightened her. "Ptuh!" Letty blew air through her teeth as if spitting the word back at the air.

She did know these women, Letty thought, as she stood at the counter smiling out at the poker game. They were oblivious to her, except for Terry. Letty remembered that was Delia's cousin's name. As Letty took her first sip, Terry called over to her. "We gonna be finished with this game in a minute, Letty, then we can talk."

"Take your time," Letty said, then went out through the foyer door and around to the living-room. She walked slowly on the carpet and adjusted her eyes to the light, which was a bit softer. The tall woman, Maryalice, had just put a record on the turntable and sat down on a love seat across from the other two women. Letty stood in the doorway a moment before the tune began:

> Hush now, don't explain
> Just say you'll remain
> I'm glad you're back
> Don't explain . . .

Letty was stunned, but the song sounded different here, among these women. Billie sang just to them, here. The isolation and sadness seemed less inevitable with these women listening. Letty watched Maryalice sitting with her long legs stretched out tensely in front of her. She was wrapped in her own thoughts, her eyes closed. She appeared curiously disconnected, after what had clearly been a long search for this record. Letty watched her face as she swallowed several times. Then Letty moved to sit on the seat beside her. They listened to the music while the other two women spoke in low voices.

When the song was over Maryalice didn't move. Letty rose from the sofa and went to the record player. Delia stood tentatively in the doorway of the living-room. Letty picked up the arm of the phongraph and replaced it at the beginning of the record. When she sat again beside Maryalice she noticed the drops of moisture on the other woman's lashes. Maryalice relaxed as Letty settled on to the seat beside her. They both listened to Billie together, for the first time.

1987

HUNGRY DOG

Agnes Rossi

W e were scrawny, scrappy, not very pretty. We weren't the sort of girls boys in our high school flipped over. Up at the Hungry Dog it was a different story. Everybody loved us there. We went to work in short shorts, tank tops, Dr. Scholl's sandals that were supposed to make our calves shapely.

Our customers were all men, truckdrivers and guys who worked on the assembly line at the Ford plant. We'd look up and see a group of Ford workers in navy blue coveralls waiting for their chance to cross Route 17. When it came, they'd run all together. Eva said they reminded her of a baseball team heading out to the field. She'd nudge me, say, "Here they come."

The Dog stood in the shadow of Stag Hill. The Jackson Whites lived there. They were a group of mulattoes who kept to themselves. We heard stories about inbreeding and truant officers being shot at with rock salt. The Jackson Whites who came into the Dog had kinky reddish hair and nervous eyes, paid with crumpled dollar bills and lots of change. It was 1975. We lived in a New Jersey town that was devoid of history—nobody's parents, even, had grown up in Montvale—and there we were selling hot dogs to the descendants of slaves who had been freed by Andrew Jackson.

Our friends worked in supermarkets and fast-food places with names everybody knew. My parents would have preferred if we'd found jobs like those but were glad we were working at all. I don't remember either one of them ever setting foot inside the Dog. When my mother had to drive us up there, she'd stop the car at the edge of the parking lot.

Eva and I couldn't believe our good fortune. Just fifteen minutes from our suburban home we'd stumbled on this pocket of tough guys in their twenties and thirties. The boys in our high school didn't thrill us. They were too much like us: sheltered, amorphous, soft. We all seemed to be standing around waiting for our lives to begin. Our customers at the Dog had declared themselves. The world had worked on them. They had calloused hands, heavy beards. Their blue jeans were darkened with grime from the road or the factory.

For a while we were in love with all of them. The way they rubbed their eyes after taking a first long swallow of coffee, the bandannas so many of them tied across their foreheads. One would chastise another for saying cocksucker or motherfucker in front of us. A truckdriver would come in dusty and bleary-eyed, go right to the men's room, emerge with his hair damp and freshly combed, the top of his T-shirt wet. He'd sit down, smile, say hey girls.

Then Bobby, a Vietnam vet with tattoos on his forearms, started bringing Eva jewelry from the Southwest, tough biker-girl stuff, a coiled snake with bright green eyes, a turquoise thunderbolt. She kept it all in a zippered compartment of her purse so my mother wouldn't see it. As we drove up to the Dog, she'd put it on piece by piece.

Eva began leaving the Dog to be with Bobby. As soon as he pulled in, she'd climb up into his truck with an agility I hadn't seen before. When she got back, hours later, she'd look pleasantly mussed, her dark eyes shining.

I liked being at the Dog without Eva. I'd lean against the counter and we—six or seven guys and I—would watch familiar sit-coms on the small black and white. I'd watched those same shows with my girl friends, even at home with my parents. Around eight o'clock we'd turn off the TV and drivers from Tennessee and Mississippi would argue with auto workers from Newark about which radio station we should listen to, country western or a black one that was all the way at the end of the dial. I liked being in the middle of that, knowing that Eva was out there in the night like a scout, riding around in Bobby's truck, wearing all her jewelry.

As was bound to happen, the headiness of close quarters, southern accents, second looks that shot straight through me coalesced into a crush on one man, Mike. He was neither a truckdriver nor a Ford worker. I didn't know what he did except that he drove a battered station wagon, one of those cars you see in parking lots, a tool chest on wheels. The backseat was permanently down to make room for ladders and push brooms. Crushed styrofoam cups and empty cigarette packs were sprinkled over everything like croutons on a salad.

Mike was in his late twenties, tall and lean, had a black man's mustache and beard. I think of him whenever I see a picture of Malcolm X. He had a sinewy intensity and sharp wit, didn't say much, hovered around the outskirts of conversations making occasional wry comments. I believed he and I were smarter than the others, made sure he knew I got his jokes.

Mike's skin was light brown like a Jackson White's, but I wasn't convinced he was one. Unlike them, he always came in alone. They were hicks, said dang and reckon, and he seemed worldly. Then one night a couple of them came in and, as usual, ordered their hot dogs to go. When they left, Kyle, a loud, stupid guy nobody much liked, started bad-mouthing them, calling them J.W.'s, saying they all had blood diseases because of incest.

Mike got up, walked over to Kyle, and just stared at him. Kyle's voice trailed off. He withered in his seat. Mike looked ready to swing. A couple of guys stood up in that call-to-action way men will when a fight is about to start. Mike turned and walked out slowly. He stood in the parking lot and I could see his shoulders rising and falling as he took deep breaths.

He started coming in every night. I was nervous around him because I'd spent so much time thinking about us. In my head our affair was progressing nicely. I'd anticipate his laugh seconds before it came and congratulate myself on knowing him so well. I interpreted everything he said to me as clear evidence of his attraction and began taking longer and longer to get ready for work. I'd emerge from the bathroom at home, eyes made up, hair blown straight, reeking of the Charlie I'd put on all my pulse points.

One night I was working alone. Bobby was on the road and Eva had begged off, said she didn't feel like being around people. The sadness in her voice hinted at the downside of all this, the treachery of love. Mike sat at the counter spiking his Cokes with rum he poured from a flat pint bottle and smiling at me in a way that seemed purposeful and sly. I could feel his eyes on me when my back was turned. The smell of his rum found its way to me through cigarette smoke and the salty steam of hot dogs. I wanted to keep whatever was going on between us alive and knew I was doing all right.

Then I put an onion on the cutting board to slice. The knives had just been sharpened. I cut my finger, blood flowed. Mike saw it happen and straightened in his seat to get a better look. His eyes, my blood. It was a peculiar and intimate moment, like when you drop something and a stranger kneels to pick it up. He came behind the counter, soaked a clean rag in cold water, wrapped it around my finger, squeezed hard. The bleeding wouldn't stop, so I couldn't work. Mike took over for me, told people he was an emergency replacement and they should keep their orders simple. I had never seen such grace.

We closed at ten o'clock. Mike did what I told him to do, put the condiments away, turned off the steam table. He didn't seem fluid and relaxed the way he had earlier. His movements were taut and deliberate now.

Flirting with this man was one thing. It was something else entirely to be alone with him in a gravel parking lot on a summer night. The air smelled of exhaust from the highway and wet leaves from the mountain. My finger throbbed and I squeezed it, felt fresh blood seep into the napkin.

He leaned against the bumper of his station wagon, put his hand on my back, pulled me toward him, said, "You're just a little thing."

We kissed and a tremor went through me, a scalding sense that all there was was me. Now he'd find out I wasn't who I'd pretended to be. I'd kissed boys in the corners of basements and backyards but there'd always been other people around, some of them kissing too, girls smirking at each other over boys' shoulders. Mike's seriousness and plain desire were new. The kiss went on and on and I began to feel the pull of something genuine, something as simple and true as the ground under my feet. I could smell the Dog on us, the sour smell of coffee and fried onions that was in our hair, on our clothes. I put my arms around his neck. When I tilted my head, his followed. I was filled with a sense that my family, friends, school were all behind me. I was marching on without encumbrance. I thought of Eva climbing into Bobby's truck and felt party to that sort of momentum.

Then Mike slid his hand under my shirt and I froze. I had no breasts to speak of, a slight swelling was all, and the way my arms were raised minimized even that. I was sure he was accustomed to breasts with some heft. I stiffened, pulled back, was solidly in the middle of my own life again. Embarrassment revived fear and I knew I wouldn't go any further.

Mike looked at me for a moment then smiled and crossed his arms. "Go on home," he said. "You need to get in your mother's car now and go home." I did exactly that, drove with my bandaged finger sticking straight out. As I pulled into the driveway, I reached down to turn off the radio but in fact turned it on. It had been off the whole way and I hadn't noticed.

I hoped Eva would be awake so I could tell her I'd kissed Mike. She wasn't. I turned on the light in our room and still she didn't wake up. I took the spiral notebook I used as a diary out of my underwear drawer, looked around for a pen, spotted Eva's purse on the dresser. I opened the zippered compartment, scooped out the jewelry, put it all on. Looking at myself in the mirror, I brought my hand to my face so the snake bracelet would show. Eva stirred and I whispered her name. She nestled deeper in her covers, licking her lips and dreaming, I was sure, of the tattooed forearms of her Vietnam vet.

1992

III. CROSSINGS

THE LOUDEST VOICE

Grace Paley

There is a certain place where dumb-waiters boom, doors slam, dishes crash; every window is a mother's mouth bidding the street shut up, go skate somewhere else, come home. My voice is the loudest.

There, my own mother is still as full of breathing as me and the grocer stands up to speak to her, "Mrs. Abramowitz," he says, "people should not be afraid of their children."

"Ah, Mr. Bialik," my mother replies, "if you say to her or her father 'Ssh,' they say, 'In the grave it will be quiet.'"

"From Coney Island to the cemetery," says my papa. "It's the same subway; it's the same fare."

I am right next to the pickle barrel. My pinky is making tiny whirlpools in the brine. I stop a moment to announce: "Campbell's Tomato Soup. Campbell's Vegetable Beef Soup. Campbell's S-c-otch Broth . . ."

"Be quiet," the grocer says, "the labels are coming off."

"Please, Shirley, be a little quiet!" my mother begs me.

In that place the whole street groans: Be quiet! Be quiet! but steals from the happy chorus of my inside self not a tittle or a jot.

There, too, but just around the corner, is a red brick building that has been old for many years. Every morning the children stand before it in double lines which must be straight. They are not insulted. They are waiting anyway.

I am usually among them. I am, in fact, the first, since I begin with "A."

One cold morning the monitor tapped me on the shoulder. "Go to Room 409, Shirley Abramowitz," he said. I did as I was told. I went in a hurry up a down staircase to Room 409, which contained sixth graders. I had to wait at the desk without wiggling until Mr. Hilton, their teacher, had time to speak.

After five minutes he said, "Shirley?"

"What?" I whispered.

He said, "My! My! Shirley Abramowitz! They told me you had a particularly loud, clear voice and read with lots of expression. Could that be true?"

"Oh yes," I whispered.

"In that case, don't be silly; I might very well be your teacher someday. Speak up; speak up."

"Yes," I shouted.

"More like it," he said. "Now, Shirley, can you put a ribbon in your hair or a bobby pin? It's too messy."

"Yes!" I bawled.

"Now, now, calm down." He turned to the class. "Children, not a sound. Open at page 39. Read till 52. When you finish, start again." He looked me over once more. "Now, Shirley, you know, I suppose, that Christmas is coming. We are preparing a beautiful play. Most of the parts have been given out. But I still need a child with a strong voice, lots of stamina. Do you know what stamina is? You do? Smart kid. You know, I heard you read 'The Lord is my shepherd' in Assembly yesterday. I was very impressed. Wonderful delivery. Mrs. Jordan, your teacher, speaks highly of you. Now listen to me, Shirley Abramowitz, if you want to take the part and be in the play, repeat after me, 'I swear to work harder than I ever did before.'"

I looked to heaven and said at once, "Oh, I swear." I kissed my pinky and looked at God.

"That is an actor's life, my dear," he explained. "Like a soldier's, never tardy or disobedient to his general, the director. Everything," he said, "absolutely everything will depend on you."

That afternoon, all over the building, children scraped and scrubbed the turkeys and the sheaves of corn off the schoolroom windows. Goodbye Thanksgiving. The next morning a monitor brought red paper and green paper from the office. We made new shapes and hung them on the walls and glued them to the doors.

The teachers became happier and happier. Their heads were ringing like the bells of childhood. My best friend Evie was prone to evil, but she did not get a single demerit for whispering. We learned "Holy Night" without an error. "How wonderful!" said Miss Glacé, the student teacher. "To think that some of you don't even speak the language!" We learned "Deck the Halls" and "Hark! The Herald Angels". . . . They weren't ashamed and we weren't embarrassed.

Oh, but when my mother heard about it all, she said to my father: "Misha, you don't know what's going on there. Cramer is the head of the Tickets Committee."

"Who?" asked my father. "Cramer? Oh yes, an active woman."

"Active? Active has to have a reason. Listen," she said sadly, "I'm surprised to see my neighbors making tra-la-la for Christmas."

My father couldn't think of what to say to that. Then he decided: "You're in America! Clara, you wanted to come here. In Palestine the Arabs would be eating you alive. Europe you had pogroms. Argentina is full of Indians. Here you got Christmas. . . . Some joke, ha?"

"Very funny, Misha. What is becoming of you? If we came to a new country a long time ago to run away from the tyrants, and instead we fall into a creeping pogrom, that our children learn a lot of lies, so what's the joke? Ach, Misha, your idealism is going away."

"So is your sense of humor."

"That I never had, but idealism you had a lot of."

"I'm the same Misha Abramovitch, I didn't change an iota. Ask anyone."

"Only ask me," says my mama, may she rest in peace. "I got the answer."

Meanwhile the neighbors had to think of what to say too.

Marty's father said: "You know, he has a very important part, my boy."

"Mine also," said Mr. Sauerfeld.

"Not my boy!" said Mrs. Klieg. "I said to him no. The answer is no. When I say no! I mean no!"

The rabbi's wife said, "It's disgusting!" But no one listened to her. Under the narrow sky of God's great wisdom she wore a strawberry-blond wig.

Every day was noisy and full of experience. I was Right-hand Man. Mr. Hilton said: "How could I get along without you, Shirley?"

He said: "Your mother and father ought to get down on their knees every night and thank God for giving them a child like you."

He also said: "You're absolutely a pleasure to work with, my dear, dear child."

Sometimes he said: "For God's sakes, what did I do with the script? Shirley! Shirley! Find it."

Then I answered quietly: "Here it is, Mr. Hilton."

Once in a while, when he was very tired, he would cry out: "Shirley, I'm just tired of screaming at those kids. Will you tell Ira Pushkov not to come in till Lester points to that star the second time?"

Then I roared: "Ira Pushkov, what's the matter with you? Dope! Mr. Hilton told you five times already, don't come in till Lester points to the star the second time."

"Ach, Clara," my father asked, "what does she do there till six o'clock she can't even put the plates on the table?"

"Christmas," said my mother coldly.

"Ho! Ho!" my father said. "Christmas. What's the harm? After all, history teaches everyone. We learn from reading this is a holiday from pagan times also, candles, lights, even Chanukah. So we learn it's not altogether Christian. So if they think it's a private holiday, they're only ignorant, not patriotic. What belongs to history, belongs to all men. You want to go back to the Middle Ages? Is it better to shave your head with a secondhand razor? Does it hurt Shirley to learn to speak up? It does not. So maybe someday she won't live between the kitchen and the shop. She's not a fool."

I thank you, Papa, for your kindness. It is true about me to this day. I am foolish but I am not a fool.

That night my father kissed me and said with great interest in my career, "Shirley, tomorrow's your big day. Congrats."

"Save it," my mother said. Then she shut all the windows in order to prevent tonsillitis.

In the morning it snowed. On the street corner a tree had been decorated for us by a kind city administration. In order to miss its chilly shadow our neighbors walked three blocks east to buy a loaf of bread. The butcher pulled down black window shades to keep the colored lights from shining on his chickens. Oh, not me. On the way to school, with both hands I tossed it a kiss of tolerance. Poor thing, it was a stranger in Egypt.

I walked straight into the auditorium past the staring children. "Go ahead, Shirley!" said the monitors. Four boys, big for their age, had already started work as propmen and stagehands.

Mr. Hilton was very nervous. He was not even happy. Whatever he started to say ended in a sideward look of sadness. He sat slumped in the middle of the first row and asked me to help Miss Glacé. I did this, although she thought my voice too resonant and said, "Show-off!"

Parents began to arrive long before we were ready. They wanted to make a good impression. From among the yards of drapes I peeked out at the audience. I saw my embarrassed mother.

Ira, Lester, and Meyer were pasted to their beards by Miss Glacé. She almost forgot to thread the star on its wire, but I reminded her. I coughed a few times to clear my throat. Miss Glacé looked around and saw that everyone was in costume and on line waiting to play his part. She whispered, "All right . . ." Then:

Jackie Sauerfeld, the prettiest boy in first grade, parted the curtains with his skinny elbow and in a high voice sang out:

> *"Parents dear*
> *We are here*
> *To make a Christmas play in time.*
> *It we give*
> *In narrative*
> *And illustrate with pantomine."*

He disappeared.

My voice burst immediately from the wings to the great shock of Ira, Lester, and Meyer, who were waiting for it but were surprised all the same.

"I remember, I remember, the house where I was born . . ."

Miss Glacé yanked the curtain open and there it was, the house—an old hayloft, where Celia Kornbluh lay in the straw with Cindy Lou, her favorite doll. Ira, Lester, and Meyer moved slowly from the wings toward her, sometimes pointing to a moving star and sometimes ahead to Cindy Lou.

It was a long story and it was a sad story. I carefully pronounced all the words about my lonesome childhood, while little Eddie Braunstein wandered upstage and down with his shepherd's stick, looking for sheep. I brought up lonesomeness again, and not being understood at all except by some women everybody hated. Eddie was too small for that and Marty Groff took his place, wearing his father's prayer shawl. I announced twelve friends, and half the boys in the fourth grade gathered around Marty, who stood on an orange crate while my voice harangued. Sorrowful and loud, I declaimed about love and God and Man, but because of the terrible deceit of Abie Stock we came suddenly to a famous moment. Marty, whose remembering tongue I was, waited at the foot of the cross. He stared desperately at the audience. I groaned, "My God, my God, why hast thou forsaken me?" The soldiers who were sheiks grabbed poor Marty to pin him up to die, but he wrenched free, turned again to the audience, and spread his arms aloft to show despair and the end. I murmured at the top of my voice, "The rest is silence, but as everyone in this room, in this city—in this world—now knows, I shall have life eternal."

That night Mrs. Kornbluh visited our kitchen for a glass of tea.

"How's the virgin?" asked my father with a look of concern.

"For a man with a daughter, you got a fresh mouth, Abramovitch."

"Here," said my father kindly, "have some lemon, it'll sweeten your disposition."

They debated a little in Yiddish, then fell in a puddle of Russian and Polish. What I understood next was my father, who said, "Still and all, it was certainly a beautiful affair, you have to admit, introducing us to the beliefs of a different culture."

"Well, yes," said Mrs. Kornbluh. "The only thing . . . you know Charlie Turner—that cute boy in Celia's class—a couple others? They got very small parts or no part at all. In very bad taste, it seemed to me. After all, it's their religion."

"Ach," explained my mother, "what could Mr. Hilton do? They got very small voices: after all, why should they holler? The English language they know from the beginning by heart. They're blond like angels. You think it's so important they should get in the play? Christmas . . . the whole piece of goods . . . they own it."

I listened and listened until I couldn't listen any more. Too sleepy, I climbed out of bed and kneeled. I made a little church of my hands and said, "Hear, O Israel . . ." Then I called out in Yiddish, "Please, good night, good night. Ssh." My father said, "Ssh yourself," and slammed the kitchen door.

I was happy. I fell asleep at once. I had prayed for everybody: my talking family, cousins far away, passersby, and all the lonesome Christians. I expected to be heard. My voice was certainly the loudest.

1958

THE MAN TO SEND
RAIN CLOUDS

Leslie Marmon Silko

They found him under a big cottonwood tree. His Levi jacket and pants were faded light blue so that he had been easy to find. The big cottonwood tree stood apart from a small grove of winterbare cottonwoods which grew in the wide, sandy arroyo. He had been dead for a day or more, and the sheep had wandered and scattered up and down the arroyo. Leon and his brother-in-law, Ken, gathered the sheep and left them in the pen at the sheep camp before they returned to the cottonwood tree. Leon waited under the tree while Ken drove the truck through the deep sand to the edge of the arroyo. He squinted up at the sun and unzipped his jacket—it sure was hot for this time of year. But high and northwest the blue mountains were still in snow. Ken came sliding down the low, crumbling bank about fifty yards down, and he was bringing the red blanket.

Before they wrapped the old man, Leon took a piece of string out of his pocket and tied a small gray feather in the old man's long white hair. Ken gave him the paint. Across the brown wrinkled forehead he drew a streak of white and along the high cheekbones he drew a strip of blue paint. He paused and watched Ken throw pinches of corn meal and pollen into the wind that fluttered the small gray feather. Then Leon painted with yellow under the old man's broad nose, and finally, when he had painted green across the chin, he smiled.

"Send us rain clouds, Grandfather." They laid the bundle in the back of the pickup and covered it with a heavy tarp before they started back to the pueblo.

They turned off the highway onto the sandy pueblo road. Not long after they passed the store and post office they saw Father Paul's car coming toward them. When he recognized their faces he slowed his car and waved for them to stop. The young priest rolled down the car window.

"Did you find old Teofilo?" he asked loudly.

Leon stopped the truck. "Good morning, Father. We were just out to the sheep camp. Everything is OK now."

"Thank God for that. Teofilo is a very old man. You really shouldn't allow him to stay at the sheep camp alone."

"No, he won't do that anymore now."

"Well, I'm glad you understand. I hope I'll be seeing you at Mass this week—we missed you last Sunday. See if you can get old Teofilo to come with you." The priest smiled and waved at them as they drove away.

Louise and Teresa were waiting. The table was set for lunch, and the coffee was boiling on the black iron stove. Leon looked at Louise and then at Teresa.

"We found him under a cottonwood tree in the big arroyo near sheep camp. I guess he sat down to rest in the shade and never got up again." Leon walked toward the old man's bed. The red plaid shawl had been shaken and spread carefully over the bed, and a new brown flannel shirt and pair of stiff new Levi's were arranged neatly beside the pillow. Louise held the screen door open while Leon and Ken carried in the red blanket. He looked small and shriveled, and after they dressed him in the new shirt and pants he seemed more shrunken.

It was noontime now because the church bells rang the Angelus. They ate the beans with hot bread, and nobody said anything until after Teresa poured the coffee.

Ken stood up and put on his jacket. "I'll see about the gravediggers. Only the top layer of soil is frozen. I think it can be ready before dark."

Leon nodded his head and finished his coffee. After Ken had been gone for a while, the neighbors and clanspeople came quietly to embrace Teofilo's family and to leave food on the table because the gravediggers would come to eat when they were finished.

The sky in the west was full of pale yellow light. Louise stood outside with her hands in the pockets of Leon's green Army jacket that was too big for her. The funeral was over, and the old men had taken their candles and medicine bags and were gone. She waited until the body was laid into the pickup before she said anything to Leon. She touched his arm, and he noticed that her hands were still dusty from the corn meal that she had sprinkled around the old man. When she spoke, Leon could not hear her.

"What did you say? I didn't hear you."

"I said that I had been thinking about something."

"About what?"

"About the priest sprinkling holy water for Grandpa. So he won't be thirsty."

Leon stared at the new moccasins that Teofilo had made for the ceremonial dances in the summer. They were nearly hidden by the red blanket. It was getting colder, and the wind pushed dust down the narrow pueblo road. The sun was approaching the long mesa where it disappeared during the winter. Louise stood there shivering and watching his face. Then he zipped up his jacket and opened the truck door. "I'll see if he's there."

Ken stopped the pickup at the church, and Leon got out; and then Ken drove down the hill to the graveyard where people were waiting. Leon knocked at the old carved door with its symbols of the Lamb. While he waited he looked up at the twin bells from the king of Spain with the last sunlight pouring around them in their tower.

The priest opened the door and smiled when he saw who it was. "Come in! What brings you here this evening?"

The priest walked toward the kitchen, and Leon stood with his cap in his hand, playing with the earflaps and examining the living room—the brown sofa, the green armchair, and the brass lamp that hung down from the ceiling by links of chain. The priest dragged a chair out of the kitchen and offered it to Leon.

"No thank you, Father. I only came to ask you if you would bring your holy water to the graveyard."

The priest turned away from Leon and looked out the window at the patio full of shadows and the dining-room windows of the nuns' cloister across the patio. They curtains were heavy, and the light from within faintly penetrated; it was impossible to see the nuns inside eating supper. "Why didn't you tell me he was dead? I could have brought the Last Rites anyway."

Leon smiled. "It wasn't necessary, Father."

The priest stared down at his scuffed brown loafers and the worn hem of his cassock. "For a Christian burial it was necessary."

His voice was distant, and Leon thought that his blue eyes looked tired. "It's OK, Father, we just want him to have plenty of water."

The priest sank down into the green chair and picked up a glossy missionary magazine. He turned the colored pages full of lepers and pagans without looking at them.

"You know I can't do that, Leon. There should have been the Last Rites and a funeral Mass at the very least."

Leon put on his green cap and pulled the flaps down over his ears. "It's getting late, Father. I've got to go."

When Leon opened the door Father Paul stood up and said, "Wait." He left the room and came back wearing a long brown overcoat. He followed Leon out the door and across the churchyard to the adobe steps in front of the church. They both stooped to fit through the low adobe entrance. And when they started down the hill to the graveyard only half of the sun was visible above the mesa.

The priest approached the grave slowly, wondering how they managed to dig into the frozen ground; and then he remembered that this was New Mexico, and saw the pile of cold loose sand beside the hole. The people stood close to each other with little clouds of steam puffing from their faces. The priest looked at them and saw a pile of jackets, gloves, and scarves in the yellow, dry tumbleweeds that grew in the graveyard. He looked at the red blanket, not sure that Teofilo was so small, wondering if it wasn't some perverse Indian trick—something they did in March to ensure a good harvest—wondering if maybe old Teofilo was actually at sheep camp corraling the sheep for the night. But there he was, facing into a cold dry wind and squinting at the last sunlight, ready to bury a red wool blanket while the faces of his parishioners were in shadow with the last warmth of the sun on their backs.

His fingers were stiff, and it took him a long time to twist the lid off the holy water. Drops of water fell on the red blanket and soaked into dark icy spots. He sprinkled the grave and the water disappeared almost before it touched the dim, cold sand; it reminded him of something—he tried to remember what it was, because he thought if he could remember he might understand this. He sprinkled more water; he shook the container until it was empty, and the water fell through the light from sundown like August rain that fell while the sun was still shining, almost evaporating before it touched the wilted squash flowers.

The wind pulled at the priest's brown Franciscan robe and swirled away the corn meal and pollen that had been sprinkled on the blanket.

They lowered the bundle into the ground, and they didn't bother to untie the stiff pieces of new rope that were tied around the ends of the blanket. The sun was gone, and over on the highway the eastbound lane was full of headlights. The priest walked away slowly. Leon watched him climb the hill, and when he had disappeared within the tall, thick walls, Leon turned to look up at the high blue mountains in the deep snow that reflected a faint red light from the west. He felt good because it was finished, and he was happy about the sprinkling of the holy water; now the old man could send them big thunderclouds for sure.

1981

AMERICAN HORSE

Louise Erdrich

The woman sleeping on the cot in the woodshed was Albertine American Horse. The name was left over from her mother's short marriage. The boy was the son of the man she had loved and let go. Buddy was on the cot too, sitting on the edge because he'd been awake three hours watching out for his mother and besides, she took up the whole cot. Her feet hung over the edge, limp and brown as two trout. Her long arms reached out and slapped at things she saw in her dreams.

Buddy had been knocked awake out of hiding in a washing machine while herds of policemen with dogs searched through a large building with many tiny rooms. When the arm came down, Buddy screamed because it had a blue cuff and sharp silver buttons. "Tss," his mother mumbled, half awake, "wasn't nothing." But Buddy sat up after her breathing went deep again, and he watched.

There was something coming and he knew it.

It was coming from very far off but he had a picture of it in his mind. It was a large thing made of metal with many barbed hooks, points, and drag chains on it, something like a giant potato peeler that rolled out of the sky, scraping clouds down with it and jabbing or crushing everything that lay in its path on the ground.

Buddy watched his mother. If he woke her up, she would know what to do about the thing, but he thought he'd wait until he saw it for sure before he shook her. She was pretty, sleeping, and he liked knowing he could look at her as long and close up as he wanted. He took a strand of her hair and held it in his hands as if it was the rein to a delicate beast.

She was strong enough and could pull him along like the horse their name was.

Buddy had his mother's and his grandmother's name because his father had been a big mistake.

"They're all mistakes, even your father. But *you* are the best thing that ever happened to me."

That was what she said when he asked.

Even Kadie, the boyfriend crippled from being in a car wreck, was not as good a thing that happened to his mother as Buddy was. "He was a medium-sized mistake," she said. "He's hurt and I shouldn't even say that, but it's the truth." At the moment, Buddy knew that being the best thing in his mother's life, he was also the reason they were hiding from the cops.

He wanted to touch the satin roses sewed on her pink T-shirt, but he knew he shouldn't do that even in her sleep. If she woke up and found him touching the roses, she would say, "Quit that, Buddy." Sometimes she told him to stop hugging her like a gorilla. She never said that in the mean voice she used when he oppressed her, but when she said that he loosened up anyway.

There were times he felt like hugging her so hard and in such a special way that she would say to him, "Let's get married." There were also times he closed his eyes and wished that she would die, only a few times, but still it haunted him that his wish might come true. He and Uncle Lawrence would be left alone. Buddy wasn't worried, though, about his mother getting married to somebody else. She had said to her friend, Madonna, "All men suck," when she thought Buddy wasn't listening. He made an uncertain sound, and when they heard him they took him in their arms.

"Except for you, Buddy," his mother said. "All except for you and maybe Uncle Lawrence, although he's pushing it."

"The cops suck the worst, though," Buddy whispered to his mother's sleeping face, "because they're after us." He felt tired again, slumped down, and put his legs beneath the blanket. He closed his eyes and got the feeling that the cot was lifting up beneath him, that it was arching its canvas back and then traveling, traveling very fast and in the wrong direction for when he looked up he saw three of them were advancing to meet the great metal thing with hooks and barbs and all sorts of sharp equipment to catch their bodies and draw their blood. He heard its insides as it rushed toward them, purring softly like a powerful motor and then they were right in its shadow. He pulled the reins as hard as he could and the beast reared, lifting him. His mother clapped her hand across his mouth.

"Okay," she said. "Lay low. They're outside and they're gonna hunt."

She touched his shoulder and Buddy leaned over with her to look through the cracks in the boards.

They were out there all right, Albertine saw them. Two officers and that social worker woman. Vicki Koob. There had been no whistle, no dream, no voice to warn her that they were coming. There was only the crunching sound of cinders in the yard, the engine purring, the dust sifting off their car in a fine light brownish cloud and settling around them.

The three people came to a halt in their husk of metal—the car emblazoned with the North Dakota State Highway Patrol emblem which is the glowing profile of the Sioux policeman, Red Tomahawk, the one who killed Sitting Bull. Albertine gave Buddy the blanket and told him that he might have to wrap it around him and hide underneath the cot.

"We're gonna wait and see what they do." She took him in her lap and hunched her arms around him. "Don't you worry," she whispered against his ear. "Lawrence knows how to fool them."

Buddy didn't want to look at the car and the people. He felt his mother's heart beating beneath his ear so fast it seemed to push the satin roses in and out. He put his face to them carefully and breathed the deep, soft powdery woman smell of her. That smell was also in her little face cream bottles, in her brushes, and around the washbowl after she used it. The satin felt so unbearably smooth against his cheek that he had to press closer. She didn't push him away, like he expected, but hugged him still tighter until he felt as close as he had ever been to back inside her again where she said he came from. Within the smells of her things, her soft skin, and the satin of her roses, he closed his eyes then, and took his breaths softly and quickly with her heart.

They were out there, but they didn't dare get out of the car yet because of Lawrence's big, ragged dogs. Three of these dogs had loped up the dirt driveway with the car. They were rangy, alert, and bounced up and down on their cushioned paws like wolves. They didn't waste their energy barking, but positioned themselves quietly, one at either car door and the third in front of the bellied-out screen door to Uncle Lawrence's house. It was six in the morning but the wind was up already, blowing dust, ruffling their short moth-eaten coats. The big brown one on Vicki Koob's side had unusual black and white markings, stripes almost, like a hyena and he grinned at her, tongue out and teeth showing.

"Shoo!" Miss Koob opened her door with a quick jerk.

The brown dog sidestepped the door and jumped before her, tiptoeing. Its dirty white muzzle curled and its eyes crossed suddenly as if it were zeroing its cross-hair sights in on the exact place it would bite her. She ducked back and slammed the door.

"It's mean," she told Officer Brackett. He was printing out some type of form. The other officer, Harmony, a slow man, had not yet reacted to the car's halt. He had been sitting quietly in the back seat, but now he rolled down his window and with no change in expression unsnapped his holster and drew his pistol out and pointed it at the dog on his side. The dog smacked down on its belly, wiggled under the car and was out and around the back of the house before Harmony drew his gun back. The other dogs vanished with him. From wherever they had disappeared to they began to yap and howl, and the door to the low shoebox-style house fell open.

"Heya, what's going on?"

Uncle Lawrence put his head out the door and opened wide the one eye he had in working order. The eye bulged impossibly wider in outrage when he saw the police car. But the eyes of the two officers and Miss Vicki Koob were wide open too because they had never seen Uncle Lawrence in his sleeping get-up or, indeed, witnessed anything like it. For his ribs, which were cracked from a bad fall and still mending, Uncle Lawrence wore a thick white corset laced up the front with a striped sneakers' lace. His glass eye and his set of dentures were still out for the night so his face puckered here and there, around its absences and scars, like a damaged but fierce little cake. Although he had a few gray streaks now, Uncle Lawrence's hair was still thick, and because he wore a special contraption of elastic straps around his head every night, two oiled waves always crested on either side of his middle part. All of this would have been sufficient to astonish, even without the most striking part of his outfit—the smoking jacket. It was made of black satin and hung open around his corset, dragging a tasseled belt. Gold thread dragons struggled up the lapels and blasted their furry red breath around his neck. As Lawrence walked down the steps, he put his arms up in surrender and the gold tassels in the inner seams of his sleeves dropped into view.

"My heavens, what a sight." Vicki Koob was impressed.

"A character," apologized Officer Harmony.

As a tribal police officer who could be counted on to help out the State Patrol, Harmony thought he always had to explain about Indians or get twice as tough to show he did not favor them. He was slow-moving and shy but two jumps ahead of other people all the same, and now, as he watched Uncle Lawrence's splendid approach, he gazed speculatively at the torn and bulging pocket of the smoking jacket. Harmony had been inside Uncle Lawrence's house before and knew that above his draped orange-crate shelf of war medals a blue-black German luger was hung carefully in a net of flat-headed nails and fishing line. Thinking of this deadly exhibition, he got out of the car and shambled toward Lawrence with a dreamy little smile of welcome on his face. But when he searched Lawrence, he found that the bulging pocket held only the lonesome-looking dentures from Lawrence's empty jaw. They were still dripping denture polish.

"I had been cleaning them when you arrived," Uncle Lawrence explained with acid dignity.

He took the toothbrush from his other pocket and aimed it like a rifle.

"Quit that, you old idiot." Harmony tossed the toothbrush away. "For once you ain't done nothing. We came for your nephew."

Lawrence looked at Harmony with a faint air of puzzlement.

"Ma Frere, listen," threatened Harmony amiably, "those two white people in the car came to get him for the welfare. They got papers on your nephew that give them the right to take him."

"Papers?" Uncle Lawrence puffed out his deeply pitted cheeks. "Let me see them papers."

The two of them walked over to Vicki's side of the car and she pulled a copy of the court order from her purse. Lawrence put his teeth back in and adjusted them with busy workings of his jaw.

"Just a minute," he reached into his breast pocket as he bent close to Miss Vicki Koob. "I can't read these without I have in my eye."

He took the eye from his breast pocket delicately, and as he popped it into his face the social worker's mouth fell open in a consternated O.

"What is this," she cried in a little voice.

Uncle Lawrence looked at her mildly. The white glass of the eye was cold as lard. The black iris was strangely charged and menacing.

"He's nuts," Brackett huffed along the side of Vicki's neck. "Never mind him."

Vicki's hair had sweated down her nape in tiny corkscrews and some of the hairs were so long and dangly now that they disappeared into the zippered back of her dress. Brackett noticed this as he spoke into her ear. His face grew red and the backs of his hands prickled. He slid under the steering wheel and got out of the car. He walked around the hood to stand with Leo Harmony.

"We could take you in too," said Brackett roughly. Lawrence eyed the officers in what was taken as defiance. "If you don't cooperate, we'll get out the handcuffs," they warned.

One of Lawrence's arms was stiff and would not move until he'd rubbed it with witch hazel in the morning. His other arm worked fine though, and he stuck it out in front of Brackett.

"Get them handcuffs," he urged them. "Put me in a welfare home."

Brackett snapped one side of the handcuffs on Lawrence's good arm and the other to the handle of the police car.

"That's to hold you," he said. "We're wasting our time. Harmony, you search that little shed over by the tall grass and Miss Koob and myself will search the house."

"My rights is violated!" Lawrence shrieked suddenly. They ignored him. He tugged at the handcuff and thought of the good heavy file he kept in his tool box and the German luger oiled and ready but never loaded, because of Buddy, over his shelf. He should have used it on these bad ones, even Harmony in his big-time white man job. He wouldn't last long in that job anyway before somebody gave him what for.

"It's a damn scheme," said Uncle Lawrence, rattling his chains against the car. He looked over at the shed and thought maybe Albertine and Buddy had sneaked away before the car pulled into the yard. But he sagged, seeing Albertine move like a shadow within the boards. "Oh, it's all a damn scheme," he muttered again.

"I want to find that boy and salvage him," Vicki Koob explained to Officer Brackett as they walked into the house. "Look at his family life—the old man crazy as a bedbug, the mother intoxicated somewhere."

Brackett nodded, energetic, eager. He was a short hopeful redhead who failed consistently to win the hearts of women. Vicki Koob intrigued him. Now, as he watched, she pulled a tiny pen out of an ornamental clip on her blouse. It was attached to a retractable line that would suck the pen back, like a child eating one strand of spaghetti. Something about the pen on its line excited Brackett to the point of discomfort. His hand shook as he opened the screen door and stepped in, beckoning Miss Koob to follow.

They could see the house was empty at first glance. It was only one rectangular room with whitewashed walls and a little gas stove in the middle. They had already come through the cooking lean-to with the other stove and washstand and rusty old refrigerator. That refrigerator had nothing in it but some wrinkled potatoes and a package of turkey necks. Vicki Koob noted that in her perfect-bound notebook. The beds along the walls of the big room were covered with quilts that Albertine's mother, Sophie, had made from bits of old wool coats and pants that the Sisters sold in bundles at the mission. There was no one hiding beneath the beds. No one was under the little aluminum dinette table covered with a green oilcloth, or the soft brown wood chairs tucked up to it. One wall of the big room was filled with neatly stacked crates of things—old tools and springs and small half-dismantled appliances. Five or six television sets were stacked against the walls. Their control panels spewed colored wires and at least one was cracked all the way across. Only the topmost set, with coathanger antenna angled sensitively to catch the bounding signals around Little Shell, looked like it could possibly work.

Not one thing escaped Vicki Koob's trained and cataloguing gaze. She made note of the cupboard that held only commodity flour and coffee. The unsanitary tin oil drum beneath the kitchen window, full of empty surplus pork cans and beer bottles, caught her eye as did Uncle Lawrence's physical and mental deteriorations. She quickly described these "benchmarks of alcoholic dependency within the extended family of Woodrow (Buddy) American Horse" as she walked around the room with the little notebook open, pushed against her belly to steady it. Although Vicki had been there before, Albertine's presence had always made it difficult for her to take notes.

"Twice the maximum allowable space between door and threshold," she wrote now. "Probably no insulation. Two three-inch cracks in walls inadequately sealed with whitewashed mud." She made a mental note but could see no point in describing Lawrence's stuffed reclining chair that only reclined, the shadeless lamp with its plastic orchid in the bubble glass base, or the three-dimensional picture of Jesus that Lawrence had once demonstrated to her. When plugged in, lights rolled behind the water the Lord stood on so that he seemed to be strolling although he never actually went forward, of course, but only pushed the glowing waves behind him forever like a poor tame rat in a treadmill.

Brackett cleared his throat with a nervous rasp and touched Vicki's shoulder.

"What are you writing?"

She moved away and continued to scribble as if thoroughly absorbed in her work. "Officer Brackett displays an undue amount of interest in my person," she wrote. "Perhaps?"

He snatched playfully at the book, but she hugged it to her chest and moved off smiling. More curls had fallen, wetted to the base of her neck. Looking out the window, she sighed long and loud.

"All night on brush rollers for this. What a joke."

Brackett shoved his hands in his pockets. His mouth opened slightly, then shut with a small throttled cluck.

When Albertine saw Harmony ambling across the yard with his big brown thumbs in his belt, his placid smile, and his tiny black eyes moving back and forth, she put Buddy under the cot. Harmony stopped at the shed and stood quietly. He spread his arms to show her he hadn't drawn his big police gun.

"Ma Cousin," he said in the Michif dialect that people used if they were relatives or sometimes if they needed gas or a couple of dollars, "why don't you come out here and stop this foolishness?"

"I ain't your cousin," Albertine said. Anger boiled up in her suddenly. "I ain't related to no pigs."

She bit her lip and watched him through the cracks, circling, a big tan punching dummy with his boots full of sand so he never stayed down once he fell. He was empty inside, all stale air. But he knew how to get to her so much better than a white cop could. And now he was circling because he wasn't sure she didn't have a weapon, maybe a knife or the German luger that was the only thing that her father, Albert American Horse, had left his wife and daughter besides his name. Harmony knew that Albertine was a tall strong woman who took two big men to subdue when she didn't want to go in the drunk tank. She had hard hips, broad shoulders, and stood tall like her Sioux father, the American Horse who was killed threshing in Belle Prairie.

"I feel bad to have to do this," Harmony said to Albertine. "But for god-sakes, let's nobody get hurt. Come on out with the boy, why don't you? I know you got him in there."

Albertine did not give herself away this time. She let him wonder. Slowly and quietly she pulled her belt through its loops and wrapped it around and around her hand until only the big oval buckle with turquoise chunks shaped into a butterfly stuck out over her knuckles. Harmony was talking but she wasn't listening to what he said. She was listening to the pitch of his voice, the tone of it that would tighten or tremble at a certain moment when he decided to rush the shed. He kept talking slowly and reasonably, flexing the dialect from time to time, even mentioning her father.

"He was a damn good man. I don't care what they say, Albertine, I knew him."

Albertine looked at the stone butterfly that spread its wings across her fist. The wings looked light and cool, not heavy. It almost looked like it was ready to fly. Harmony wanted to get to Albertine through her father but she would not think about American Horse. She concentrated on the sky blue stone.

Yet the shape of the stone, the color, betrayed her.

She saw her father suddenly, bending at the grille of their old gray car. She was small then. The memory came from so long ago it seemed like a dream—narrowly focused, snapshot-clear. He was bending by the grille in the sun. It was hot summer. Wings of sweat, dark blue, spread across the back of his work shirt. He always wore soft blue shirts, the color of shade cloudier than this stone. His stiff hair had grown out of its short haircut and flopped over his forehead. When he stood up and turned away from the car, Albertine saw that he had a butterfly.

"It's dead," he told her. "Broke its wings and died on the grille."

She must have been five, maybe six, wearing one of the boy's T-shirts Mama bleached in Hilex-water. American Horse took the butterfly, a black and yellow one, and rubbed it on Albertine's collarbone and chest and arms until the color and the powder of it were blended into her skin.

"For grace," he said.

And Albertine had felt a strange lightening in her arms, in her chest, when he did this and said, "For grace." The way he said it, grace meant everything the butterfly was. The sharp delicate wings. The way it floated over grass. The way its wings seemed to breathe fanning in the sun. The wisdom of the way it blended into the flowers or changed into a leaf. In herself she felt the same kind of possibilities and closed her eyes almost in shock or pain, she felt so light and powerful at that moment.

Then her father had caught her and thrown her high into the air. She could not remember landing in his arms or landing at all. She only remembered the sun filling her eyes and the world tipping crazily behind her, out of sight.

"He was a damn good man," Harmony said again.

Albertine heard his starched uniform gathering before his boots hit the ground. Once, twice, three times. It took him four solid jumps to get right where she wanted him. She kicked the plank door open when he reached for the handle and the corner caught him on the jaw. He faltered, and Albertine hit him flat on the chin with the butterfly. She hit him so hard the shock of it went up her arm like a string pulled taut. Her fist opened, numb, and she let the belt unloop before she closed her hand on the tip end of it and sent the stone butterfly swooping out in a wide circle around her as if it was on the end of a leash. Harmony reeled backward as she walked toward him swinging the belt. She expected him to fall but he just stumbled. And then he took the gun from his hip.

Albertine let the belt go limp. She and Harmony stood within feet of each other, breathing. Each heard the human sound of air going in and out of the other person's lungs. Each read the face of the other as if deciphering letters carved into softly eroding veins of stone. Albertine saw the pattern of tiny arteries that age, drink, and hard living had blown to the surface of the man's face. She saw the spoked wheels of his iris and the arteries like tangled threads that sewed him up. She saw the living net of springs and tissue that held him together, and trapped him. She saw the random, intimate plan of his person.

She took a quick shallow breath and her face went strange and tight. She saw the black veins in the wings of the butterfly, roads burnt into a map, and then she was located somewhere in the net of veins and sinew that was the tragic complexity of the world so she did not see Officer Brackett and Vicki Koob rushing toward her, but felt them instead like flies caught in the same web, rocking it.

"Albertine!" Vicki Koob had stopped in the grass. Her voice was shrill and tight. "It's better this way, Albertine. We're going to help you."

Albertine straightened, threw her shoulders back. Her father's hand was on her chest and shoulders lightening her wonderfully. Then on wings of her father's hands, on dead butterfly wings. Albertine lifted into the air and flew toward the others. The light powerful feeling swept her up the way she had floated higher, seeing the grass below. It was her father throwing her up into the air and out of danger. Her arms opened for bullets but no bullets came. Harmony did not shoot. Instead, he raised his fist and brought it down hard on her head.

Albertine did not fall immediately, but stood in his arms a moment. Perhaps she gazed still farther back behind the covering of his face. Perhaps she was completely stunned and did not think as she sagged and fell. Her face rolled forward and hair covered her features, so it was impossible for Harmony to see with just what particular expression she gazed into the head-splitting wheel of light, or blackness, that overcame her.

Harmony turned the vehicle onto the gravel road that led back to town. He had convinced the other two that Albertine was more trouble than she was worth, and so they left her behind, and Lawrence too. He stood swearing in his cinder driveway as the car rolled out of sight. Buddy sat between the social worker and Officer Brackett. Vicki tried to hold Buddy fast and keep her arm down at the same time, for the words she'd screamed at Albertine had broken the seal of antiperspirant beneath her arms. She was sweating now as though she'd stored up an ocean inside of her. Sweat rolled down her back in a shallow river and pooled at her waist and between her breasts. A thin sheen of water came out on her forearms, her face. Vicki gave an irritated moan but Brackett seemed not to take notice, or take offense at least. Air-conditioned breezes were sweeping over the seat anyway, and very soon they would be comfortable. She smiled at Brackett over Buddy's head. The man grinned back. Buddy stirred. Vicki remembered the emergency chocolate bar she kept in her purse, fished it out, and offered it to Buddy. He did not react, so she closed his fingers over the package and peeled the paper off one end.

The car accelerated. Buddy felt the road and wheels pummeling each other and the rush of the heavy motor purring in high gear. Buddy knew that what he'd seen in his mind that morning, the thing coming out of the sky with barbs and chains, had hooked him. Somehow he was caught and held in the sour tin smell of the pale woman's armpit. Somehow he was pinned between their pounds of breathless flesh. He looked at the chocolate in his hand. He was squeezing the bar so hard that a thin brown trickle had melted down his arm. Automatically he put the bar in his mouth.

As he bit down he saw his mother very clearly, just as she had been when she carried him from the shed. She was stretched flat on the ground, on her stomach, and her arms were curled around her head as if in sleep. One leg was drawn up and it looked for all the world like she was running full tilt into the ground, as though she had been trying to pass into the earth, to bury herself, but at the last moment something had stopped her.

There was no blood on Albertine, but Buddy tasted blood now at the sight of her, for he bit down hard and cut his own lip. He ate the chocolate, every bit of it, tasting his mother's blood. And when he had the chocolate down inside him and all licked off his hands, he opened his mouth to say thank you to the woman, as his mother had taught him. But instead of thank you coming out he was astonished to hear a great rattling scream, and then another, rip out of him like pieces of his own body and whirl onto the sharp things all around him.

1983

EL PATRÓN

Nash Candelaria

My father-in-law's hierarchy is, in descending order: Dios, El Papá, y el patrón. It is to these that mere mortals bow, as in turn el patrón bows to El Papá, and El Papá bows to Dios.

God and the Pope are understandable enough. It's this el patrón, the boss, who causes most of our trouble. Whether it's the one who gives you work and for it pay, the lifeblood of hardworking little people—or others: our parents (fathers affectionately known as jefe, mothers known merely as mama, military commanders el capitán), or any of the big shots in the government el alcalde, el gobernador, el presidente and never forget la policía).

It was about some such el patrón trouble that Señor Martínez boarded the bus in San Diego and headed north toward L.A.—and us.

Since I was lecturing to a mid-afternoon summer school class at Southwestern U., my wife, Lola, picked up her father at the station. When I arrived home, they were sitting politely in the living room talking banalities: "Yes, it does look like rain. But if it doesn't rain, it might be sunny. If only the clouds would blow away."

Lola had that dangerous look on her face that usually made me start talking too fast and too long in hope of shifting her focus. It never worked. She'd sit there with a face like a brown-skinned kewpie doll whose expression was slowly turning into that of an angry maniac. When she could no longer stand it, she'd give her father a blast: "You never talk to me about anything important, you macho, chauvinist jumping bean!" Then it would escalate to nastiness from there.

But tonight it didn't get that far. As I entered Señor Martínez rose, dressed neatly in his one suit as for a wedding or a funeral, and politely shook my hand. Without so much as a glance at Lola, he said, "Why don't you go to the kitchen with the other women."

"There are no other women," Lola said coldly. She stood and belligerently received my kiss on the cheek before leaving.

Señor Martínez was oblivious to her reaction, sensing only the absence of "woman," at which he visibly relaxed and sat down.

"Rosca," he said, referring to me as he always did by my last name. "Tito is in trouble with the law."

His face struggled between anger and sadness, tinged with a crosscurrent of confusion. Tito was his pride and joy. His only son after four daughters. A twilight gift born to his wife at a time when he despaired of ever having a son, when their youngest daughter, Lola, was already ten years old and their oldest daughter twenty.

"He just finished his examinations at the state university. He was working this summer to save money for his second year when this terrible thing happened."

I could not in my wildest fantasies imagine young Vicente getting into any kind of trouble. He had always impressed me as a bright, polite young man who would inspire pride in any father. Even when he and old Vicente had quarreled about Tito going to college instead of working full-time, the old man had grudgingly come around to seeing the wisdom of it. But now. The law! I was stunned.

"Where is he?" I asked, imagining the nineteen-year-old in some filthy cell in the San Diego jail.

"I don't know." Then he looked over his shoulder toward the kitchen, as if to be certain no one was eavesdropping. "I think he went underground."

Underground! I had visions of drug-crazed revolutionary zealots. Bombs exploding in federal buildings. God knows what kind of madness.

"They're probably after him," he went on. Then he paused and stared at me as if trying to understand. "Tito always looked up to you and Lola. Of all the family it would be you he would try to contact. I want you to help me." Not help *Tito*, I thought, but help *me*.

I went to the cabinet for the bottle that I keep there for emergencies. I took a swallow to give me enough courage to ask the question. "What . . . did . . . he do?"

Señor Martínez stared limply at the glass in his hand. "You know," he said, "my father fought with Pancho Villa."

Jesus! I thought. If everyone who told me his father had fought with Pancho Villa was telling the truth, that army would have been big enough to conquer the world. Besides—what did this have to do with Tito?

"When my turn came," he continued, "I enlisted in the Marines at Camp Pendleton. Fought los Japonés in the Pacific." Finally he took a swallow of his drink and sat up stiffly as if at attention. "The men in our family have never shirked their duty!" He barked like the Marine corporal he had once been.

It slowly dawned on me what this was all about. It had been *the* topic all during summer school at Southwestern U. Registration for the draft. "No blood for Mideast oil!" the picket signs around the campus post office had shouted. "Boycott the Exxon army!"

"I should have never have let him go to college," Señor Martínez said. "That's where he gets such crazy radical ideas. From those rich college boys whose parents can buy them out of all kinds of trouble."

"So he didn't register," I said.

"The FBI is probably after him right now. It's a federal crime, you know. And the Canadians don't want draft dodgers either."

He took a deep swallow and polished off the rest of his drink in one gulp, putting the empty glass on the coffee table. There, his gesture seemed to say, now you know the worst.

Calmer now, he went on to tell me more. About the American Civil War; a greater percentage of Spanish-speaking men of New Mexico had joined the Union Army than the men from any other group in any other state in the Union. About the Rough Riders, including young Mexican-Americans, born on horseback; riding roughest of all over the Spanish in Cuba. About the War-to-End-All-Wars, where tough, skinny, brown-faced doughboys from farms in Texas, New Mexico, Arizona, Colorado, and California gave their all "Over There." About World War II, from the New Mexico National Guard captured at Bataan to the tough little Marines whom he was proud to fight alongside; man for man, there were more decorations for bravery among Mexican-Americans than among any other group in this war. Then Korea, where his younger brother toughed it out in the infantry. Finally Vietnam, where kids like his nephew, Pablo, got it in some silent, dark jungle trying to save a small country from the Communists.

By now he had lost his calm. There were tears in his eyes, partly from the pride he felt in this tradition of valor in war. But partly for something else, I thought. I could almost hear his son's reply to his impassioned call to duty: "Yes, Papá. So we could come back if we survived, to our jobs as busboys and ditch diggers: *that's* why I have to go to college. I don't want to go to the Middle East and fight and die for some oil company when you can't even afford to own a car. If the Russians invaded our country, I would defend it. If a robber broke into our house, I would fight him. If someone attacked you, I would save you. But this? No, Papá."

But now Tito was gone. God knows where. None of his three sisters in San Diego had seen him. Nor any of his friends in the neighborhood or school or work.

I could hear preparations for dinner from the kitchen. Señor Martínez and I had another tragito while Lolita and Junior ate their dinner early, the sounds of their childish voices piercing through the banging of pots and pans.

When Lola called me Emiliano instead of by my nickname, Pata, I knew we were in for a lousy meal. Everything her father disliked must have been served. It had taken some kind of perverse gourmet expending a tremendous amount of energy to fix such rotten food. There was that nothing white bread that presses together into a doughy flat mass instead of the tortillas Papá thrived on. There was a funny little salad with chopped garbage in it covered by a blob of imitation goo. There was no meat. No meat! Just all those sliced vegetables in a big bowl. Not ordinary vegetables like beans and potatoes and carrots, but funny, wiggly long things like wild grass . . . or worms. And quivering cubes of what must have been whale blubber.

Halfway through the meal, as Señor Martínez shuffled the food around on his plate like one of our kids resisting what was good for them, the doorbell rang.

"You'd better get that, Emiliano," Lola said, daring me to refuse by her tone of voice and dagger-throwing glance.

Who needs a fight? In a sense I was the lucky one because I could leave the table and that pot of mess-age. When I opened the door, a scraggly young man beamed a weak smile at me. "I hitchhiked from San Diego," Tito said.

Before I could move onto the steps and close the door behind me, he stumbled past me into the house. Tired as he was, he reacted instantly to seeing his father at the table. "You!" he shouted, then turned and bolted out the door.

Even tired he could run faster than I, so I hopped into the car and drove after him while Lola and Señor Martínez stood on the steps shouting words at me that I couldn't hear.

Two blocks later Tito finally climbed into the car after I bribed him with a promise of dinner at McDonald's. While his mouth was full, I tried to talk some sense into him, but to no avail. He was just as stubborn as his father and sister. Finally, I drove him to the International House on campus where the housing manager, who owed me a favor, found him an empty bed.

"You should have *made* him come back with you," Lola nagged at me that night.

"He doesn't want to be under the same roof with his father." From her thoughtful silence I knew that she understood and probably felt the same way herself. When I explained to her what it was all about—her father had said nothing to her—it looked for a moment as if she would get out of bed, stomp to the guest room, and heave Señor Martínez out into the street.

The next day seemed like an endless two-way shuttle between our house and the I House. First me. Then Lola. If Señor Martínez had had a car and could drive, he would have certainly followed each of us.

Our shuttle diplomacy finally wore them down. I could discern cracks in father's and son's immovable positions.

"Yes. Yes. I love my son."

"I love my father."

"I know. I know. Adults should be able to sit down and air their differences, no matter how wrong he is."

"Maybe tomorrow. Give me a break. But definitely not at mealtime. I can't eat while my stomach is churning."

The difficulty for me, as always, was in keeping my opinion to myself. Lola didn't have that problem. After all, they were her brother and father, so she felt free to say whatever she pleased.

"The plan is to get them to talk," I said to her. "If they can talk they can reach some kind of understanding."

"Papá has to be set straight," she said. "As usual, he's wrong, but he always insists it's someone else who messed things up."

"He doesn't want Tito to go to jail."

"That's Tito's choice!" Of course she was right; they were both right.

The summit meeting was set for the next afternoon. Since I had only one late morning lecture, I would pick up Tito, feed him a Big Mac or two, then bring him to the house. Lola would fix Señor Martínez some nice tortillas and chili, making up for that abominable dinner of the night before last. Well fed, with two chaperones mediating, we thought they could work something out.

When Tito and I walked into the house, my hope started to tremble and develop goose bumps. It was deathly silent and formal. Lola had that dangerous look on her face again. The macho, chauvinist jumping bean sat stiffly in his suit that looked like it had just been pressed—all shiny and sharply creased, unapproachable and potentially cutting, an inanimate warning of what lay behind Señor Martínez's stone face.

Tito and I sat across from the sofa and faced them. Or rather I faced them. Both Tito and Señor Martínez were looking off at an angle from each other, not daring to touch glances. I smiled, but no one acknowledged it so I gave it up. Then Lola broke the silence.

"What this needs is a woman's point-of-view," she began.

That's all Señor Martínez needed. The blast his eyes shot at her left her open-mouthed and silent as he interrupted. "I don't want you to go to jail!" He was looking at Lola, but he meant Tito.

Tito's response was barely audible, and I detected a trembling in his voice. "You'd rather I got killed on some Arabian desert," he said.

The stone face cracked. For a moment it looked as if Señor Martínez would burst into tears. He turned his puzzled face from Lola toward his son. "No," he said. "Is that what you think?" Then, when Tito did not answer, he said, "You're my only son, and damn it! Sons are supposed to obey their fathers!"

"El patrón, El Papá, and Dios," Tito said with a trace of bitterness.

But Lola could be denied no longer. "Papá, how old were you when you left Mexico for the U.S.?" She didn't expect an answer, so didn't give him time to reply. "Sixteen, wasn't it? And what did your father say?"

Thank God that smart-ass smile of hers was turned away from her father. She knew she had him, and he knew it too, but he didn't need her smirk to remind him of it.

He sighed. The look on his face showed that sometimes memories were best forgotten. When he shook his head but did not speak, Lola went on. She too had seen her father's reaction, and her voice lost its hard edge and became more sympathetic.

"He disowned you, didn't he? Grandpa disowned you. Called you a traitor to your own country. A deserter when things got tough."

"I did not intend to stay in Mexico and starve," he said. He looked around at us one by one as if he had to justify himself. "He eventually came to Los Estados Unidos himself. He and Mamá died in that house in San Diego."

"What did you think when Grandpa did that to you?"

No answer was necessary. "Can't you see, Papá?" Lola pleaded, meaning him and Tito. He could see.

Meanwhile Tito had been watching his father as if he had never seen him before. I guess only the older children had heard Papá's story of how he left Mexico.

"I don't intend to go to jail, Papá," Tito said, "I just have to take a stand along with thousands of others. In the past old men started wars in which young men died in order to preserve old men's comforts. It just has to stop. There's never been a war without a draft. Never a draft without registration. And this one is nothing but craziness by el patrón in Washington, D.C. If enough of us protest, maybe he'll get the message."

"They almost declared it unconstitutional," I said. "They may yet."

"Because they aren't signing women," Papá said in disgust. But from the look on Lola's face, I'd pick her over him in any war.

"If they come after me, I'll register," Tito said. "But in the meantime I have to take this stand."

There. It was out. They had had their talk in spite of their disagreements.

"He's nineteen," Lola said. "Old enough to run his own life."

Señor Martínez was all talked out. He slumped against the back of the sofa. Even the creases in his trousers seemed to have sagged. Tito looked at his sister, and his face brightened.

"Papá," Tito said. "I . . . I'd like to go home, if you want me to."

On Papá's puzzled face I imagined I could read the words: "My father fought with Pancho Villa." But it was no longer an accusation, only a simple statement of fact. Who knows what takes more courage — to fight or not to fight?

"There's a bus at four o'clock," Señor Martínez said.

Later I drove them in silence to the station. Though it felt awkward, it wasn't a bad silence. There are more important ways to speak than with words, and I could feel that sitting shoulder to shoulder beside me, father and son had reached some accord.

Papá still believed in el patrón, El Papá, and Dios. What I hoped they now saw was that Tito did too. Only in his case, conscience overrode el patrón, maybe even El Papá. In times past, popes too declared holy wars that violated conscience. For Tito, conscience was the same as Dios. And I saw in their uneasy truce that love overrode their differences.

I shook their hands as they boarded the bus, and watched the two similar faces, one old, one young, smile sadly at me through the window as the Greyhound pulled away.

When I got back home, Junior and Lolita were squabbling over what channel to watch on TV. I rolled my eyes in exasperation, ready to holler at them, but Lola spoke up first.

"I'm glad Papá got straightened out. The hardest thing for parents with their children is to let go."

Yeah, I started to say, but she stuck her head into the other room and told Junior and Lolita to stop quarreling or they were going to get it.

1988

THANK GOD FOR THE JEWS

Tahira Naqvi

On a morning like any other August morning with its promising bright sunshine, its late summer aura of capricious warmth so unlike the faithful, torrid heat of August mornings in Lahore, Ali said, "Kamal is bringing his mother over for dinner."

"Aunt Sakina? When?" Fatima asked, forgetting how many teabags she had dropped into the small white Corningware teapot. Five would be too many and three not enough. Peering into the pot she counted: three bags were clearly visible, the fourth could be an illusion. She tore off a Tetley tag and threw an extra one in. The water gurgled with a familiar sound as she poured it into the pot and steam rose to embrace her face warmly. "But she said she was going to be in New Jersey for another week."

"She must have changed her mind. Anyway, Kamal called me at the hospital and I told him Sunday would be fine." Ali was speaking from the bedroom. He had this knack of starting a serious conversation with Fatima when he was not in the same room with her.

Fatima wasn't sure whether she should be glad at the prospect of seeing her cousin who got along well with Ali, excited at the thought of meeting Aunt Sakina who would have more gossip about the relatives from Lahore, or upset that Ali hadn't checked with her before giving Kamal the okay for dinner. After all, preparations had to be made.

The unwashed plates in the sink and the two Farberware pots crusty with over-cooked spices from last night's supper fed her aggravation. The disarray on the cramped kitchen counters—bottles of the baby's food, assorted Beech-Nut juices, and cans of formula huddling together as if seeking safety in numbers—didn't help either. After Ali had left for the hospital around eleven to attend to an emergency, she had settled comfortably on the sofa in the living room to watch the *Eleven o'Clock Movie* on channel 9. *The Snows of Kilimanjaro.* Gregory Peck. The man who had invaded her daydreams many an afternoon when she was a teenager. Even now he smiled and she wished she were Ava Gardner. Nobody's going to come and inspect my kitchen at this hour of the night. She had waved the dishes away.

Leaving the tea to steep under the only tea cozy she possessed, Fatima walked into bedroom determined to have it out with her husband. She found him thrashing through a drawer, looking for clean underwear.

"But that's the day after tomorrow," she said, picking up his white cotton pajama and kurta from the bedroom floor with one hand, his discarded socks with the other.

"Yes," Ali replied. Now he was rummaging for socks.

He's already beside a patient, no doubt. Taking a pulse. The round ends of the stethoscope snug into the little cavities of his ears. Playing God with such a casual air, nonchalantly. A face she does not know, does not understand. She turned to straighten the bedsheets and he was gone from there.

"And she'll eat only halal meat!" Fatima ran after him. In the kitchen now, he was pouring himself a cup of tea.

"We don't have any in the freezer?" he asked, seemingly unmoved by the panic in her voice. Uf! Gulping tea again. It's not mango squash. Sip it, slowly, savor it. He was pouring a second cup already. His long, dark brows formed short uneven waves over his nose as he picked up a piece of toast and crunched it noisily.

"Of course we don't. We bought a couple of pounds from Halal Meats in Queens when we were there last month to see *Mughal-e-Azam.* Remember? It's all gone."

Sometimes Fatima and Ali bought halal meat, meat prepared the Islamic way, from one of the many Pakistani shops that ubiquitously lined Jackson Boulevard in Queens. Every once in a while they also ventured into the small, busy place called Halal Meats on Lexington in Manhattan. But for the most part it was beef, chicken, and lamb from Grand Union for them. Packed in shiny, neat packages that led Fatima to believe that someone had gone through a great deal of trouble to give the shoppers only the best, the meat always had a fresh, clean color, and the packages were so easy to pick up and throw into the shopping cart. Whenever Fatima remembered to, she recited, "There is no God but Allah and Muhammad is his

Prophet" while she rinsed the meat with cold water. Remembering to undertake that little ritual made her feel pious and wise beyond her years.

"It's not like we're giving her pork," she protested. "Once we've said the kalima while washing the meat, it's okay, isn't it? Aba said that's all the Quran requires us to do. That's all I do. All this nonsense about bleeding the animal, or pronouncing the name of Allah at the time the poor animal is put to the knife—it's ridiculous!" Frustration hung in her head like the beginnings of a migraine and she realized she hadn't had any tea yet; also, this wasn't a good time to engage her husband in a discussion about rational approaches to the preparation of halal meat.

He finished his second cup of tea and vigorously rubbed down the corners of his moustache with a paper napkin. "Your father's a rationalist, Fatima. But we both know there's more to Islam than what's in the Quran. Anyway, that's not the point. In Pakistan you ate only halal, didn't you?"

"Yes, but this is different..." Why, he might ask. She knew why, but there wasn't enough time to explain.

He was saying, "Well, some people are more conservative; they don't want to compromise. They'll eat halal wherever they go."

"I know," Fatima said glumly.

"Anyway, what about fish?" he asked. They were standing in the foyer now, his hand reaching for the door knob. Was he going to kiss her or was he going to forget?

"Fish?" She leaned over to brush a tiny crumb that dangled invitingly from his dark, thick moustache.

True, fish was not subject to the same stringent laws as other types of meat. It had probably been spared because there was no blood to contend with; what else could it be? But Fatima had such bad luck with fish, always. Whenever she tried to fry fillets dripped in gram flour batter, invariably the fish and the batter separated as soon as the piece was dropped into hot oil. Curried fish suffered a worse fate: no sooner had she turned the cubed chunks over than the chunks disintegrated, becoming mush. Usually she just threw everything into the trash and started all over again with something else. If her mother saw her, she would cringe at her wastefulness.

"Fish?" She looked at Ali to make sure he wasn't teasing. "In the first place I don't make very good fish, and in the second place how many kinds of fish are we going to serve? Who knows, maybe Aunt Sakina hates fish."

"Maybe not. Try the fish. It's never that bad." Surely he is desperate. He doesn't want to upset Aunt Sakina. And what tales she might take back home. They've already forgotten their ways. Imagine not eating halal. What will it be next, pork?

"Okay," Fatima said, "I'll try the fish. But don't blame me if it's a disaster. I hope they have some bluefish at Grand Union, that's the only kind that works well with curry. I'm not going to try the frying recipe."

"All right, all right. And don't forget to use some oregano." He glanced at the clock on the living room wall, tweaked her cheek and was out of the door with a smile and a "Bye," before she could ask, "But what do you know about oregano?" It probably reminded him of something his mother used in her fish recipe, perhaps ajwain. He had forgotten to kiss her.

Left alone, Fatima dawdled in the foyer as if she were a guest in her own home. Looking down at her feet she observed the scuff marks made by Haider's walker on the yellow and beige linoleum; looking above she glanced upon the throng of cobwebs that looped with silken finesse in two corners of the white ceiling. She must do some cleaning this afternoon. Her son, Haider, impervious to the trivialities and banalities of custom and habit gone awry in Westchester County, was still asleep. From the kitchen, tea beckoned as a deliverer's promise would. All else must wait and be taken care of after this one cup of Tetley tea, Tetley which had become their choice after a protracted dalliance with the likes of Earl Grey and other "Indian" teas; the Americans had done something right with tea after all.

With the cup cradled in her palm, she came into the living room, pulled down the shades from force of habit to shut out the bright morning sun, turned on the TV, and sat down on the settee. The warmth from the first gulp slunk down her throat and made her feel good, sure of herself. She took another sip and crossed her legs. The *Eight o'Clock News* had just begun. The Jews and Muslims were fighting again in the Middle East. A tall, handsome reporter, who, with his upturned coat collar and straw-colored, wind-swept hair, seemed to belong in an ad for Burberry's in *The New Yorker*, was saying something about "recent acts of terrorism" in a faraway voice. An Israeli school bus had been bombed. Its carcass sat forlornly on a hill; some children had been killed, some injured; a girl, who was perhaps four years older than Haider, ran away wildly from the soldier who scrambled after her to hold her. The camera moved abruptly to another scene before he caught up with her. An Arab village in ruins. Nearly all the houses had been demolished, the survivors of the attack moving in slow motion like zombies. An old woman whose face looked familiar squatted before a crumbled, hollowed-out dwelling and cried without restraint, her mouth hanging open in a grotesque caricature of a smile.

During a commercial break Fatima decided to make a list so she wouldn't forget anything when Ali took her to Grand Union this evening. She wrote down "oregano." *Now I know, the old woman in the news. Crying in despair. She resembled Aunt Sakina. All old women look the same at some point, I suppose.*

Aunt Sakina was Fatima's father's cousin. Last summer, when Fatima visited her in Pakistan, Aunt Sakina confessed secretively that she missed Kamal terribly, especially now that she had lost her husband and her daughter was also married. "A daughter-in-law will make this house come to life again," she said in a quavering voice. She confessed Kamal had been begging her to come to America for a visit. Her eyes, set far into their sockets and glazed over with age, filled quickly with tears. "But don't say anything to him," she entreated, wiping with a corner of her white dupatta the moisture that had trickled thickly over her grooved, leathery cheeks. "You must come then, Auntie," Fatima had said. "Why are you so reluctant to come?" Fatima knew Aunt Sakina was biding her time, waiting until Kamal begged. *Her mother would do the same. Mothers like their grown sons to beg, to fawn over them. That's because they usually ignore them altogether. Stay away.*

Still feeling uncomfortable about fish, Fatima put an oversized question mark after "Boston Blue" on the grocery list. A segment about Jerusalem was on the air. The handsome, roving reporter, unchanged in his appearance, disconnected still from his surroundings, was speaking in a crisp accent that wasn't anything like what she heard on the streets in New York or Westville: "Jerusalem, named Yeroshalayim by the Jews and Bayt al Mugaddas by the Muslims, is a city which the Muslims want as much as the Jews and Christians do." Jewish pilgrims stood in grave postures at the Wailing Wall, called the Wall of Suleiman by the Arabs, she remembered from her high school history book. Suddenly she felt guilty for not having offered prayers or read the Quran in what was surely a very long time. *If Aunt Sakina found out she had been so lazy, she'd certainly tell her a thing or two.* Just then the muezzin's call to prayer, the azan, arose and rang like a siren song, insinuating its way into the murmurings of Hebrew prayer and the hubbub of the bazaars. *Poor King Hussein. So debonair, so patient. An unhappy monarch who had let Jerusalem slip from his hands.*

"O Fab, we're glad / There's lemon-freshened borax in you!" Remembering she was out of laundry detergent, she jotted down "detergent—Fab" on her list.

But why not consult the Quran anyway? That was the spring of Islamic law. The source.

She leafed through the Pickthall translation. "*The Cow:* 2:168. Believers, eat of the wholesome things with which we have provided you. . . . He has forbidden you carrion, blood, and the flesh of swine; also any flesh that is consecrated other than in the name of Allah."

So, the issue was no issue at all. The commandment clear-cut. But will Aunt Sakina accede to such an argument? No. We're all creatures of custom and habit.

At that moment Fatima envied the women in Lahore who didn't have to torment themselves with such absurd doubts when they were planning a feast for a husband's friend's mother. Their concern would be with the menu, with having enough sugar and milk for kheer, with getting to the market early so that the best portions of mutton or beef could be had, with finding a plump chicken for a reasonable price, and with securing enough ice for drinking water. How her cousin Zenab would laugh if she were to see her now. How she would snicker if she knew that Fatima's dinner party was preceded by scholarly research on the matter of halal meat. Fatima blushed at her own foolishness. But Zenab wasn't around to see her in her moment of weakness. She was alone, and Haider was too young to know anything.

She riffled through the paperback Quran. On page 357 she read: "Women shall have rights similar to those exercised by men, although men have a status above women. Allah is mighty and wise." Adeeba, she thought. Why hadn't she thought of Adeeba before?

Adeeba knew most things there were to know. She and her husband, a second year resident, had been in the U.S. a little longer than Fatima and Ali and many others. Often Fatima had heard Samina, or one of the other Pakistani wives say in a tone of absolute trust, "Ask Adeeba, she'll know." As a matter of fact Samina was getting to be rather good herself. Already adept at keeping a close watch on sales and where to buy the best 220-volt appliances for taking back to Pakistan as gifts, she was also developing an eye for eligible young women who might be suitable for the Pakistani bachelors at Westville Hospital.

However, Adeeba wasn't home, which didn't surprise Fatima at all; Adeeba was rarely to be found at home. After all, how could she know so much if she didn't window-shop and hunt for bargains early in the day, before shoppers crowded the stores looking for discounts? Fatima decided to try Samina instead and dialed her number. After a few rings Samina's sluggish "Hallo" greeted her. Since Samina didn't have any children, there was a silent agreement among the women that she be allowed to sleep late. Fatima apologized for having woken her.

"Don't be silly," Samina said sleepily. "I was awake, just lying down." For a whole minute she and Fatima chatted energetically about the fabric sale at Singer's. "Don't forget to look over the dollar-a-yard table at the far end of the shop," Samina advised.

"No, I won't," Fatima acceded hastily. Who cares about that, and anyway, I've already done my fabric shopping for the month. Now, how to do this. "By the way, Samina, is there any halal meat available around here?" Fatima finally asked. She knew by asking this she had condemned herself; surely her ignorance would now be evident to all.

"Halal? Are you joking? We always get ours from Queens. Are you out?"

"Yes," Fatima said, playing with her wedding band. "And I need some desperately. We're having company on Sunday and there's no time to go to New York." Will she offer me some of hers? I don't think so, unless I ask. I wish she had offered. One packet would make all the difference.

"What about kosher?" Samina's voice rang out with authority.

"Kosher?" Fatima queried inanely. The word had a familiar ring, like the name of an acquaintance whose face one can't place. Oh my God! Yes! I've seen it on hot dog labels at Grand Union. Jewish, surely. But what does Samina mean? Afraid of exposing her ignorance further and fully, Fatima didn't elaborate her question. Samina loved to talk, so she let her.

"Yes, kosher chicken," Samina was saying, seemingly undisturbed by Fatima's perplexity on the matter of kosher. "There's kosher hot dogs too, and all the meat's prepared just like ours. They recite God's name before slaughtering the animal and bleed the animal afterward."

They? Fatima winced at her own stupidity.

"Anyway, what's kosher is okay for us." Samina spoke with greater authority than before. Fatima could picture her at the other end, her small, beady eyes shining, her face flushed, the expression on it triumphant with the knowledge that she had offered valuable advice, that she could now move closer to Adeeba's league.

"Does Adeeba use kosher too?" I have to be sure. Know everything. What if Aunt Sakina decides to quiz me.

"Of course. We all do."

All? Ohhhh. . . .

"Especially in the winter. It's difficult to make frequent trips to New York when the weather's bad, you know. Thank God for the Jews."

"Yes." Fatima's voice floundered.

"Pathmark always has a good supply." Samina volunteered more information quickly.

Should I put my trust wholly in Samina's word? After all, she's only a fledging disciple. And isn't a Jewish prayer different from a Muslim prayer?

Chamber's Twentieth Century Dictionary had traveled with her from Pakistan, one of the few books Fatima had brought along with her. Inside, on the first blank page, was her brother's name, below hers, while her sister's girlish flourish lurched precariously immediately under his. The pages of the dictionary were sere, curling at the edges, and brittle. Gingerly she worked on the top right corner of each page until she had it secure between her forefinger and thumb. Then she lifted it slowly, with care. Twice she went through J and twice, arriving at L, missed K. Finally she wet a finger, slowly leafed this time, found "junk" and, running a finger down, came to "kosher" in the column at the left. Right under "Koran." It said: "pure, clean according to the Jewish ordinances—as of meat killed and prepared by Jews. [Hebrew, from *yashar*, to be right]."

Fatima crossed out "Boston Blue" on her grocery list and put down "kosher chicken—Pathmark" instead. The segment on fighting in the Middle East was winding down. A mist had settled over Jerusalem. The prayer shawls and *abas* appeared like dabs of white paint on a dark canvas. The handsome roving reporter was nowhere in sight. Fatima switched the channel to PBS so that Haider, who was now awake and whimpering, could watch "Sesame Street."

The rest of the day dragged. At eleven she watched Hitchcock's *To Catch a Thief* on channel 9. When Haider dozed off around two, she also took a nap during which she dreamt she and Aunt Sakina were roaming around in an Arab village looking for oregano. In the dream she led her aunt by her arm through a maze of dust-ridden streets bright with torrid sunshine, encountering on her way her son who ran from her as if she were a stranger. When she woke up she was sweating and her throat was dry. Just as she was about to get up from the bed to get a drink of water she heard Ali's key turn in the front door.

Breathless with excitement, she left her bed and ran to the door. No sooner had Ali stepped into the foyer than she said, "Ali, our troubles are over. Thank God for the Jews!"

1991

GUSSUK

Mei Mei Evans

The float plane touched down so smoothly that it felt to Lucy as though the surface of the lake had risen to meet it. From below, the encircling mountains seemed more imposing than ever. The pilot taxied steadily across the reflection of the snow-flecked peaks toward the cluster of houses that formed the village of Kigiak, and Lucy saw a group of people waiting for them on the narrow beach.

As she clambered out of the cockpit and stepped onto the flimsy aluminum wing, she could see that her welcoming committee was mostly women. Many of them had brightly colored scarves tied over their long black hair, and all of them wore pants. Lucy felt conspicuous suddenly in her khaki skirt and tasseled loafers—clothes she had worn more to make a good impression than because she liked them. The women giggled and looked away when she tried to meet their eyes, which added to Lucy's feeling of self-consciousness.

A smooth-faced young man stepped forward and offered to help her down. Their eyes met. Lucy smiled. His brows furrowed in a frown, and then he too looked away, but she thought from the way he held onto her hand a moment longer than necessary that he, too, had noticed their resemblance to each other.

She stepped down. He released her hand and murmured words she couldn't make out in a soft monotone. At first Lucy thought she hadn't understood him because her ears were still vibrating with the drone of the plane, but when he repeated his question, she realized that he must be speaking to her in Yup'ik.

"My name is Robert," he said in English, dropping his eyes again. "I thought you were Eskimo."

"Lucy," she said, extending her hand. "I'm Chinese-American. My grandmother was Chinese."

He studied her closely. His eyes were very intense. He was a handsome man, his dark skin so smooth that it seemed to shine. This time it was she who looked away.

Then the women and children overcame their shyness and pressed forward. Robert introduced his wife, a tall stringy woman, and their fat-cheeked baby. The villagers formed a procession to carry Lucy's luggage up the path to the trailer that was to be her office and home. Behind her, Lucy heard the plane's motor start up again as it took off across the water, gaining speed. She was really on her own now, she thought. Sink or swim.

From the air, the houses that dotted the shoreline of Lake Kigiak looked as though they'd been shaken out like dice and come to rest in loose clusters. From the ground, however, Lucy could see that most of the structures were government-issue: pre-fabricated wooden boxes on poorly constructed foundations. The village looked shabby to her, and the huge mountains that rose on all sides of the lake were intimidating: dormant creatures that might awaken at a moment's notice and send the houses tumbling into the water as carelessly as children's blocks on a piece of suddenly stretched fabric. But the mountains were also greener and more lush than anything she had been led to expect about the "far, frozen north," and it was actually warm here, almost hot. The mountainsides reflected the scattered sunlight, playing back every nuance of light and shadow.

Her welcoming committee left her at the door of the trailer. Lucy was grateful for the privacy; she needed to absorb this rush of impressions.

She'd made it. She was here, in the Alaskan "bush," away from the east coast and her own people for the very first time in her life. It was, in fact, a summer of firsts for her: just graduated from college, out here in this remote Eskimo village in western Alaska to undertake her first real job, as the region's new public health nurse. She'd been told that she'd probably experience "culture shock" the first few weeks, but right now she was more concerned about being accepted. She hoped that looking like a Native would work to her advantage.

The health department people in Anchorage had let her know in various ways—some making it sound like a warning, others like a joke—that she would very likely be mistaken for a Native. Now that she was out here, face to face, she felt a little overwhelmed by the similarity her skin coloring and features bore to theirs.

The trailer was furnished with tacky furniture, cheap acetate curtains and synthetic carpeting, but Lucy got the feeling that it was probably a cut above the villagers' housing, and it was hers, rent-free, courtesy of the state. She hadn't done too badly for herself on her very first job.

She carried her suitcases down the hall to the bedroom, and then returned to the front, which was one long room containing both kitchen and office. She lay her briefcase on the formica-topped cabinet, and then the two lower ones, in turn. Each contained rows of neatly labeled files, which Lucy flipped through. Everything seemed to be in order. She wondered again why her predecessor had left so abruptly. She had asked that question at the main office, and although no one seemed to know, neither had they seemed particularly concerned.

Lucy pulled open the drawers in the kitchen counter. The top one held a plastic silverware tray containing an assortment of cutlery. The bottom drawer, the deep one, held all kinds of medical paraphernalia: two blood pressure cuffs, stethoscope, bottles of medicine, disposable syringes. Feeling more comfortable, Lucy smiled and slid the drawer shut.

There was a soft tapping at the door, and muffled voices. She opened it to find two of the smaller children, a boy and a girl.

"Hello," she said. "Would you like to come in?"

The children looked at their feet and then at each other. Finally, the little boy mumbled towards the floor, "You want to come outside?"

"I'd like that. Let me change into some dungarees."

"Dungarees?"

"Blue jeans."

"Levi's?"

"Levi's."

They all laughed, and when she went down the hallway to change her clothes, the children followed her. They stood side by side in front of the double bed, watching her undress. The boy's name was Amos, his sister's Mary. Mary sucked her thumb with a serious expression and left the talking to her brother.

They led Lucy around the village, making special mention of the houses that had television. Theirs didn't. Three husky-type dogs with matted fur followed them around, even coming inside the schoolhouse. Amos assured her it was all right for them to be in there when Lucy tried to shoo them out. She asked him if they were sled dogs.

"What's that?"

Lucy had never seen a pool table in a schoolhouse before. Outside again, the kids pointed out the old Russian Orthodox church, perched peak-roofed and solitary on the upper hillside, its three-barred cross askew. Lucy wanted to take a closer look, but the kids were anxious to go down to the water.

By now Mary had a tight grip on Lucy's hand. Lucy stood beside her on the little beach and gazed out across the water. With the village at their backs, there was nothing in the vista to indicate what year, or even century, this was. The lake stretched for miles, flat and expansive, surrounded by mountains. The slopes themselves were mottled with sunlight and new growth. Lucy noticed a single house in a cleft in the hills, approximately a mile to the left.

"Who lives over there?" she asked.

"Abners," Amos said.

Mary spoke in her little voice. *"Gussuks."*

"Gussuks?"

"Missionaries," Amos explained.

The kids laughed at the puzzled look on Lucy's face. Amos ran around collecting pebbles and sticks from the shore, which he flung as hard as he could into the glassy water.

Later in the evening, although it was still fully light outside, Lucy was going through her files, making occasional notes on a yellow legal tablet. She was so absorbed in her work that the knock on the door startled her. When she opened it, Robert smiled at her from behind mirror sunglasses. Lucy had always disliked those glasses because they took unfair advantage.

"How's it going?" he asked.

"Fine. I think I'm going to like it here."

Amos and Mary came running up the path just then, jostling Robert as they pushed past him into the trailer. Amos spoke breathlessly; Mary reached for Lucy's hand.

"Mom says you eat with us."

"Looks like you're pretty popular with my niece and nephew already," Robert said, grinning.

"You're their uncle?"

"Their mom and my wife, they're sisters." He waved a hand as he walked down the trail.

Mercy was scraping Hamburger Helper around with some ground beef in an electric skillet when they arrived. She welcomed Lucy with a wide, mostly toothless, smile. "Hi, nurse!"

The house was cramped and cluttered. It smelled of food and cooking and the closeness of people in a small space. Lucy sat down stiffly at a rickety metal table, the surface of which was strewn with magazines, empty soda cans, and used paper plates. Mercy came over, gathered everything up in her arms, and dumped it in a large cardboard box that sat on the floor beside the stove. She served out two portions from the skillet onto paper plates, set them on the table, and told the kids to eat. Then she reached up on top of the refrigerator and brought down a green plastic cup of what she explained was seal oil, and a paper plate of dried fish, pale and fibrous and almost translucent where it was not encrusted with salt. Mercy set these dishes down on the table and proceeded to pick several dead mosquitoes out of the oil with her fingers. She wiped her hands on her polyester slacks.

She showed Lucy how to eat the fish, by first breaking off a portion, sucking on it to soften it, dipping it into the oil, and then biting off the oily part. She then redipped the remainder. Lucy wondered how long this particular cup of oil had been recycled for how many mouths, but she plunged a piece of fish in and popped it into her mouth. Although all she could taste at first was salt and the bitterness of the oil, she came to enjoy the chewy texture.

"You like it? Want some more?" Mercy's chin and fingers were slathered in oil.

"Sure. It's good."

"You're all right, girl." Mercy grinned and handed Lucy another strip of fish.

Amos suddenly got up from the table, his food only half-eaten, and went over to a blue plastic utility bucket that stood in the farthest corner of the house. He casually unzipped his fly and peed into the bucket, watching them at the table the whole time, as if he didn't want to miss anything. Lucy realized that they had no plumbing, and that what was in the bucket was one of the odors she had smelled when she first walked in. Her throat constricted. She quickly broke off another piece of fish and put it in her mouth. She was glad her trailer had plumbing.

Amos stopped on his way back to the table to check the clock on the stove. "Mary!" he said sharply. "Nine o'clock!"

Mary's eyes widened. She set her fork on the table and slipped down from her chair. They ran out of the house.

Although Mercy shook her head, she didn't look particularly annoyed. "TV," she said. She looked at Lucy. "So you're a nurse, huh?"

"Well, I just graduated."

"College? Hey, you must be plenty smart."

Lucy laughed, relaxing for the first time. "I don't know about that."

"You like it here?"

"Yes." She reached for another piece of fish, which caused Mercy to smile in approval.

"That other nurse," Mercy shook her head with a disgusted expression, "she didn't belong here."

"Why'd she leave?"

"Who knows?" Mercy shrugged. They ate in silence.

"So where you been all your life? Anchorage?"

"No, Boston."

"Where the hell is that?"

"The east coast. New England."

"Then how come you look Native?" Mercy asked shrewdly.

"My grandmother was Chinese."

"And she ate lots of rice, right? With chopsticks!" Mercy tittered as though this was a big joke. Lucy smiled. "You sure don't look *gussuk*," Mercy went on.

"What does that mean, *gussuk*?"

"You know, white. Like those missionaries."

"Well, I'm probably *not* like them."

"No. You look Eskimo. Now you gotta act Eskimo."

"Okay," Lucy said, breaking off another piece of fish. "You can teach me."

Mercy got up from the table and went to the refrigerator.

"You want a pop?"

"No, thanks."

Mercy returned with a Pepsi Light, sat down, popped the top, and reached for a pack of Salems. She lit one of the cigarettes with a disposable lighter and resumed her interrogation. "So how come you're not married?"

Lucy laughed. "Because I'm not."

"How old are you?"

"Twenty-three."

"Brother. You gonna be an old maid?"

Mercy apparently found Lucy's indignation amusing. She started laughing again, coughing out smoke. She stared at Lucy for a minute without speaking, then she shook her head. "Damn, girl. You *look* Eskimo. Maybe not a hundred percent, but—" She thought for a moment, then said, "*Avuk!*"

"What's that mean?"

"Halfbreed." Mercy laughed at Lucy's expression. "Hey, it's a joke, you know? Don't get all bent out of shape."

Lucy told herself to calm down. Mercy didn't mean any harm. Maybe this was just Eskimo humor.

"You sure you don't want some pop?" Mercy offered her the can.

Lucy shook her head.

"Hey, you're not a virgin, are you?"

Lucy stared at her. This was going too far. She was on the verge of saying something, but Mercy had erupted in her high-pitched laughter again, slapping her lap to emphasize her mirth. "You're all right, girl. Eskimo, *gussuk*, what the hell, right?"

"Right," Lucy said carefully. "What the hell." She reached for the can of soda and raised it to her mouth. "As a matter of fact," she said, not looking at Mercy, "I'm not."

"Good. That other one, I think she was."

It didn't much matter to Lucy that Mercy had a strange sense of humor, that the seal oil was a little bit rancid, or that the dried fish had gotten caught between her teeth. The point was that she was sitting in an Eskimo house, eating real Eskimo food. Her predecessor had probably holed up in that trailer night after night eating peanut butter and jelly sandwiches.

Lucy spent her first week reorganizing the filing system and visiting the older, housebound villagers. She communicated with those who didn't speak English by having their children act as interpreters. She set up office hours, took blood pressures, administered TB tests and polio vaccinations. She took pride in her efficiency.

It was almost solstice, staying light all night now as dusk merged with dawn. Someone told her it wouldn't get dark again until August. The extended daylight made her feel energized and productive. She liked Kigiak; she wanted to stay there for at least a year.

The first of the green and red sockeye salmon entered the lake, swimming in soundless and inexorable procession to their spawning grounds. Day after day they'd been journeying, these silent swimmers, focused on a single intent. The village children tossed stones and sticks into the water, but the fish merely passed around them, undeterred, too mesmerized and single-minded now to be startled or hurried or prevented from achieving their end. Lucy was fascinated by their strength, by their beauty and brightness.

She walked out beside the lake one night to watch them. She wandered along the shoreline, swatting at mosquitoes from time to time, enjoying the iridescent greenery and the breezes that wafted down from the snow-covered peaks. Occasionally, the dorsal fin of one of the fish broke the surface of the water with a faint splash.

She stopped when she came to a recess in the shore, where the alder ended and the ground gave way to peat and marsh. *Muskeg* was what they called it here. The mosquitoes were not so bad in this little cove, and the shallow water seemed to be some sort of resting place for fish. They milled offshore in shadowy clumps, swimming in long, slow circles, as though gathering strength to resume their journey. Lucy sat down on a grassy hummock, brushing some insects away from her face.

Robert's approach was stealthy. She never even heard him until he stepped out of the shrubbery behind her and asked her if she wanted a cigarette. He was wearing his mirror sunglasses again.

"I don't smoke. Neither should you."

He grinned and sat down on the damp earth beside her. "You like it here?" he asked.

"I'm still not used to the mountains, but yes. It's so lovely, and peaceful."

"Just like a calendar picture, right?"

Something in his voice made her glance at him. "Don't you like it?"

He shrugged. "It's my home, you know? But I feel trapped here." When he spoke there were pauses between his sentences, and his voice was soft, unhurried. "I've only been to one other place, to live, I mean."

"Where'd you go?"

"Fairbanks."

"Did you like it?"

He shook his head. "Too cold. Too many *gussuks*. I got homesick." He was quiet for so long that she thought he'd exhausted the subject. "Now I want to go away again, but there's nowhere to go."

"But Kigiak's so beautiful. You're so lucky to live here—" Lucy hesitated, and when Robert didn't say anything more, she kept silent, too.

Instead, she watched the fish milling offshore, their fins sometimes breaking the sheen that was the surface of the water at this hour. She watched the water and felt Robert watching her. They sat like this, not speaking, for perhaps ten or fifteen minutes, and it struck Lucy that it was probably the longest period of time that she had ever shared silence with anyone. It surprised her when Robert spoke.

"These fish, they depress the hell out of me."

"Why's that?"

"I can't help thinking how they're all gonna die."

It hadn't occurred to Lucy that the salmon were already dying, having stopped eating once they entered fresh water. She considered the fact that none of these thousands of fish would ever swim in the ocean again, and would in fact be dead in a matter of weeks. It was an awesome thought.

Robert sighed and she glanced at him, thinking that he was going to say something else, but all he did was to reach for her hand, as casually as though they'd known each other for some time. She pulled away in alarm and stood up. She couldn't look him in the face.

"I have to get back," she said, starting off. She didn't like the way her voice sounded apologetic. She hurried away. Only when she had reached the curve in the shoreline did she dare to glance behind her. He was sitting exactly as she'd left him, gazing across the lake. The mountains glowed with rose and violet light. It was hard to tell if it was sunset or dawn.

It was a few nights later that he came to her trailer, waking her with his insistent knocking. When she opened the door, wearing her nightgown, he stepped in without hesitation and sat down at the table. He was wearing the dark glasses, and this time she appreciated the irony of living in a place where you wore dark glasses in the middle of the night. She also noticed that he was really not much taller than she, and that he had a slight frame. She thought she could fight him if she had to. She also admitted to herself for the first time that she was attracted to him, in spite of the fact that he frightened her. Or maybe because of it.

She remained standing beside the door. "What do you want?" She had intended to sound indignant, or at least annoyed, but it didn't come out like that at all.

His face was turned towards her expectantly, his eyes unreadable behind the mirror lenses.

"Robert." Now her voice sounded firmer, more businesslike.

He took off the glasses then and looked at her standing there in her long flannel nightgown, her hands on her hips. He smiled.

"You'll have to leave," she said.

He hooked the glasses back over his ears and stood up. Lucy opened the door wide and then locked it behind him. As she got back into bed, she realized that he'd never said a word.

She took to locking her door every night after that, the only one in the village to do so, she was sure. If the others learned of it, it would make them feel bad, she knew. But she wasn't one of them; she had to look out for herself.

She didn't see Robert again for over a week and was beginning to think he'd lost interest. It was a relief, but she had to admit to feeling a little disappointed, too. She asked herself if she would have gotten involved with him if he hadn't been married, and decided that there were just too many cultural differences. She told herself that his interest in her was purely sexual, an extramarital fling.

One day Mercy asked her, "Got your party dress ready, nurse?"

"What for?"

"The big bash. The glorious Fourth. Robert and them, they already went to Dillingham to get the booze."

The night before the holiday, she was awakened by a rhythmic tapping on her bedroom window. It came from the back of the trailer, the side that faced away from the village. Lucy always kept the blue curtains drawn across the glass.

"Who is it?" This time she was scared.

"Robert."

"What do you want?"

"Let me in." Then, as an afterthought, "Please."

She wondered if he was drunk. He continued to rap on the glass. "Go home, Robert. Go to sleep."

But he didn't go home. He tapped at her window for what seemed like hours, maybe all night. Lucy burrowed under the covers and piled the pillows and her clothes on top of her head. Still she could hear it. The sound seemed to have moved into her brain. She would doze for a time, and then awaken, and he would still be there, tapping. She was amazed by his persistence, and also by the fact that he didn't just smash the window with his fist or a piece of wood. Occasionally, along with the percussion on the glass, she would hear his voice, tired and patient, saying, "Let me in."

When she woke up, exhausted, in the morning, the noise had stopped. She stood to one side of the window and drew the curtain back cautiously. There was no one there.

The Fourth of July party was held in the one-room schoolhouse. All the desks and chairs had been pushed back against the walls to allow room for dancing. The music, played on someone's tape deck, was exclusively country-Western: Waylon Jennings, Willie Nelson, Dolly Parton, and other voices Lucy didn't recognize.

There were cases and cases of beer. Lucy had never seen so much beer other than in a package store. Olympia, Hamm's, Rainer, Heineken, Budweiser. Cans and bottles, in six-packs and cartons, ferried up by boat from Dillingham all week long, and all illegal, since Kigiak had been voted "dry" the year before. Lucy wondered if the presence of alcohol was responsible for the absence of some of the villagers.

The drinking had already started. Lucy noticed right away that these people drank fast, guzzling their beer, drinking to get drunk. The women drank as much and as deliberately as the men, and as the evening wore on several people crumpled to the floor, unconscious. The children had disappeared early, and now Lucy understood why.

She danced with some of the men, enjoying herself. At one point, someone suggested loudly that they sing the national anthem, and Mercy nominated Lucy to lead it, pushing her into the center of the room. Lucy protested in embarrassment. "I don't know the words. Honest."

Robert stood beside his wife all evening. For some reason, they struck Lucy as an Eskimo version of that "American Gothic" painting. Esther was a tall, skinny woman who seemed to derive no pleasure from either the occasion or the beer she sipped. Lucy realized she had never seen Esther smile. Robert looked preoccupied. He didn't seem to be drinking, which surprised Lucy, since even she was putting away her share of beer.

When she slipped out the door to make her retreat, Lucy was aware of two things. The first was that she had drunk a lot more that she'd meant to, and the other was that someone had followed her out.

Robert quickly caught up to her on the trail. He took her hand and asked her to go with him to his house, to talk.

Lucy took a deep breath. "I'll talk to you. But I don't want to hold hands."

But Robert's grip was firm and he wouldn't let go.

They sat side by side on the living room carpet, their backs against the sofa. Robert still hadn't let go of her hand, and he raised it now in a gesture of frustration before returning it to the floor. Then he tried to kiss her.

"You said you just wanted to talk," Lucy said. She felt flushed. She was worried that Esther would come home and see them.

Robert was silent for a long time. Then he looked at her and said, "Why do you hate me?"

They heard footsteps on the porch just then. Lucy jerked away from him and stood up.

Mercy kicked open the door with her foot and entered the kitchen. She stood in the middle of the linoleum floor, swaying unsteadily, beer spilling from an open can of Budweiser in one hand, a six-pack of Rainier dangling from the other. With an effort, she focused on Robert and Lucy and smiled broadly. "Merry Christmas, kids! Merry Christmas!"

Lucy spoke in a tired voice. "It's not Christmas, Mercy. It's the Fourth of July. You know that."

"Yeah, yeah, yeah. Freedom and liberty and all that jazz." She hoisted the six-pack, as though to offer them some, gave a sudden lurch, and toppled over at their feet.

Lucy watched Mercy fall with utter detachment, and when it finally registered that she felt neither friendly nor professional concern, she knew that she was drunker than she'd thought. She looked at Robert. His eyes were closed.

She studied Mercy's broad, flat face, her right cheek crumpled against the beige carpet, her mouth all scrunched up and already leaking saliva. She was snoring. Lucy watched the pale, toothless gums appear and disappear with each rasping breath. Mercy's long black hair lay scattered around her head. Her blouse had ridden up around her stomach, exposing the faint caterpillar-like trails of stretchmarks where her flesh folded against the top of her blue jeans.

Lucy sat down and reached for Robert's hand. He opened his eyes and leaned toward her, swiveling his torso awkwardly in the attempt to embrace her, crushing her knuckles into the rug as his weight shifted onto his arm. She turned her face to him, but then, losing nerve, pulled away. She tensed, anticipating his anger, but when she looked at him again, he was crying.

Her own eyes pooled with tears. "It's not that I don't like you, Robert. It's just that—Well, look, you *are* married, after all." I shouldn't even be here, she thought, looking down at their joined hands.

"I don't love her," he said quietly. "I love you."

"How can you love me? You don't even know me."

"Your world is different from mine."

"That doesn't mean it's better." Lucy paused. "What about your baby? Robert, you have to at least try."

He shook his head. Lucy felt utterly confused. She had only come out here to do a job. It wasn't *her* fault that he was unhappily married.

When she stood to go, he didn't protest or try to stop her. It required all of her concentration to get out the door and down the slanted steps without falling, and as she picked her way along the grassy path to her trailer, she felt the alcohol surging against the front of her skull like surf. My God, she thought, as she stumbled through the door, I'm really drunk. Another first.

Later, she couldn't remember even entering the trailer, let alone falling into bed fully dressed. But she would remember that Robert had come and tugged off her clothes, and that when they made love she had cried out— something she'd never done before.

When she awoke with a splitting headache late in the morning, he was already gone. She wondered if anyone had seen him leave, if there was going to be trouble, if she might lose her job. She'd acted recklessly, unprofessionally. She would make certain that it never happened again. At least she was reasonably sure that she hadn't risked pregnancy. She stayed in the shower a long time, until the throbbing in her head subsided.

When she went outside at last, to walk down to the lake, it was afternoon. It seemed to her that the volume of salmon had thinned, as if overnight, but there were still hundreds of them, proceeding silently, empowered with purpose. She saw a few kids on the public dock, jigging for fish with hand-held lines.

It was unnaturally quiet and subdued for that time of day. No one else was about. She thought of small Western towns in movies, when disease struck and entire households were put under quarantine. She had an urge to go back to bed herself.

She noticed that the door of Robert's house was ajar, and before she thought about what she was doing, she was standing on the porch, looking in.

Mercy was lying on the floor pretty much where she had fallen, but she lay on her back now, her hair still flung out around her head, her mouth open. Her blue jeans and pink underpants were bunched around her ankles. Her pubic hair was gray, Lucy saw, as shocked by that as by anything. A man Lucy had never seen before was snoring on the couch.

She pulled the door closed and made her way quickly back to the trailer, where she threw up in the sink almost as soon as she got inside. She locked the door and lay down on the sofa. She'd change the sheets on the bed when she felt better.

Robert came over around suppertime. He knocked politely, but firmly. No more tapping at windows, Lucy thought.

She opened the door and stood in the doorframe. He was wearing his dark glasses again. He smiled at her. "Just wanted to make sure you were okay."

"I'm fine," Lucy said. She didn't smile. "I'm very busy. Is there something I can do for you?"

Robert was happy. "How about a cup of coffee?" he said, stepping forward, expecting her to move. Her outstretched arm blocked his chest. He stopped smiling.

"I'm busy, Robert. Look, you can't go on bothering me anymore."

His face was expressionless as he turned and walked away. She could read no emotion in the set of his shoulders, in his walk.

Later, when he came rapping at her bedroom window again, she got quietly out of bed and went to sit in the front room. After a couple of hours, he left. Lucy realized later that this was the moment when she decided she would leave Kigiak at the end of the summer. She could see what Robert meant about it being too small, and for all her dark hair and coloring, she was and always would be a *gussuk*. She didn't belong here.

He didn't come anymore after that, and she learned that he had gotten a job in Dillingham.

She didn't see him again until late in August, when the nights were darkening and the very last straggling salmon, their skin tattered and infected with freshwater fungus, had passed beyond the village. Every now and then the pale carcass of a dead fish washed ashore. She heard that Robert had lost his job.

She'd taken to going down to the dock after supper, to sit and think. When she saw him, she held very still. He was some distance away, down by the river, straining to push a wooden skiff off the shore. When the boat was free, he stepped lightly into the stern, leaned from the waist, and pulled once on the engine's starter cord.

He turned the boat with a smooth, uninterrupted motion, gave it full throttle, and sped away across the darkening lake. He drove standing up. Lucy watched until his figure and the outline of the boat became one silhouette, and then she continued to watch until she could neither see the skiff nor hear the motor.

In September she left Kigiak and Alaska to go back to Boston. She'd decided to return to school. The administration in Anchorage told her she'd done an outstanding job, and said that if she ever wanted to come back they could always find a place for her.

Lucy was gone for two years. She'd been back in Anchorage less than three months, working for the health department, when a middle-aged Native woman approached her one night in the lobby of a downtown movie theatre. Lucy had planned to meet her boyfriend there, to see a foreign film.

"Hello," the woman said, approaching Lucy with a hesitant smile. "You probably don't remember me."

Lucy was sure she had never seen this woman before in her life.

"My name is Anna. I met you in Kigiak. On the Fourth of July, maybe three, four years ago. I'm Robert's cousin.

"I'm sorry, I don't remember." Lucy looked around. Rick was late. "I remember Robert, of course. How is he?"

Anna continued to smile, but her voice became very soft, almost a whisper. "He died. Last year. Drowned."

Lucy felt her face grow flushed. "Drowned?" Her voice sounded unnaturally shrill. "But he was so good with those boats. How could he—"

Anna reached out and touched Lucy's sleeve, giving her another gentle smile. "You look even more like him now than when I met you."

"Who?" Lucy looked desperately for Rick. For no reason at all, she felt exasperated with this woman. She wished that she would stop smiling, for one thing.

"Robert. You look like him."

Lucy was relieved to see Rick enter the lobby. She turned abruptly from Anna and went to meet him, taking his arm. They walked toward the theatre, where the lights were already going down.

"Who was that?" Rick asked.

"Just some Native woman. I really don't know what she was talking about." Lucy shrugged. Then she began to cry.

1989

BARBIE-Q

Sandra Cisneros

Yours is the one with mean eyes and a ponytail. Striped swimsuit, stilettos, sunglasses, and gold hoop earrings. Mine is the one with bubble hair. Red swimsuit, stilettos, pearl earrings, and a wire stand. But that's all we can afford, besides one extra outfit apiece. Yours, "Red Flair," sophisticated A-line coatdress with a Jackie Kennedy pillbox hat, white gloves, handbag, and heels included. Mine, "Solo in the Spotlight," evening elegance in black glitter strapless gown with a puffy skirt at the bottom like a mermaid tail, formal-length gloves, pink chiffon scarf, and mike included. From so much dressing and undressing, the black glitter wears off where her titties stick out. This and a dress invented from an old sock when we cut holes here and here and here, the cuff rolled over for the glamorous, fancy-free, off-the-shoulder look.

Every time the same story. Your Barbie is roommates with my Barbie, and my Barbie's boyfriend comes over and your Barbie steals him, okay? Kiss kiss kiss. Then the two Barbie's fight. You dumbbell! He's mine. Oh no he's not, you stinky! Only Ken's invisible, right? Because we don't have money for a stupid-looking boy doll when we'd both rather ask for a new Barbie outfit next Christmas. We have to make do with your mean-eyed Barbie and my bubblehead Barbie and our one outfit apiece not including the sock dress.

Until next Sunday when we are walking through the flea market on Maxwell Street and *there!* Lying on the street next to some tool bits, and platform shoes with the heels all squashed, and a fluorescent green wicker wastebasket, and aluminum foil, and hubcaps, and a pink shag rug, and windshield wiper blades, and dusty mason jars, and a coffee can full of rusty nails. *There!* Where? Two Mattel boxes. One with the "Career Gal" ensemble, snappy black-and-white business suit, three-quarter-length sleeve jacket with kick-pleat skirt, red sleeveless shell, gloves, pumps, and matching hat included. The other, "Sweet Dreams," dreamy pink-and-white plaid nightgown and matching robe, lace trimmed slippers, hairbrush and hand mirror included. How much? Please, please, please, please, please, please, please, until they say okay.

On the outside you and me skipping and humming but inside we are doing loopity-loops and pirouetting. Until at the next vendor's stand, next to boxed pies, and bright orange toilet brushes, and rubber gloves, and wrench sets, and bouquets of feather flowers, and glass towel racks, and steel wool, and Alvin and the Chipmunks records, *there!* And *there!* And *there!* And *there!* and *there!* and *there!* and *there!* Bendable Legs Barbie with her new page-boy hairdo. Midge, Barbie's best friend. Ken, Barbie's boyfriend. Skipper, Barbie's little sister. Tutti and Todd, Barbie and Skipper's tiny twin sister and brother. Skipper's friends, Scooter and Ricky. Alan, Ken's buddy. And Francie, Barbie's MOD'ern cousin.

Everybody today selling toys all of them damaged with water and smelling of smoke. Because a big toy warehouse on Halsted Street burned down yesterday—see there?—the smoke still rising and drifting across the Dan Ryan Expressway. And now there is a big fire sale at Maxwell Street, today only.

So what if we didn't get our new Bendable Legs Barbie and Midge and Ken and Skipper and Tutti and Todd and Scooter and Ricky and Alan and Francie in nice clean boxes and had to buy them on Maxwell Street, all water-soaked and sooty. So what if our Barbies smell like smoke when you hold them up to your nose even after you wash and wash and wash them. And if the prettiest doll, Barbie's MOD'ern cousin Francie with real eyelashes, eyelash brush included, has a left foot that's melted a little—so? If you dress her in her new "Prom Pinks" outfit, satin splendor with matching coat, gold belt, clutch, and hair bow included, so long as you don't lift her dress, right?—who's to know.

1991

BIRTHDAY

David Wong Louie

There's a man outside the door. He pounds away at it with his fists, and that whole side of the room shakes. He can pound until the house falls. I don't care, it's his house; he can do with it what he pleases.

He talks to me through the door. His talk is nothing like his knock. His voice is gentle, soothing, contrite. I might even be tempted to say it's sweet, only he's a man, and the man that he is.

I came to see the boy. It's true I have no rights except those that come with love. And if I paid any attention to what the court says, I wouldn't be here. The court says the boy belongs to the man, the boy's father. This has been hard to take. After all, the boy calls us both by our first names, and as far as I'm concerned that means we're equals.

It's the boy's birthday, and back in the days when the world was cold and rainy and sane, back in the days when we still lived together, I had promised we'd go for an afternoon of baseball—sunshine, pop, hotdogs. I told the man I was coming. I kept calling his number, but no one answered. I left plenty of messages on his machine, detailing what I had planned for my date with the boy. No response. When the boy first moved into this house, I tried phoning him every couple of weeks. I just wanted to hear him say my name again, Wallace Wong—the clearest three syllables in his vocabulary when his mother introduced us. But all I ever got for my troubles was the man's recorded voice—until yesterday, that is, when he interrupted the message I was leaving to say, "Wong, why don't you leave us alone?"

I just hung up on him. I couldn't talk to someone who used that tone of voice.

The boy's mother is gone from the picture. She's in New York; I say New York because that's where she's from originally, but she might be in Topeka for all I know. Losing the boy almost killed her. All those days in court for nothing. What did that black robe know about the weave of our three hearts? The man won custody. Perhaps he bribed the judge; it's happened before. More likely it's because he's making money now writing movies, and in this town that's everything. He had written a script based on their marriage and breakup, which was made into a film and did well at the box office, so now he's in big demand.

One day I came home from the shop, and she was gone. No note then, and not a word from her since. But I'm confident she'll come home once her heart's on the mend. Her disappearance wasn't a complete surprise. She's a quirky one. I've learned to expect such behavior. When we first started going out, she wanted me to prove that I really loved her. She was still recovering from the marriage then and didn't trust what anyone said about anything, especially love. So she said she needed proof. I told her okay, but for weeks she couldn't decide what she wanted me to do. Then one day while we were having lunch at a restaurant, she said, "This is it."

"What?"

"Steal his radio." She pointed across the street.

"You crazy?"

The radio went into a health club with a man built like a heavyweight boxer.

I crossed the street, and as I followed the radio into the building, I imagined the possible headline for tomorrow's paper: CHINESE ROMEO BITES GYM FLOOR. Having accepted the possibility of severe bodily injury, I found the actual theft of the radio surprisingly easy. I just hung around the locker room, watching him strip and flex, and when he got up to relieve himself, I snatched up the radio left sitting on the bench.

She met me on the street in front of the gym. "Keep it," she said. "A present from me to you."

This I didn't appreciate. I reminded her the size of that man's fist was bigger than my entire head.

"Frank," she said, laughing in a mean sort of way, "wouldn't hurt anyone he wasn't married to."

That's Frank out there, punching the door.

I'm sitting on a kiddie chair. My knees are pressed against the bottom of a table that's under two feet tall. It's as if I'm crammed in a crate. In front of me I have a drawing pad and eight thick crayons. Sooner or later, the man will find the key to the lock and poke his fist through the door. Before that happens, I want to leave the boy a note, just to let him know I didn't forget his birthday. But unless he's learned to read in the past few months, words will be useless. So I have to say my piece with pictures, and I'm not much when it comes to pictures.

I take up the red crayon and draw a circle; then I put in some eyes. I'm trying for a self-portrait but it's sizing up more feline than *Homo sapien*. Soon I admit defeat and finish off the cat with a pair of triangles for ears.

The man calls my name. "Don't do anything funny while I'm away," he says. His footsteps go down the stairs.

I hurry to the window. The man's walking up the front path. He goes about halfway, turns, and looks back at the house. He catches my eyes and gestures with his hand, like an umpire thumbing a guy out.

I try a yellow crayon. I make another circle, but now I'm distracted by the man's absence. Can't draw with him there, can't draw without him. I go to the window. He's standing at the curb, waiting for the boy, or maybe he's called the police.

Back at the table again, I give my drawing some teeth, big yellow squares. My creation reminds me of my father, though no one else would make the connection.

"What good's a son that doesn't know who his own father is?" That's what my father said when I told my parents about the boy and how the three of us planned to set up housekeeping. He didn't care for the idea of his only son adopting a used family. He gritted his false teeth, which he does when he's mad, and said, "Wallace" (he never uses my American name), "don't be such a jerk. There are millions of available Chinese girls. And I'll tell you a secret. The basic anatomy's the same no matter where it comes from. Just say yes, and we'll go to China and find you a nice girl."

My mother nodded, her hair jet black from a beautician's bottle. She said, "Love between lions and sheep has but one consequence." She talks in aphorisms. I don't know if they're the real thing or if she makes them up.

My parents had their hearts set on Connie Chung. "Marry your mother a girl she can talk to without having to use her hands," said my father.

"What makes you think Connie Chung can even speak Chinese?" I said.

"Because she's smart; otherwise, she wouldn't be on TV," said my father.

My mother said, "Only a fool whistles into the wind." At this, even my father shot her a funny look.

On the drive over here I heard a story on the radio about California condors going extinct. I tried to imagine myself as a condor at the dead end of evolution. In my veins I felt the primordial soup bubbling, and my whole entropic bulk quaked as I gazed at the last females of my species. I knew I was supposed to mate, but I wasn't sure how. Yeah, I'd probably have to start by picking a partner. But which one? I looked them over, the last three in creation; she'd need to have good genes. Finally, after careful consideration, I chose—her, the bird with blond tail feathers. Then I heard my father's voice: "No, not that one, that one."

I wonder if he might be right. Maybe I'd be wise to pack a few suitcases full of Maybelline and soft Italian shoes and go over to China. Plenty of women there in that lipstick-free society. Seduce them with bourgeois decadence, and they'll gladly surrender their governmentally mandated 1.2 children to me.

This morning I taped a sign on the door for my customers, saying that I had to attend a funeral. Even though Saturdays show my best profit, for the boy's birthday I didn't bother to open the shop. I operate an Italian-style café. I traffic in slow death: buttery eggs, pinguid coffee, and sweets on top of sweets. At first business was slow. People didn't believe a Chinaman could produce a decent cappuccino. I could hardly blame them. I'd shy away, too, from moo shu pork from a Sicilian's pan. But I do all right now, and take off when the need comes up.

So I drove over to the man's house, and when I first caught sight of it I was surprised by its size, its thick Greek columns, its funereal cypresses, its imposing terra-cotta roof.

Seated on a white cast-iron love seat by the front door, the man was hunched over a book in which he appeared to be writing. I walked up the long front path, flanked on both sides by enormous expanses of chipped white stone where there should've been grass. He acted as if I weren't there. He just kept scribbling. This reminded me of his courtroom manner: done up in a pinstriped suit, he sat at his table, writing feverishly on a yellow legal pad, as if he were an agent of the law.

I hated that time. The boy and his mother stayed downtown in a hotel to be near the court building. Each night my father would call to ask who was winning. Of course he was rooting against us. My mother wanted to know if I was eating rice again, now that the girl was gone. I got so confused talking to them that I moved out of the house just to avoid their calls. I set up a cot in the café storeroom and slept next to egg cartons, milk crates, and hot exhaust from the refrigerator fan. Those nights I fell asleep listening to talk shows on the radio.

They were good company. So much misery on the airwaves, it was a comfort. I heard this one guy complaining about his chronic indigestion, and the radio doctor, without so much as laying a stethoscope on him, diagnosed that the caller had cancer. I listened to too many women with a similar story. The husband's a hitter, they'd say, and in the morning she's ready to hit back, but by then the bum's gone off somewhere, so she smacks the kids instead, and wants to know why she doesn't feel sorry for doing so. We were all half-crazed insomniacs, one big aching family.

I even called a radio psychologist the night of the day the boy's mother left me. The second I got through to the station I realized how desperate I was, and felt pretty silly. But I didn't hang up. I had a conversation with the show's producer. He said my story was too complex. He wanted me to simplify it. He advised me that if I wanted the listeners' sympathy I should consider dropping the "Chinese stuff." Before I listened to another word, I told him that I hoped one day he'd be lonesome and heartbroken in the back roads of China, thousands of miles from Western ears, and the nearest ones carved from stone.

"I've been expecting you," said the man. He motioned for me to sit next to him on the love seat. I held my ground. He crossed his legs and reopened his book to a page marked with a greeting card. "You like poetry?" he asked, then bowed his head and finished copying a poem from the book onto the card. "I read this one back in high school, so I guess it must be good." He handed me the card when he was through. His handwriting looked like ants set end to end, painfully tiny words crawling all over the place.

I said, "Would you mind calling the boy?"

"We should talk," he said, taking back the card and slipping it into a hot-pink envelope. "I don't know you from the Gang of Four, and here you are asking for Welby."

I had braced myself for that. Welby. I can hardly say it. Named the poor kid after a TV doctor. The boy's mother swears it was all the man's doing. When she comes home and we're settled, we'll go to court and have his name changed.

"It's his birthday," I said. "We have plans. The ball game, remember?"

"And don't think he hasn't talked about seeing you," the man said.

"Well then, let's not disappoint the boy." I took a step forward and reached for the doorbell.

"That's not necessary," said the man, rising from his seat. "We're talking now."

He pushed back the cuff of his long-sleeved shirt and checked his watch. "Can you spare me a few minutes?" he said and, with a sweep of his hand, invited me to sit again. This time I did.

"The scene opens in a supermarket," he began. "Rows of fruits and vegetables. People, carts fill the aisle. Close-up on Welby; he's about eighteen months old, sitting in the kiddie seat. I go squeeze avocados. Reverse angle: Welby watches as I join the swarm of shoppers. Pan of aisle, finally zeroing in on a nice-looking lady, who parks her cart next to mine. Zoom in: she's talking to her own kid, who's too big for the kiddie seat and looks awkward and clumsy in it. His head's bowed, eyes dim and sad. His mother says, 'Here's another little boy,' and she disappears among the shoppers. Zoom in on me in the crowd. I look over at Welby. Cut back to kids. Welby's leaning across the cart and pats the new boy, nothing rough, just finding out what the other kid feels like. Twin shot: big boy freezes, letting Welby do his thing, the way people let mean dogs sniff all they want, instead of trying to get away. I return to the cart. See the kid's crying, no noise, just these tears on his cheeks. Mom comes back. I apologize. Close-up on Mom: she's eating a candy bar right in front of her kid's face. You know something's wrong with the picture, but you can't figure out what. It takes a few seconds, but then you realize the kid's blind. Fade out."

"Scene from a new movie?" I asked.

"No, from real life."

"Oh. Look, we have to get going." I stood up and stepped away from the door. "So what's your point?"

He looked at his watch again. "Look, she left me, she left you. On that score, we're dead even." He came up behind me and put his hand on my shoulder. "Say, what kind of car you driving?" He gave me the gentlest push, and we started walking up the front path. "You know what Welby thought when he came to live here? He thought he was being punished for breaking up our marriage. How do you think that made me feel? We all do things we don't mean, and end up hurting people. I hurt her, she hurt me; now you're hurt."

We were still walking toward the curb. The man nudged me whenever my feet slowed down.

"Frank, look, thanks for the talk."

"Sure," he said. "It's about time we had a man-to-man." He touched me on the shoulder again.

"But you're forgetting something—where's Welby? We really should hit the road. I promised him batting practice."

"Say, that reminds me, what kind of tickets you buy? I'll reimburse you for them."

We reached the curb. He opened the driver-side door and rolled down the window. "The ballpark express," he said, sweeping his hand past the opening, like a model on a game show showing off a prize.

I slid in behind the wheel. "Okay. Now call Welby."

He shut the door and crouched, his big forearms resting against the bottom of the window. "Listen to me," Frank said. "To Welby, you're big time. You're like a living, breathing video game. There've been times I couldn't stand being around him. He'd tell stories: 'One day me and Wallace Wong' did this, did that. I'm never in any of his stories." The man looked into the side-view mirror and fixed his hair. "But I'm his father, right? Come on, give me a chance. Leave us alone, okay? He's starting to get used to me."

It was obvious he wasn't going to hand the boy over. So I proposed a trade: I'd do what he wanted, but in exchange I'd get the boy for the afternoon. We'd have so much fun, the man would need all of geologic time to chase those nine innings from the boy's memory.

He drummed his fingers against the door and looked at his watch. "It's late," he said. "You better get rolling." He reached across my body and pointed at the ignition switch.

My equal and opposite reaction: I leaned on the horn. I got in two long blasts before he stopped my hand. "The people in this neighborhood are still sleeping," he said. "Now listen up, friend, I'm telling you for your own good—you don't want to be here."

"So get the boy," I said. I brought my fist down on the dashboard to show I meant business. The glove compartment flew open. Things spilled onto the passenger seat.

"Hey, my radio," said the man.

"Your what? What do you mean, your radio?" I had brought it along so we could listen to the play-by-play in the stands.

"That's her. Zenith eight transistor with a crack in back where the battery goes."

I shook my head.

"Don't be that way," he said. "I know all about it. Sylvie told me she made you steal it."

"She what?"

"Sylvie always was a touch *loco en la cabeza*." He tapped his finger against his temple. "She always had funny ideas, don't you think so?"

"Here," I said, "take the radio."

"No, you keep her."

"I don't want it. I never did."

"No, keep her," he said. "Must feel like she belongs to you now anyway."

He stood up from his crouch and checked the time. "We need to stop fooling around. I have an appointment in a few minutes with someone. So, if you don't mind—"

"You mean like a date, Frank? You have a girlfriend?"

He didn't answer.

"Well, don't let me stand in the way of romance. Just call the boy, and we'll be off. Think of me as his sitter. Then you two will have the whole afternoon free to yourselves."

The man put his hands on his hips and arched his back. "Nothing's clicking with you, is it? Come with me," he said. "I have something to show you."

We walked up the front path, and I followed him into the kitchen. "Smell that?" he said. "Welby's birthday cake. My first ever, and I'm doing it from scratch. Fudge swirl topped with chocolate mousse frosting." He caught my eye and grinned. He was proud of his achievement. The place was a mess—bowls, spoons, measuring cups, cookbook, batter, eggshells, flour scattered and smeared everywhere. The cake layers were cooling on racks. "I'm trying my best," he said.

I was standing in an archway that separated the kitchen from the dining area. Past the round glass table, the wall of glass bricks, the giant earthenware horse, just to the left of the dwarf lemon tree, I spotted the staircase to the second floor. I had a clear path, an easy dash, and I'd be upstairs where the boy was waiting for me.

"Say, you cook in a restaurant," he said, picking the cookbook off the counter. "Maybe you can help. What do they mean by fold egg mixture into the chocolate?" he asked. "Am I supposed to pour the whole thing out and fold it with my hands?" He had his nose in the book and reread the passage.

I didn't hang around to give my expert advice.

The boy's room was the second off the hallway. I locked the door. Why there was a lock on the boy's door, I'll never know. But I was glad it was there. At first, I thought I had the wrong room. It didn't look like a child's room. At least not one the boy's age. The wall were covered with posters of TV starlets. So much cleavage and bare thigh couldn't be good for someone that young. I wondered what a social worker would think if I sent one up here.

The man knocked on the door. "Can't you see," he said, "Welby's not home? I sent him to a friend's for the night so I can bake his cake. It's a surprise."

It was my surprise. "He has to come home sometime," I said.

"Get out of there!" he shouted. "You can still make the game if you leave now."

I didn't answer. The man then started to pound on the door. I went over and inspected the boy's toy shelves. I couldn't tell if the boy had chosen the toys or, like the posters, they were a reflection of the man's tastes. There was such an emphasis on angles, gadgetry, and intimidation. Very high-tech stuff. Mostly robots, rockets, and space-guns. So much plastic and chrome. Do kids instinctively gravitate to these materials? Whatever happened to animal love, the considerate petting of fur? I searched for the stuffed rabbit I had given him back in the good times. It was nowhere in sight. I wanted to believe it had accompanied him on the overnight but knew that wasn't likely. Then I tried to imagine the boy playing with these contraptions. I tried to hear the accompanying narrative as he sailed the toys through outer space. But I couldn't remember his voice. It was lost to me, just as my own boyhood voice is forever gone, tumbling across light-years and, like radio signals, bouncing off the four corners of the universe.

I watch the man coming toward the house. I hear him climb the stairs. He goes past my room. Then, a few minutes later, he knocks at my door. "You're in there now," he says. "So stay put. Got it?" He hurries downstairs. I go to the window. He's in a sports coat now, as he jogs to the curb. In one hand is a bunch of flowers wrapped in pink paper, in the other the greeting card. I don't know what to think. First killer robots and now poetry and roses?

The man runs off the curb. He surveys the sun-washed street, checks his watch once more, and then looks back at me.

Soon a car pulls up behind mine. I look for the boy in the backseat. If I do seventy all the way, we can still catch the first pitch.

The driver gets out: a woman with coral-red hair, cropped close to her scalp, earrings like a set of handcuffs, and miles of doodads around her neck. She's wearing a sleeveless purple jumpsuit that shifts like leather. I try my best to see into the car. But there's no sign of life.

The woman adjust her sunglasses and throws her arms around the man. He crushes the flowers against the small of her back. I had forgotten about her coming. Quite a change from the boy's mother. But that's none of my business.

I return to the little table and look at what I've drawn. I wish I had some talent. At least a bit of imagination. On the page is a flock of animals, ones the boy used to ask me to draw. "How about a horse," he'd say, handing me a crayon. And no matter how the drawing turned out, I'd say, "That's a horse," and he'd generously say, "That's a horse."

I don't know if he'll still be so generous, now that he's abandoned rabbits for ray guns, but he'll know who did the drawings. It troubles me, though, that I haven't said what I want to say, that no matter how hard I try, I'm stuck doing the same old things in the same old ways. What have I accomplished but a page full of nouns—a camel, a dog, a cat, a cow, a bird, and my famous horse. Sure, I can try adopting a new vocabulary, sketch in a rocket ship, a rectangle, and a few well-placed triangles. That shouldn't be too hard. But that's not how he knows me. Ours was a simpler world. He must be a different boy now. The universe he knows has expanded, just as his palette broadened during our time together. This is inevitable. But in this expansion have I been eclipsed? Am I like a rattle, once a favorite toy, then—not so much discarded, but neglected with the discovery of blocks and things with wheels? I wish there was some way for me to know what he's up to, the way my father came home one day from Sears with a bat and ball and glove for me. There he was, son of China's great famines, who knew nothing of earned-run averages or the number of homers Mantle hit in '56, but somehow he anticipated my next step. With the boy, I didn't know what to think. Will the drawings delight him? That's what I mean— I should know.

I look our at the street. The trunk of the woman's car is open, and there's a ton of luggage stacked on the sidewalk. She must be here on an extended visit or else she's moving in. None of that's my business either, but she better not think she can take the boy's mother's place.

The woman goes over to my car. It's just an old VW square-back, but she's really checking it over. She does a lap around it, then sticks her head in the driver's window. She holds the radio up in her hand. The man's saying things that don't seem to please her. She spins away from him and starts up the front path. The man points at the house. She flips up her sunglasses. She sees me. I see her, too. I've waited a long time for this day. But it isn't how I've imagined it would feel when Sylvie finally came home.

The man catches her halfway up the front walk. They argue, but I can't hear them. About a minute later, they move slowly toward the street, turn at her luggage, and keep walking until they're gone from sight. It's plain they're giving me a chance to leave.

I go downstairs. The house is still sweet with baking. I reach the foyer but then make a U-turn and go to the kitchen. The layers of cake have cooled nicely.

What else is there for me to do? It is his birthday.

I crack an egg and separate the yolk from the whites. I repeat this three more times. I add sugar to the yolks and beat them with a whisk. This feels good. Then I heat up a pan of water and melt the chocolate in a second pan. In the meantime I beat the egg whites. I'm not thinking now. The whites hold their peaks perfectly. I mix the chocolate with the sugar and the yolks. Then I fold in the whipped whites.

I work briskly. And for the first time in a long time, perhaps for the first time ever, I feel at peace. I'm not familiar with this recipe, but I know what I need to do.

I spread the mousse on the layers of cake. I spread it on thick. This, I know, the boy will like.

1991

BORDERS

Thomas King

When I was twelve, maybe thirteen, my mother announced that we were going to go to Salt Lake City to visit my sister who had left the reserve, moved across the line, and found a job. Laetitia had not left home with my mother's blessing, but over time my mother had come to be proud of the fact that Laetitia had done all of this on her own.

"She did real good," my mother would say.

Then there were the fine points to Laetitia's going. She had not, as my mother liked to tell Mrs. Manyfingers, gone floating after some man like a balloon on a string. She hadn't snuck out of the house, either, and gone to Vancouver or Edmonton or Toronto to chase rainbows down alleys. And she hadn't been pregnant.

"She did real good."

I was seven or eight when Laetitia left home. She was seventeen. Our father was from Rocky Boy on the American side.

"Dad's American," Laetitia told my mother, "so I can go and come as I please."

"Send us a postcard."

Laetitia packed her things, and we headed for the border. Just outside of Milk River, Laetitia told us to watch for the water tower.

"Over the next rise. It's the first thing you see."

"We got a water tower on the reserve," my mother said. "There's a big one in Lethbridge, too."

"You'll be able to see the tops of the flagpoles, too. That's where the border is."

When we got to Coutts, my mother stopped at the convenience store and bought her and Laetitia a cup of coffee. I got an Orange Crush.

"This is real lousy coffee."

"You're just angry because I want to see the world."

"It's the water. From here on down, they got lousy water."

"I can catch the bus from Sweetgrass. You don't have to lift a finger."

"You're going to have to buy your water in bottles if you want good coffee."

There was an old wooden building about a block away, with a tall sign in the yard that said "Museum." Most of the roof had been blown away. Mom told me to go and see when the place was open. There were boards over the windows and doors. You could tell that the place was closed, and I told Mom so, but she said to go and check anyway. Mom and Laetitia stayed by the car. Neither one of them moved. I sat down on the steps of the museum and watched them, and I don't know that they ever said anything to each other. Finally, Laetitia got her bag out of the trunk and gave Mom a hug.

I wandered back to the car. The wind had come up, and it blew Laetitia's hair across her face. Mom reached out and pulled the strands out of Laetitia's eyes, and Laetitia let her.

"You can still see the mountain from here," my mother told Laetitia in Blackfoot.

"Lots of mountains in Salt Lake," Laetitia told her in English.

"The place is closed," I said. "Just like I told you."

Laetitia tucked her hair into her jacket and dragged her bag down the road to the brick building with the American flag flapping on a pole. When she got to where the guards were waiting, she turned, put the bag down, and waved to us. We waved back. Then my mother turned the car around, and we came home.

We got postcards from Laetitia regular, and, if she wasn't spreading jelly on the truth, she was happy. She found a good job and rented an apartment with a pool.

"And she can't even swim," my mother told Mrs. Manyfingers.

Most of the postcards said we should come down and see the city, but whenever I mentioned this, my mother would stiffen up.

So I was surprised when she bought two new tires for the car and put on her blue dress with the green and yellow flowers. I had to dress up, too, for my mother did not want us crossing the border looking like Americans. We made sandwiches and put them in a big box with pop and potato chips and some apples and bananas and a big jar of water.

"But we can stop at one of those restaurants, too, right?"

"We maybe should take some blankets in case you get sleepy."

"But we can stop at one of those restaurants, too, right?"

The border was actually two towns, though neither one was big enough to amount to anything. Coutts was on the Canadian side and consisted of the convenience store and gas station, the museum that was closed and boarded up, and a motel. Sweetgrass was on the American side, but all you could see was an overpass that arched across the highway and disappeared into the prairies. Just hearing the names of these towns, you would expect that Sweetgrass, which is a nice name and sounds like it is related to other places such as Medicine Hat and Moose Jaw and Kicking Horse Pass, would be on the Canadian side, and that Coutts, which sounds abrupt and rude, would be on the American side. But this was not the case.

Between the two borders was a duty-free shop where you could buy cigarettes and liquor and flags. Stuff like that.

We left the reserve in the morning and drove until we got to Coutts.

"Last time we stopped here," my mother said, "you had an Orange Crush. You remember that?"

"Sure," I said. "That was when Laetitia took off."

"You want another Orange Crush?"

"That means we're not going to stop at a restaurant, right?"

My mother got a coffee at the convenience store, and we stood around and watched the prairies move in the sunlight. Then we climbed back in the car. My mother straightened the dress across her thighs, leaned against the wheel, and drove all the way to the border in first gear, slowly, as if she were trying to see through a bad storm or riding high on black ice.

The border guard was an old guy. As he walked to the car, he swayed from side to side, his feet set wide apart, the holster on his hip pitching up and down. He leaned into the window, looked into the back seat, and looked at my mother and me.

"Morning, ma'am."

"Good morning."

"Where you heading?"

"Salt Lake City."

"Purpose of your visit?"

"Visit my daughter."

"Citizenship?"

"Blackfoot," my mother told him.

"Ma'am?"

"Blackfoot," my mother repeated.

"Canadian?"

"Blackfoot."

It would have been easier if my mother had just said "Canadian" and been done with it, but I could see she wasn't going to do that. The guard wasn't angry or anything. He smiled and looked towards the building. Then he turned back and nodded.

"Morning, ma'am."

"Good morning."

"Any firearms or tobacco?"

"No."

"Citizenship?"

"Blackfoot."

He told us to sit in the car and wait, and we did. In about five minutes, another guard came out with the first man. They were talking as they came, both men swaying back and forth like two cowboys headed for a bar or a gunfight.

"Morning, ma'am."

"Good morning."

"Cecil tells me you and the boy are Blackfoot."

"That's right."

"Now, I know that we got Blackfeet on the American side and the Canadians got Blackfeet on their side. Just so we can keep our records straight, what side do you come from?"

I knew exactly what my mother was going to say, and I could have told them if they had asked me.

"Canadian side or American side?" asked the guard.

"Blackfoot side," she said.

It didn't take them long to lose their sense of humor, I can tell you that. The one guard stopped smiling altogether and told us to park our car at the side of the building and come in.

We sat on a wood bench for about an hour before anyone came over to talk to us. This time it was a woman. She had a gun, too.

"Hi," she said. "I'm Inspector Pratt. I understand there is a little mis-understanding."

"I'm going to visit my daughter in Salt Lake City," my mother told her. "We don't have any guns or beer."

"It's a legal technicality, that's all."

"My daughter's Blackfoot, too."

The woman opened the briefcase and took out a couple of forms and began to write on one of them. "Everyone who crosses our border has to declare their citizenship. Even Americans. It helps us keep track of visitors we get from the various countries."

She went on like that for maybe fifteen minutes, and a lot of the stuff she told us was interesting.

"I can understand how you feel about having to tell us your citizenship, and here's what I'll do. You tell me, and I won't put it down on the form. No one will know but you and me."

Her gun was silver. There were several chips in the wood handle and the name "Stella" was scratched into the metal butt.

We were in the border office for about four hours, and we talked to almost everyone there. One of the men bought me a Coke. My mother brought a couple of sandwiches in from the car. I offered part of mine to Stella, but she said she wasn't hungry.

I told Stella that we were Blackfoot and Canadian, but she said that didn't count because I was a minor. In the end, she told us that if my mother didn't declare her citizenship, we would have to go back to where we came from. My mother stood up and thanked Stella for her time. Then we got back in the car and drove to the Canadian border, which was only a few hundred yards away.

I was disappointed. I hadn't seen Laetitia for a long time, and I had never been to Salt Lake City. When she was still at home, Laetitia would go on and on about Salt Lake City. She had never been there, but her boyfriend Lester Tallbull had spent a year in Salt Lake at a technical school.

"It's a great place," Lester would say. "Nothing but blondes in the whole state."

Whenever he said that, Laetitia would slug him on his shoulder hard enough to make him flinch. He had some brochures on Salt Lake and some maps, and every so often the two of them would spread them out on the table.

"That's the temple. It's right downtown. You got to have a pass to get in."

"Charlotte says anyone can go in and look around."

"When was Charlotte in Salt Lake? Just when the hell was Charlotte in Salt Lake?"

"Last year."

"This is Liberty Park. It's got a zoo. There's good skiing in the mountains."

"Got all the skiing we can use," my mother would say. "People come from all over the world to ski at Banff. Cardston's got a temple, if you like those kinds of things."

"Oh, this one is real big," Lester would say. "They got armed guards and everything."

"Not what Charlotte says."

"What does she know?"

Lester and Laetitia broke up, but I guess the idea of Salt Lake stuck in her mind.

The Canadian border guard was a young woman, and she seemed to be happy to see us. "Hi," she said. "You folks sure have a great day for a trip. Where are you coming from?"

"Standoff."

"Is that in Montana?"

"No."

"Where are you going?"

"Standoff."

The woman's name was Carol and I don't guess she was any older than Laetitia. "Wow, you both Canadians?"

"Blackfoot."

"Really? I have a friend I went to school with who is Blackfoot. Do you know Mike Harley?"

"No."

"He went to school in Lethbridge, but he's really from Browning."

It was a nice conversation and there were no cars behind us, so there was no rush.

"You're not bringing any liquor back, are you?"

"No."

"Any cigarettes or plants or stuff like that?"

"No."

"Citizenship?"

"Blackfoot."

"I know," said the woman, "and I'd be proud of being Blackfoot if I were Blackfoot. But you have to be American or Canadian."

When Laetitia and Lester broke up, Lester took his brochures and maps with him, so Laetitia wrote to someone in Salt Lake City, and, about a month later, she got a big envelope of stuff. We sat at the table and opened up all the brochures, and Laetitia read each one out loud.

"Salt Lake City is the gateway to some of the world's most magnificent skiing.

"Salt Lake City is the home of one of the newest professional basketball franchises, the Utah Jazz.

"The Great Salt Lake is one of the natural wonders of the world."

It was kind of exciting seeing all those color brochures on the table and listening to Laetitia read all about how Salt Lake City was one of the best places in the entire world.

"That Salt Lake City place sounds too good to be true," my mother told her.

"It has everything."

"We got everything right here."

"It's boring here."

"People in Salt Lake City are probably sending away for brochures of Calgary and Lethbridge and Pincher Creek right now."

In the end my mother would say that maybe Laetitia should go to Salt Lake City, and Laetitia would say that maybe she would.

We parked the car to the side of the building and Carol led us into a small room on the second floor. I found a comfortable spot on the couch and flipped through some back issues of *Saturday Night* and *Alberta Report*.

When I woke up, my mother was just coming out of another office. She didn't say a word to me. I followed her down the stairs and out to the car. I thought we were going home, but she turned around and drove back towards the American border, which made me think we were going to visit Laetitia in Salt Lake City after all. Instead she pulled into the parking lot of the duty-free store and stopped.

"We're going to see Laetitia?"

"No."

"We going home?"

Pride is a good thing to have, you know. Laetitia had a lot of pride, and so did my mother. I figured that someday, I'd have it too.

"So where are we going?"

Most of that day, we wandered around the duty-free store, which wasn't very large. The manger had a name tag with a tiny American flag on one side and a tiny Canadian flag on the other. His name was Mel. Towards evening, he began suggesting that we should be on our way. I told him we had nowhere to go, that the neither the Americans nor the Canadians would let us in. He laughed at that and told us that we should buy something or leave.

The car was not very comfortable, but we did have all that food and it was April, so even if it did snow as it sometimes does on the prairies, we wouldn't freeze. The next morning my mother drove to the American border.

It was a different guard this time, but the questions were the same. We didn't spend as much time in the office as we had the day before. By noon, we were back at the Canadian border. By two we were back in the duty-free shop parking lot.

The second night in the car was not as much fun as the first, but my mother seemed in good spirits, and, all in all, it was as much an adventure as an inconvenience. There wasn't much food left and that was a problem, but we had lots of water as there was a faucet at the side of the duty-free shop.

One Sunday, Laetitia and I were watching television. Mom was over at Mrs. Manyfingers's. Right in the middle of the program, Laetitia turned off the set and said she was going to Salt Lake City, that life around here was too boring. I had wanted to see the rest of the program and really didn't care if Laetitia went to Salt Lake City or not. When Mom got home, I told her what Laetitia had said.

What surprised me was how angry Laetitia got when she found out that I had told Mom.

"You got a big mouth."

"That's what you said."

"What I said is none of your business."

"I didn't say anything."

"Well, I'm going for sure, now."

That weekend, Laetitia packed her bags, and we drove her to the border.

Mel turned out to be friendly. When he closed up for the night and found us still parked in the lot, he came over and asked us if our car was broken down or something. My mother thanked him for his concern and told him that we were fine, that things would get straightened out in the morning.

"You're kidding," said Mel. "You'd think they could handle the simple things."

"We got some apples and a banana," I said, "but we're all out of ham sandwiches."

"You know, you read about these things, but you just don't believe it. You just don't believe it."

"Hamburgers would be even better because they got more stuff for energy."

My mother slept in the backseat. I slept in the front because I was smaller and could lie under the steering wheel. Late that night, I heard my mother open the car door. I found her sitting on her blanket leaning against the bumper of the car.

"You see all those stars," she said. "When I was a little girl, my grandmother used to take me and my sisters out to the prairies and tell us stories about all the stars."

"Do you think Mel is going to bring us any hamburgers?"

"Every one of those stars has a story. You see that bunch of stars over there that look like fish?"

"He didn't say no."

"Coyote went fishing, one day. That's how it all started." We sat out under the stars that night, and my mother told me all sorts of stories. She was serious about it, too. She'd tell them slow, repeating parts as she went, as if she expected me to remember each one.

Early the next morning, the television vans began to arrive, and guys in suits and women in dresses came trotting over to us, dragging microphones and cameras and lights behind them. One of the vans had a table set up with orange juice and sandwiches and fruit. It was for the crew, but when I told them we hadn't eaten for a while, a really skinny blonde woman told us we could eat as much as we wanted.

They mostly talked to my mother. Every so often one of the reporters would come over and ask me questions about how it felt to be an Indian without a country. I told them we had a nice house on the reserve and that my cousins had a couple of horses we rode when we went fishing. Some of the television people went over to the American border, and then they went to the Canadian border.

Around noon, a good-looking guy in a dark blue suit and an orange tie with little ducks on it drove up in a fancy car. He talked to my mother for a while, and, after they were done talking, my mother started the engine, Mel came over and gave us a bag of peanut brittle and told us that justice was a damn hard thing to get, but that we shouldn't give up.

I would have preferred lemon drops, but it was nice of Mel anyway.

"Where are we going now?"

"Going to visit Laetitia."

The guard who came out to our car was all smiles. The television lights were so bright they hurt my eyes, and, if you tried to look through the windshield in certain directions, you couldn't see a thing.

"Morning, ma'am."

"Good morning."

"Where you heading?"

"Salt Lake City."

"Purpose of your visit?"

"Visit my daughter."

"Any tobacco, liquor, or firearms?"

"Don't smoke."

"Any plants or fruit?"

"Not any more."

"Citizenship?"

"Blackfoot."

The guard rocked back on his heels and jammed his thumbs into his belt. "Thank you," he said, his fingers patting the butt of the revolver. "Have a pleasant trip."

My mother rolled the car forward, and the television people had to scramble out of the way. They ran alongside the car as we pulled away from the border, and, when they couldn't run any farther, they stood in the middle of the highway and waved and waved and waved.

We got to Salt Lake City the next day. Laetitia was happy to see us, and, that first night, she took us out to a restaurant that made really good soups. The list of pies took up a whole page. I had cherry. Mom had chocolate. Laetitia said that she saw us on television the night before and, during the meal, she had us tell her the story over and over again.

Laetitia took us everywhere. We went to a fancy ski resort. We went to the temple. We got to go shopping in a couple of large malls, but they weren't as large as the one in Edmonton, and Mom said so.

After a week or so, I got bored and wasn't at all sad when my mother said we should be heading back home. Laetitia wanted us to stay longer, but Mom said no, that she had things to do back home and that, next time, Laetitia should come up and visit. Laetitia said she was thinking about moving back, and Mom told her to do as she pleased, and Laetitia said that she would.

On the way home, we stopped at the duty-free shop, and my mother gave Mel a green hat that said "Salt Lake" across the front. Mel was a funny guy. He took the hat and blew his nose and told my mother that she was an inspiration to us all. He gave us some more peanut brittle and came out into the parking lot and waved at us all the way to the Canadian border.

It was almost evening when we left Coutts. I watched the border through the rear window until all you could see were the tops of the flag-poles and the blue water tower, and then they rolled over a hill and disap-peared.

1993

HOW TO DATE A
BROWNGIRL, BLACKGIRL,
WHITEGIRL, OR HALFIE

Junot Díaz

Wait for your brother and your mother to leave the apartment. You've already told them that you're feeling too sick to go to Union City to visit that tía who likes to squeeze your nuts. (He's gotten big, she'll say.) And even though your moms knows you ain't sick you stuck to your story until finally she said, Go ahead and stay, malcriado.

Clear the government cheese from the refrigerator. If the girl's from the Terrace stack the boxes behind the milk. If she's from the Park or Society Hill hide the cheese in the cabinet above the oven, way up where she'll never see. Leave yourself a reminder to get it out before morning or your moms will kick your ass. Take down any embarrassing photos of your family in the campo, especially the one with the half-naked kids dragging a goat on a rope leash. The kids are your cousins and by now they're old enough to understand why you're doing what you're doing. Hide the pictures of yourself with an Afro. Make sure the bathroom is presentable. Put the basket with all the crapped-on toilet paper under the sink. Spray the bucket with Lysol, then close the cabinet.

Shower, comb, dress. Sit on the couch and watch TV. If she's an outsider her father will be bringing her, maybe her mother. Neither of them want her seeing any boys from the Terrace—people get stabbed in the Terrace—but she's strong-headed and this time will get her way. If she's a whitegirl you know you'll at least get a hand job.

The directions were in your best handwriting, so her parents won't think you're an idiot. Get up from the couch and check the parking lot. Nothing. If the girl's local, don't sweat it. She'll flow over when she's good and ready. Sometimes she'll run into her other friends and a whole crowd

will show up at your apartment and even though that means you ain't getting shit it will be fun anyway and you'll wish these people would come
over more often. Sometimes the girl won't flow over at all and the next day
in school she'll say sorry, smile and you'll be stupid enough to believe her
and ask her out again.

Wait and after an hour go out to your corner. The neighborhood is full
of traffic. Give one of your boys a shout and when he says, Are you still waiting on that bitch? say, Hell yeah.

Get back inside. Call her house and when her father picks up ask if
she's there. He'll ask, Who is this? Hang up. He sounds like a principal or
a police chief, the sort of dude with a big neck, who never has to watch his
back. Sit and wait. By the time your stomach's ready to give out on you, a
Honda or maybe a Jeep pulls in and out she comes.

Hey, you'll say.

Look, she'll say. My mom wants to meet you. She's got herself all worried about nothing.

Don't panic. Say, Hey, no problem. Run a hand through your hair like
the whiteboys do even though the only thing that runs easily through your
hair is Africa. She will look good. The white ones are the ones you want the
most, aren't they, but usually the out-of-towners are black, blackgirls who
grew up with ballet and Girl Scouts, who have three cars in their driveways. If she's a halfie don't be surprised that her mother is white. Say, Hi.
Her moms will say hi and you'll see that you don't scare her, not really. She
will say that she needs easier directions to get out and even though she has
the best directions in her lap give her new ones. Make her happy.

You have choices. If the girl's from around the way, take her to El
Cibao for dinner. Order everything in your busted-up Spanish. Let her correct you if she's Latina and amaze her if she's black. If she's not from around
the way, Wendy's will do. As you walk to the restaurant talk about school. A
local girl won't need stories about the neighborhood but the other ones
might. Supply the story about the loco who'd been storing canisters of tear
gas in his basement for years, how one day the canisters cracked and the
whole neighborhood got a dose of the military-strength stuff. Don't tell her
that your moms knew right away what it was, that she recognized its smell
from the year the United States invaded your island.

Hope that you don't run into your nemesis, Howie, the Puerto Rican kid
with the two killer mutts. He walks them all over the neighborhood and every
now and then the mutts corner themselves a cat and tear it to shreds, Howie

laughing as the cat flips up in the air, it neck twisted around like an owl, red meat showing through the soft fur. If his dogs haven't cornered the cat, he will walk behind you and ask, Hey, Yunior, is that your new fuckbuddy?

Let him talk. Howie weighs about two hundred pounds and could eat you if he wanted. At the field he will turn away. He has new sneakers, and doesn't want them muddy. If the girl's an outsider she will hiss now and say, What a fucking asshole. A homegirl would have been yelling back at him the whole time, unless she was shy. Either way don't feel bad that you didn't do anything. Never lose a fight on a first date or that will be the end of it.

Dinner will be tense. You are not good at talking to people you don't know. A halfie will tell you that her parents met in the Movement, will say, Back then people thought it a radical thing to do. It will sound like something her parents made her memorize. Your brother once heard that one and said, Man, that sounds like a whole lot of Uncle Tomming to me. Don't repeat this.

Put down your hamburger and say, It must have been hard.

She will appreciate your interest. She will tell you more. Black people, she will say, treat me real bad. That's why I don't like them. You'll wonder how she feels about Dominicans. Don't ask. Let her speak on it and when you're both finished eating walk back into the neighborhood. The skies will be magnificent. Pollutants have made Jersey sunsets one of the wonders of the world. Point it out. Touch her shoulder and say, That's nice, right?

Get serious. Watch TV but stay alert. Sip some of the Bermúdez that your father left in the cabinet, which nobody touches. A local girl may have hips and a thick ass but she won't be quick about letting you touch. She has to live in the same neighborhood you do, has to deal with you being all up in her business. She might just chill with you and then go home. She might kiss you and then go, or she might, if she's reckless, give it up, but that's rare. Kissing will suffice. A whitegirl might just give it up right then. Don't stop her. She'll take her gum out of her mouth, stick it to the plastic sofa covers and then will move close to you. You have nice eyes, she might say.

Tell her that you love her hair, that you love her skin, her lips, because, in truth, you love them more than you love your own.

She'll say, I like Spanish guys, and even though you've never been to Spain, say, I like you. You'll sound smooth.

You'll be with her until about eight-thirty and then she will want to wash up. In the bathroom she will hum a song from a radio and her waist will keep the beat against the lip of the sink. Imagine her old lady coming to get her, what she would say if she knew her daughter had just lain under you and blown your name, pronounced with her eighth-grade Spanish, into your ear. While she's in the bathroom call one of your boys and say, Lo hice, loco. Or just sit back on the couch and smile.

But usually it won't work this way. Be prepared. She will not want to kiss you. Just cool it, she'll say. The halfie might lean back, breaking away from you. She will cross her arms, say, I hate my tits. Stroke her hair but she will pull away. I don't like anybody touching my hair, she will say. She will act like somebody you don't know. In school she is known for her attention-grabbing laugh, as high and far-ranging as a gull, but here she will worry you. You will not know what to say.

You're the only kind of guy who asks me out, she will say. Your neighbors will start their hyena calls, now that the alcohol is in them. You and the blackboys.

Say nothing. Let her button her shirt, let her comb her hair, the sound of it stretching like a sheet of fire between you. When her father pulls in and beeps, let her go without too much of a good-bye. She won't want it. During the next hour the phone will ring. You will be tempted to pick it up. Don't. Watch the shows you want to watch, without a family around to debate you. Don't go downstairs. Don't fall asleep. It won't help. Put the government cheese back in its place before your moms kills you.

1996

IV. REMEMBERING

OLD WEST

Richard Bausch

1950

Don't let my age or my clothes fool you. I've traveled the world. I've read all the books and tried all the counsels of the flesh, too. I've been up and down and I've lived to see the story of my own coming of age in the Old West find its way into the general mind, if you will. In late middle age, for a while, I entertained on the vaudeville stage, telling the story. It's easy to look past an old man now, I know. But in those days I was pretty good. The Old West was my subject. I had that one story I liked to tell, about Shane coming into our troubled mountain valley. You know the story. Well, I was the one, the witness. The little boy. I had come from there, from that big sky, those tremendous spaces, and I had seen it all. And yet the reason I could tell the story well enough to work in vaudeville with it was that I no longer quite believed it.

What I have to tell now is about that curious fact.

I've never revealed any of this before. Back then, I couldn't have, because it might've threatened my livelihood; and later I didn't because — well, just because. But the fact is, he came back to the valley twelve, thirteen years later. Joe Starrett was dead of the cholera, and though Mother and I were still living on the place, there really wasn't much to recommend it anymore. You couldn't get corn or much of anything green to grow. That part of the world was indeed cattle country and for all the bravery of the homesteaders, people had begun to see this at last.

We'd buried Joe Starrett out behind the barn, and Mother didn't want to leave him there, wouldn't move to town. Town, by the way, hadn't really changed, either: the center of it was still Grafton's one all-purpose building —

though, because it was the site of the big gunfight, it had somewhat of the
aspect of a museum about it now, Grafton having left the bullet hole in the
wall and marked out the stains of blood on the dusty floor. But it was still the
center of activity, still served as the saloon and general store, and lately, on
Sundays, it had even become a place of worship.

I should explain this last, since it figures pretty prominently in what
happened that autumn I turned twenty-one: one day late in the previous
winter a short, squat old bird who called himself the Right Reverend Bagley
rode into the valley on the back of a donkey and within a week's time was
a regular sight on Sunday, preaching from the upstairs gallery of the saloon.
What happened was, he walked into Grafton's, ordered a whiskey and
drank it down, then turned and looked at the place: five or six cowhands,
the cattle baron's old henchmen, and a whore that Grafton had brought
back with him from the East that summer. (Nobody was really *with* anybody; it was early evening. The sun hadn't dropped below the mountains
yet.) Anyway, Bagley turned at the bar and looked everybody over, and then
he announced in a friendly but firm tone that he considered himself a man
of the gospel, and it was his opinion that this town was in high need of some
serious saviorizing. I wasn't there, but I understand that Grafton, from
behind the bar, asked him what he meant, and that Bagley began to explain
in terms that fairly mesmerized everyone in the place. (It is true that the
whore went back East around this time, but nobody had the courage—or
the meanness—to ask Grafton whether or not there was a connection.)

But as I was saying, the town wasn't much, and it wasn't going to *be*
much. By now everybody had pretty well accepted this. We were going on
with our lives, the children were growing up and leaving, and even some of
the older ones, the original homesteaders who had stood and risked themselves for all of it alongside Joe Starrett, who had withstood the pressure of
the cattlemen, had found reasons to move on. It's simple enough to say
why: the winters were long and harsh; the ground, as I said, was stingy;
there were better things beyond the valley (we had heard, for instance, that
in San Francisco people were riding electric cars to the tops of buildings;
Grafton claimed to have seen one in an exhibit in New York).

I was restless. It was just Mother and me in the cabin, and we weren't
getting along too well. She'd gone a little crazy with Joe Starrett's death; she
wasn't even fifty yet, but she looked at least fifteen years older than that. In
the evenings she wanted me with her, and I wanted to be at Grafton's. Most
of the men in the valley were spending their evenings there. We did a lot of

heavy drinking back in those days. A lot of people stayed drunk most of the time during the week. Nobody felt very good in the mornings. And on Sundays we'd go aching and sick back to Grafton's, the place of our sinful pastimes, to hear old Bagley preach. Mother, too. The smell of that place on a Sunday—the mixture of perfume and sweat and whiskey, and the deep effuvium of the spittoons, was enough to make your breathing stop at the bottom of your throat.

Life was getting harder all the time, and we were not particularly deserving of anything different, and we knew it.

Sometimes the only thing to talk about was the gunfight, though I'm willing to admit that I had contributed to this; I was, after all, the sole witness, and I did discover over the years that I liked to talk about it. It was history, I thought. A story—my story. I could see everything that I remembered with all the clarity of daytime sight, and I *believed* it. The principal actors, through my telling, were fixed forever in the town's lore—if you could call it lore. Three of them were still buried on the hill outside town, including Wilson, the gunfighter who was so fast on the draw and who was shot in the blazing battle at Grafton's by the quiet stranger who had ridden into our valley and changed it forever.

He came back that autumn, all those years later, and, as before, I was the first to see him coming, sitting atop that old paint of his, though of course it wasn't the same horse. Couldn't have been. Yet it was old. As a matter of harsh fact, it was, I would soon find out, a slightly swaybacked mare with a mild case of lung congestion. I was mending a fence out past the creek, standing there in the warm sun, muttering to myself, thinking about going to town for some whiskey, and I saw him far off, just a slow-moving speck at the foot of the mountains. Exactly like the first time. Except that I was older, and maybe half as curious. I had pretty much taken the attitude of the valley: I was reluctant to face anything new—suspicious of change, afraid of the unpredictable. I looked off at him as he approached and thought of the other time, that first time. I couldn't see who it was, of course, and had no idea it would actually turn out to be him, and for a little aching moment I wanted it to *be* him—but as he was when I was seven; myself as I was then. The whole time back, and Joe Starrett chopping wood within my hearing, a steady man, good and strong, standing astride his own life, ready for anything. I stood there remembering this, some part of me yearning for it, and soon he was close enough to see. I could just make him out. Or rather, I could just make out the pearl-handled six-shooter. Stepping away from the fence, I waited for him, aching, and then quite suddenly I wanted to signal him to turn around, find another valley. I wasn't even curious. I knew, before I could distinguish the changed shape of his body and the thickened features of his face, that he would be far different from my memory of him, and I recalled that he'd left us with the chance for some progress, the hope of concerning ourselves with the arts of peace. I thought of my meager town, the years of idleness in Grafton's store. I wasn't straight or tall, particularly. I was just a dirt farmer with no promise of much and no gentleness or good wishes anymore, plagued with a weakness for whiskey.

Nothing could have prepared me for the sight of him.

The shock of it took my breath away. His buckskins were frayed and torn, besmirched with little maplike continents of salt stains and sweat. He was huge around the middle—his gunbelt had been stretched to a small homemade hole he'd made in it so he could still wear it—and the flesh under his chin was swollen and heavy. His whole face seemed to have dropped and gathered around his jaws, and when he lifted his hat I saw the bald crown of his head through his blowing hair. Oh, he'd gone very badly to seed. "You wouldn't be—" he began.

"It's me all right," I said.

He shifted a little in the saddle. "Well."

"You look like you've come a long way," I said.

He didn't answer. For a moment, we simply stared at each other. Then he climbed laboriously down from the nag and stood there holding the reins.

"Where does the time go," he said, after what seemed a hopeless minute.

Now I didn't answer. I looked at his boots. The toes were worn away; it was all frayed, soiled cloth there. I felt for him. My heart went out to him. And yet as I looked at him I knew that more than anything, more than my oldest childhood dream and ambition, I didn't want him there.

"Is your father—" he hesitated, looked beyond me.

"Buried over yonder," I said.

"And Marian?" He was holding his hat in his hands.

"Look," I said. "What did you come back for, anyway?"

He put the hat back on. "Marian's dead, too?"

"I don't think she'll be glad to see you," I said. "She's settled into a kind of life."

He looked toward the mountains, and a little breeze crossed toward us from the creek. It rippled the water there and made shadows on it, then reached us, moved the hair over his ears. "I'm not here altogether out of love," he said.

I thought I'd heard a trace of irony in his voice. "Love?" I said. "Really?"

"I mean love of the valley," he told me.

I didn't say anything. He took a white handkerchief out of his shirt—it was surprisingly clean—and wiped the back of his neck with it, then folded it and put it back.

"Can I stay here for a few days?" he asked.

"Look," I said. "It's complicated."

"You don't want me to stay even a little while?"

I said nothing for a time. We were just looking at each other across the short distance between us. "You can come up to the cabin," I told him. "But I need some time to prepare my mother for this. I don't want—and you don't want—to just be riding in on her."

"I understand," he said.

Mother had some time ago taken to sitting in the window of the cabin with my old breech-loading rifle across her lap. When she'd done baking the bread and tending the garden, when she'd finished milking the two cows and churning the butter, when the eggs were put up and the cabin was swept and clean and the clothes were all hanging on the line in the yard, she'd place herself by the window, gun cocked and ready to shoot. Maybe two years earlier, some poor, lost, starved, lone Comanche had wandered down from the north and stopped his horse at the edge of the creek, looking at us, his hands visored over his eyes. He was easily ninety years old, and when he turned to make his way west along the creek, on out of sight, Mother took my rifle off the wall, loaded it, and set herself up by the window.

"Marian," I said. "It was just an old brave looking for a good place to die."

"You let me worry about it, son."

Well, for a while that worked out all right, in fact; it kept her off me and my liquid pursuits down at Grafton's. She could sit there and take potshots at squirrels in the brush all day if she wanted to, I thought. But in the last few months it had begun to feel dangerous approaching the cabin at certain hours of the day and night. You had to remember that she was there, and sometimes, coming home from Grafton's, I'd had enough firewater to forget. I had her testimony that I had nearly got my head blown off more than once, and once she had indeed fired upon me.

This happened about a week before he came back into the valley, and I felt it then as a kind of evil premonition—I should say I *believe* I felt it that way, since I have the decades of hindsight now, and I do admit that the holocaust which was coming to us might provide anyone who survived it with a sense that all sorts of omens and portents preceded the event. In any case, the night Marian fired on me, I was ambling sleepily along, drunk, barely able to hold on to the pommel, and letting the horse take me home. We crossed the creek and headed up the path to the house. The shot nicked me above the elbow— a tiny cut of flesh that the bullet took out as it went singing off into the blackness behind me. The explosion, the stinging crease of the bullet just missing bone, and the shriek of my horse sent me flying into the water of the creek.

"I got you, you damn savage Indian," Marian yelled from the cabin.

I lay there in the cold water and reflected that my mother had grown odd. "Hey!" I called, staying low, hearing her put another shell into the breech. "It's me! It's your son!"

"I got a repeating rifle here," she lied. She'd reloaded and was aiming again. I could actually hear it in her voice. "I don't have any children on the place."

There is no sound as awful and startling as the sound of a bullet screaming off rock, when you know it is aimed earnestly at you.

"Wait!" I yelled. "Goddammit, Marian, it's me! For God's sake, it's your own family!"

"Who?"

"Your son," I said. "And you've wounded me."

"I don't care what he's done," she said and fired again. The bullet buzzed over head like a terribly purposeful insect.

"Remember how you didn't want any more guns in the valley?" I shouted. "You remember how much you hate them?"

She said, "Who is that down there?"

"It's me," I said. "Good Christ, I'm shot."

She fired again. This one hit the water behind me and went off skipping like a piece of slate somebody threw harder than a thing can be thrown. "Blaspheming marauders!" she yelled.

"It's me!" I screamed. "I'm sick. I'm coming from Grafton's. I'm shot in the arm."

I heard her reload, and then there was a long silence.

"Marian?" I said, keeping low. "Would you shoot your own son dead?"

"How do I know it's you?"

"Well, who else would it be at this hour?"

"You stay where you are until I come down and see, or I'll blow your head off," she said.

So I stayed right where I was, in the cold running creek, until she got up the nerve to approach me with her lantern and her cocked rifle. Only then did she give in and tend to me, her only son, nearly killed, hurting with a wound she herself had inflicted.

"You've been to Grafton's drinking that whiskey," she said, putting the lantern down.

"You hate guns," I told her. "Right?"

"I'm not letting you sleep it off in the morning, either."

"Just don't shoot at me," I said.

But she had already started up on something else. That was the way her mind had gone over the years, and you never knew quite how to take her.

And so that day when he rode up, I told him to stay out of sight and went carefully back up to the cabin. "Mother," I said. "Here I come."

"In here," she said from the barn. She was churning butter, and she simply waited for me to get to the window and peer over the sill. I did so, the same way I almost always did now: carefully, like a man in the middle of a gunfight.

"What?" she said. "What?"

I had decided during my stealthy course up the path that my way of preparing her for his return would be to put her out of the way of it, if I could. Any way I could. She was sitting there in the middle of the straw-strewn floor with a floppy straw hat on her head as though the sun were beating down on her. Her hands looked so old, gripping the butter churn. "Mother," I said. "The Reverend Bagley wants you to bring him some bread for Sunday's communion."

"Who's dead?"

On top of everything else, of course, she'd begun to lose her hearing. I repeated myself, fairly shrieking it at her.

"Bagley always wants that," she said, looking away. "I take the bread over on Saturdays. This isn't Saturday. You don't need to yell."

"It's a special request," I said. "He needs it early this week." If I could get her away from the cabin now, I could make some arrangements. I could find someplace else for our return visitor to stay. I could find out what he wanted, and then act on it in some way. But I wasn't really thinking very clearly. Marian and old Bagley had been seeing each other for occasional Saturday and Sunday afternoon picnics, and some evenings, too. There could have been no communication between Bagley and me without Marian knowing about it. I stood there trying to think up some other pretext, confused by the necessity of explaining the ridiculous excuse for a pretext I had just used, and she came slowly to her feet, sighing, touching her back low, shaking her head, turning away from me.

"Hitch the team up," she said.

It took a moment for me to realize that she'd actually believed me. "I can't go with you," I told her.

"You don't expect me to go by myself." She wiped her hands on the front of her dress. "Go on. Hitch the team."

"All right," I said. I knew there would be no arguing with her. She'd set herself to my lie, and once her mind was set you couldn't alter or change it. Besides, I was leery of giving her too much time to ponder over things. I'd decided the best thing was to go along and deal with everything as it came. There was a chance I could get away after we got to town; I could hightail it back home and make some adjustment or some arrangement. "I have to tie off what I'm doing with the fence," I told her. "You change and I'll be ready."

"You're going to change?"

"You change."

"You want *me* to change?"

"You've got dirt all over the front of you."

She shook her head, lifted the dress a little to keep it out of the dust, and made her slow way across to the cabin. When she was inside, I tore over to the fence and found him sitting his horse, nodding, half dozing, his hat hanging from the pommel of his saddle, his sparse hair standing up in the wind. He looked a little pathetic.

"Hey," I said, a little louder than I had to, I admit.

He tried to draw his pistol. The horse jumped, stepped back, coughing. His hand missed the pearl handle, and then the horse was turning in a tight circle, stomping his hat where it had fallen, and he sat there holding on to the pommel, saying. "Whoa. Hold it. Damn. Whoa, will you?" When he got the horse calmed, I bent down and retrieved his hat.

"Here," I said. "Lord."

He slapped the hat against his thigh, sending off a small white puff of dust, then put it on. The horse turned again, so that now his back was to me.

"For God's sake," I said. "Why don't you get down off him?"

"Damn spooky old paint," he said, getting it turned. "Listen, boy, I've come a long way on him. I've slept on him and just let him wander where he wanted. I've been that hungry and that desperate." The paint seemed to want to put him down as he spoke. I thought it might even begin to buck.

"Look," I said. "We need to talk. We don't have a lot of time, either."

"I was hoping I could ride up to the cabin," he said.

I shook my head. "Out of the question."

"No?"

"Not a chance," I said.

He got down. The paint coughed like an old sick man, stepped away from us, put its gray muzzle down in the saw grass by the edge of the water, and began to eat.

"A little congestion," he said.

The paint coughed into the grass.

"I can't ride in?"

"On that?"

He looked down.

"Look," I said. "It would upset her. You might get your head shot off."

He stared at me. "Marian has a gun?"

"Marian shoots before she asks questions these days," I said.

"What happened?" he wanted to know.

"She got suspicious," I said. "How do I know?" And I couldn't keep the irritation out of my voice.

He said nothing.

"You can use the barn," I told him. "But you have to wait until we leave, and you can't let her see you. You're just going to have to take my word for it."

Again he took the hat off, looking down. Seeing the freckles on his scalp, I wished he'd put it back on.

"Wait here and keep out of sight until you see us heading off toward town," I said. I couldn't resist adding, "There's a preacher who likes her, and she likes him back." I watched his face, remembering with a kind of sad satisfaction the way—as I had so often told it—he'd leaned down to me, bleeding, from his horse and said, "Tell your mother there's no more guns in the valley."

He put the hat back on.

I said, "I'm hoping she'll be tied up with him for a while, anyway, until I can figure something out."

"Who's the preacher?" he said, staring.

"There's nothing you can do about it," I said.

"I'd just like to know his name."

I said the name, and he nodded, repeating it almost to himself. "Bagley."

"Now will you do as I say?" I asked.

"I will," he said. "If you'll do something for me." And now I saw a little of the old fire in his eyes. It sent a thrill through me. This was, after all, the same man I remembered single-handedly killing the old cattle baron and his hired gunfighter in the space of a half second. I had often talked about the fact that while my shouted warning might have been what saved him from the backshooter aiming at him from the gallery, the shot he made — turning into the explosion and smoke of the ambush and firing from reflex, almost as if the Colt in his flashing hand had simply gone off by accident — was the most astonishing feat of gun handling and shooting that anyone ever saw: one shot, straight through the backshooter's heart, and the man toppled from the gallery like a big sack of feed, dead before he even let go of his still smoking rifle. That was how I had told the story; that was how I remembered everything.

"All right," I said.

He took a step away from me, then removed his hat again, stood there smoothing its brim, folding it, or trying to. "This Bagley," he said over his shoulder. "How long's he been here?"

"I don't know," I said, and I didn't exactly. Nobody ever counted much time in those days, beyond looking for the end of winter, the cold that kills. "Sometime last winter, I guess."

"He's your preacher."

"I guess."

"Ordained?"

In those days, I didn't know the word.

"What church is he with?"

"No church," I said. "Grafton's. His own church."

"Set up for himself, then."

"Every Sunday. He preaches from the gallery."

"Does he wear a holster?"

"Not that I know of."

"You ever see him shoot?"

"No," I said. Then: "Listen, shooting the preacher won't change any-thing."

He gave me a look of such forlorn unhappiness that I almost corrected myself. "Maybe I won't be staying very long at all," he said.

"Just wait here," I told him.

He nodded, but he wasn't looking at me.

On the way to town, I kept thinking of the hangdog way he'd stood watching me go back to the cabin for Marian—the vanquished look of his face and the dejection in his bowed stance. I wasn't prepared to think I could've so defeated him with news, or with words. Certainly there was something else weighing him down. Marian rode along beside me, staring off at the mountains, her rough, red hands lying in her lap. To tell the truth, I didn't want to know what she might be thinking. Those days, if asked, she was likely to begin a tirade. There was always something working on her sense of well-being and symmetry. Entropy and decline were everywhere. She saw evil in every possible guise. Moral decay. Spiritual deprivation and chaos. Along with her window sitting, armed to the teeth and waiting for marauders, I'm afraid she'd started building up some rather strange hostili-ties toward the facts of existence: there had even been times, over the years, when I could have said she meant to demand all the rights and privileges of manhood, and I might not have been far from wrong. That may sound advanced, to your ears; in her day, it was cracked. In any case, way out there in the harsh, hard life of the valley, I had managed to keep these more bizarre aspects of her decline from general knowledge. And I'd watched with gladness her developing attachment to old Bagley, who had a way of agreeing with her without ever committing himself to any of it.

"So," she said now. "Why'd you want to get me away from the house?"

For a moment I couldn't speak.

"I can't believe you remember it's the anniversary of our coming here."

Now I was really dumbfounded. Things had worked into my hands, in a way, and I was too stupefied to take advantage of the fact.

"Well?" she said.

I stammered something about being found out in my effort to surprise her, then went on to make up a lie about taking her to Grafton's for a glass of the new bottled Coke soda. Grafton had tried some of it on his last trip to New York and had been stocking it ever since. Now and then Marian liked to be spoiled, driven in the wagon to some planned destination and treated like a lady. For all her crazy talk, she could be sweet sometimes; she could remember how things were when Joe Starrett was around and she was his good wife.

"We're not going to see Bagley?"

"We can stop by and see him," I said.

The team pulled us along the road. It was a sunny day, clear and a little chilly. She turned and looked behind us in that way she had sometimes of sensing things. "Look," she said.

It was the dust of a lone rider, a long way off, following, gaining on us. I didn't allow myself to think anything about it.

"I thought I heard you talking to somebody down at the spring," she said. "Could this be him?"

"Who?" I said. It was amazing how often her difficulty hearing yielded up feats of overhearing, long distances bridged by some mysterious transmutation of her bad nerves and her suspicions.

"I don't know," she said. "Whoever you were talking to."

"I wasn't talking to anybody," I said, and I knew I sounded guilty.

"I thought I heard something," she mumbled, turning again to look behind us.

I had ahold of the reins, and without having to think about it I started flapping them a little against the hindquarters of the team. We sped up some.

"What're you doing?" she said. "It's not Indians, is it?"

We were going at a pretty good gait now.

"It's Comanches," she said, breathless, reaching into her shawl and bringing out a big six-shot Colt. It was so heavy for her that she had to heft it with both hands.

"Where in God's name did you get that thing?" I said.

"Bagley gave it to me for just this purpose."

"It's not Indians," I said. "Jesus. All the Indians are peaceful now anyway."

She was looking back, trying to get the pistol aimed that way and managing only to aim it at me.

"Will you," I said, ducking. "Marian."

"Just let me get turned," she said.

When she had got it pointed behind us, she pulled the hammer back with both thumbs. It fired, and it was so unwieldy in her hands, going off toward the blue sky as she went awry on the seat, that it looked like something that had got ahold of her.

"Marian!" I yelled.

The team was taking off with us; it was all I could do to hold them. She was getting herself right in the seat again, trying to point the Colt.

"Give me that," I said.

"Faster!" she screamed, firing again. This time she knocked part of a pine branch off at the rim of the sky. Under the best circumstances, if she'd been aiming for it and had had the time to draw a good bead on it, anyone would have said it was a brilliant shot. But it knocked her back again, and I got hold of the hot barrel of the damn thing and wrenched it from her.

"All right!" she yelled. "Goddammit, give me the reins, then!"

I suppose she'd had the time to notice, during her attempts to kill him on the run, that he was quickly catching up to us. Now he came alongside me, and he had his own Colt drawn. I dropped Marian's into the well of the wagon seat and pulled the team to a halt, somehow managing to keep Marian in her place at my side. She was looking at him now, but I don't think she recognized him. Her face was registering relief—I guess at the fact that he wasn't a Comanche.

He still had his gun drawn. "So," he said. "You were going to warn him."

"What the hell are you talking about?" I said. I was pretty mad now. "Will you put that Colt away, please?"

He kept it where it was, leveled at me.

"I know," I said. "I'm going to get shot. It must be God's plan. First her, and now you."

"You were shooting at me."

"No, he wasn't," Marian said. "I was."

He looked at her, then smiled. It was a sad, tentative, disappointed smile. I don't think he could quite believe what time had done to her. She was staring back at him with those fierce, cold, pioneer-stubborn, unrecognizing eyes. "Marian?" he said.

"What."

"You were going to warn him, weren't you."

"Warn who?" I said.

"She knows." He looked past me at her. "Well, Marian?"

"I can't believe it," she said. "After all these years. Look at you. What happened to you?"

He said nothing to this.

"Will you please holster your Colt," I said to him.

"Marian," he said, doing as I asked with the Colt. "You were going to tell him I was here, right?"

"Will somebody tell me what's going on here?" I said.

Marian stared straight ahead, her hands folded on her lap. "My son was taking me to Grafton's for a bottle of Coke soda."

"That's the truth," I said to him. "I was trying to spare her the shock of seeing you. I told you I had to make some arrangements."

"I—I was sorry to hear about Joe," he said, looking past me again.

"Joe," she said. She merely repeated the name.

He waited.

"She thought you were an Indian," I said.

"I'm here to get a man named Phegley—self-styled preacher. Squarish, small build. Clean-shaven. Rattlery voice. I was hired to chase him, and I think I chased him here."

"This one's name is Bagley," I said. "And he's got a beard."

"He's used other names. Maybe he's grown a beard. I'll know him on sight."

Through all this Marian simply stared at him, her hands still knotted on her lap. "You're going to kill him," she said now.

"I'm going to take him back to Utah, if he'll come peacefully."

"Look at you," she said. "I just don't believe it."

"You haven't changed at all," he said. It was almost charming.

"I don't believe it," my mother said under her breath.

He got down off his horse and tied it to the back of the wagon, then climbed up on the back bench.

"I hope you don't mind," he said, nodding politely.

"We really are going to Grafton's," I said.

"That's fine."

"I don't think Bagley will be there."

"I'm sure I'll run into him sooner or later."

"If somebody doesn't warn the poor man," Marian said.

"Well," he said. "Phegley—or Bagley—will use a pistol."

Then we were just going along toward town. In a way, we were as we had once been—or we were a shade of it. The wagon, raising its long column of dust, and the horse trotting along, tethered to the back. I held the reins as Joe Starrett had held them, and wondered what the woman seated to my right could be thinking about.

Bagley lived in a little shed out in back of the stables. The smell of horses was on him all the time, though he never did any riding to speak of, and he never quite got himself clean enough for me to be able to stand him at close quarters for very long. Back then, of course, people could go several seasons without feeling it necessary to be anywhere near the vicinity of a bath, and Bagley was one of them. On top of this, he was argumentative and usually pretty grumpy and ill-tempered. And for some reason—some unknown reason fathomable only to her, and maybe, to give him the credit of some self-esteem, to Bagley, too—Marian liked him. He had a way of talking to her as if the two of them were in some sort of connivance about things (I had heard him do this, had marveled at it, wondered about it). And he'd done some reading. He'd been out in the world, and around some. He'd told Marian that when he was a younger man, he'd traveled to the farthest reaches of the north and got three of his toes frozen off, one on one foot and two on the other. Marian said she'd seen the proof of this. I didn't care to know more.

What I found interesting was the fact that Bagley was usually available for our late-night rounds of whiskey drinking and was often enough among the red-eyed and half-sick the following morning—even, sometimes, Sunday morning. In fact, it was when he was hung over that he could be really frightening as an evangelist; the pains of hell, which he was always promising for all sinners, were visible in his face: "Hold on, brethren, for this here is the end times!" he'd shout. "This is the last of civilized humankind. Hold on. We've already broken the chain! The end has already begun. Hold on. Storms are coming! War! New ways of killing! Bombs that cause the sun to blot out, hold on! I said, Hold on! Death falling from the sky and floating up out of the ground! I don't believe you heard me, brethren. Plagues and wars and bunched towns clenched on empty pleasures and fear, it's on its way, just hold on! Miseries and diseases we ain't even named! Pornography and vulgar worship of possessions, belief in the self above all else, abortion, religious fraud, fanatic violence, mass murder, and killing boredom, it's all coming, hold on! Spiritual destitution and unbelievable banality, do hold on!"

He was something.

And you got the feeling he believed it all: when he really got going, he looked like one of those crazed, half-starved prophets come back from forty days and nights in the desert.

I hadn't had a lot to do with him in the time he'd been in town, but I had told him the story of the gunfight. It was one of those nights we were all up drinking whiskey and talking. We were sitting in Grafton's around the stove, passing a bottle back and forth. It was late. Just Grafton and Bagley and me. I went through the whole story: the cattle baron and his bad men trying to run us all off, and the stranger riding into the valley and siding with us, the man with the pearl-handled Colt and the quick nervous hands who seemed always on the lookout for something. The arrival of Wilson, a killer with the cold blood of a poisonous snake. And the inevitable gunfight itself, my memory of Wilson in black pants with a black vest and white shirt, drawing his Colt, and the speed of the hands that beat him to the draw. Bagley listened, staring at me like consternation itself.

"Wilson was fast," I said to him. "Fast on the draw."

"Young man, you should tell stories of inspiration and good works. Do I detect a bit of exaggeration in your story?"

"Exaggeration," I said. I couldn't believe I was being challenged.

"A little stretching of things, maybe?"

"Like what?" I said, angry now.

"I don't know. What about this Wilson? Was he really so cold-blooded?"

"He shot a man dead outside on the street. He picked a fight with him and then slaughtered him with no more regard than you'd give a bug. We buried the poor man the day before the fight."

"And this Wilson—he wore black?"

I nodded. "Except for the white shirt."

"I knew a Wilson," he said. "Of course, that's a common name. But this one was a sort of professional gunfighter, too. Sort of. Not at all like the one you describe. I heard he was shot somewhere out in the territories, a few years back."

This had the effect of making me quite reasonlessly angry, as though Bagley were trying to cast some doubt on me. It also troubled something in my mind, which glimmered for a second and then went on its unsettling way. I was drunk. There were things I didn't want to talk about anymore. I was abruptly very depressed and unhappy.

"What is it, son?" he said.

"Nothing."

He leaned back in his chair and drank from the bottle we had all been passing around.

"I seem to remember Wilson as wearing buckskins," Grafton said.

"No," I said. "He was wearing black pants and a black vest over a white shirt. And he had a two-gun rig."

"Well," said Bagley. "The Wilson I knew carried this old heavy Colt. Carried it in his pants."

"Come to think of it, I don't believe I remember two guns on him," said Grafton.

"It was two guns," I said. "I saw them. I was there."

"Boy *was* there," Grafton said to Bagley. "You have to hand him that."

"Must not be the same Wilson," Bagley said.

"You ever been in a gunfight, Reverend?" Grafton asked him.

"No, I usually run at the first sign of trouble."

"Do you own a gun?" I asked him.

He shook his head. "I had once. Matter of fact, this Wilson fellow—the one I knew—he gave it to me. Come to think of it, he had three of them. And he carried them all on his person. But the one he used most was always stuck down in his belt."

"Why would he give you a Colt?" I asked him.

"I don't recall. Seems to me I won it from him, playing draw poker. We were both a little drunk. He could be an amiable old boy, too. Give you the shirt off his back if he was in a good mood. Trouble was, he wasn't often disposed to be in a good mood."

"Was he fast on the draw?" I asked.

He made a sound in his throat, cleared it, looking at me. "You read a lot, do you?"

"Some," I lied. I was barely able to write my name, then, for all Marian's early efforts.

"Well," said Bagley, clearing his throat again. "I seem to recall that when old Wilson was upset he was quick to shoot people, if that's what you mean."

"Was he fast?"

"I don't think he thought in those terms. He usually had his six-shooter out and already cocked if he thought there would be any reason to use it."

Grafton said, "You know quite a bit about this sort of thing, don't you, Reverend?"

Bagley nodded, folding his pudgy hands across his chest. He looked at me. "I guess I saw some things over the years of my enslavement to the angels of appetite and sin."

'But you were in a gunfight?"

"I said I usually run."

"Did you ever find yourself in a circumstance where you couldn't run?"

"Once or twice," he said, reaching for the bottle.

"And?" I said.

He smiled, drank, wiped his whiskered mouth. "Why, I shot from ambush, of course." Then he laughed loud, offering me the bottle. "There are several states of this tragic and beautiful union which I am not particularly anxious to see again."

"Do you mean you're wanted?" Grafton asked him.

"I don't really know," he said. "It's been a long time. And I've traveled so far."

When he wasn't preaching, he seemed fairly inactive. Marian had never had any trouble figuring where he'd be. His sole support was what he could collect on Sunday, and what he could make helping out with the work of keeping the stables. He was fond of saying that no task was too low for sinners. Sometimes when he preached, if he wasn't getting on about the dire troubles the world was heading for, he was inclined to talk about the dignity provided by simple work. He could be almost sweet about that sort of idea. And sometimes, too, he talked about odd, unconnected things: Galileo and Napoleon; the new English queen; the tragic early death of the English writer, Dickens. Everything was a lesson. He'd fix you with his old, hooded eyes, and his thin lips would begin to move, as though he were chewing something unpalatable that was hurting his gums, and then he would begin to talk, the sentences lining up one after the other, perfectly symmetrical and organized as well as any written speech. We had all got to trusting him, not as the figure we could look to for succor or solace, particularly, but as a predictable and consistent form of diversion, of entertainment.

At least that was how I felt about him.

And so some coloration of that feeling was rising in me as I drove the wagon into town and stopped in front of Grafton's wondering if Bagley was there and what would happen if indeed he was. The street was empty. There weren't even any other horses around. Wind picked up dust and carried it in a drunken spiral across the way, where the dirt lane turned toward the stables.

"Grafton," Marian called, getting down. "You open or not?"

The door was ajar. She went up on the wooden sidewalk and down to the end of it, looked up and down that part of the crossing street. She waited there a minute. Then she came back and went into the saloon. In the wagon now it was just me and our returning visitor.

I said, "Tell me. What did Bagley—Phegley—do?"

"I can't say I know for sure. His name was posted. There's a reward."

"How much?" I asked.

He shrugged. "Six hundred dollars dead."

"And alive?"

"Five hundred twenty-five."

I looked at him.

"It was a private post."

"And you don't even know what he did?"

"I could use the extra seventy-five dollars," he said. "But I'm willing to take him back alive."

"You're—you're a peace officer, then?"

He shook his head, looking beyond me at the tall façade of Grafton's building.

"Is it personal?" I said.

"It's business," he mumbled. "Old business, too."

"Listen," I said. "Where'd you go when you left us that day? After the fight here."

He looked at me. "Fight?"

I waited.

He seemed to consider a moment. "Chinook Falls, I guess."

"Chinook Falls?" I said. "That's the next town over. That's only a day's ride."

He nodded. "Guess it is."

"How long did you stay there?"

Again, he thought a moment. "I don't know—four or five years, maybe."

"Four or five years?"

"I got married."

I stared at him.

"Yep. Got married and settled down awhile. But she wasn't much for sitting around in the evenings."

"She left you."

"In a way," he said. "I guess so."

"What happened?"

"Got sick on gin," he muttered, chewing on something he'd brought out of his shirt pocket; it looked like a small piece of straw. "Got real sick on gin one night. Died before I could do much of anything for her."

A moment later I said. "*Then* where'd you go?"

He shrugged, took a piece of straw from his mouth. "Around."

"Around where?" I asked, and he named several other towns, not one of which was farther than two days' ride from where we were sitting.

"That's it?" I said.

He nodded, not quite looking at me. "Pretty much."

"You're just a bounty hunter," I said. "Right?"

And he gave me a quizzical look, as if he hadn't understood the question. "What do you think?"

"Well, for God's sake," I said. "And you wanted me to grow straight and tall."

"You were a little boy. That's what you say to little boys. Some of them do, you know. Some of them grow straight and tall. Look at Joe Starrett."

"I don't want to think about that," I said. "I was thinking about you."

Now Marian came out of the saloon, and behind her Grafton stood, looking worried. "Don't come in," he said. "I don't want any trouble here. I'm too old for it." He squinted, peering at us.

"We're looking for Bagley," I said. By now I simply wanted to see what would happen.

"I don't think you should come here."

"Is he in there?" I said.

"He's where he always is this time of day," Grafton said. "The stables, sleeping it off."

Marian had climbed back onto the wagon seat. "Took me a strain getting that much out of him," she muttered. Then she turned to me. "Take me to the stables."

"Wait," said Grafton. "I'm coming along, too." And he hurried down and climbed up into the back of the wagon, arranging his besmirched white apron over his knees.

So it was the four of us who rode around to the stables and pulled up at the shady, open entrance. We sat there for a while. Then Marian got down and stood in the rising dust and looked at me. "I'm going to tell him we're here."

"He's a man who will use a gun," Shane said.

"This isn't your man," said Marian.

And Bagley's voice came from one of the windows above the street, I couldn't see which one. "Who wants to see the preacher?"

Now Grafton got down, too. He and Marian were standing there next to the wagon.

"Bagley," I said. "There's a man here looking for somebody named—"

But then Marian went running toward the open doorway. "Don't shoot!" she yelled. "Don't anybody shoot!"

Grafton had moved to take hold of her arms as she swept past him. She was dragging him with her toward the shade of the building.

From the nearest window, I saw Bagley's black gun barrel jutting out.

"Everybody just be calm!" Marian was shouting. "Let's all just wait a little bit! Please!"

But nobody waited for anything. Bagley fired from the window and the bullet hit the planks just below my foot. I have no idea what he could've been trying to hit, but I assumed he had through some mistake been aiming at me, so I dove into the back of the wagon—and there I collided painfully with the balding, deeply lined face of my childhood hero.

I had struck him on the bridge of the nose with my forehead, and instantly there was blood. It covered both of us. We looked at each other. I saw blind, dumb terror in his eyes. All around us was the roar of gunfire, explosions that seemed to come nearer, and we were crouching here, bloody and staring at each other. "Save me," I said, feeling all the more frightened for what I saw in his eyes—the scared little life there, wincing back from danger, sinking, showing pain and confusion and weakness, too. I never hated any face more, all my long life.

I had been a boy when the other thing happened. I had remembered it a certain way all those years, and had told the story a certain way, and now, here, under the random explosive, struck-wood sound of ricocheting bullets, I was being given something truer than what I'd held in my mind all that time.

At least that is what I've been able to make of it. I know that everything seemed terribly familiar, and that something about it was almost derisively itself, as if I could never have experienced it in any fashion but like this, face down in a wagon bed with my hands over my head.

"Everybody shut up!" Marian was yelling. "Everybody stop!"

From somewhere came the sound of someone reloading, and I heard Bagley's voice. "One, two, three." He voice was imbued with an eerie kind of music, like happiness.

"Bagley!" I screamed. "It's me!"

"I'm going to have to shoot all of you," he said. "That's the way it's going to have to be now. Unless you turn that wagon around and get out fast. And take him with you."

"John Bagley, you listen to me." Marian said from somewhere in the dust.

But then everything was obliterated in the din, the tumult which followed. It seemed to go on and on, and to grow louder. I didn't know where anyone was. I lay there in the wagon bed and cried for my life, and then it was over and in the quiet that followed—the quiet that was like something muffled on the eardrums, a physical feeling, a woolly, prickly itch on the skin, coupled with the paralyzed sense of a dreadful dumbfoundedness—I heard my own murmuring, and came to understand that I had survived. After a long wait, I stood in the wagon bed and looked at Marian sitting, alive and untouched, in the dust of the street, her hands held tight over her ears like a child trying to drown out the thunderous upheaval of a storm. Poor Grafton was sitting against one of the bales of hay by the stable door, his hands open on his thighs as though he had just paused there to get out of the brilliant autumn sun that was beating down out of the quiet sky. Bagley lay in the upstairs window, his head lolling down over the pocked sill. A stray breeze stirred his hair. The man who had brought his gun back into the valley lay at the back wheel of the wagon, face up to the light, looking almost serene. The whole thing had taken ten seconds, if that.

I have come from there to here.

I helped Marian up onto the wagon seat and drove her home. We didn't say anything; we didn't even go near each other for several days (and then it was only to stare across the table at each other while we ate the roast she'd made; it was as if we were both afraid of what might be uncovered if we allowed ourselves to speak at all). Someone else, I don't know—someone from the town—took the others away and buried them. The next time I went into town, Grafton's was closed, and people were sitting around on the sidewalk in front, leaning against the side of the building. Apparently Grafton's whore was challenging the arrangements or something: nobody could touch a thing in the place until it got settled, one way or the other. Anyway, it wasn't going to be Grafton's anymore.

Some years later, when she'd grown too tired and too confused to know much of anything, Marian passed on quietly in her sleep. I buried her with Joe Starrett out behind the barn of that place. I traveled far away from the valley—much farther than the next town—and never went back. I have grown old. My life draws back behind me like a long train. I never knew what it was Shane intended for himself, nor what Bagley had done to be posted, nor what had caused him to open fire in that way, any more than I was ever to know what poor Grafton must've thought when he dropped down in the street with the bullet in his lungs.

When I think of it, though, I find a small truth that means more to me than all my subsequent reading, all my late studies to puzzle out the nature of things: of course, nothing could be simpler, and perhaps it is already quite obvious to you, but what I remember now, in great age, is that during the loudest and most terrifying part of the exchange of shots, when the catastrophe was going on all around me and I was most certain that I was going to be killed, I lay shivering in the knowledge, the discovery really, that the story I'd been telling all my life was in fact not true enough—was little more than a boy's exaggeration.

And this is what I have come to tell you.

That the clearest memory of my life is a thing I made up in my head. For that afternoon at the stables, in the middle of terror, with the guns going off, I saw it all once again, without words, the story I'd been telling and that I'd believed since I was seven years old, only this time it was just as it had actually been. I saw again the moment when the gunfighter Wilson went for his Colt, and he was indeed not all in black, not wearing two guns or any holster, but sloppily draped in some flannels of such faded color as to be not quite identifiable. I saw it like a searing vision, what it had *really* been—a man trying to get a long-barreled pistol out of the soiled tangle of his pants, catching the hammer of it on the tail of his shirt. And the other, the hero struggling with his own weapon, raising it, taking aim, and firing— that shattering detonation, a blade of fire from the end of the pistol, and Wilson's body crashing down between a chair and table. The hero then turning to see the cattle baron on the other side of the room reach into his own tight coat, and a boy watching the hero raise his heavy Colt to fire upon the cattle baron, too—the cattle baron never even getting his weapon clear of the shoulder holster he had.

And it was all over. Like murder, nothing more.

Do you see? No backshooter firing from the gallery. Just the awful moment when the cattle baron realized he would be shot. And the boy who watched from under the saloon door saw the surprised, helpless, frightened look on the old whiskered face, saw this and closed his eyes, hearing the second shot, the second blast, squeezing his eyes shut for fear of looking upon death anymore, but hearing the awful, clattering fall and the stillness that followed, knowing what it was, what it meant, and hearing, too, now, the little other sounds—the settling in of ragged breath, the sigh of relief. Beginning, even then, in spite of himself—in spite of what he had just seen—to make it over in his young mind, remembering it already like all the tales of the Old West, the story as he would tell it for more than eighty years, even as he could hear the shaken voice, almost garrulous, of the one who had managed to stay alive—the one who was Shane, and who, this time, hadn't been killed in the stupid, fumbling blur of gunfighting.

1990

ELETHIA

Alice Walker

A certain perverse experience shaped Elethia's life, and made it possible for it to be true that she carried with her at all times a small apothecary jar of ashes.

There was in the town where she was born a man whose ancestors had owned a large plantation on which everything under the sun was made or grown. There had been many slaves, and though slavery no longer existed, this grandson of former slaveowners held a quaint proprietary point of view where colored people were concerned. He adored them, of course. Not in the present—it went without saying—but at that time, stopped, just on the outskirts of his memory: his grandfather's time.

This man, whom Elethia never saw, opened a locally famous restaurant on a busy street near the center of town. He called it "Old Uncle Albert's." In the window of the restaurant was a stuffed likeness of Uncle Albert himself, a small brown dummy of waxen skin and glittery black eyes. His lips were intensely smiling and his false teeth shone. He carried a covered tray in one hand, raised level with his shoulder, and over his other arm was draped a white napkin.

Black people could not eat at Uncle Albert's, though they worked, of course, in the kitchen. But on Saturday afternoons a crowd of them would gather to look at "Uncle Albert" and discuss how near to the real person the dummy looked. Only the very old people remembered Albert Porter, and their eyesight was no better than their memory. Still there was a comfort somehow in knowing that Albert's likeness was here before them daily and that if he smiled as a dummy in a fashion he was not known to do as a man, well, perhaps both memory and eyesight were wrong.

The old people appeared grateful to the rich man who owned the restaurant for giving them a taste of vicarious fame. They could pass by the gleaming window where Uncle Albert stood, seemingly in the act of sprinting forward with his tray, and know that though niggers were not allowed in the front door, ole Albert was already inside, and looking mighty pleased about it, too.

For Elethia the fascination was in Uncle Albert's fingernails. She wondered how his creator had got them on. She wondered also about the white hair that shone so brightly under the lights. One summer she worked as a salad girl in the restaurant's kitchen, and it was she who discovered the truth about Uncle Albert. He was not a dummy; he was stuffed. Like a bird, like a moose's head, like a giant bass. He was stuffed.

One night after the restaurant was closed someone broke in and stole nothing but Uncle Albert. It was Elethia and her friends, boys who were in her class and who called her "Thia." Boys who bought Thunderbird and shared it with her. Boys who laughed at her jokes so much they hardly remembered she was also cute. Her tight buddies. They carefully burned Uncle Albert to ashes in the incinerator of their high school, and each of them kept a bottle of his ashes. And for each of them what they knew and their reaction to what they knew was profound.

The experience undercut whatever solid foundation Elethia had assumed she had. She became secretive, wary, looking over her shoulder at the slightest noise. She haunted the museums of any city in which she found herself, looking, usually, at the remains of Indians, for they were plentiful everywhere she went. She discovered some of the Indian warriors and maidens in the museums were also real, stuffed people, painted and wigged and robed, like figures in the Rue Morgue. There were so many, in fact, that she could not possibly steal and burn them all. Besides, she did not know if these figures—with their valiant glass eyes—would wish to be burned.

About Uncle Albert she felt she knew.

What kind of man was Uncle Albert?

Well, the old folks said, he wasn't nobody's uncle and wouldn't sit still for nobody to call him that, either.

Why, said another old-timer, I recalls the time they hung a boy's privates on a post at the end of the street where all the black folks shopped, just to scare us all, you understand, and Albert Porter was the one took 'em down and buried 'em. Us never did find the rest of the boy though. It was just like *always*—they would throw you in the river with a big old green log tied to you, and down to the bottom you sunk.

He continued:

Albert was born in slavery and he remembered that his mama and daddy didn't know nothing about slavery'd done ended for near 'bout ten years, the boss man kept them so ignorant of the law, you understand. So he was a mad so-an'-so when he found out. They used to beat him severe trying to make him forget the past and grin and act like a nigger. (Whenever you saw somebody acting like a nigger, Albert said, you could be sure he seriously disremembered his past.) But he never would. Never would work in the big house as head servant, neither—always broke up stuff. The master at that time was always going around pinching him too. Looks like he hated Albert more than anything—but he never would let him get a job anywhere else. And Albert never would leave home. Too stubborn.

Stubborn, yes. My land, another one said. That's why it do seem strange to see that dummy that sposed to be old Albert with his mouth open. All them teeth. Hell, all Albert's teeth was knocked out before he was grown.

Elethia went away to college and her friends went into the army because they were poor and that was the way things were. They discovered Uncle Alberts all over the world. Elethia was especially disheartened to find Uncle Alberts in her textbooks, in the newspapers, and on TV.

Everywhere she looked there was an Uncle Albert (and many Aunt Albertas, it goes without saying).

But she had her jar of ashes, the old-timers' memories written down, and her friends who wrote that in the army they were learning skills that would get them through more than a plate glass window.

And she was careful that, no matter how compelling the hype, Uncle Alberts, in her own mind, were not permitted to exist.

1979

VISITORS, 1965

Oscar Hijuelos

1.

Down in the cool basement of the hotel restaurant, Alejo Santinio looked over a yellowed newspaper clipping dating back to 1961. He had not looked at it recently, although in the past had always been proud to show it to visitors. And why? Because it was a brief moment of glory. In the newspaper picture Alejo and his friend Diego were in their best dress whites standing before a glittering cart of desserts. Beside them was a fat, cheery, beaming face, the Soviet premier Nikita Khrushchev, who was attending a luncheon in his honor at the hotel.

Alejo always told the story: The governor and mayor were there with the premier, who had "great big ears and a bright red nose." The premier had dined on a five-course meal. The waiters and cooks, all nervous wrecks, had fumbled around in the kitchen getting things into order. But outside they managed an orderly composed appearance. After the meal had been served, the cooks drew lots to see who would wheel out the dessert tray. Diego and Alejo won.

Alejo put on his best white uniform and apron and waited in the foyer, chainsmoking nervously, while, outside, news reporters fired off their cameras and bodyguards stood against the walls, watching. Alejo and Diego did not say anything. Alejo was bewildered by the situation: Only in America could a worker get so close to a fat little guy with enormous power. These were the days of the new technology: mushroom-cloud bombs and satellites and missiles. And there he was, a hick from a small town in Cuba, slicked up by America, thinking, "If only my old compañeros could see me now! and my sisters and Mercedes."

When the time came, they went to the freezer, filled up shiny bowls with ice cream, brought out the sauces and hot fudge, and loaded them all onto a dessert cart. Alejo was in charge of cherries. They went out behind the maître d' and stood before the premier's table. They humbly waited as the smiling premier looked over the different cakes, tarts, pies, fruits, sauces, and ice creams. Through a translator the premier asked for a bowl of chocolate and apricot ice cream topped with hot fudge, cocoanut, and a high swirl of fresh whipped cream. This being served, Alejo picked out the plumpest cherry from a bowl and nimbly placed it atop the dessert.

Delighted, the premier whispered to the translator, who said, "The premier wishes to thank you for this masterpiece."

As Diego and Alejo bowed, lightbulbs and cameras flashed all around them. They were ready to wheel the cart back when the premier rose from the table to shake Diego's and Alejo's hands. Then through the translator he asked a few questions. To Alejo: "And where do you come from?"

"Cuba," Alejo answered in a soft voice.

"Oh yes, Cuba," the premier said in halting English. "I would like to go there one day. Cuba." And he smiled and patted Alejo's back and then rejoined the table. A pianist, a violinist, and a cellist played a Viennese waltz.

Afterward reporters came back into the kitchen to interview the two cooks, and the next morning the *Daily News* carried a picture of Alejo, Diego, and Khrushchev with a caption that read: DESSERT CHEFS CALL RUSKY PREMIER HEAP BIG EATER! It made them into celebrities for a few weeks. People recognized Alejo on the street and stopped to talk with him. He even went on a radio show in the Bronx. The hotel gave him a five-dollar weekly raise, and for a while Alejo felt important, and then it played itself out and became the yellowed clipping, stained by grease on the basement kitchen wall.

In Alejo's locker Khrushchev turned up again, on the cover of *Life* magazine. He was posed, cheek against cheek, with the bearded Cuban premier Fidel Castro. "What was going to happen to Cuba?" Alejo wondered. He shook his head. "How could Cuba have gone 'red'?" It had been more than six years since the fall of Batista on New Year's Eve, 1958, the year of getting rid of the evil in Cuba, and now Alejo and Mercedes were going to sponsor the arrival of Aunt Luisa, her daughters, and a son-in-law, Pedro. They were coming to the United States via *un vuelo de la libertad*, or freedom flight, as the U.S. military airplane trips from Havana to Miami were called. Khrushchev was going to eat up Cuba like an ice cream sundae. Things had gotten out of hand, bad enough for Luisa, who had loved her life in Holguín, to leave. Gone were the days of the happy-go-lucky Cubans who went on jaunts to Miami and New York to have a high time ballroom hopping; gone were the days when Cubans came to the States to make money and see more of the world. Now Cubans were leaving because of Khrushchev's new pal, Fidel Castro, the Shit, as some Cubans called him.

2.

Alejo had supported Castro during the days of the revolution. He had raised money for the pro-Castro Cubans in Miami by hawking copies of the *Sierra Maestra* magazine to pals on the street. This magazine was printed in Miami by pro-Castro Cubans and was filled with pictures of tortured heroes left on the streets or lying in the lightless mortuary rooms with their throats cut and their heads blood-splattered. They were victims of the crooked Batista regime, and now it was time for Batista and his henchmen to go! Alejo was not a political creature, but he supported the cause, of course, to end the injustices of Batista's rule. When someone brought him a box of Cuban magazines to sell, Alejo went down on Amsterdam Avenue and sold them to friends. Alejo always carried one of those magazines in his pocket, and he was persuasive, selling them. In his soft calm voice he would say, "Come on, it's only a dollar and for the cause of your countrymen's freedom!" And soon he would find himself inviting all the buyers back to his apartment, where they sat in the kitchen drinking and talking about what would save the world: "An honest man with a good heart, out of greed's reach," was the usual consensus. Political talk about Cuba always led to nostalgic talk, and soon Alejo's friends would soften up and bend like orchid vines, glorying in the lost joys of childhood. Their loves and regrets thickened in the room in waves, until they began singing along with their drinking and falling down. With their arms around each other and glasses raised, they toasted Fidel as "the hope for the future."

Alejo and Mercedes had been happy with the success of the revolution. The day Castro entered Havana they threw a party with so much food and drink that the next morning people had to cross into the street to get around the stacks of garbage bags piled on the sidewalk in front of the building. Inside, people were sprawled around everywhere. There were sleepers in the kitchen and in the hall, sleepers in the closet. There was a *dudduhduh* of a skipping needle over a phonograph record. A cat that had come in through the window from the alley was going around eating left-over scraps of food.

Soon the papers printed that famous picture of Castro entering Havana with his cowboy-looking friend, Camilio Ciefuegos, on a tank. They were like Jesus and John the Baptist in a Roman epic movie. The *Sierra Maestra* magazine would later feature a centerfold of Castro as Jesus Christ with his hair long and golden brown, almost fiery in a halo light. And for the longest time Cubans, Alejo and Mercedes among them, referred to Castro with great reverence and love, as if he were a saint.

In a few years, however, kids in the street started to write slogans like *Castro eats big bananas!* The New York press ran stories about the Castro visit to New York. Alejo and Hector stood on the corner one afternoon, watching his motorcade speed uptown to a Harlem hotel. There, the press said, Castro's men killed their own chickens and ate them raw. Castro even came to give a talk at the university. Alejo and Hector were among a crowd of admirers that clustered around him to get a look. Castro was very tall for a Cuban, six-feet-two. He was wearing a long raincoat and took sips from a bottle of Pepsi-Cola. He listened to questions intently, liked to smile, and kept reaching out to shake hands. He also signed an occasional autograph. He was, the newspapers said, unyielding in his support of the principles of freedom.

In time Castro announced the revolutionary program. Alejo read the *El Diario* accounts intently while Mercedes wandered around the apartment asking, "What's going to happen to my sisters?" By 1962, after the Bay of Pigs invasion and the beginning of the Cuban ration-card program, an answer to her question came in the form of letters. Standing by the window Mercedes would read the same letter over and over again, sighing and saying out loud, "Oh my Lord! They are so unhappy!"

"Ma, what's going on?" Hector would ask her.

"Things are very bad. The Communists are very bad people. Your aunts have nothing to eat, no clothes to wear, no medicine. The Communist go around taking things away from people! And if you say anything they put you in jail!"

Mercedes's stories about the new life in Cuba made Hector think of a house of horrors. In his sleep he pictured faceless, cowled abductors roaming the streets of Holguín in search of victims to send to brain-washing camps. He pictured the ransacking of old mansions, the burning of churches, deaths by firing squads. He remembered back many years and saw the door of Aunt Luisa's house on Arachoa Street, and then he imagined guards smashing that door open to search Luisa's home.

All the news that came into the house in those letters fed such visions: "Ai, Hector, do you remember your cousin Paco? He has been sent to prison for a year and all he did was get caught with a pound of sugar under his shirt!" A year later: "Oh your poor cousin Paco! He just came out of prison and now my sister can hardly recognize him. Listen to what Luisa says: 'He has lost most of his hair and is as thin as a skeleton with yellowed, jaundiced skin. He has aged twenty years in one.'" Another letter: "Dear sister, the headaches continue. Everything is upside down. You can't even go to church these days without someone asking, 'Where are you going?' Everyone in the barrio watches where you go. No one has any privacy. If you are not in the Party then you're no good. Many of them are Negroes, and now that they have the power, they are very bad to us. I don't know how long we can endure these humiliations. We hope for Castro's fall." Another letter: "Dear sister, last week your niece Maria was kicked out of dental school, and do you know what for? Because she wouldn't recite 'Hail Lenin!' in the mornings with the other students! I went to argue with the headmaster of the school, but there was nothing I could do. On top of that, poor Rina's roof was hit by lightning but she can't get the materials to fix it. When it rains the floors are flooded—all because she is not in the Party. . . . As usual I ask for your prayers and to send us whatever you can in the way of clothing, food, and medicine. Aspirins and penicillin are almost impossible to find these days, as are most other things. I know I'm complaining to you, but if you were here, you would understand. With much love, Luisa."

To help her sisters, Mercedes went from apartment to apartment asking neighbors for any clothing they might not need. These clothes were packed into boxes and sent down to Cuba at a cost of fifty dollars each. Mercedes paid for this out of her own pocket. She had been working at night cleaning in a nursery school since the days of Alejo's illness. Alejo too contributed. He came home with boxes of canned goods and soap and toothpaste from the hotel and he bought such items as rubbing alcohol, aspirins, mercurochrome, iodine, Tampax, Q-Tips, cotton, and toilet paper to send to Cuba.

"The world is going to the devil," Mercedes would say to Alejo as she packed one of the boxes. "Imagine having to use old newspapers for toilet paper! The Russians are the new masters, they have everything, but what do Luisa and Rina have? Nothing!"

Of the family, Mercedes was the most outspoken about the revolution. Alejo was very quiet in his views. He didn't like Castro, or, for that matter, Khrushchev. But he would never argue with a friend about politics. He was always more concerned about keeping his friendships cordial. To please two different sets of neighbors he subscribed to both the *Daily Worker* and to the *Republican Eagle*. He read neither of them, but still would nod emphatically whenever he came upon these neighbors in the hallway and they bombarded him with their philosophies. "Certainly," Alejo would say to them, "why don't you come inside and have a drink with me?" When there was a gathering of visitors with different points of view, Alejo used liquor to keep the wagging tongues in line. Get them drunk and make them happy, was his motto.

But Mercedes didn't want to hear about Fidel Castro from anyone, not even from Señor Lopez, a union organizer and good friend of the family who lived in the building. He would come to the apartment to recount the declines in illiteracy, prostitution, and malnutrition in Cuba. "No more of this!" he would declare, showing Mercedes and Alejo and Hector a picture from *La Bohemia* of a decrepit old Negro man dying in bed, with bloated stomach, festering sores on his limbs, and a long gray worm literally oozing out of his navel. "You won't see this anymore now that Castro is in power!"

"And what about the decent people who supported Castro in the first place, and who now have nothing but troubles?" she would ask.

"Mercita, the revolution is the will of the majority of the Cuban people!"

"You mean people who were the good-for-nothings?"

"No, the people who had nothing because they were allowed nothing."

"Oh yes? And what about my family?"

"Mercita, use your brains. I don't like to put it this way, but as the saying goes, 'To make an omelet you have break a few eggs.'"

"My family are not eggs! If you like eggs so much, why don't you go down to Cuba and live there? Chickens have more to eat than what you would get. Go there and see what freedom is like!"

By 1965 it was becoming clear that Castro was not going to fall from power. Cubans who had been hoping for a counterrevolution were now growing desperate to leave. Luisa and her family were among them. One evening an errand boy from the corner drugstore knocked at the door. There was a call from Cuba. Mercedes and Hector hurried down the hill. The caller was Aunt Luisa. Her sad voice was so far away, interrupted by sonic hums and clicking static echoes. It sounded like the voices of hens reciting numbers in Spanish. With the jukebox going, it was a wonder that Luisa's voice could be heard over mountains and rivers and across the ocean.

"How is it over there now?" Mercedes asked.

"It's getting worse here. There are too many headaches. We want to leave. Pedro, Virginia's husband, lost his mechanic's shop. There is no point in our staying."

"Who wants to come?"

"Me, Pedro, Virginia, and Maria."

"And what about Rina?"

"She is going to stay for the time being with Delores and her husband." Delores was Rina's daughter. She had a doctorate in pedagogy that made her a valuable commodity in those days of literacy programs. "Delores has been appointed to a government post and she is too afraid to refuse the Party, for fear they will do something to Rina or to her husband. But we will come. I have the address of the place where you must write for the sponsorship papers. We've already put our name on the government waiting list. When our name reaches the top of the list we'll be able to go."

The only other way was to fly either to Mexico or Spain, but at a cost of two thousand dollars per person to Mexico, three thousand dollars to Spain. The family did not have that kind of money.

Mercedes then gave Hector the telephone. He listened to his aunt's soft voice, saying, "We will be with you soon, and you will know your family again. Pray for us so that we will be safe." Her voice sounded weak. There was clicking, like a plug being pulled. Perhaps someone was listening in the courthouse, where the call was being made.

Luisa spoke with Mercedes for another minute, and then their time was up and Mercedes and Hector returned home.

Alejo took care of the paperwork. He wrote to immigration authorities in Miami for their visa and for the special forms that would be mailed out by him, approved by the U.S. Immigration Department, and sent to Cuba.

In February 1966 Luisa and her daughters and son-in-law left Cuba. First they waited in front of the house on Arachoa Street in Holguín, where they had all been living, for the army bus that would take them on the ten-hour journey west to Havana. When they arrived at the José Marti Airport, they waited in a wire-fenced compound. A Cuban official went over their papers and had them stand in line for hours before they boarded the military transport jet to America.

On the day that Alejo looked at the clipping of Khrushchev again, they received word that Luisa and her daughters and a son-in-law were coming, and a sort of shock wave of apprehension and hope passed through them.

3.

For Hector the prospect of Aunt Luisa's arrival stirred up memories. He began to make a conscious effort to be "Cuban," and yet the very idea of Cubanness inspired fear in him as if he would grow ill from it, as if micróbios would be transmitted by the very mention of the word Cuba. He was a little perplexed because he also loved the notion of Cuba to an extreme. In Cuba there were so many pleasant fragrances, like the smell of Luisa's hair and the damp clay ground of the early morning. Cuba was where Mercedes had once lived a life of style and dignity and happiness. And it was the land of happy courtship with Alejo and the land where men did not fall down. Hector was tired of seeing Mercedes cry and yell. He was tired of her moroseness and wanted the sadness to go away. He wanted the apartment to be filled with beams of sunlight, like in the dream house of Cuba.

He was sick at heart for being so Americanized, which he equated with being fearful and lonely. His Spanish was unpracticed, practically nonexistent. He had a stutter, and saying a Spanish word made him think of drunkenness. A Spanish sentence wrapped around his face, threatened to peel off his skin and send him falling to the floor like Alejo. He avoided Spanish even though that was all he heard at home. He read it, understood it, but he grew paralyzed by the prospect of the slightest conversation.

"Hablame en espanol!" Alejo's drunken friends would challenge him. But Hector always refused and got lost in his bedroom, read Flash comic books. And when he was around the street Ricans, they didn't want to talk Spanish with Whitey anyway, especially since he was not getting high with them, just getting drunk now and then, and did not look like a hood but more like a goody-goody, round-faced, mama's boy: a dark dude, as they used to say in those days.

Even Horacio had contempt for Hector. Knowing that Hector was nervous in the company of visitors, he would instigate long conversations in Spanish. When visiting men would sit in the kitchen speaking about politics, family, and Cuba, Horacio would play the patrón and join them, relegating Hector to the side, with the women. He had disdain for his brother and for the ignorance Hector represented. He was not interested in "culture." He had returned from England a complete European who listened to Mozart instead of diddy-bop music. His hair was styled as carefully as Beau Brummell's. His wardrobe consisted of English tweed jackets and fine Spanish shoes; his jewelry, his watches, his cologne, everything was very European and very far from the gutter and the insecurity he had left behind. As he put it, "I'm never going to be fuckin' poor again."

He went around criticizing the way Mercedes kept house and cooked, the way Alejo managed his money (buying everything with cash and never on credit) and the amounts of booze Alejo drank. But mostly he criticized Hector. The day he arrived home from the Air Force and saw Hector for the first time in years, his face turned red. He could not believe his eyes. Hector was so fat that his clothes were bursting at the seams, and when Hector embraced him, Horacio shook his head and said, "Man, I can't believe this is my brother."

And now the real Cubans, Luisa and her daughters and son-in-law, were coming to find out what a false life Hector led. Hector could not sleep at night, thinking of it. He tried to remember his Spanish, but instead of sentences, pictures of Cuba entered into his mind. But he did not fight this. He fantasized about Cuba. He wanted pictures to enter him, as if memory and imagination would make him more of a man, a Cuban man.

The day before Luisa arrived he suddenly remembered his trip to Cuba with Mercedes and Horacio in 1954. He remembered looking out the window of the plane and seeing fire spewing from the engines on the wing. To Cuba. To Cuba. Mercedes was telling him a story when the plane abruptly plunged down through some clouds and came out into the night air again. Looking out the window he saw pearls in the ocean and the reflection of the moon in the water. For a moment he saw a line of three ships, caravels with big white sails like Columbus's ships, and he tugged at Mercedes's arm. She looked but did not see them. And when he looked again, they were gone.

Hector tried again for a genuine memory. Now he saw Luisa's house on Arachoa Street, the sun a haze bursting through the trees.

"Do you remember a cat with one eye in Cuba?" he asked Horacio, who was across the room reading *Playboy* magazine.

"What?" he said with annoyance.

"In Cuba, wasn't there a little cat who used to go in and out of the shadows and bump into things? You know, into the steps and into the walls, because it only had one eye. And then Luisa would come out and feed it bits of meat?"

"You can't remember anything. Don't fool yourself," he replied.

But Hector could not stop himself. He remembered bulldozers tearing up the street and that sunlight again, filtering through the flower heads, and flamingos of light on the walls of the house. He remembered the dog with the pathetic red dick running across the yard. Then he remembered holding an enormous trembling white sunhat. His grandmother, Doña Maria, was sitting nearby in a blue-and-white dotted dress, and he took the sunhat to show her. But it wasn't a sunhat. It was an immense white butterfly. "¡Ai, que linda!" Doña Maria said. "It's so pretty, but maybe we should let the poor thing go." And so Hector released the butterfly and watched it rise over the house and float silently away.

Then he saw Doña Maria, now dead, framed by a wreath of orchids in the yard, kissing him—so many kisses, squirming kisses—and giving advice. She never got over leaving Spain for Cuba and would always remain a proud Spaniard. "Remember," she had told Hector. "You're Spanish first and then Cuban."

He remembered sitting on the cool steps to Luisa's kitchen and watching the road where the bulldozers worked. A turtle was crawling across the yard, and iguanas were licking up the sticky juice on the kitchen steps. Then he heard Luisa's voice: "Come along, child," she called. "I have something for you." And he could see her face again through the screen door, long and wistful.

Inside, she had patted Hector's head and poured him a glass of milk. Cuban milk alone was sour on the tongues of children, but with the Cuban magic potion, which she added, it was the most delicious drink Hector ever tasted. With deep chocolate and nut flavors and traces of orange and mango, the bitter with the sweet, the liquid went down his throat, so delicious. "No child, drink that milk," Luisa said. "Don't forget your *tia*. She loves you."

Then a bam! bam! came from the television and Hector could hear voices of neighbors out in the hallway. No, he wasn't used to hearing Luisa's niceties anymore, and he couldn't remember what was in the milk, except that it was Cuban, and then he wondered what he would say to his aunt and cousins, whether he would smile and nod his head or hide as much as possible, like a turtle on a hot day.

4.

It was late night when a van pulled up to the building and its four exhausted passengers stepped onto the sidewalk. Seeing the arrival from the window, Mercedes was in a trance for a moment and then removed her apron and ran out, almost falling down the front steps, waving her arms and calling, "Aaaaiiii, aaaaiiii, aaaaiiii! Oh my God! My God! My God," and giving many kisses. Alejo followed and hugged Pedro. The female cousins waited humbly, and then they began kissing Mercedes and Alejo and Hector and Horacio, their hats coming off and teeth chattering and hair getting all snarled like ivy on an old church... kisses, kisses, kisses... into the warm lobby with its deep, endless mirrors and the mailbox marked *Delgado / Santinio*. The female cousins, like china dolls, were incredibly beautiful, but struck dumb by the snow and the new world, silent because there was something dreary about the surroundings. They were thinking Alejo had been in this country for twenty years, and yet what did he have? But no one said this. They just put hands on hands and gave many kisses and said, "I can't believe I'm seeing you here." They were all so skinny and exhausted-looking, Luisa, Virginia, Maria, and Pedro. They came holding cloth bags with all their worldly possessions: a few crucifixes, a change of clothing, aspirins given to them at the airport, an album of old photographs, prayer medals, a Bible, a few Cuban coins from the old days, and a throat-lozenge tin filled with some soil from Holguín, Oriente province, Cuba.

After kissing and hugging them Alejo took them into the kitchen where they almost died: There was so much of everything! Milk and wine and beer, steaks and rice and chicken and sausages and ham and plantains and ice cream and black bean soup and Pepsi-Cola and Hershey chocolate bars and almond nougat, and popcorn and Wise potato chips and Jiffy peanut butter, and rum and whiskey, marshmallows, spaghetti, flan and pasteles and chocolate cake and pie, more than enough to make them delirious. And even though the walls were cracked and it was dark, there was a television set and a radio and lightbulbs and toilet paper and pictures of the family and crucifixes and toothpaste and soap and more.

It was "Thank God for freedom and bless my family" from Luisa's mouth, but her daughters were more cautious. Distrusting the world, they approached everything timidly. In the food-filled kitchen Alejo told them how happy he was to have them in his house, and they were happy because the old misery was over, but they were still without a home and in a strange world. Uncertainty showed in their faces.

Pedro, Virginia's husband, managed to be the most cheerful. He smoked and talked up a storm about the conditions in Cuba and the few choices the Castro government had left to them. Smoking thick, black cigars, Horacio and Alejo nodded and agreed, and the conversation went back and forth and always ended with "What are you going to do?"

"Work until I have something," was Pedro's simple answer.

It was such a strong thing to say that Hector, watching from the doorway, wanted to be like Pedro. And from time to time, Pedro would look over and wink and flash his Victor Mature teeth.

Pedro was about thirty years old and had been through very bad times, including the struggle in 1957 and 1958 to get Castro into power. But wanting to impress Hector with his cheeriness, Pedro kept saying things in English to Hector like, "I remember Elvis Presley records. Do you know *You're My Angel Baby?*" And Hector would not answer that. But Pedro would speak on, about the brave Cubans who got out of Cuba in the strangest ways. His buddy back in Holguín stole a small airplane with a few friends and flew west to Mexico, where they crash-landed their plane on a dirt road in the Yucatán. He ended up in Mexico City, where he found work in the construction business. He was due in America soon and would one day marry Maria, who wanted a brave man. These stories only made Hector more and more silent.

As for his female cousins, all they said to him was: "Do you want to eat?" or "Why are you so quiet?" And sometimes Horacio answered for him, saying: "He's just dumb when it comes to being Cuban."

Aunt Luisa, with her good heart, really didn't care what Hector said or didn't say. Each time she encountered him in the morning or the afternoon, she would take his face between her hands and say, "Give me a kiss and say 'Tia, I love you.'" And not in the way Alejo used to, falling off a chair and with his eyes desperate, but sweetly. Hector liked to be near Luisa with her sweet angelic face.

He felt comfortable enough around Aunt Luisa to begin speaking to her. He wasn't afraid because she overflowed with warmth. One day while Aunt Luisa was washing dishes, Hector started to think of her kitchen in Cuba. He remembered the magic Cuban drink.

"Auntie," he asked her. "Do you remember a drink that you used to make for me in the afternoons in Cuba? What was it? It was the most delicious chocolate but with Cuban spices."

She thought about it. "Chocolate drink in the afternoon? Let me see…" She wiped a plate clean in the sink. She seemed perplexed and asked, "And it was chocolate?"

"It was Cuban chocolate. What was it?"

She thought on it again and her eyes grew big and she laughed, slapping her knee. "Ai, bobo. It was Hershey syrup and milk!"

After that he didn't ask her any more questions. He just sat in the living room listening to her tell Mercedes about her impressions of the United States. For example, after she had sat on the stoop or gazed out the window for a time, she would make a blunt declaration: "There are a lot of airplanes in the sky." But usually when Mercedes and Luisa got to talking, they drifted toward the subject of spirits and ghosts. When they were little girls spiritualism was very popular in Cuba. All the little girls were half mediums, in those days. And remembering this with great laughter, Luisa would say, "If only we could have seen what would happen to Papa! Or that Castro would turn out to be so bad!"

"Yes, Papa, that would have been something," Mercedes answered with wide hopeful eyes. "But Castro is something else. What could a few people do about him?"

"Imagine if you're dead in Cuba," said Luisa, "and you wake up to that mess. What would you do?"

"I would go to Miami, or somewhere like that."

"Yes, and you would go on angel wings."

It was Luisa's ambition to ignore America and the reality of her situation completely. So she kept taking Mercedes back to the old days; "You were such a prankster, so mischievous! You couldn't sit down for a moment without being up to something. Poor Papa! What he had to do with you!" And then, turning to Hector, she would add, "Look at your Mama. This innocent over here was the fright of us all. She was always imagining things. Iguanas, even little baby iguanas, were dragons. A rustle in the bushes was ghosts of fierce Indians looking for their bones!" She laughed. "There are ghosts, but not as many as she saw. She was always in trouble with Papa. He was very good to her but also strict. But his punishments never stopped your mother. My, but she was a fresh girl!"

When she wasn't talking to Mercedes, Luisa watched the Spanish channel on the television or ate, or prayed. Pedro went out with Alejo and Horacio, looking for work. Maria and Virginia helped with the housecleaning and the cooking, and then they studied their books. They were very quiet, like felines, moving from one spot to another without a sound. Sometimes everyone went out to the movies; Alejo paid for it. Or they all went downtown to the department stores to buy clothing and other things they needed. Again, Alejo paid for everything, angering Mercedes, for whom he bought nothing.

"I know you're trying to be nice to my family, but remember we don't have money."

Still, he was generous with them, as if desperate to keep Luisa and her daughters in the apartment. Their company made him as calm and happy as a mouse. Nothing pleased Alejo more than sitting at the head of the dinner table, relishing the obvious affection that Luisa and her daughters and son-in-law felt for him. At meals Alejo would make toast after toast to their good health and long life, drink down his glass of rum or whiskey quickly, and then fill another and drink that and more. Mercedes always sat quietly wondering. "What does my sister really think of me for marrying him?" while Hector waited for Alejo suddenly to fall off his chair, finally showing his aunt and cousins just who the Santinios really were.

One night Alejo fell against the table and knocked down a big stack of plates. The plates smashed all around Alejo, who was on the floor. Hector scrambled to correct everything before Virginia and Maria and Pedro came to look. He scrambled to get Alejo up before they saw him. He pulled with all his strength, the way he and Horacio used to, but Alejo weighed nearly three hundred pounds. As the cousins watched in silence, Hector wished he could walk through the walls and fly away. He thought that now they would know one of his secrets, that the son is like the father. He tried again to pull Alejo up and had nearly succeeded when Pedro appeared and, with amazing strength, wrapped his arms around Alejo's torso and heaved him onto a chair with one pull.

Hector hadn't wanted them to see this, because then they might want to leave and the apartment would be empty of Pedro and Luisa and her daughters, those fabulous beings. He didn't want them to see the dingy furniture and the cracking walls and the cheap decorative art, plaster statues, and mass-produced paintings. He didn't want them to see that he was an element in this world, only as good as the things around him. He wanted to be somewhere else, be someone else, a Cuban . . . And he didn't want the family perceived as the poor relations with the drunk father. So he tried to laugh about Alejo and eventually went to bed, leaving Luisa and Pedro and his cousins still standing in the hall. Eventually, they did move away. Virginia and Maria found work in a factory in Jersey City, and Pedro came home one evening with news that he had landed a freight dispatcher's job in an airport. Just like that. He had brought home a big box of pastries, sweet cakes with super-sweet cream, chocolate eclairs, honey-drenched cookies with maraschino cherries in their centers.

As Alejo devoured some of these, he said to Pedro, "Well, that's good. You're lucky to have such good friends here. Does it pay you well?"

Pedro nodded slightly and said, "I don't know, it starts out at seven thousand dollars a year, but it will get better."

Alejo also nodded, but he was sick because after twenty years in the same job he did not make that much, and this brought down his head and made him yawn. He got up and went to his bedroom where he fell asleep.

A few months later, they were ready to rent a house in a nice neighborhood in Jersey. The government had helped them out with some emergency funds. ("We never asked the government for even a penny," Mercedes kept saying to Alejo.) Everyone but Luisa was bringing home money. They used that money to buy furniture and to send Virginia to night computer school taught by Spanish instructors. Instead of being cramped up in someone else's apartment with rattling pipes and damp plaster walls that seemed ready to fall in, they had a three-story house with a little yard and lived near many Cubans who kept the sidewalks clean and worked hard, so their sick hearts would have an easier time of it.

Hector was bereft at their leaving, but more than that he was astounded by how easily they established themselves. One day Pedro said, "I just bought a car." On another, "I just got a color TV." In time they would be able to buy an even larger house. The house would be filled with possessions: a dishwasher, a washing machine, radios, a big stereo console, plastic-covered velour couches and chairs, electric clocks, fans, air conditioners, hair dryers, statues, crucifixes, lamps and electric-candle chandeliers, and more. One day they would have enough money to move again, to sell the house at a huge profit and travel down to Miami to buy another house there. They would work like dogs, raise children, prosper. They did not allow the old world, the past, to hinder them. They did not cry but walked straight ahead. They drank but did not fall down. Pedro even started a candy and cigarette business to keep him busy in the evenings, earning enough money to buy himself a truck.

"Qué bueno," Alejo would say.

"This country's wonderful to new Cubans," Mercedes kept repeating. But then she added, "They're going to have everything, and we . . . what will we have?" And she would go about sweeping the floor or preparing chicken for dinner. She would say to Alejo, "Doesn't it hurt you inside?"

Alejo shrugged. "No, because they have suffered in Cuba."

He never backed off from that position and always remained generous to them, even after their visits became less frequent, even when they came only once a year. And when Pedro tried to repay the loans, Alejo always waved the money away. By this time Virginia was pregnant, so Alejo said, "Keep it for the baby."

"You don't want the money?"

"Only when you don't need it. It's important for you to have certain things now."

But Mercedes stalked around the apartment, screaming, "What about the pennies I saved? What about us?"

1983

THE DISAPPEARANCE

Jeanne Schinto

"You can drive the devil out of your garden, but you
will find him again in the garden of your son."
— Pestalozzi

The glare of the wet, white sheets as Rosario untwisted them, and of his
wife's enormous underpants, also white, also twisted, reminded him, as his
pinned the laundry to the clothesline outside his back door, of "Snow-
bound"... by John Greenleaf Whittier. He'd memorized a portion of the
poem in tenth grade, and he'd recited it, wearing his itchy woolen pants
and standing in front of the classroom. He'd done it all right, too—the
teacher, with her apple breasts, had praised him; but Rosie, as he had been
called since he was a boy, had to leave school shortly afterward and go to
work as a gardener on one of the estates in the rich town next door to the
cramped, unkempt little city where he'd lived all his life and where his
father had gotten into so much trouble down at one of the mills.

Now, this father's son was a man of seventy with silver locks of oily hair,
almost like rows of sardines, and fierce black eyes set in a permanent squint
from his years spent outdoors. And he was recently retired. That was why
he had no more excuses to get out of hanging the laundry. His wife Ignatia
was too arthritic to do the job herself. Lena, Ignatia's sister, had been doing
it for them all summer, but she was sickly now, too, or so she claimed. A
widow who lived alone in a large house three blocks away, Lena clung so
to Ignatia, they were like two sides of a peach. Earlier this week Rosie even
had to take Lena to the doctor's office. Like *she* was his wife! Lena complained that she felt dizzy and had difficulty drawing breath. But as Rosie
had walked with her toward Dr. Fettinger's door, she'd confessed to him
that she sometimes *held* her breath. Rosie had stopped short, stared at her
lifting her glasses to dab at her eyes and heavily powdered nose with a

balled-up Kleenex, and said to her, *"Breathe,"* bending his knees on his own intake. "Take a breath of air, for Chrissakes! What else have you got to do?" Lena also had complaints the doctor could not name. But Rosie could. "It's nerves," he told a neighbor, Mr. Pasquerelli. Other people on the block called Mr. Pasquerelli "The F.B.I." He hung around the street corner, wearing dark glasses, watching out for "things—funny business . . . kids—you know, the jerks." Rosie told Mr. Pasquerelli that Lena should take a shot now and then, the way he himself did. "That'd fix her right up." Then he paused. Something about the waiting room had upset him, he told Mr. Pasquerelli's dark glasses, the cracked white lips waiting under them: "There were all *old* people in there. Nobody young. Don't kids get sick anymore or what?"

Inside their ground-floor apartment, Rosie's and Ignatia's grandson Vin, who used to let himself be called "Vinnie" until just this school year, stood by the glossy kitchen table. His black eyelashes were closely bunched, he was tall for fourteen, and his muscles were long and lean, so mostly hidden. "How'd you get here?" Ignatia asked him, shuffling over to the table from the stove. She wore men's bedroom slippers with holes cut out for her bunions. "You hitchhike? You're going to get murdered one of these days. Who picked you up? A man or a woman? The women are worse than the men sometimes. You have to be careful, every minute of your life."

The boy told his grandmother that he was very careful and that he had ridden his bike.

"Your hair looks good," she said, reaching up to smooth it. "Before you were born, boys wanted to look like girls. Like your Uncle Patsy. And don't think Luca didn't cut his hair for him but good one time." Luca, their landlord, an old friend of Rosie's father, was a retired tailor who lived upstairs and always wore a white shirt and dark tie knotted up close to his throat. He was slightly bent now, but still moved quickly, like a young person with an injury.

"Rosie held Patsy down right out there in the garden while Luca did the cutting," Ignatia said. "You don't believe me?"

"I believe you, Gram," Vin said.

"Our own son. I did nothing to stop it. Now I'm sorry. Well, sit, sid-down," Ignatia said, sitting heavily herself, as if to show how it was done. "Sit, sit, have a cup of coffee."

"Just tell me why you wanted me to come over," Vin said.

"I'm going to ask you a favor."

"I know, Gram. Just tell me what it is."

"Did that storm wake you up last night?" Ignatia pressed a clutched fist in the middle of her chest. "I had the sheet pulled up over my head just like Lena and I used to do when we were kids. St. Christopher here, St. Michael there." She touched the top of each of her breasts, doughy cushions. "And the rosary beads around my hand!" She laughed girlishly, then gathered together the two parts of her housecoat, its color the green of cheap ice cream, the print worn to illegibility. She adjusted the safety pins that had replaced its lost buttons, holding them in her mouth at intervals, like a mother doing a diaper; then pushed a plate of almond cookies at him. He took one, but just held it in his hand, didn't bite down. She herself was never much on sweets, either, she said. The real food—the meat!—that was the important thing. She poured coffee into her cup from a thermos, then she poured it from the cup into the saucer and lapped it up from there, lifting it to her mouth with both hands.

"I didn't sleep a wink the night *before* the storm, either," she said. She had felt the pains in her heart again. And then the palpitations. "But as long as I can talk about it, I'm all right. Right?"

"Right," said Vin, but she could see he'd grown impatient. He'd come all the way from the next town. He was a good boy to obey her.

Finally she told him what he was to do: buy her a money order that she would give to Patsy, so he could pay his rent. She gave Vin cash: $400 in twenty-dollar bills. He was to bring the money order back to her tomorrow and then she'd mail it to Patsy in Boston for a surprise.

"He wasn't dishonest—that's why he's a failure," Ignatia said. "He could have made a lot of money at one time, you know."

As Vin started to leave, Ignatia pressed an extra twenty into the hand of his that was in his jeans pocket.

"No, Gram, I can't take that," he said, finally eating the cookie he still held, needing his other hand free to try resisting her.

"Take."

"I don't want to."

"But I want."

"Just say me a prayer or something."

Ignatia hugged him hard just as Rosie came in from the garden, tomatoes, not quite ripe, rolling around in the plastic laundry basket. "I wanted to pick them before the frost got them," he said, looking suspiciously from

Ignatia to Vin and back. It was a little unusual for the boy to show up here like this after school. What would Rosie think when the boy showed up here again tomorrow?

"You put them in a paper bag to ripen," Ignatia said. "Did you know that, Vinnie?"

"Yes, Gram."

"How does a boy like you know a thing like that?" One more time she reached up to touch his closely shorn head.

Rosie bent down to pinch suckers from the tomato vines while Vin retrieved his bike from the tool shed. Rosie had made him stash it in there, not just lock it. So many Slippery Sam's walking the streets of Lawrence nowadays. "Puerto Ricans!" Near the peeling, warped-boarded shed, roses, red and white, still bloomed, heavy heads touching the ground, the sleepy scent wafting up. Ladies in church wore roses like that on their hats: artificial. At least they used to: Rosie hadn't been to church in years. How many real roses had he pruned, sprayed, been stuck by?

"You have a girlfriend yet?" Rosie lifted his white-stubbled chin to ask Vin his dead-serious question. "Or are you going to be a fruit like your Uncle Patsy? Your brother has a beautiful girlfriend. Doesn't she have a younger sister for you?" Rosie scratched his behind, smiling to himself, thinking about Peter's girlfriend. "She's a real girl."

Vin agreed. Sometimes he spied on Peter and Maggie. Today, after school, on his way over here, he'd watched them whacking golfballs on her front lawn. Vin had crouched down behind some bushes, watching until they went into the house by the side door: an immense house. It was made of honey-colored stone and the lawn was like green snow, that perfect. A gardener had been moving along the edge of it, a pair of clippers in his hand. Then he spotted Vin, who ran to his bike, surprised that the man could be so angry, acting as if it were his own property.

"What did you want to come over here for today?" Rosie asked Vin. He gestured toward the kitchen, his fingers stained yellow by tomato plants.

"A favor," Vin said simply.

"Something about Patsy, am I right?"

"A favor, that's all."

Rosie nodded grimly at the kitchen window. "I don't know what happened to that one in there," he said, catching a glimpse of Ignatia fuming at him through the curtains. "She let herself go, watching those stories, stuffing herself with candy. She used to be like this, you know." Rosie blew a breath across his palm. "See where I got calluses?" He pointed. "On either side of the wedding band. See that? Nowhere else. See? Feel them. *Feel.*" Vin touched his grandfather's hand.

Ignatia went into her bedroom and put on a wide dress. She rouged her face, making two red circles, swiped her eyelids with a blue dust, and hung a dangling ornament from each ear. Then she forced her arms through the sleeves of an old black cloth coat. Rosie softly swore when he saw her. This was her going-out look. He'd forgotten that today he took her food shopping. He trudged through the garden to back the car out of the garage. The furry white sun was gone. Another storm coming? Rosie swore under his breath again. He'd let the clothes stay on the line, anyway. Maybe it would pass over.

While Rosie waited for Ignatia, he watched a downtown smoke stack puffing purple, and a sullen orange cat saunter across the street. It was a tom just like the one his mother had chased with a broom after she'd found it on her bed, eating the drying spaghetti. A stranger's cat, no less; that had upset her the most. She and Rosie were living with her sister Rocchina by then. This was shortly after Rosie's father's disappearance, during the strike of '31. Twenty-three thousand had walked out of the mills, but Saverio Rosario had to be one of the few arrested on the picket line. His crime? Assaulting a policeman for arresting another picketer, who had called the officer "a cucumber," in dialect. Not such a terrible insult, in any language. Even if he'd said something worse, the policeman shouldn't have been so rough with him.

The papers said that all the arrested men's claims of citizenship would be investigated. Saverio's face burned with anger under his cap at that one; or so Rosie imagined. After the day of his arrest, neither Rosie nor his mother ever saw Rosie's father again. Where had he gone? The police claimed Saverio escaped. The Reds from Harvard cried: "Murder!" saying he'd been beaten to death in his cell, the body disposed of. But neither the police not the Reds had ever produced a body, dead or living. Still, Rosie's mother had cried into the bloodied clothes that a member of the Young Communists had brought her. What did Rosie think? Even after all these years, he wasn't sure, though he'd never much liked policemen—never mind that his own daughter had married one: Vin's and Peter's father. Rosie wasn't too crazy for Communists, either, but if he didn't believe what they had said, if his father had escaped after all, and had never called for Rosie and his mother, that meant he had deserted them.

"Nice!" Ignatia said on her way down the back-yard path to the car. She was admiring the boughs of roses falling against the shed, though she couldn't help but point out that she and Rosie didn't own them. Or the house.

"You were *afraid* to buy a house," she said to begin their old argument. "We could have had this house, upstairs *and* down."

"I paid for this house, every month," Rosie said quietly.

"You could have paid for your own house," she said. "But no: 'What if the roof caves in?' That's what you always said."

"Do you have any idea how much a new roof costs?"

"Oh, you're so smart," she said.

"Well, do you?"

She flung her hand to signal that she had given up on him again.

"Well, you're traveling light, look at it that way," Rosie said.

"Traveling light? Honey. Where am I traveling *to?*"

In the grocery store Rosie walked broodingly behind her as she pushed the cart along, using it as a kind of walker, then made leaps away from it for the food, once embracing a whole armload of tomato cans before dumping them in. Sometimes, Rosie noticed, she forgot her "arthritis" completely, for example, when she pinched and prodded a bag of seeded rolls to see how fresh they felt through the plastic. "Corn on the cob should have handles on *both* ends," she told herself and others at the vegetable bins. She criticizes God himself, thought Rosie, who, as usual, just followed along with his hands knotted behind his back, knowing from long years of experience that if he even picked so much as a roll of toilet paper, there'd be something wrong with it; she'd have to put it back and choose another. Then, wouldn't you know it, today, in the frozen foods aisle, a man about Patsy's age, forty-five this month, began to glare accusingly at Rosie while Ignatia stood on her toes to reach across the frosty bins to claim the exact canister of bread crumbs she wanted.

"What's your problem, pal?" Rosie asked the kinky-haired man. The glasses he wore were round black circles like those drawn on posters to deface them.

"She's having trouble. You could help her."

"Says who?"

"I say. I see her struggling."

"Yeah. She struggles like a snake."

The man glared at Rosie again through the portholes of his glasses.

"You think she needs so much help," said Rosie, "you help her. See what happens."

"Oh, thank you, no thank you," said Ignatia to the man, who shrugged and moved along, still glaring at Rosie over his shoulder.

"He's smoking reefers, that guy," said Rosie.

At the check-out counter he wearily took out his wallet to pay while Ignatia supervised the boy in his apron who loaded the food into the bags. She waited until they were wheeling the cart out to the parking lot before she said: "He was right, you know."

"Who?"

"The one that told you to help me. You could, you know."

"That guy should be in a straightjacket somewheres."

"You should be as crazy as he is. He looks like a smart boy."

"Living with you, I'm crazier."

"Lena! She's the only one who understands me."

"Go! Live with Lena. Who's stopping you?"

"We'll both be living with her soon enough, when Luca goes."

"I'd rather chew grape seeds with the bums down under the bridge."

"You might be. Don't laugh."

Rosie mumbled something else, then drove recklessly up and over a curb on his way out of the parking lot. "Jesus, Mary, and Joseph," Ignatia said as they headed for the highway ramp. The car wheezed and lurched up the incline, and then, just as they were about to join the traffic barreling up behind them, lost power. Rosie pressed the pedal to the floor, but they still crept dangerously along the edge of the highway. When another driver trying to get into the flow of cars finally got the chance to screech past them, swearing out the window at Rosie, shaking his index finger at him, Rosie drew his elbow across his face, as if ready to strike anyone who could be as impatient as that. Couldn't he see a man in trouble? "Jesus Christ!" Rosie said as he steered into the breakdown lane.

They sat. "My Mother, My Confidence, My Mother, My Confidence," Ignatia droned. Then Rosie saw in the rear-view mirror a little pickup truck had pulled over behind them. A woman in jeans and boots hopped out and walked purposefully to Ignatia's side of the car.

"Have you got far to go?" the young woman asked; she looked rugged and healthy and unafraid of anything; her lips were thin, her eyes clear.

"God bless you!" Ignatia said. "One exit. My husband was showing off. He doesn't have any business driving on here."

"I can run you home."

"Could you, honey?"

"No problem."

"My husband'll ride in the truck part," Ignatia offered for Rosie.

"I think we could all fit up front, if we squeeze," the woman said.

"Good-bye," said Rosie.

"You really want to stay here?" the woman asked.

"Good-bye, I told you."

"I'll call Jimmy," Ignatia said. "Our son-in-law, a policeman," she proudly explained, struggling to get herself and her big black oily bird of a pocketbook out of the car. "Jimmy would say not to take a ride with any-body, but would a bad person stop and be so nice?"

When the door had latched shut behind her, and the truck was a speck disappearing down the highway, Rosie closed his eyes. *Peace.* If he had to walk home, so what? It'd do him good. Since he'd retired, he'd put on some weight, though his twenty-year-old pants and cardigan had never fit him well. Besides, the storm clouds were moving away, ragged and swift; through the breaks he could see blue.

"The sun, a snowblown traveler, sank / From sight beneath the smoth-ering bank. . . ." He'd recited "Snow-bound" for his father. Habitually, when he was in trouble, Rosie thought of him and his neat black mous-tache, trim waist and thighs, strong arms that reached for the lunch pail Rosie would run down to the mill to deliver. The man was just thirty-four years old when Rosie saw him last; that was in the fall of '31, when they sat together at the kitchen table and drank coffee while Rosie read him the strike news in the paper, translating it into Italian as he went along. Saverio had come in late and eaten the fried dough, sprinkled with sugar, that they had saved him from supper. After that he'd settled into his stuffed armchair in the living room, the antimacassar crocheted by Rosie's mother in place behind his head, plastered to the edge of the upholstery by his hair oil. Rosie was fifteen. When he was four or five, he'd hidden behind that same chair, counting on his fingers to come up with the right answer when his father drilled him in his sums. Though the man knew few English words, he knew English numbers well enough: that was money. The big armchair was also the place where Rosie's father sat to write letters for people—in Italian; they came to the house and told him what they wanted to say; he wrote in his small straight hand on whatever scraps of paper they had brought with them.

After the disappearance, however, everything changed. Rosie got old, fast—especially since he'd had to leave school. One minute, he was a boy full of the devil, sitting in the back of the class, whittling away at a pencil; the next, he had a shovel in his hand, standing in someone else mud. He was a gray-haired boy in no time. And he still hadn't stopped daydreaming that his father had become rich and would return to rescue him. His night dreams included him, too—in the rare times when he dreamt. He had trouble sleeping. To make it worse, Ignatia snored. He could hear the racket— like a door opening and slamming shut, over and over—even from the next room where his bed was.

And where would he sleep at Lena's? She lived in the big cedar-shingled house across the street from the German Old Folks Home. Alfred had done well. A saint, to hear Lena tell it. He had risen to a supervisor role in the Bradford Silk Underwear Mills, and wasn't it just his dumb good luck to be gone by the time the company went under? When he died in his forties, Alfred left Lena with a fat insurance payoff. His early death may have been a good thing in disguise for Lena; she seemed happier without him. And she couldn't claim to be lonely. Not only a widow, she'd had no children—she was all sealed up: even her hair, in tight bronzed curls, looked impenetrable, like rows of spray-painted seashell macaroni—but, except in the dead of night, Lena's constant companion was her sister Ignatia.

And if he and Ignatia moved in with her? No, something would have to prevent that. But if it did happen, would he have to go back to sharing a bedroom with Ignatia? Or would Lena give them each their own room? Or would the two sisters share a room, so they could whisper in the dark? Whatever the arrangement, he'd be humiliated. He'd be a guest, everyone would know his business. This would be the slowest death. And if Ignatia were to die? Would he have to spend the rest of his days in the same house with Lena? That would be the worst possibility of all. Or would she kick him out? Well, why give her a chance to? He could avoid all that by never agreeing to live there in the first place.

After a while, Rosie got out of the car and looked under the hood. A distributor wire was disconnected. So that was the trouble. He reconnected it and got the car to start. I could just keep driving, he thought. But he didn't. He merely drove cautiously home. For one thing, he had to urinate badly.

The old man's disease. Ignatia was in the garden cutting roses when he pulled up outside the gate.

"I called Jimmy. They're sending somebody to go find you, for nothing, I guess," she said. "And don't forget the packages. We'll have garbage in five minutes more."

He watched her with narrowed eyes from the bathroom window, unseen. She'd taken off her shoes and put her slippers back on, though she still wore her black coat. She'd brought her wooden cane out to the garden to lean on; she had a pair of red-handled scissors in her other hand, and she'd laid a piece of newspaper on the grass. As she snipped the roses, she dropped them onto the paper. Then she stopped, as if to listen hard to something. "Rosie!" she called. Rosie glowered, saying nothing, still spying on her. Couldn't a man have a little peace, even in the bathroom? Where would his dignity go in Lena's house? She only had one bathroom, right next to her bedroom. Ignatia continued to call him. She was swearing at him, too. When he was finished, he went to see what her hollering was all about.

He reached the threshold of the back door in time to see her fall. As if she'd waited for him, so that he might see the spectacle: she rolled, like a great black boulder, or two men fighting, rolling over one another on the ground. Rosie picked up the scissors first. Wasn't that what any sensible man would do? The rose heads were strewn everywhere as if a flower girl had done it.

She wouldn't let him help her up. She just lay on the ground, yelling at him in her mother's language. She was wishing to God that her father had never left the *fattoria*, meaning "farm," but Rosie reminded her that *fattoria* also meant "factory"—on this side of the world it did.

"I wouldn't have fallen if you'd come to help me when I called you the first time," she said with her cheek to the ground.

"Damn roses," he mumbled. "I had to go to the bathroom. Is that a crime?" He gathered the roses up on the newspaper. A headline caught his eye, something about an ex-priest. He carried the roses into the house and put them on the kitchen table, then returned to the garden.

"I went to work—I should have gone to school." She was still on the ground, digging her elbows into the grass. "Left sole, left shoe, right sole, right shoe—you think it was easy? Everybody used to walk to work, all those feet wearing down shoes. Good for business. Nobody walks anywhere anymore. Ooooh, but I feel like somebody just walked all over me."

Rosie put his hands underneath her moist armpits, and pulled her to her feet. He handed her the cane. "I was getting roses to put by the statue. His flower. The Sacred Heart," she said.

"Good thing this didn't happen on the stairs," said Rosie. "See? You're lucky we don't live in a whole big house."

"I was getting roses for Him and look what happens," she said, and gave her cane a little shake, pointing up toward Heaven.

"Well, the roses'll cheer you up," he said when she finally got her bearings and they were standing in the garden together.

When Vin heard that evening of his grandmother's fall, he lay across the bed and started writing a poem called "Maggie." His grandmother was like a mountain to him, with one of those rock-slide warnings at the bottom. You looked up and saw rocks about to topple, but you couldn't believe that they ever would. His mother Lobelia talked about how old her mother Ignatia looked, but to Vin she was like a mountain in that, too—not aging except in ways you wouldn't notice. *Fourteen years old.* Was that young? He thought so, but every time he saw himself in the mirror, he was shocked. The top of his head was edging up toward the top of the mirror. He could make his chest look broad, especially if he held his breath. His father and brother had noticed his growth. So now they had started testing him, holding him down on his bed and fighting with him, both of them together, to toughen him up, they said.

Vin wrote another line of his poem: "Maggie, your eyes are like two blue daisies . . . ," then crossed out the word "two." How many eyes did anybody ever have, unless they were a cyclops or something, dodo bird.

Bored by the poem, he began to think about the money his grandmother had given him for Patsy's money order. Maybe he could say the money was lost, or stolen. Then he could spend it. But could he do that to his Uncle Patsy? The turd. As his grandfather said, "Lawyers are supposed to make a lot of money, right? Not Patsy. Noooo. He's too smart for that. He's just like my father," Rosie said. "Couldn't leave well enough alone. Had the Devil in him. Had to meddle. Had to tell people what he thought. Now Patsy's going around doing the same: defending bums. His own people aren't good enough for him."

Peter came into the room after Vin had written a few more lines to Maggie. "What's that? What is it?" He grabbed the piece of notebook paper out of Vin's hand. Vin leapt and landed on his brother's back and pounded him with his fists; Vin tore the paper into bits in order to get it away from him. "All right, God, you're a wild man," said Peter, who, lucky for Vin, had not been able to see that his own girlfriend's name was written on it.

The next day at school, Vin showed Maggie the roll of bills. "Yeah? So?" She was dressed entirely in pink, including scuffless pink leather aerobic shoes. Vin's eyes searched for a speck of dirt. How did she keep so clean? She pretended to yawn. "So what?" Of course, she'd be unimpressed with money, but she did seem interested in where a kid like him might have gotten it. Peter was even more interested. His eyes grew wide. "Where'd you get that? You stole it!" He snatched the money.

"I did not."

"Got any more? Gimme that."

Peter grabbed the money out of his hand—easily, because Vin would not get risk tearing that. Peter slid it into his jeans pocket, and he and Maggie strolled down the corridor. If Peter spent it, if he didn't give it back, that *was* stealing. If Peter told his parents what Vin had brought to school, Vin would tell the truth, and his grandmother would back him up. Unless she died. Unless she was already dead, this morning. Why didn't all old people just die? Why didn't everybody—just get it over with and die?

After school, Vin again rode his bike to see Ignatia and told her what Peter had done. "You'll get it back from him, honey," she said, lying on her bed; the dark pigment around her eyes looked like a burglar's mask. She said she was sore all over. She really didn't care about anything right now except getting better. She would take care of it later. "Tell Peter to come see me in a couple of days. I'll tell him what I think about things. I'll give him one of these. You know? "She made a motion, half karate chop, half a spank for a baby's bottom. "Have an apple or a banana on the way out. On the kitchen table in the nice big bowl. Ahhh, I used to feed the birds. They used to see me coming. I'd walk home from work along Union Street, and they'd flock all around me, like I was St. Francis or something. Now I feed birds like you."

Rosie didn't speak to Vin as he left by the way of the garden. The two of them—Vin and Ignatia—were in cahoots, doing something for Patsy, and Rosie would find out sooner or later what it was. Rosie had phoned Patsy last night to tell him about his mother's fall, and to say that a call from him would cheer her up. But he hadn't been able to get through to Patsy. Not even after midnight. At six, this morning, Rosie had been awake, but didn't think of Patsy until seven. And by then there was no answer once again.

Patsy, gone to work early. Or else he hadn't spent any time at all in his apartment last night.

Luca, his landlord, his father's friend, hadn't been home upstairs last night, for certain. Doctor's orders. Yesterday he'd been told that he wasn't to spend the night alone anymore, so he had stayed with his son Dennis and daughter-in-law in West Boxford. He wasn't allowed to drive, either, but shortly after Vin pedaled away, along came Luca driving without permission, like a teenager. He had things to attend to in the apartment, he told Rosie in his accented English. "There's something in there for you, too, you'll see. You'll get it. You wait." And the way he said it, Rosie could guess that meant he'd have to wait until after Luca was dead.

Luca took a few wobbly steps to the garden border and pinched off a yellow coreopsis head. He slipped the short stem into the breast pocket of his jacket; the flower poked out. He broke off another one and handed it to Rosie, who could never help but get annoyed whenever Luca acted like he owned the place, even if he was the landlord. Luca had heard about Ignatia's fall. He wanted to see her. Together he and Rosie walked inside. Luca weaved; Rosie took hold of his elbow. "I'm all right," the old man said, brushing him away.

The house smelled of burned food. Rosie had ruined some fried peppers and onions he'd tried to make for lunch, though he'd done all right with breakfast. The only thing he'd done wrong was to spill the coffee trying to pour it into the thermos. He wore a bandage on his forearm where the liquid had scalded him. He had affixed a square of gauze and tape with the help of Lena, who'd been there around mid-morning. Her dizziness had miraculously disappeared, she had said as she fussed over Ignatia and puttered in the kitchen.

When Luca walked into Ignatia's room, she was sitting up, cleaning the statue of the Sacred Heart, polishing it with a cotton dish towel. She was sorry now for what she had said against God in the garden.

As she and Luca chatted, Rosie began to wonder what Luca had for him upstairs. Could it be money? Wouldn't it have to be? What if it was the deed to the whole house? Luca's children would fight it, but Rosie would win the case. He'd get Patsy to help him. Then Rosie scolded himself; Luca was not going to leave him his property; that was a ridiculous thought. If anybody looked inside his head while that was passing through it, they'd have said he was nuttier than Patsy.

"One thing about being sick, everybody comes to see you," Luca laughed.

"Lobelia's been here, and Vinnie. Peter's busy with his girlfriend. And Patsy, he's so busy, too," said Ignatia.

Rosie watched Luca closely. Why was he going to make him wait until after he was dead to get whatever he was going to give him? Driving around in his condition, Luca'd probably be dead before the day was out. And take two or three people with him. But what are you gonna do? Asfter Luca went creakily up the stairs to his apartment, Rosie phoned Dennis to tell him his father was here. The sooner Luca died, the sooner he'd get his gift, if it was a gift; but also the sooner he and Ignatia would be packing off to Lena's.

"My wife thought somebody *stole* the car," Dennis told Rosie on the phone from his office. "Then she figured it out. She's on her way."

Later, Rosie saw the old man walking to his daughter-in-law's car with his hands out, like someone in pitch darkness feeling for walls.

A few weeks after that, Rosie dressed in his one good suit to attend Luca's wake. Outside it was a bright fall day, leaves crackled underfoot; inside the funeral home, it was spring: wreaths and flowers made the whole place stink, thought Rosie, who recognized many of his own old acquaintances among the throng, including his neighbor Pasquerelli.

Rosie knelt solemnly at the casket. Luca's waxen face was rouged, wearing lipstick, too. Behind Rosie, people talked loudly, reminiscing. "Fabrizio Pitocchelli's bank. Remember how it went bankrupt? Five hundred thousand dollars. That's the Depression. Today, a football player couldn't buy his underwear with that. . . ." "Neapolitans didn't have much money in that bank—they ate their money. . . ." "LoPiano ate his and everybody else's after he went to New Jersey with those stolen money orders. . . ." They laughed.

Eighty-nine years old. That was Luca's age. Rosie's father would be that age, too, if he had lived. If he still did live somewhere today. Rosie moved to the receiving line to pay his respects to Luca's family.

"How's Ignatia?" Dennis asked Rosie as they shook hands. He had a tan. He was one of those fifty-year-olds who still dressed like a kid.

"She was sorry she couldn't be here herself to tell you how bad she feels," Rosie said, though, at home, Ignatia, hearing the news of Luca's death, had been not sad but elated. Now they really could go live with Lena. They might have gone sooner, but it was only polite to wait until the old man died, considering his kindnesses to them over all these years. He would never have gotten new tenants as good as they were, not in a million years. Of course Dennis and the others would have had him sell the building long ago, but Luca wouldn't stand for that. Now all Ignatia and Rosie had to do was wait for Lena's formal invitation.

The wake was followed by a huge funeral the next day. Then, after the burial, a party back at the house of Luca's daughter, in Methuen. At the buffet table, where Rosie had gone to hide from Mr. Pasquerelli, he found himself standing right next to Dennis again.

"Doesn't that guy have a home?" Rosie asked Dennis of Pasquerelli.

"He used to deliver mail to my father's shop," Dennis said.

Rosie nodded, remembering that Pasquerelli's first career, as a postal worker, reading everybody's envelopes and postcard messages, had prepared him for his second career as a neighborhood spy. Rosie was about to make this observation to Dennis, but when he turned to him Dennis said, solemnly as a judge, "Rosie, I know you're probably concerned about what we're going to do with the house. I want you to know that we'd like you to take all the time you need to get resettled. I'm going to have some people come over and look at the property, but they're not to disturb you. Nothing's going to happen quickly. You take all the time in the world. You'll hear me cleaning things out upstairs. Don't worry. I think there's something up there for you, as a matter of fact."

Rosie ate a black olive. He knew these words must be considered one more kindness of the Luca family, and he knew he should thank Dennis, but he could bring himself to say nothing. He nodded and watched Dennis filling his plate with cole slaw, and Pasquerelli drifting toward him.

"Where've you been?" Pasquerelli asked. "I haven't seen you around."

"You know us gardeners. We're like the bears. We hibernate. In the spring, you'll see us again."

"Ignatia. How's she doing?"

"She still got complaints. Arthuritis, her heart . . ."

"Woman trouble?"

"Me? I'm too old for that."

"You know what I mean. Ignatia."

"I don't know if she's got any or not. I haven't checked lately."

"That's what it always is with them, don't you think?"

"Myself, I don't speak for women," said Rosie.

When Rosie returned home, Ignatia said, "What happened? What did people say?" He told her what Dennis had told him. "Well, Ro, Lena has said she'd have us come live with her. It's all set. All we have to do is say the word."

*   *   *

The first snow came early that year, just a few weeks after the funeral, while Dennis was cleaning out his father's apartment. Rosie could hear him overhead and see the white flakes falling past the blackness of the tree branches spread out across his downstairs window. The snow was falling wet and fast, sticking as if each piece were carrying a bit of glue. The chatter of the television was coming from Ignatia's room. Rosie had convinced her to stay here, to put off moving to Lena's, at least until they had received the gift promised, whatever it was, from Luca. "You never know," Rosie said. "Oh, yes you do," said Ignatia, but she agreed to wait.

Dennis came to the door as he was leaving, with a bundle of letters.

"Come in, come in," Rosie said.

"No, I gotta get home, but these are for you. Your name. From my father."

The dates of the postmarks began 1931, '32, '33 . . . The handwriting that had written Luca's name and address looked familiar; then Rosie saw the return address: a place in Italy and the name and first initial, S. Rosario.

Rosie sat and read of his father's life, gripped by a fear that he wouldn't get to the end of the letters. His heart pounded irregularly against the wall of his chest. So! he kept saying as he read the faded ink written in his father's patchwork Italian. So! The Reds had *paid* Saverio to disappear, to go back to Italy. At a time when men were waiting in line for a slice of bread and salt pork, they had enticed him with money, saying that, with him gone, they could more easily claim, as they had done, that the police had murdered him in his cell and hidden his body. Produce the body of Saverio Rosario, the Reds would demand of the police; and of course they wouldn't be able to. The deal was that they would send Rosie and his mother back to Italy soon after, and this was what Rosie's father had intended all along. And so he fled.

Rosie's mother had not followed that plan, however. She was paralyzed, with fear. She wouldn't budge; she'd just gotten here to America, she said, though it had already been nearly seventeen years. Rocchina, her sister, who had just then lost her husband in a mill fire, was begging her to stay; she would die of loneliness, otherwise. And so they did stay. And Saverio had written Luca all these letters to urge him to get Rosie's mother to change her mind, to consider his own state of loneliness. Apparently, he had been writing letters, too, but she hadn't answered. And Saverio couldn't return to America because of the new immigration laws.

After he finished reading the letters, Rosie just stared out the window; for a long time, he just watched the crazy people driving by in the slippery snow. Then Ignatia was calling him from her bedroom. "Ro, Vinnie's here. I can see him coming through the gate, wheeling his bike."

"Don't you listen to weather reports?" Rosie asked him at the door.

"Yeah, I listen, but I don't always believe them."

"Come in, come in."

Vin knocked the snow off his shoes and shed his clothes for warm ones of Rosie's.

"Where were you going on your bike on a day like today?"

"Out."

"Out where?"

"Away."

"Running away?"

Vin said nothing, just covered his face with the towel he was using to dry his hair.

"I thought so. I saw that look. Come on, come on now, get warm. Go sit on the radiator."

Vin obeyed while Rosie fixed him some coffee and two large fried-egg sandwiches.

"Where's the bike?"

"Out there."

"Not in the shed?"

"I didn't even lock it," Vin shrugged.

"Why not?"

"Who's going to steal a bike in this weather?"

"Thieves'll steal anytime."

Rosie went out to attend to the bike. He found it leaning up against the house. He wheeled it toward the snow-topped shed. It had been a while since he'd walked along with a bike at his side. The movement brought with it a feeling of freedom he used to know. Or maybe he'd only dreamed of such a feeling, of being free to go anywhere, to make himself at home anywhere in the world.

Inside the house, Ignatia called to Vin from her bedroom. "What'sa matter? You're mad at me."

"Sure I'm mad."

"About the money."

"Peter took it and spent it and you let him get away with it. Why?"

"He must have needed it if he took it like that."

"He didn't *need* it! He spent it on his girlfriend!"

"Shhh. Rosie'll be coming back in."

"I thought *Patsy* needed it so badly."

"Shhh. Shhh. I can only do so much. Here I am an old woman, honey. I can't even get out of bed. The doctor says there's a black mass over my heart. 'Those are my sins,' I told him." Ignatia managed a laugh. "*My* sins, honey. I can't be worrying about anyone else's."

Throughout the early evening, the three of them—Rosie, Ignatia, Vin—watched the falling snow together, alternating with watching the TV. Jimmy would come to pick up Vin and his bike on his way home from the police station. But then, after they had eaten a little dinner that Rosie had prepared, Jimmy called back to say that Vin should stay there for the night.

"It's just like having Patsy here again," Ignatia told Lena on the phone from her bed. "He's sitting here in one of Ro's old sweaters and big old pairs of woolen pants. I should have some of Patsy's things here for an emergency like this with one of my grandsons. The both of them—Vin and Rosie—are all wrapped up. You should see. I'm perspiring as usual. Oh, I'm all right. No. I'm always all right. You know me."

At bedtime, Rosie told Vin to go to sleep in his room; the boy was chilled. Rosie said he would take the couch, though he knew he couldn't sleep. Or, out of habit, he didn't even try, and after midnight, he put on his coat and went outside. The snow had stopped. In the distance, he could hear a car stuck, trying to get free. A city sand truck went by noisily. Nothing else moved. He got out his shovel and started digging out the driveway.

He had thought of running away so many times in the past—to get away from Ignatia, this Godforsaken city, his life, yes, but also to look for his father—but he'd never known in which direction to go first. Now he knew it didn't matter.

He had begun to see how it could be: he could take the car wherever he might go. Ignatia had no need for it. She and Lena could figure a way to get around without him. He shoveled without stopping for an hour, until the driveway was completely clear.

Walking back to the house through the garden, to throw some things into a bag, he made another decision: he would introduce himself as Leo from now on—his real name, not his nickname: a lousy flower. His cousins had given him that name when he went to work as a gardener. He would never call himself that name again. It wasn't too late. He could still be like his father, a man who had trusted strangers, who wasn't afraid. Then he saw many big black birds descend. What in the world were birds doing out on a night like tonight? Crazy birds. He chased them away once, but they descended again, folded their wings and watched him, blinking their calm yellow eyes.

It began to snow again. Rosie was buried by the snow that fell all during the early morning hours; and, for an hour or two after that, until, that is, his grandson found him, Ignatia cursed Rosie, even envying him a little, believing that he had finally done what for so long he had silently intended.

1988

THE CHANDELIER

Gregory Orfalea

Mukhlis drives up Asbury Street in Pasadena and brings his green Buick to an easy, slow stop underneath the largest flowering eucalyptus in southern California. The first door cracked is that of his wife, Wardi, who gets out as she has every week for the past forty years, as if she were with child. She has not been with child for many years, but her body at center is like the large burl of a cedar and her legs are as bowed as an old chair's. Mukhlis emerges from the Buick. He looks left and right for cars—a short, searing look either way. And the sun tries to plant its white seed on the center of his bald head.

Mukhlis has made a small fortune in real estate. He has apartment complexes here and there in the city, and many of his tenants are black or brown. He himself is brown, or rather almond, and his eyes, like those of many Lebanese and Syrians, are blue. He owes this hue to the Crusaders. A continent man, Mukhlis' eyes are the last blue twinkle of a distant lust.

What words there are to say, Mukhlis rarely says. His eyes and body speak—a body made to withstand. As he ascends the steps of his sister's home, the collar of his gray suit pulls taut around his neck. And his neck has the thickness of a foundation post; it welds his head to the shoulders. For years it has been bronzed by the sun. So tight is the tie and collar around his neck that his nape stands up in a welt of muscle. It is not a fat neck—nothing about the man is fat, save a slight bulge to his belly, brought on, no doubt, by forty years of Wardi's desserts, among the finest Arabic delights in Los Angeles. Mukhlis has learned it is useless to compliment her because Wardi (Rose, in English), like most Arabs, does not react to compliments; she prefers to go to great lengths to pay a compliment, instead. But not Mukhlis. He says not two crooked words about Wardi's *knafi*, the bird's nest whose wafer-like shell must be rolled with the patience of Job before it is filled with pistachios as green as Mukhlis' Buick—and probably greener—then topped with a spoon of rosewater syrup.

Mukhlis kisses his sister, Matile, and booms a greeting to the air behind her in a robust voice that speaks in simple sentences and laughs silently. His large head, sapphire eyes, and corded neck all shake with his laughter.

And if it is on a summer evening, with a large group of people chatting on Matile's porch, all will be aware of Mukhlis, though he will surely say the least, and when his hands come apart after having been clasped tightly on his belly for so long, people will take a drag on their cigarettes and turn in his direction.

"No one wants to work, and so the devil has his pick of the young people."

Wardi, who clasps her hands on a more bulbous belly, will nod and sip her coffee from the demitasse.

"Matile, do you have any cream?" Mukhlis asks his sister.

"Certainly, my honey," she sings. "Anything for you."

When Matile's voice sings it is to smooth over rough spots in conversation; her feigned joy or fright has saved many a wounded soul. But when Mukhlis sang—the fact that he once did sing is his most guarded secret—it was with the voice of the *hassoun*, the national bird of Lebanon, multi-colored red, yellow, and black, prized for its rich warble, and fed marijuana seeds by children.

Sitting among immigrants from the First World War, Mukhlis was asked to fill the gaps in all hearts over the strange Atlantic, which in Arabic is called "The Sea of Darkness." Please, Mukhlis, sing the praise to the night! Sing of the moon and its white dress! Huddled on the stoops in Brooklyn, they asked for the song of two lovers separated by a river. The one of the nine months of pregnancy, in which Mukhlis stuffed a pillow under his shirt. Sing, cousin Mukhlis, for we are tired of the dress factories, we are tired of the fish market. Sing the Old Land on the Mediterranean!

And sing he did. His voice was effortless and sweet; it was made all the sweeter by the immense power everyone knew lay under it. Then one day this unschooled tenor, this voice dipped in rosewater, simply stopped. It stopped cold when Mukhlis' mother died in a little loft above a funeral parlor in Brooklyn. It died when he covered the four long white scars of her back, from the lashes of the Turks, for the last time. No one in California has ever heard him sing.

All of this is whispered from time to time behind Mukhlis' back. None of it is spoken directly to his ears. He will not tolerate it. His usual response to any mention of the latest atrocity in Lebanon is: "How is your dog?" or "The apricots are too thick on the boughs this year. They need to be snapped off."

But today the large porch is empty, except for Matile herself and her oldest grandson, Mukhlis' great-nephew. This young man has been traveling for years. He is a restless soul, thinks Mukhlis, as they take their places on the porch—he on the legless couch, his wife on a white wrought-iron chair with a pillow of faded flowers made by Matile. The great-nephew takes to the old iron swing. What is it about this day? Mukhlis says to himself, noticing a vine in the yard. The wind is hurting the grape leaves.

Matile brings a tray of coffee and announces dinner is not too far off, and all must stay.

"It is never too far off with you, Matile," Mukhlis says, blowing over the coffee.

"You *must* stay," she sings. "I am making stuffed zucchini."

"Never mind," he says. "Have you got a *ghrabi?*"

"*Ghrabi?*" Matile stands so quickly she leaves her black shoes. And goes into a litany of food that last five minutes.

"No, no, no," Mukhlis punctuates each breathless pause in her list. "*Ghrabi*—just give me one."

"One!" she cries. "I have a hundred."

"One, please, is all I want."

She brings a dish piled high with small hoops of butter, sugar, and dough, each with a mole or two of pistachio.

"Eat," she says.

Wardi takes one. Mukhlis shakes his head and breaks off half a *ghrabi*.

"Isn't that delicious?" Matile asks, preempting the compliment. Mukhlis chews. "You look real good today," she smiles with a brightened face, disregarding his nodding. Mukhlis turns to the young man.

"And so, what are you doing here?"

"Looking for work," says the great-nephew, a dark, slender fellow with broad shoulders. These eyes of his, Mukhlis thinks, have a dark sparkle. He's cried and laughed too much for his age; his laugh is a cry and his cry is a laugh.

"It's time for you to get serious and stop this wandering and get a good job in business," Mukhlis says rather loudly.

"You are playing with your life. When are you going to get married?"

Mukhlis gleams his crocodile smile and laughs silently. Then he becomes solemn, and touches the pistachio on a *ghrabi* with a thick forefinger, taps it several times, then removes it.

"Aren't you ever really hungry, Uncle Mukhlis?"

The old realtor looks out past the stanchions of the porch, past the thickened apricots.

"Boy, have you ever seen a person eat an orange peel?"

"I've eaten them myself. They're quite good."

"No, no, boy. I mean rotten orange peels, with mud and dung on them. Have you had that?"

The great-nephew purses his lips.

"Well, I want to tell you a story. I want to tell you about hunger, and I want to tell you about disgrace."

Matile gets up again, and lets out in her falsetto, "Don't go no further till I come back."

Mukhlis disregards her and squeezes a faded pillow on the legless couch, as if he were squeezing his brain. What is it about the breeze and the light today, the crystal light? Will he go on? He does not know. His great-nephew is too silent. Mukhlis does not like silence waiting for silence. He likes his silence to be hidden in a crowd. From the dome of his almond head, he takes some sweat and smells it. Wardi continues to eat.

"I was the oldest of us in Lebanon when we lived in the mountain, but when the World War started I was still a young boy. They cut off Beirut harbor in 1914. You see, the Germans were allied with the Turks who had hold over all the Arab lands. And so the Germans become our masters for a time. When it was all we could do to steer clear of the Turks! The Allies blockaded Beirut harbor, and for four years there was no food to be had in Mount Lebanon."

At this moment Matile puts a heap of grapes in front of him.

"Nothing like this purple grape, I can assure you! These were treacherous times of human brutality. People were hungry and hunger is the beginning of cruelty. The Turks themselves would tolerate no funny business. If people refused to cooperate with them they would take it out on the children. I saw them seize a small boy by the legs and literally rip him in half. I saw this happen with my own eyes; one half of the child flew into the fountain we had in Mheiti, which is near Bikfaya. The fountain was empty, but even after the war when it had water and the remains of the child were dried up no one would drink there."

"Yi! You tell them, Mukhlis! You tell this to show what happen to us!" Matile's voice rises as she lays down a plate of goat's cheese and bread. "It was terrible."

"Food was so scarce people would pick up horse dung, wash it, and eat the grains of hay left. It was common to go days without eating or drinking, because the Nahr Ibrahim and the Bardowni rivers were contaminated by dead bodies. The Germans and the Turks would throw traitors into the river . . . then there was the chandelier."

Matile clicks her tongue, "I could tell you story, boy, I could tell you story."

"Did you know 'Lebanon' means 'snow'?" Mukhlis raises his pointer finger. "It means 'white as yogurt' because the mountains are covered with snow. It was very cold in the winter, and we had to stay in. Without food, it was colder."

"What about restaurants?" the great-nephew ventures.

"Restaurant? You are an idiot, young man, forgive me for saying. Any restaurant was destroyed in the first year, any market plundered by the soldiers. We had to find food for ourselves. Each day for four years was a battle for food."

"I could tell you story," Matile puts her eyes up to the stucco ceiling of the porch and shakes her hands. "*Thoobs!* A crust of bread was so rare it was like communion. My mother she had to go away for days to trade everything we had for food on the other side of the mountain—"

"Matile, I . . ."

"—she give us a slice of bread before she leaves and she shake her finger at us and say—Matile, Mukhlis, Milhem—you don't take this all at once. Each day you cut one piece of the bread. One piece! No more. And you cut this piece into four pieces—three for you, and then you break the last one for the infants. You understand? Like one cracker a day for each of us. Little Milhem and Leila, they cry all day. They want more. They too little to understand, and the baby . . . ah! Milhem hit us for the rest of the slice of bread. I hide it under my pillow one night. And that night . . . oh, I could tell you story to make your ears hurt!"

Mukhlis shifts in his seat and flings out his arms, "Now, when I went off in the snow . . ."

"The chandelier, you remember."

"Yes, Matile, of course I do."

"You remember, Wardi, you wouldn't believe it."

Wardi's eyes are as large as a night creature behind her thick eyeglass lenses, and she nods.

Mukhlis clears his throat loudly. "My mother gave me the last piastres we had and told me to go through the snow over the mountain to the village in the dry land, to fetch milk and bread. I was not as strong as my mother but I was strong, and so I tried. But the first day out I was shot at by a highwayman, a robber. I hid behind a rock; still he found me and stripped off my jacket and took the piastres. I was glad he did not kill me. But what was I to do? I could not go home. I continued walking until I came to the monastery. I thought I would ask the monks for some milk. They were not there."

"They die."

"Matile, please. They were not there. Perhaps they went to Greece. They were Greek monks. The place was empty. The door to the chapel opening with the wind that moved it back and forth. Inside the candles were snuffed. And the candlesticks were cold, and all the pews were covered with frost. It was winter, inside and out. Up above was a . . ."

"Chandelier!"

"Yes, Matile, a huge crystal chandelier. In all my life I have never seen one larger. Its branches were as far across as this couch, made of solid gold. Inlaid in the arms were rubies the size of your eyes, nephew! I remember standing in that chapel that day thinking how we had come to worship there with my father when I was a very young child; the chandelier was something I would worship. I would look up and its great shining light would say to me—God. This is your God. Mukhlis, here on Mount Lebanon. He brims with light and He will sit in your eyes, in your dreams. I had never thought of touching it. For one thing, it was too high. It was at least fifteen feet above my head. Well, so help the Almighty, I was hungry. And my mother was hungry. And so were my brothers . . . and my sisters. And we had not heard from our father, who was in America, for two years. Before God and man, I committed a sacrilege. The mosaics, you see, on the wall were shot out and in tatters. I crawled up the wall where the tile was gone. I crawled up that mosaic until I made it to the crossbeams of the ceiling. And I had to be very careful not to knock loose the mosaic where I was hanging—a mosaic of Our Lady it was, and who knows? Maybe my foot was in her mouth."

"How sad!" sighs Matile.

"But I hoisted myself onto the crossbeam and slid—like this, yes—slid across the beam. It was cold enough to hold my hands fast as I tried to balance. But finally I made it out over the nave of the chapel, to the chandelier."

"Yi!"

"The chandelier was held to the ceiling with tall iron nails. Carefully, carefully I put my hands through the crystal teardrops, to latch onto the gold arms. And then you know what I did, young man? I became a monkey. I swung free on that chandelier! I pulled up and heaved down on it, trying to loosen it. I yanked and yanked with the crystal hitting my eyes and the rubies sweating in my hands. And I swung back and forth in the cold air. For a long time the chandelier would not loosen. It seemed like God Himself was holding onto the chandelier through the ceiling and saying to me: No you don't, Mukhlis! You do not take the chandelier from this church. This is mine, Mukhlis! This chandelier was given to the worship of the Almighty. And you—you are a puny human being who deserves to rot in hell for this.

"I am not talking about playing in the acacias. I am not talking about swinging from those miserable apricot trees, which need to be cut back by the way, Matile."

"Anything you say, my honey."

"I am talking about a tree of crystal and gold. I am talking about food."

"Wardi, would you like more coffee, dear?"

"Matile, I am talking about food."

"So am I!"

Wardi's enlarged eyes close and her big bosom vibrates with mirth, like a dreaming horse.

"Oh it's useless. Why talk about it?" Mukhlis folds his hands, as if to tie up the story once and for all and leave everyone hanging on the chandelier.

Matile speaks with alarm: "Please, tell them, tell them. I won't get up no more. This is story you never heard the like of before. It can't be no worse!"

Mukhlis gets up, paces on the clay porch, and goes over to the apricot, breaking off a branch crowded with fruit.

"Here, Matile, here is your dessert," he spits and continues, still standing. "Finally, I heard it come loose. The plaster dust rained on my face and I heaved on this chandelier one more time. And then I fell."

Mukhlis raises his thick forearms and grips the air.

"It breaks, ah!"

"No, Matile, it does not break. Please, you are killing my story at every juncture."

She laughs and gets up for some rice pudding that is cooling in the refrigerator.

"I fall with it. I fall with it and I fall directly on my rump. This is why I walk slowly to this day, young man. Because of the chandelier. That chandelier had to become milk. It was going to save my life, our lives. What did my bones mean? Nothing. But I was a tough young fellow—not like you soft people today—and not one teardrop of that crystal was scratched. I got up, and my hip was partially cracked. But I got up. I carried the chandelier to the entrance of the church. No one was around. No one saw me do it."

"God finally let go?" the great-nephew asks, with a smirk.

"God never lets go. I yanked it out of His hands. But I could not carry the chandelier far—it weighed a ton. In the vestibule of the chapel was a small Oriental rug. I placed the chandelier on top of that, took the cord of chain, tied it around the branches of gold, and dragged the whole mess out into the snow. No, Matile, no rice pudding. For the next three days, I dragged the chandelier over the snow to get to the village over the mountain in the hot land of the Bekaa. For three days I walked and pulled it behind me."

Mukhlis stops and wipes his brow. He is sweating heavily now, even though the California air is dry.

"I was exhausted by the end of the first day. I lay down in the snow by a cedar. I did not want to damage the chandelier, so I left it on the rug and tried to sleep on the snow with as much of my body as I could against the cedar. I was so tired and fell fast alseep."

"Did you dream?" asks the great-nephew, taking a spoonful of the sweet rice pudding.

"I don't remember. No, I don't dream. Dreams are for soft times," Mukhlis grunts. "You've dropped some pudding." His listener takes up the white spot on the porch with a finger. For a while Mukhlis says nothing, and listens to them eating. His blue eyes stare out into the warm air past the apricots, past the flowering eucalyptus, to the cloudless sky.

"I awoke to the sound of licking in the dark. I felt warm breath near my face. I sat up. There were six eyes, six greenish eyes in the darkness. My blood went cold. Wolves. I got up fast, grabbed the chandelier and swung it around and around, turning inside it myself. It made a tinkling noise that was loud in the dead forest and the wolves howled and scattered back into the night. I was breathing so hard my heart felt like it would come out of me.

I was much too awake now and decided to go on dragging the chandelier in the dark. All through the night the teardrops clinked against each other and the rug rubbed over the snow. My eyes have never been so wide as that night. I looked on all sides and hurried until dawn, then rested. I remember lying down by a boulder, hooking the chandelier with my arm. When it dawned, the sun sent it sparkling. It made rays of red all over the snow, and the rubies looked like drops of glistening blood. I rested a while, my eyes opening and closing, but I did not let them close completely. No, not again! The second day I met a family trudging in the snow—a mother, daughter, and two babies. The mother asked if I had any milk. I said I was going to get some for the chandelier. She shook her head and kissed me on the head. Her daughter's eyes were rimmed with blue and she was shaking. She had nothing on but a nightgown and thin sweater, and her toes showed through her leather shoes. They went on—they were going to Zahle, they said. I said I thought Zahle had no food, because my mother had been there and had bought the last scoop of flour in town. The mother asked where my family lived and I told her. They said they would try and go there. I said, Please do. The mother stared at me a while with her own blue-rimmed eyes. One baby had blue lips. The other was whimpering and breathing quickly in the daughter's arms. I went on. I went on and on, with the snow wedged in my socks and pants. That night I slept with my head inside the chandelier, my arms coiled it, my legs twisted inside it so that if wolves came they would not want me, for they would think I was part of the chandelier. It worked. I was not bothered by wolves that night. The third day I descended from the mountain. I saw the dry lands in the distance—the rust-colored sand and rock of the Bekaa—and I broke out laughing, I was so happy. But I descended too quickly, and a thread of the rug snagged on a twig raised out of the snow. The chandelier slid off and down a smooth embankment of snow which the sun had turned into a plate of ice. I plunged down the cliff after the chandelier. But when it reached a ledge it fell. It fell about twenty feet. I cried out and rolled like a crazy dog down the snowbank and fell on my face in front of the chandelier. Luckily it had landed on snow that had not iced over, that had some shade from the ledge. I moved it slowly. One of the gold arms was bent and five or six teardrops of crystal were shattered. I turned it and stepped back. It did not look too bad if one looked from this perspective, with the broken part to the back. The rug was still above, so I fetched it and carefully laid the chandelier on it, like a wounded human being, and went on. Slow now, Mukhlis, slow now. I did not let myself be

excited any more because of the nearness of the Bekaa. I have never let
myself be excited again because of that chandelier breaking over the ledge.
That day, around four o'clock, I reached the small village my mother had
told me about. The villagers there were healthy. They still had some fields
producing corn and wheat and lentils, and the road to Damascus was open.
When they saw me—a little runt dragging this chandelier on the dry, dusty
road—they gathered around me, asking all sorts of questions. I was too tired
to answer. I just said, 'Take me to a cow-farmer. Please, as soon as you can.'
They led me to such a man. I said to him, 'Look, I have come from the
mountain where it is very cold and no food is there. My family is starving. I
will give you this chandelier for milk and anything else I can carry.' The
farmer inspected the chandelier, God damn his soul. Our people! They will
try to strike a deal no matter what. You may be flat on the ground, your legs
chopped off, and they will throw dust in your eyes while they cheat at
backgammon. This farmer held up the chandelier with the aid of another
man and said, 'It is broken. It can't be worth much.' I said to him, 'Please,
sir. It is made of gold and rubies and crystal.' Where did you get it from?' he
asked. I said, 'I got it from the mountain.' He nodded. He did not want to
ask me the next questions. 'I'm not sure,' he said. It was then that his wife,
God save her soul, slapped him on the eyes. He pushed her away. 'All right,'
he said, "Two jugs of milk and we will put a pack of bread on your back. Can
you carry all that?' I said, 'Yes, yes, I can carry as much as you can give me.'
And he gave me two lambskins of milk and hoisted the bread on my back.
The wife put in two bags of dates and dried apricots when he wasn't looking.
And she kissed me on the head.

"I stayed in that town to rest for the night. They fed me a good meal. It
felt good to sleep, to sleep thoroughly. But by morning I was ready to go. I
walked back up the mountain, rising from the warm air to the cold, walking back into the snow world and the dark forest. I walked steadily, though
my back and pelvis were hurting. When I made it back to Mheiti in a few
days, I found myself running through the worn path in the snow up to my
little house—a house made of limestone blocks, a good, sturdy house in
normal times. My mother spotted me through the window and came running. She shouted in a hoarse voice, 'Mukhlis! Oh Mukhlis, you've come!'"

Matile is standing rigid. She does not speak, or offer food. She watches
her brother's sapphire eyes melting in their own fire.

"My mother threw me above her—*ya rubi*, she was strong—and then
carried me into the house before she even saw the milk. When she did, she

nearly tore it off my neck. She gave some to Matile, to my brother Milhem, and to the baby Leila. But there was the infant to go—my brother Wadie. She frantically squeezed the lambskin's tip into his mouth as he lay in his crib. It was a wooden crib. A small wooden crib. I watched her force it on him. I saw that his eyes were stunned open as if he had seen a large rock toppling on top of him. She kept squeezing the lambskin of milk until half of it was dripping out of his mouth to the floor. 'Mother!' I called to her. 'Don't, don't! You're wasting it.' She wouldn't stop. I had to pull it from her hands. She squeezed the infant's cold cheeks and then took her nails directly to the wall and clawed it. She claws it, yes. After a while she put a sheet over the whole crib."

Mukhlis looks down, then far up to the ceiling of the porch. "I never knew him."

"Ach!" Mukhlis stands slowly. "Let's go, Wardi."

"No, no," Matile wakes from her trance. "You must stay for supper."

"We can't. I must go pick up a rent."

But Matile will not be swayed. She lifts her urgent voice, as if the food were gold and they were turning their backs on precious things. Mukhlis relents while shaking his head. All move into the dining room.

They sit under the chandelier, and pass the grape leaves, the stuffed zucchini, the swollen purple eggplant. They eat in silence, the unlit chandelier struck by the California sundown. It breaks into light above the food; it breaks in pieces of light on Mukhlis' almond head. When he finishes he stands, and ticks one of the crystal droplets with the thick nail of his finger, and does not speak.

"You hear what we went through?" Matile says after they are gone. "That was not all of it." She hugs her grandson, but not long. Even before she is through crying she has opened her mammoth horizontal freezer and said, "We need more bread, more bread."

1984

FIVE JACK COOL

Michael Stephens

He's dead. The old man's dead. Poor old bastard.

His sons—how many of them are here?—and daughters, none of them the first night, and not many sons either, have gathered in the old neighborhood. In this funeral parlor across from the shrine church of Our Lady of Lourdes, the elevated subway train rattling past every couple of minutes. The Broadway elevated, the KK, the QJ. A few blocks over: the bocci courts and Eastern Parkway, the abandoned LIRR, the Canarsie Line. East New York. The old ghetto in Brooklyn. That mythical land between Bushwick and Bed-Stuy, between Hell and Brownsville. High crime, low rent, none of the buildings more than a few stories except the projects. The projects. Hmmm. Not a familiar face on the street. This neighborhood hasn't seen our kind in three decades maybe. The last time I was here was when we had the funeral for the old man's mother.

Then a year or two later the funeral for his crazy sister Augusta, she of the flaming red hair and the temper tantrums, of the knuckle sandwiches on Pitkin Avenue, shopping for bargains from the carts of the Jewish merchants on Sunday; Aunt Augusta of the brawls at Rangers hockey games at the old Garden, where they asked her to behave or leave—at a Rangers game!—and Aunt Augusta of the brawls in the boardwalk bars of Coney Island. It's been that long since any of us have been in East New York.

But the old man, ever perverse, left instructions in his will that he was not to be buried in Florida next to the wife—our dearly beloved mother, Rose Coole née Moody—whom all of us thought would outlive him and us by twenty years, and the old man demanded that a service be held at the old funeral parlor underneath the "el" and across from Our Lady of Lourdes, and afterward we were to wake him in the bars along Broadway, after which he would be interred across from his beloved Tromer's Brewery and Beer Garden, up the block on Bushwick Avenue, and then into the land of cemeteries beyond the eerie reservoir and park system that separate East New York and Bushwick from the more gentrified world of Ridgewood and the outer boroughs right on to the city limits, outside of which he raised us in County Watchamacallit out on Long Island.

The old man himself was supposedly from County Clare.

But I was saying how many of us, his children, were there in the funeral parlor and how many were absent and who they were and why they were here or not here. There were five of us, only five, but I recall at least twice that many children, maybe even three times that number at an earlier stage of our development. Half of them were daughters, I thought. But I could be mistaken about that. Maybe it was only about a third of them daughters and two thirds sons, the boys always in the ascendancy numberwise in the household.

My father never knew any of his sons' or daughters' names, and so he called us Jack or Mack or shithead. He called us all such names sometimes I forget why I even bothered to come here in the first place. But then I tell myself, he was your father, Mack, and these are your siblings. They are all you have left.

The sons of Inspector Coole clomped into the main room of the funeral parlor, wielding his coffin on their shoulders.

Our father, he art in his pangs, a hollow little fat man full of terror and that most Brooklyn of things—dentalized T's. It was a habit he picked up after he stepped off the boat from the old country with his own old man, not to live in this outermost outpost of civilization in Brooklyn, but on the Upper West Side in Manhattan, first in Hell's Kitchen and later up in Irishtown in the Eighties, a rundown tenement between Broadway and Amsterdam, just half a block from where Zabar's is today. Back then, there was no Zabar's, though, no designer bagels and salmon salads, no espresso machines and lingonberry jams. It was a new land, the promised land.

He called himself Leland Coole, but his real name was James Coole, but because his father was James, his mother and other relatives called him by his middle name. But why he called his oldest son Leland, I don't understand, because my brother Leland's real name was James, too. To make matters worse, both Lelands had the nickname Jack, the same nickname as my father's father and my brother's grandfather. His name was James (or Jems), but they also called him Jack once in a while, too.

So I had better make clear from the start that when I refer to Leland as James, or James as Jems, or Jems as Jack, I mean all the same person, except if I am referring to my brother or father or maybe even my grandfather or the great Fenian warrior of the same name or maybe even the lyric poet of such Keltic Twilitic renown, Seamus Coole, bard-extraordinaire. I hope I make myself clear since I am the lone seanachie (the airish balladeer and bardic warrior and hysterical historian) in the family; I am the chronicler of deeds, Mack the Knife. Mickey Mack is back.

This all reminds me of other Jacks, real and imagined, living and dead, from near and far, of the old and new countries, who come to mind when the old man is conjured. One way or the other we are all Jacks here. But specifically there are five Jack Cooles I might spout about from the top of my head. This is just like tonight where there are five sons the first night of the wake in the funeral parlor underneath the el in East New York, across from Our Lady of Lourdes Church, right here on Broadway.

"There's still time for the others," I say, "still time for the other brothers to pay their respects."

"Ha," one of my brothers says.

But I can't remember which brother made the remark as we all had our assigned places at the coffin, carrying it from the back room to the main room of the funeral parlor. I couldn't see who said it, but it was one of the three brothers on the other side of the casket.

Then, of course, an endless stream of aunts and uncles might show up. Not the old man's relations, though. They were either dead or out of town or out of their minds somewhere. The relations were all Moodys from my mother's side, still living in Brooklyn, though not in East New York, out in Flatbush further out on the Eastern Parkway or over the hump from the reservoir and Highland Park in Ridgewood. Some of these relatives still might show.

Then, too, a long list of the old man's gin-mill cronies might appear. Also his dockside partners, reprobates, priests, and friends to say a prayer over his wilted form.

How wilted was my father?

When I was a boy, he was a huge man, not tall, but wide, no more than five and half feet tall, but nearly that wide, too, weighing in at 220 pounds in his boxer shorts and stockinged feet. Now he was no more than a light-weight, or worse, maybe even a featherweight or junior lightweight.

One of the people from his past showed up as we prepared to carry him from the back room to the front parlor.

"Good old Jack," the man said, though none of us knew who he was. "He looks better than ever."

But the fellow wasn't kidding. Dad looked pretty good in repose. There was none of his typical anger and spite, the knitted black eyebrows, the scowl lines along his cheeks, the intense madness of his eyes. I thought maybe he never looked better than he did that night.

One of my brothers on the other side of the coffin put it best—though, again, I can't say which of my brothers said it. He said: "He looks like he did when he stepped off the boat back then, way back when."

"How would you know?" a brother next to him asked.

"It's just a thought," the first answered.

"You weren't even born when he came from the old country," the second brother said. "Besides, I don't think he ever did come from the old country. I think maybe he was born right here in Brooklyn, and that everything else he said was a lie: where he came from, who his father was, and how his mother died. Why do you think he wants to waked here on Broadway in East New York and why do you think he wants to be interred, not in Florida next to his wife, but in those tombs at the Brooklyn-Queens border?"

"Why, indeed?" I asked.

But this brother had a point. For years I never understood why my own birth certificate didn't list where my father was born, and when I mentioned this to the other brothers, they likewise had blank spots on their certificates where it was supposed to say where he was born. Our mother, Rose Moody, was less ambiguous, having been born not too many blocks from here on Madison in Bed-Stuy, sprung in a birthing room of the twenty-six-room house of her lace-curtain father, William Moody of Albany and Brooklyn, and her equally lacy mother, Elizabeth Moody née McGillicutty, the daughter of Richard Mojo McGillicutty the radical newspaperman and Solange Cold-Veal (my translation from the French—Froidveaux). There was no question that our mother was a Brooklomaniac, like all of us except myself, born as was my wantonness in Washington, D.C. at the close of WW II. But don't let me bore you to death at my own father's funeral; after all, this is his show, and it is a mockery of my father to speak of genealogies here, because the man had none to speak of, whether he was born in the old country as half my brothers claimed or here in Brooklyn as another contingent of us were wont to pronounce. The funeral was a low-budget affair for a back-door-type man who drank in shot-and-a-beer places on Broadway underneath the el or drank out of paper bags as he played snooker with his fellow East New Yorkolinos—Jackie Gleason, just one name that comes to mind. Poor Jimmy-Jack Leland Coole looks fine just where he is, a man without lineage to speak of but for these vagrant sons attending the cortege.

"Dad looks fine," another one of those yapping brothers on the other side of the coffin says.

As we lug his deathless form into the main room I am reminded that he called me Jack, too, though my name is Mickey Mack. He called me terrible things. Some I remember bitterly. Others I've cast away as so much childish experience. So much cargo that ain't worth dragging into my grown life. I left Brooklyn a long time ago. Then I left this family out on Long Island. I've been gone from them for the better part of my life. Like a traitor, I moved to Manhattan, that mauve land of ideas and sensibility so foreign to everyone in this room. I betrayed the clan by writing books about them, by making a living off the misery they inflicted upon me, and probably inflicted even worse upon themselves. Tit for tat, one of them called it. Old stab-em-in-the-back Mickey Coole, still another brother said of me.

When I saw the old man there, earlier in the afternoon, supine, flowers about his head, rosary gnarled between his pudgy alabaster and rubescent fingers, fresh new white shirt and plain black tie, I thought of all those Cooles before him. Each one of them had that hawk nose. Each was small and stout. If a Coole was not short and stout, then he was tall and stout or short and thin. But no matter his morphology, no matter the physique, a Coole always had that bird beak. Or at least that is what I thought as we weeped and keened and wended in our cortege, rear room to front.

"It's no bed of roses if your name is Jack Coole," I said.

"What's that supposed to mean?"

"I'll tell you what it's supposed to mean," his brotherly companion answered, shoving him in the chest, nearly spilling the coffin of its cargo.

"Keep your end of it up!" a third brother shouted.

"The old man used to say there were three strains of blood in our family," I went on.

"Cro-Magnon via Europe and Africa," one brother laughed. "Long head, long-limbed, try that blood on for size."

"That wasn't it," I said.

An older brother said, "How about the long-limbed, short-bodied Iberni?"

"The fucking Micks!" a young one shouted.

"There you go," I said. "That's what he called them. He called them that, all right."

"The fucking Micks," the young one said again, not because he was redundant but because he thought of himself in possession of a fine musical sense of life and death.

"Hey, who's tilting?" the big one up front asked.

I bolstered my end, hoping the others would carry their load equitably. I was thinking of what my father called the ghoulish Kelts or the salty Gauls. The old man wasn't much for history. And yet I recall him, in his cups, calling out other names which made no sense whatsoever, whether he had a sense of history or not. These were more curses than appellations, and yet nonetheless all relations, the bloodline, as it were, of the Coole family. He once told me in a saloon down the block from here—I think it was Grim's Tavern near Marion Street—that it was from the Caspian where the last group came from, in the Valley of the Danube, herdsmen, some even descended from sheep, he said, and from there they journeyed across the Rhine, no doubt drinking much wine, and then later to the Seine and the Marne, and so on and so forth, until they entered the Valley of the Black Pig. Of course, it might not have been the old man who said any of this. Perhaps I imagined it. For I've imagined a great deal in my life, Brooklyn lending itself more to the imagination than facts, more to feelings and drifts than actual truths.

Sometimes I would refer, for instance, to *The Book of Cooles*, but now I can't remember if there really was a book or if I made the book up. And yet my father was the sort of man that if your story was good enough, he didn't concern himself with its veracity, and though he never patted me on the back and said, "Good for you, Mackey Mick," I often thought that if he did not approve of my procrastinating art of storytelling, he didn't disapprove either. That book, referred to as *The Cooles* in our family, whether real or fictive, was nonetheless a despicable work of obscenity and ungrammatical intentions in this world of grief-stricken fraternity and even evil-intentioned fratricidal madness, brother fume to cock-eyed belligerence.

But then I was taken from my own miserable reveries by one of the younger brothers at the coffin.

"Tell the one about Fenian Jack Coole," the brother said to me, a boy eager for the old legends.

"It's not his time or place to eulogize," the second oldest brother in attendance spat. "That's the oldest Jack among us, his prerogative if you catch my drift."

Still, I couldn't resist putting in my two cents before the floor was relinquished completely.

"It goes back deeper than Fenian Jack," I said. "All the way back to King Cormorant in the Land of Tantrum."

That got them quiet, for a profound respect for the legends ran through us all on occasion, especially as we came upon the full domain of the half-lit main room of the funeral parlor. Evening was upon us. Sparks blew down from the elevated train outside the broken and patched stained glass windows. Mounds of empty beer and whiskey bottles from the past afternoon were stacked in a corner, still not removed by the funeral parlor director. Suddenly it dawned on me that our father never did much for any of us, and I wondered what the hell I was doing here. King Cormorant be damned!

Besides, if any of my sisters were present, I know they would disagree about any lineage to King Cormorant and insist that we were descended from Francisco de Cuellar—where the name Coole came from, I was told—who was one of the few Spaniards, beached by the wrecking Armada in 1588 off the western shores of the old country, to make it safely ashore and even find safe passage out of the country and back to his native Spain, but not before he deflowered the fair-skinned virgins, impregnating many of them with the dark-haired, black-eyed, hawk-nosed children who would become known as the scions of Coole. Of course, I didn't believe any of this, not about Francisco de Cuellar, not about King Cormorant. But I was not going to pass up the chance to pontificate on subjects about which I knew hardly anything, especially to a roomful of brothers who knew even less than I did and so could not verify anything I said, could not prove the veracity of any historical or imaginative facts I cared to put forward to them in their grief and cups. They did not call me Mack the Knife because I was a big fan of Bobby Darin, although the fact is I was a big fan of Darin's and particularly that Brechtian rendition, but that is another story and I feel I am failing already to render unto Jack Coole the things that are Jack's and to render unto the tallow merchant the renderings that are his. Let me get back to the present.

One bare lightbulb in the center of the ceiling lit the main room of the funeral parlor. Business had not been good here, the assistant director told us. For one thing people died younger and younger, and so therefore poorer and poorer, each year, from gunshot wounds, from stabbings, from drug overdoses, from broken bottles to the neck of irate lovers, or even from children dismantling avenging parents on drug and alcohol orgies of death and destruction. East New York is not a happy place, the assistant director said.

His name was Sean Carlos Padilla O'Brady, and he should know. The Spanish used another funeral parlor up the block; the blacks went to the old parlor over on Gates Avenue or down the block on Stone or over by Rockaway Avenue. The Irish and Italians were gone for good from the old neighborhood, he said, and they were the last to use the parlor. When the last of Mother Teresa's nuns died, Sean Carlos intended to close up the place and move to Miami. I didn't blame him. This place didn't just smell of death; the funk was more primordial than that, like a gaping hole in the festering universe that needed stitches to close its wound. More than once in this day I had gone to the wash closet and tossed up my cookies.

The radiators clanked, but they were regularly drowned out by the subway train sparking and screeching overhead, the elevated train tracks weaving and shaking above. The panes of glass that were not mottled by rocks and bullets were smashed by fists (some our own).

Finally we came to that point in the room where we needed to dislodge the coffin from our shoulders. The casket had become quite heavy by now. We struggled to dislodge it from the shoulders, then attempted to line it up on the row of chairs, three on either side of the wooden crate. Up to this point my brothers had dragged their heels in unison. With the coffin between us and lowered onto the chairs, I saw them now. There was Jack, of course, the oldest, the brother familias, then Emmett of the crime waves and the sorrows. I was the third of Jack Coole's sons, followed this evening by Patrick and Terry. Wolfe, the youngest, was away from us, playing a championship softball game on the south shore of Long Island.

Dermott of the Love Spot, Oisin, Finn—there were so many names I could have made up for my brothers—but I decided to stick with the names their parents dropped upon their heads. Those names which resonated of the uniformed services in the city—cops and firemen.

But enough of my grousing and quibblings, my dicing and cutting and perambulations. We had struggled into the room under the enormous weight of our father, carrying the plain wooden casket a few inches at a time. The old man weighed a ton, felt like a load of bricks, like a brick shithouse. He was our cross to bear this evening. Along the way from the back room, along the vestibule—that most Brooklyn, that most old East New York word—and into the main parlor just off Broadway and underneath the el, just across from Our Lady of Lourdes and the nuns of Mother Teresa's convent, those hermetically sealed virgins of Calcutta and the South Bronx.

In this journey from the back room to the front, my brothers' speech was garbled, with such likeness of tone, of emotion, inflection, cadence, of drunkenness, and their words were like each other's, flat and nasal, lazy-tongued like the old man's. Thick with alcohol they seemed to speak in tongues. It was a kind of city babble which blends with the radiator and the elevated subway, with sirens, honking horns, gunshots and firecrackers, popped bottles, flick of cigarette lighters over the clear white coals of crack in glass pipes, the new high of the ghetto. The street outside was full of holler and yell. Rattle and hum from the passing trains, so appropriate to this Keltic ruin. I could almost hear U-2's Bono humming and rattling in the background, could hear Van Morrison, even Sinead O'Connor, that horror of liberation and imprisonment, old baldy. Once I remembered this neighborhood as one long undercurrent of Chieftain songs, of John McCormack scratchily audible from an old 78 record. Now the sounds were—Fight the Power!—Public Enemy, Willie Colon, salsa, meringue, the old guaguanco of the jibaros and their slick sons and ruby-lipped daughters. But no matter what the beat, East New York was always dangerous and raunchy, violent and sexual, dirty and down. The street smelled of greasy meat and burnt vegetables; the foyers reeked of underwear and sweat.

Sparks flew down from the elevated train again, another passing subway in the night. Spaldeen high bouncers whanged off the chipped brick of the funeral parlor's outer wall, and I pictured a kid practicing his pitches for the summer stickball season. Stoop ball was the old man's game. That and pool. While my own recreations here were basketball—Go whiteboy, go whiteboy, go!—and paddleball, once the Jewish game at the schoolyard on MacDougal and now the sport of Hispanic lovers and intellectuals.

East New York: not really New York and not east of anything. Really just the heart of Brooklyn, its heart and soul. This was a place without pretense, without ambitions, without hope. My Uncle Tommy's sister used to live above this craphole funeral parlor, their kids Annie and Howie, runty and bent and thin and carroty-haired. At any moment I expected Mamie— the streetlady who rented the top floor of my grandmother's two-story house down the block—to walk in, wearing her five or six dresses, sucking on a quart of Rheingold beer or Ballantine ale, cursing God and St. Francis and even Our Lady of Lourdes, where she daily robbed the poor boxes. She was poor, after all.

If I had not attended my aunt's and grandmother's funerals in this very parlor, I'd even expect them to come in the door, telling my father to knock it off, get sober, that he had a wife and ten or fifteen children to support. Let's stop the shenanigans, Jimmy or Jack or Lee or whatever his name was.

Earlier when we began this journey from rear to front room it felt as if there were six of us, three on each side, but I counted five upon dislodging the box, the one corner mysteriously buoyant where Wolfe should have been from the commencement of the journey.

The brothers—their ritual at an end—waddled off to their respective wooden benches, the pews with kneelers as unadorned as the old man's final home. The kneelers were murderous objects on the kneecaps, things meant to make us feel our own mortality. One day soon we would hop inside that odd-shaped box, hands folded with rosary beads entwined in the pudgy fingers, black plain suit, white shirt, single-colored tie, etc. I wondered if the funeral director had placed Dad's beat-up brogues on his calloused, pain-spattered feet?

This got me to thinking about the old man's feet: they appeared like duck's fangs. At other times they were like cleft hoofs, sort of ungulate. Still, there were other times when they seemed to be stumps which he stuffed into his old brogues. Then out the door he waddled to his job on the docks.

Jack, the eldest son, sat next to me.

"What was it about King Cormorant that possessed you to mention his name earlier, Mack?"

"I don't know," I answered as honestly as I could.

"Yeah," Terry wanted to know, "what made you say that earlier?"

I tried to shoo this young one away, the time being inapposite to legend.

"Later," I said.

"It's Jack Coole we should talk about."

"He's dead," I said.

"Dead?" Terry asked.

"I'm all right," brother Jack said. "I'm just a little under the weather, as who wouldn't be. Once the event sinks into my thick skull, I'll be able to talk."

Poor old fart, I thought.

The funeral director—supposedly my father's dearest friend, but a title he ascribed to anyone he knew for more than a few minutes when he was in his cups, and as long as the person wasn't related to him by blood or marriage—the director entered the room. He carried a pile of worn-out morning coats for us to wear, saying that our clothing was not "appropriate" to a wake. (He wanted us to don the coats, but I would prefer to doff them.) Five of us gathered in a queue to pick up these coats, placing them over flannel shirts and sweatshirts and old T-shirts full of the stains of labor and of eating in greasy spoons.

Besides the clothes that they wore, I noticed my brothers were dressed oddly in other ways. It was the middle of winter, but none had on shoes or boots. Instead they wore sneakers or running shoes—I had on a pair of walking shoes—and one wore sandals, and one (Jackie Wackie) was barefoot or maybe removed his shoes at the door, his feet being sore or whatever. Jackie Wackie weighed at least four hundred pounds, his ankles were swollen, and I'm sure his feet appreciated the breather.

"A dear man," the director said.

Of course, I didn't believe him, not his sentiment, not his words, not anything about this man. His name was Sal—"Call me Sally," he said—Malatesta, but everyone knew that his real name was Hymie Rabinowitz, the old pickle merchant from over on Chauncey Street, who inherited Featherstone Funeral Parlor as the settlement of a gambling debt with the former owner of the parlor—Dukie O'Flynn. But this was a little bit too late for old Duke, who nonetheless was found with an ice pick in his ear near the bocci courts on Eastern Parkway, and the one problem with Malatesta running the parlor was that he was not, technically speaking, a funeral director but a picklemaker, though in the neighborhood it was reputed that his pickles and his corpses stewed in the same brine.

"A dear man," Hymie repeated.

One of my brothers gave him the Bronx cheer.

"A little respect," I said.

"Here! Here!" Jackie Wackie shouted.

Hymie had red hair like his assistant, but when he bowed obsequiously to us, I saw a huge bald spot. The sound of keens and the odd belch filled his ears upon leaving. In his wake was left behind a bouquet of wilting flowers, sent anonymously, the director claimed, but it was felt generally and individually that he was going to tack this on as an extra expense. One of his optionals, I thought, which in turn would price us out of the action. We were all of us—to the last one—poor slobs.

Now with that intrusion ended, we sank into our pews, the keens growing, at times, into gnashing. Questions were asked. "Why was I born?" "Who is he?" "Why am I here?" Will I get towed from the street meters after seven?" "Will my car be there if I parked it on a side street?" Then these questions were answered: "I don't know." "I don't know." "I don't know." "Maybe." "Yes."

1991

TO DA-DUH, IN MEMORIAM

Paule Marshall

"... Oh Nana! all of you is not involved in this evil business Death,
Nor all of us in life."
 —from "At My Grandmother's Grave," by Lebert Bethune

I did not see her at first I remember. For not only was it dark inside the crowded disembarkation shed in spite of the daylight flooding in from outside, but standing there waiting for her with my mother and sister I was still somewhat blinded from the sheen of tropical sunlight on the water of the bay which we had just crossed in the landing boat, leaving behind us the ship that had brought us from New York lying in the offing. Besides, being only nine years of age at the time and knowing nothing of islands I was busy attending to the alien sights and sounds of Barbados, the unfamiliar smells.

I did not see her, but I was alerted to her approach by my mother's hand which suddenly tightened around mine, and looking up I traced her gaze through the gloom in the shed until I finally made out the small, purposeful, painfully erect figure of the old woman headed our way.

Her face was drowned in the shadow of an ugly rolled-brim brown felt hat, but the details of her slight body and of the struggle taking place within it were clear enough—an intense, unrelenting struggle between her back which was beginning to bend ever so slightly under the weight of her eighty-odd years and the rest of her which sought to deny those years and hold that back straight, keep it in line. Moving swiftly, toward us (so swiftly it seemed she did not intend) stopping when she reached us but would sweep past us out the doorway which opened onto the sea and like Christ walk upon the water!), she was caught between sunlight at her end of the building and the darkness inside—and for a moment she appeared to contain them both: the light in the long severe old-fashioned white dress she wore which brought the sense of a past that was still alive into our bustling present and in the snatch of white at her eye; the darkness of her black high-top shoes and in her face which was visible now that she was closer.

It was stark and fleshless as a death mask, that face. The maggots might have already done their work, leaving only the framework of bone beneath the ruined skin and deep wells at the temple and jaw. But her eyes were alive, unnervingly so for one so old, with a sharp light that flicked out of the dim clouded depths like a lizard's tongue to snap up all in her view. Those eyes betrayed a child's curiosity about the world, and I wondered vaguely seeing them, and seeing the way the bodice of her ancient dress had collapsed in on her flat chest (what had happened to her breasts?), whether she might not be some kind of child at the same time that she was a woman, with fourteen children, my mother included, to prove it. Perhaps she was both, both child and woman, darkness and light, past and present, life and death—all the opposites contained and reconciled in her.

"My Da-duh," my mother said formally and stepped forward. The name sounded like thunder fading softly in the distance.

"Child," Da-duh said, and her tone, her quick scrutiny of my mother, the brief embrace in which they appeared to shy from each other rather than touch, wiped out the fifteen years my mother had been away and restored the old relationship. My mother, who was such a formidable figure in my eyes, had suddenly with a word been reduced to my status.

"Yes, God is good," Da-duh said with a nod that was like a tic. "He has spared me to see my child again."

We were led forward then, apologetically because not only did Da-duh prefer boys but she also liked her grandchildren to be "white," that is, fair-skinned; and we had, I was to discover, a number of cousins, the outside children of white estate managers and the like, who qualified. We, though, were as black as she.

My sister being the oldest was presented first. "This one takes after the father," my mother said and waited to be reproved.

Frowning, Da-duh tilted my sister's face toward the light. But her frown soon gave way to a grudging smile, for my sister with her large mild eyes and little broad winged nose, with our father's high-cheeked Barbardian cast to her face, was pretty.

"She's goin' be lucky," Da-duh said and patted her once on the cheek. "Any girl child that takes after the father does be lucky."

She turned then to me. But oddly enough she did not touch me.

Instead leaning close, she peered hard at me, and then quickly drew back. I thought I saw her hand start up as though to shield her eyes. It was almost as if she saw not only me, a thin truculent child who it was said took after no one but myself, but something in me which for some reason she found disturbing, even threatening. We looked silently at each other for a long time there in the noisy shed, our gaze locked. She was the first to look away.

"But Adry," she said to my mother and her laugh was cracked, thin, apprehensive. "Where did you get this one here with this fierce look?"

"We don't know where she came out of, my Da-duh," my mother said, laughing also. Even I smiled to myself. After all I had won the encounter. Da-duh had recognized my small strength—and this was all I ever asked of the adults in my life then.

"Come, soul," Da-duh said and took my hand. "You must be one of those New York terrors you hear so much about."

She led us, me at her side and my sister and mother behind, out of the shed into the sunlight that was like a bright driving summer rain and over to a group of people clustered beside a decrepit lorry. They were our relatives, most of them from St. Andrews although Da-duh herself lived in St. Thomas, the women wearing bright print dresses, the colors vivid against their darkness, the men rusty black suits that encased them like strait-jackets. Da-duh, holding fast to my hand, became my anchor as they circled round us like a nervous sea, exclaiming, touching us with their calloused hands, embracing us shyly. They laughed in awed bursts: "But look Adry got big-big children!" / "And see the nice things they wearing, wrist watch and all!" / "I tell you, Adry has done all right for sheself in New York. . . . "

Da-duh, ashamed at their wonder, embarrassed for them, admonished them the while. "But oh Christ," she said, "why you all got to get on like you never saw people from 'Away' before? You would think New York is the only place in the world to hear wunna. That's why I don't like to go anyplace with you St. Andrews people, you know. You all ain't been colonized."

We were in the back of the lorry finally, packed in among the barrels of ham, flour, cornmeal and rice and the trunks of clothes that my mother had brought as gifts. We made our way slowly through Bridgetown's clogged streets, part of a funereal procession of cars and open-sided buses, bicycles and donkey carts. The dim little limestone shops and offices along the way marched with us, at the same mournful pace, toward the same grave ceremony—as did the people, the women balancing huge baskets on top their heads as if they were no more than hats they wore to shade them from the sun. Looking over the edge of the lorry I watched as their feet slurred the dust. I listened, and their voices, raw and loud and dissonant in the heat, seemed to be grappling with each other high overhead.

Da-duh sat on a trunk in our midst, a monarch amid her court. She still held my hand, but it was different now. I had suddenly become her anchor, for I felt her fear of the lorry with its asthmatic motor (a fear and distrust, I later learned, she held of all machines) beating like a pulse in her rough palm.

As soon as we left Bridgetown behind though, she relaxed, and while the others around us talked she gazed at the canes standing tall on either side of the winding marl road. "C'dear," she said softly to herself after a time. "The canes this side are pretty enough."

They were too much for me. I thought of them as giant weeds that had overrun the island, leaving scarcely any room for the small tottering houses of sunbleached pine we passed or the people, dark streaks as our lorry hurtled by. I suddenly feared that we were journeying, unaware that we were, toward some dangerous place where the canes, grown as high and thick as a forest, would close in on us and run us through with their stiletto blades. I longed then for the familiar: for the street in Brooklyn where I lived, for my father who had refused to accompany us ("Blowing out good money on foolishness," he had said of the trip), for a game of tag with my friends under the chestnut tree outside our aging brownstone house.

"Yes, but wait till you see St. Thomas canes," Da-duh was saying to me. "They's canes father, bo," she gave a proud arrogant nod. "Tomorrow, God willing, I goin' take you out in the ground and show them to you."

True to her word Da-duh took me with her the following day out into the ground. It was fairly large plot adjoining her weathered board and shingle house and consisting of a small orchard, a good-sized canepiece and behind the canes, where the land sloped abruptly down, a gully. She had purchased it with Panama money sent her by her eldest son, my Uncle Joseph, who had died working on the canal. We entered the ground along a trail no wider than her body and as devious and complex as her reasons for showing me her land. Da-duh strode briskly ahead, her slight form filled out this morning by the layers of sacking petticoats she wore under her working dress to protect her against the damp. A fresh white cloth, elaborately arranged around her head, added to her height, and lent her a vain, almost roguish air.

Her pace slowed once we reached the orchard, and glancing back at me occasionally over her shoulder, she pointed out the various trees.

"This here is a breadfruit," she said. "That one yonder is a papaw. Here's a guava. This is a mango. I know you don't have anything like these in New York. Here's a sugar apple." (The fruit looked more like artichokes than apples to me.) "This one bears limes. . . ." She went on for some time, intoning the names of the trees as though they were those of her gods. Finally, turning to me, she said, "I know you don't have anything this nice where you come from." Then, as I hesitated: "I said I know you don't have anything this nice where you come from. . . ."

"No," I said and my world did seem suddenly lacking.

Da-duh nodded and passed on. The orchard ended and we were on the narrow cart road that led through the canepiece, the canes clashing like swords above my cowering head. Again she turned and her thin muscular arms spread wide, her dim gaze embracing the small field of canes, she said—and her voice almost broke under the weight of her pride, "Tell me, have you got anything like these in that place where you were born?"

"No."

"I din't think so. I bet you don't even know that these canes here and the sugar you eat is one and the same thing. That they does throw the canes into some damn machine at the factory and squeeze out all the little life in them to make sugar for you all so in New York to eat. I bet you don't know that."

"I've got two cavities and I'm not allowed to eat a lot of sugar."

But Da-duh didn't hear me. She had turned with an inexplicably angry motion and was making her way rapidly out of the canes and down the slope at the edge of the field which led to the gully below. Following her apprehensively down the incline amid a stand of banana plants whose leaves flapped like elephant's ears in the wind, I found myself in the middle of a small tropical wood—a place dense and damp and gloomy and tremulous with the fitful play of light and shadow as the leaves high above moved against the sun that was almost hidden from view. It was a violent place, the tangled foliage fighting each other for a chance at the sunlight, the branches of the trees locked in what seemed an immemorial struggle, one both necessary and inevitable. But despite the violence, it was pleasant, almost peaceful in the gully, and beneath the thick undergrowth the earth smelled like spring.

This time Da-duh didn't even bother to ask her usual question, but simply turned and waited for me to speak.

"No," I said, my head bowed. "We don't have anything like this in New York."

"Ah," she cried, her triumph complete. "I din' think so. Why, I've heard that's a place where you can walk till you near drop and never see a tree."

"We've got a chestnut tree in front of our house," I said.

"Does it bear?" She waited. "I ask you, does it bear?"

"Not anymore," I muttered. "It used to, but not anymore."

She gave the nod that was like a nervous twitch. "You see," she said. "Nothing can bear there." Then, secure behind her scorn, she added, "But tell me, what's this snow like that you hear so much about?"

Looking up, I studied her closely, sensing my chance, and then I told her, describing at length and with as much drama as I could summon not only what snow in the city was like, but what it would be like here, in her perennial summer kingdom.

". . . And you see all these trees you got here," I said. "Well, they'd be bare. No leaves, no fruit, nothing. They'd be covered in snow. You see your canes. They'd be buried under tons of snow. The snow would be higher than your head, higher than your house, and you wouldn't be able to come down into this gully because it would be snowed under. . . ."

She searched my face for the lie, still scornful but intrigued. "What a thing, huh?" she said finally, whispering it softly to herself.

"And when it snows you couldn't wear a dress like you are now," I said. "Oh no, you'd freeze to death. You'd have to wear a hat and gloves and galoshes and ear muffs so your ears wouldn't freeze and drop off, and a heavy coat. I've got a Shirley Temple coat with fur on the collar. I can dance. You wanna see?"

Before she could answer I began, with a dance called the Truck which was popular back then in the 1930's. My right forefinger waving, I trucked around the nearby trees and around Da-duh's awed and rigid form. After the Truck I did the Suzy-Q, my lean hips swishing, my sneakers sidling zigzag over the ground. "I can sing," I said and did so, starting with "I'm Gonna Sit Right Down and Write Myself a Letter," then without pausing, "Tea for Two," and ending with "I Found a Million Dollar Baby in a Five and Ten Cent Store."

For long moments afterwards Da-duh stared at me as if I were a creature from Mars, an emissary from some world she did not know but which intrigued her and whose power she both felt and feared. Yet something about my performance must have pleased her, because bending down she slowly lifted her long skirt and then, one by one, the layers of petticoats until she came to a drawstring purse dangling at the end of a long strip of cloth tied around her waist. Opening the purse she handed me a penny. "Here," she said half-smiling against her will. "Take this to buy yourself a sweet at the shop up the road. There's nothing to be done with you, soul."

From then on, whenever I wasn't taken to visit relatives, I accompanied Da-duh out into the ground, and alone with her amid the canes or down in the gully I told her about New York. It always began with some slighting remark on her part: "I know they don't have anything this nice where you come from," or "Tell me, I hear those foolish people in New York does do such and such . . ." But as I answered, recreating my towering world of steel and concrete and machines for her, building the city out of words, I would feel her give way. I came to know the signs of her surrender: the total stillness that would come over her little hard dry form, the probing gaze that like a surgeon's knife sought to cut through my skull to get at the images there, to see if I were lying; above all, her fear, a fear nameless and profound, the same one I had felt beating in the palm of her hand that day in the lorry.

Over the weeks I told her about refrigerators, radios, gas stoves, elevators, trolley cars, wringer washing machines, movies, airplanes, the Cyclone at Coney Island, subways, toasters, electric lights: "At night, see, all you have to do is flip this little switch on the wall and all the lights in the house go on. Just like that. Like magic. It's like turning on the sun at night."

"But tell me," she said to me once with a faint mocking smile, "do the white people have all these things too or it's only the people looking like us?"

I laughed. "What d'ya mean," I said. "The white people have even better." Then: "I beat up a white girl in my class last term."

"Beating up white people!" Her tone was incredulous.

"How you mean!" I said, using an expression of hers. "She called me a name."

For some reason Da-duh could not quite get over this and repeated in the same hushed, shocked voice, "Beating up white people now! Oh, the lord, the world's changing up so I can scarce recognize it anymore."

One morning toward the end of our stay, Da-duh led me into the part of the gully that we had never visited before, an area darker and more thickly overgrown than the rest, almost impenetrable. There in a small clearing amid the dense bush, she stopped before an incredibly tall royal palm which rose cleanly out of the ground, and drawing the eye up with it, soared high above the trees around it into the sky. It appeared to be touching the blue dome of sky, to be flaunting its dark crown of fronds in the blinding white face of the late morning sun.

Da-duh watched me a long time before she spoke, and then she said very quietly, "All right, now tell me if you've got anything this tall in that place you're from."

I almost wished, seeing her face, that I could have said no. "Yes," I said. "We've got buildings hundreds of times this time in New York. There's one called the Empire State Building that's the tallest in the world. My class visited it last year and I went all the way to the top. It's got over a hundred floors. I can't describe how tall it is. Wait a minute. What's the name of that hill I went to visit the other day, where they have the police station?"

"You mean Bissex?"

"Yes, Bissex. Well, the Empire State Building is way taller than that."

"You're lying now!" she shouted, trembling with rage. Her hand lifted to strike me.

"No, I'm not," I said. "It really is, if you don't believe me I'll send you a picture postcard of it soon as I get back home so you can see for yourself. But it's way taller than Bissex."

All the fight went out of her at that. The hand poised to strike me fell limp to her side, and as she stared at me, seeing not me but the building that was taller than the highest hill she knew, the small stubborn light in her eyes (it was the same amber as the flame in the kerosene lamp she lit at dusk) began to fail. Finally, with a vague gesture that even in the midst of her defeat still tried to dismiss me and my world, she turned and started back through the gully, walking slowly, her steps groping and uncertain, as if she were suddenly no longer sure of the way, while I followed triumphant yet strangely saddened behind.

The next morning I found her dressed for our morning walk but stretched out on the Berbice chair in the tiny drawing room where she sometimes napped during the afternoon heat, her face turned to the window beside her. She appeared thinner and suddenly indescribably old.

"My Da-duh," I said.

"Yes, nuh," she said. Her voice was listless and the face she slowly turned my way was, now that I think back on it, like a Benin mask, the features drawn and almost distorted by an ancient abstract sorrow.

"Don't you feel well?"

"Girl, I don't know."

"My Da-duh, I goin' boil you some bush tea," my aunt, Da-duh's youngest child, who lived with her, called from the shed roof kitchen.

"Who tell you I need bush tea?" she cried, her voice assuming for a moment its old authority. "You can't even rest nowadays without some malicious person looking for you to be dead. Come girl," she motioned me to a place beside her on the old-fashioned lounge chair, "give us a tune."

I sang for her until breakfast at eleven, all my brash irreverent Tin Pan Alley songs, and then just before noon we went out into the ground. But it was a short, dispirited walk. Da-duh didn't even notice that the mangoes were beginning to ripen and would have to be picked before the village boys got to them. And when she paused occasionally and looked out across the canes or up at her trees it wasn't as if she were seeing them but something else. Some huge, monolithic shape had imposed itself, it seemed, between her and the land, obstructing her vision. Returning to the house she slept the entire afternoon on the Berbice chair.

She remained like this until we left, languishing away the mornings on the chair at the window gazing out at the land as if it were already doomed; then, at noon, taking a brief stroll with me through the ground during which she seldom spoke, and afterwards returning home to sleep till almost dusk sometimes.

On the day of our departure she put on the austere, ankle length white dress, the black shoes and brown felt hat (her town clothes she called them), but she did not go with us to town. She saw us off on the road outside her house and in the midst of my mother's tearful protracted farewell, she leaned down and whispered in my ear, "Girl, you're not to forget now to send me the picture of that building, you hear."

By the time I mailed her the large colored picture postcard of the Empire State Building she was dead. She died during the famous '37 strike which began shortly after we left. On the day of her death England sent planes flying low over the island in a show of force—so low, according to my aunt's letter, that the downdraft from them shook the ripened mangoes from the trees in Da-duh's orchard. Frightened, everyone in the village fled into the canes. Except Da-duh. She remained in the house at the window so my aunt said, watching as the planes came swooping and screaming like monstrous birds down over the village, over her house, rattling her trees and flattening the young canes in her field. It must have seemed to her lying there that they did not intend pulling out of their dive, but like the hardback beetles which hurled themselves with suicidal force against the walls of the house at night, those menacing silver shapes would hurl themselves in an ecstasy of self-immolation onto the land, destroying it utterly.

When the planes finally left and the villagers returned they found her dead on the Berbice chair at the window.

She died and I lived, but always, to this day even, within the shadow of her death. For a brief period after I was grown I went to live alone, like one doing penance, in a loft above a noisy factory in downtown New York and there painted seas of sugar-cane and huge swirling Van Gogh suns and palm trees striding like brightly-plumed Tutsi warriors across a tropical landscape, while the thunderous tread of machines downstairs jarred the floor beneath my easel, mocking my efforts.

1967

ELECTION DAY, 1984

Michelle Cliff

A woman stands on a snake of a line in the back of a born-again church in a coastal town in California. In places the line is slender, in others it bunches like a python after swallowing a calf, in a shot from *Wild Kingdom*. This is the polling place.

On the wall to the woman's right is a map, straight pins with colored beads indicating the positions of missionaries. She glances at the map, to see if any pins are fixed to her native land. Indeed. Her island so small that the huge blue head practically obliterates its outline.

On her left, through a glass, brightly, a Bible study class sits around a conference table on red plastic chairs, lips moving without a sound behind a window; all are women. She begins to hate them, fights it; whatever have they done to her? God.

She recites in her head: *Though I speak with the tongues of men and of angels and have not charity I am as a sounding brass or a tinkling cymbal.* If there is a hell (which she doesn't really believe but childhood is hard to shake) and if I am chosen to burn it will be because of this— which a teacher noted in the third grade, Palmer script flowing across the report card. *She holds herself aloof from the others.* There it was. Way back then.

"Where you from?" The woman in front of her, in a tan raincoat, a yellow fisherman's hat on her head, brown leather handbag strapped across her chest, turns suddenly to make conversation.

"New York." She answers with the place she last was, not the place she is made of. Anyhow, she belongs there no longer. Her voice would not be recognized by her people. They are background.

"How long you been out here?"

"Two months."

She is not being very friendly. The land is about to slide for Ronnie and surely this old lady is part of it, partly to blame, just as the parroting Bible class is. *Live and let live.* Her mother echoed in her head. *Slow to anger and abounding in steadfast love. I hate their hate. Two wrongs don't make a right. Judge not lest ye be judged.* Your father and I want for you and your brother a better life. There's no chance back there, that's all.

"How d'you get out here?"

"I drove."

"Married?"

"No."

"Alone?"

"Yes."

"You weren't scared?"

"Not really." *Liar.*

The line inches forward. People drip with unaccustomed rain. Every now and then someone says, "But we need it." And someone else nods.

"Isn't this country something?"

"Yes, it is." She does not say beautiful, desolate.

"And where did you stop?"

The younger woman begins to recite her route. Her mind glosses her spoken words. Images flash like lantern slides. As if someone dropped the tray. Out of order.

"Detroit first. I visited friends."

A rat sprints across the highway and a woman in a big Buick brakes— hard. Laughing with her friends in their backyard we brake for rats. The Heaven Hill is out of hand. She brakes hard, just like a woman. The totem pole—eagle on high—shadows them. Inside a turtle shell is sweetgrass. Indians inside cities raising corn. Totems. They turn to her, serious. Has she made the right decision? She stokes the sweetgrass, traces the quadrants of the turtle shell. Yes. I think so. The center fell out.

You're not running are you? No. I don't think so. Sure?

Desert. In the distance a cluster of trailers. Wires crossing like spiders' webs. Smoke rises from thin pipes. Pick-ups. Children. Laundry supported on a slender thread. Everything slender, small, minute, at this distance.

Nothing in the Rand-McNally. A cluster of people against red monuments, landscape laced with barbed wire. Dust cloud raised in the foreground as a roadrunner speeds by.

Labor Day Parade. Union floats. Reagan in an outhouse at the back of a UAW flatbed. A woman asks for a cigarette. "Got a light too, sugar?" A dime? A dollar? A house? A home, honey?

"You got a place to put your head?"

"Yes."

"You got kids?"

"No."

"God bless, sister."

River Rouge. Black Madonna. GOSPEL CHICKEN—OUR BIRD IS THE WORD! boarded up.

FREEDOM ROAD USED CARS: WE TOTE THE NOTE—rusts.

Mississippi. A plain green sign announces the King of the Waters. The Mici Sibi of the Chippewa. The final resting place of DeSoto. The river nobody wanted to be sold down. As wide as the Styx.

This is a country of waters and no water.

Glorious, ordinary the river runs.

Platte. Republican. Ohio. Little Blue. Des Moines.

In a backwater town of grain elevators and railway lines, roundhouses and old hotels, three women run a lunchroom. The wall behind the register is hung with their families. Beyond the lunchroom, the town, fields are a deep gold, pumps bow and rise, rhythm breaking the still of the landscape, in the distance a windbreak shelters a house.

She remembers from a history book in the eighth grade the photograph of a family, posed outside their sod house, amongst their valuables, chattel—Singer, piano, settee—brought into the light. *Moses Speese Family, Custer County, 1888.* That plain identification, with this opinion: *not all Negroes were downtrodden.*

FDR smiles from a wall in a lunchroom.

In the converted bank in Red Cloud hangs a letter from Langston Hughes to Willa Cather. Upstairs a diorama illustrates the Professor's room. Ántonia's cup and saucer are found behind glass. A few streets away is the perfect small white house. A small white house with an attic room where a girl plotted and planned to get away.

1961. Small apartment over a drugstore. World map over her bed. Jam jar with babysitting geld. Lying there in the heat of a summer night, regarding France, her goal back then, the woman above them playing over and over, "I always knew I'd find someone like you, so welcome to my little corner of the world." Husband shouting to shut the goddamned phonograph off. The woman chanting. "Hit me, hit me, go ahead and hit me." Quiet then.

Farmland turns high plains.

A stone is fixed to the ground. ON THIS SPOT CRAZY HORSE OGALLALA CHIEF WAS KILLED SEPT 5, 1877.

This one will stand for the others.

She sends a postcard of the market to her brother.

> Dear Bill,
> I'm okay. Thought you'd like (stupid word) to have this. Visited Cather's house and museum in Red Cloud. Lots of stuff. But no red carnation. Was it a *red* carnation?
>
> Love, Jess

Salt Lake. A city set in yellow. In the tabernacle, imposing, a family, intact, divine, walks on air.

At a gas station a man throws her change at her and calls her a wetback. What tipped him off? Her speech is plain. Her skin has a tinge but could deceive the untutored eye. Her hair curls at the edges. But permanents are "in." Perhaps not in Salt Lake. She almost laughs but realizes the danger. She revs the Mustang and lets the silver rattle on the floor.

She fought the desire to call out *Adios!* Spanish is her third language.

A tired waitress in an all-night diner serves her eggs and coffee, her skin sallow from the atmosphere. "You're not from around here, are you?"

"No."

The great white lake lies on either side of her. Black highway a thin ribbon between water and salt. Light refracting color here and there.

She turns on the tape deck and Bob Marley sings about loss and future and past and, no, woman, no cry. And she does. Her tears run salt into her mouth.

She crosses into Nevada. Stops at a restaurant on a bright Sunday morning and feeds a machine until she feels refreshed. An old man with a cup of quarters wedged in his belt feeds the one beside her. As she turns to leave, a woman in a cowboy hat, wild bird feather garnishing its rim, storms in, pushing the old man from his spinning cherries, bells, oranges. "Jesus Christ! A person can't even go get something to eat!"

"Don't mind her," the old man says, "she's just protecting her investment."

In her silver Motown prairie schooner, packed with books and all else she owns, she is driving west. She crosses into California at the Donner Pass, observes the monument to the pioneer spirit, and heads down the Sierra to the Pacific.

"My last stop before here was Reno."

"When you passed through Nebraska, did you drive through Omaha?"

"Yes. Is that where you're from?"

"No. I'm native Californian. From Bakersfield. But I was in Omaha once. In and out."

"Oh."

"Did you visit Boys' Town when you passed through?"

The old woman asks this matter-of-factly, as if an orphanage was one of the top ten tourist attractions. Right beside Disneyland, Mount Rushmore, Wounded Knee.

"No."

"That's too bad. It's a wonderful place. At least it was when I was there. Nineteen thirty-five. Of course, everything changes. That Father Flanagan was a saint. But you're probably too young to remember him."

The younger woman nods politely. She sees only Spencer Tracy, in black and white, on a nineteen-inch screen, getting tough with Mickey Rooney.

"I took a boy there once."

The old woman declares this quietly, dropping her voice, moving closer, at once transforming the dialogue.

The younger woman is startled. Brother? Cousin? Nephew? Son? Who? She doesn't dare ask. She thinks she has met an ancient mariner, one who walks the coast, telling.

"Really?"

"Yes. Really. Like I said, it was nineteen thirty-five. The depth of the Depression. Just took him and drove from Bakersfield to Omaha. Almost nonstop. Didn't take that long, you know. Most of the traffic was going in the other direction." She smiles.

The child slept in the back for most of the journey. Covered with a plaid blanket. He twitched in his sleep, whimpered now and then. The desert. Her black car eating up the rays. The child remained wrapped in the blanket, suffering from a coldness, seeming not to notice the heat, light, LAST CHANCE FOR GAS BEFORE wherever. She was washed in sweat.

She sang to pass the time, to keep them—herself—company. The desert past, they cross the Sierra. Oh, mine eyes have seen the glory of the coming of the Lord / He is trampling out the vintage where the grapes of wrath are stored. It is written in her will that they will sing it at her graveside.

She tried to get the boy to join her, but he hadn't the heart to sing. Else he didn't know the words, but she did try to teach him. The boy was too shy, frightened, to ask for food, for a drink of water, to use the bathroom. So she stopped when she thought it might be necessary and that seemed to work. It was a spinster's best solution—what did she know about children?

She stopped the car for a rest. Poured a canvas bag of water into the desperate radiator. Sitting on the running board while the car drank, sitting there they watched the people from the Dust Bowl pass them by. Each traveling band had a song. California, here I come.

People sang back then. Sang themselves through all kinds of things.

"Just you and the boy?"

"Yes." Yes, me and the boy and I didn't even know his name. Finally got it out of him in Colorado. He didn't know the year of his birth, so I made one up.

"Yes. Just the two of us. We were in a big hurry, you see, so they picked me. I had the most reliable car, for one thing. And there wasn't any reason for anyone else to come along."

"Who was 'they'?"

"A group of women from my church. Baptist. Anyway, my car was pretty good, four new tires, and I was unattached and could get away at a moment's notice, and there wasn't anyone to miss me. Being a single woman and all. I just put a sign on the door. Closed due to illness. I ran a small grocery store. Inherited it from my father. The kind of place you hardly ever see nowadays."

"What happened?"

"Well, we got to Omaha and I turned the boy over to Father Flanagan."

"I mean what happened before? Why? Why did you have to take him there? Didn't anyone want him?"

She, the child-immigrant, knows intimately the removal of children. She takes the boy's part, her suspicion drenched in assumption. "Didn't you want him?"

"Wasn't mine to want, dear. Listen, it's a long story, but I've come this far. And this line is moving awfully slow—and not much at the end of it." She smiled again and the younger woman couldn't help but join her.

"He was ten years old about. He lived with his mother and father on a small ranch at the edge of town—they were tenants, not owners—poor people. Once, when one of the church women visited the ranch with a basket for the family—which is what we need to be doing now, especially with Thanksgiving just around the corner; you can't just do it holiday time, though. Well, anyway, this was in the summer, and the church woman called on the family. She noticed, couldn't help *but* notice, that the woman who answered the door, the boy's mother, was bruised, all purple and yellow, on her face, hands, neck—everywhere not covered by her clothes. So the visitor gave the woman the basket and asked her who had beaten her—not right out, mind you, but as clear as she could make the question. And of course the woman said no one. What else could she say? The visitor told the woman that if things got so bad she couldn't stand it, she should call the minister's wife and talk to her and the minister would come and talk to the woman's husband.

"Well, they woman explained to the visitor that they had no telephone, but the visitor persisted, so the woman said, okay, if things got too bad she'd call from the pay phone at the filling station down the road. I don't think she ever intended to call on her own account. I mean, getting a minister, a stranger . . . it wasn't the brightest suggestion . . . probably would have only made things worse for her . . . anyway, the visitor left and the woman nodded and thanked her for the basket and that was that.

"Then one night the minister's wife took a call, and the voice at the other end was expressing itself in these fierce whispers. The voice was very upset, but the woman was taking care not to be overheard. Finally, the minister's wife put two and two together; she called me and I called a couple of other women – we were the ladies' auxiliary of the church, you see. Well, we got in my car and went out to the ranch."

She paused for breath and looked around, but no one else was listening.

Her voice slowed, each syllable carefully pronounced. "It was the damnedest sight I ever saw, or ever hope to see. Not even as a Red Cross girl, in the war, in New Guinea.

"The ranch house had a dutch door—remember those?—the kind where the top is separate from the bottom?"

The younger woman nodded. Fifties TV. A woman dressed in a frilly apron calls the boys in for brownies.

"Well, the top half was swinging wide open. On the porch, outside the door, was this man, lying on his back, his face just gone. Blowed off. Nothing.

"Inside, you could see this little boy sitting on some steps, holding a shotgun, crying and wiping his nose on his sleeve. His mother was sitting next to him, face as blank as they come. Ugly red line under her chin.

"We decided then and there to get him out of town. I mean, he had his whole life ahead of him. Why should he be punished? It was an easy choice, believe me.

"It was much harder convincing these Baptists that Father Flanagan's place would be the place to take the boy. But *we* were the Baptists, Lord knows what the boy and his people were. Better there than a reform school. I told them about an article I had read in the *Saturday Evening Post* and all about Father Flanagan and him saying 'there is no such thing as a bad boy' and so on, and it was decided. And we didn't even think to call the men in on this, that was for later.

"We packed up and left that very night. We told the mother it was for the boy's own good and she seemed to agree, though she didn't say much. Shock."

"Did *he* say anything?"

"Hardly a word between there and Omaha. Not even when we reached the freedom road—you know, where the Mormons are supposed to have planted sunflowers along the way? I wanted to tell him what I knew, tried too, to tell him it wasn't the Mormons, it was the Indians—his people, you see."

"You didn't say they were Indians."

"Well, I think they were. They never said for sure. But I think it was a safe guess. They looked like it. Even if he wasn't, it was a nice story I told him: how they weren't just flowers, but holding the flower to the ground was something like a potato. Food the Indians planted during the wars on the plains. But I don't know how much got through to him, all wrapped up in the back."

"Couldn't you have found out from his mother where their people were?"

The old woman sighed. "I was trying to do what I thought was best. There wasn't time and, well, the woman wasn't talking. Indians can be difficult, but coming from New York you wouldn't know that."

The younger woman says nothing.

"I tried to tell him that if someone bullies and beats up on people they have to expect what they get—shouldn't expect no better. And he was only trying to come between his mother and another beating—or worse. Are you listening?"

"Pardon?"

"I didn't think so . . . Look, better Boys' Town than some God-forsaken reservation . . . where he would drown in whiskey or die from TB."

"I understand what you are saying. But . . ."

"His mother wouldn't talk. He wouldn't talk—even if he knew who his people were. Even if all the Indians had mailing addresses and I had all the time in the world . . . I don't know. Maybe his mother didn't talk because she thought I was doing what was best for him."

The younger woman withdraws further into silence, waiting now only for the end of the story, the end of the line.

"I don't know how much he understood of what I told him. Most of the time he seemed to be sleeping. Or I could hear him crying. Most of the time I talked—or sang. What a pair, eh?"

She will not relinquish her reminiscence, the flavor of it, the goodness of it. And what did you get out of it? Adventure? Righteousness?

The younger woman thinks she sees the boy clearly. The tracks of children running from the Christian boarding schools, feet frozen in the snow. She's not a historian for nothing.

She asks the inevitable question: "Whatever happened to him?"

"I don't know. I never saw him after I left him at Boys' Town. But the police never found out where he was, either. That was good. I mean, that was the point of the whole journey. A safe place."

"What about . . . ?" The younger woman is caught up again.

"The mother? She wasn't so lucky. She went to prison for life, Manslaughter."

"Didn't she try to get away? I mean why didn't she run?"

"And where would she go? A woman like that—traveling alone?"

"Maybe she was heartbroken."

They reached the voting booths, having traveled the last few yards in silence.

1990

A DRUG CALLED TRADITION

Sherman Alexie

"Goddamn it, Thomas," Junior yelled. "How come your fridge is always fucking empty?"

Thomas walked over to the refrigerator, saw it was empty, and then sat down inside.

"There," Thomas said. "It ain't empty no more."

Everybody in the kitchen laughed their asses off. It was the second-largest party in reservation history and Thomas Builds-the-Fire was the host. He was the host because he was the one buying all the beer. And he was buying all the beer because he had just got a ton of money from Washington Water Power. And he just got a ton of money from Washington Water Power because they had to pay for the lease to have ten power poles running across some land that Thomas had inherited.

When Indians make lots of money from corporations that way, we can all hear our ancestors laughing in the trees. But we never can tell whether they're laughing at the Indians or the whites. I think they're laughing at pretty much everybody.

"Hey, Victor," Junior said. "I hear you got some magic mushrooms."

"No way," I said. "Just Green Giant mushrooms. I'm making salad later."

But I did have this brand new drug and had planned on inviting Junior along. Maybe a couple Indian princesses, too. But only if they were full-blood. Well, maybe if they were at least half-Spokane.

"Listen," I whispered to Junior to keep it secret. "I've got some good stuff, a new drug, but just enough for me and you and maybe a couple others. Keep it under your warbonnet."

"Cool," Junior said. "I've got my new car outside. Let's go."

We ditched the party, decided to save the new drug for ourselves, and jumped into Junior's Camaro. The engine was completely shot but the exterior was good. You see, the car looked mean. Mostly we just parked it in front of the Trading Post and tried to look like horsepowered warriors. Driving it was a whole other matter, though. It belched and farted its way down the road like an old man. That definitely wasn't cool.

"Where do you want to go?" Junior asked.

"Benjamin Lake," I said, and we took off in a cloud of oil and exhaust. We drove down the road a little toward Benjamin Lake when we saw Thomas Builds-the-Fire standing by the side of the road. Junior stopped the car and I leaned out the window.

"Hey, Thomas," I asked. "Shouldn't you be at your own party?"

"You guys know it ain't my party anyway," Thomas said. "I just paid for it."

We laughed. I looked at Junior and he nodded his head.

"Hey," I said. "Jump in with us. We're going out to Benjamin Lake to do this new drug I got. It'll be very fucking Indian. Spiritual shit, you know?"

Thomas climbed in back and was just about ready to tell another one of his goddamn stories when I stopped him.

"Now, listen," I said. "You can only come with us if you don't tell any of your stories until after you've taken the drug."

Thomas thought that over awhile. He nodded his head in the affirmative and we drove on. He looked so happy to be spending the time with us that I gave him the new drug.

"Eat up, Thomas," I said. "The party's on me now."

Thomas downed it and smiled.

"Tell us what you see, Mr. Builds-the-Fire," Junior said.

Thomas looked around the car. Hell, he looked around our world and then poked his head through some hole in the wall into another world. A better world.

"Victor," Thomas said. "I can see you. God, you're beautiful. You've got braids and you're stealing a horse. Wait, no. It's not a horse. It's a cow."

Junior almost wrecked because he laughed so hard.

"Why the fuck would I be stealing a cow?" I asked.

"I'm just giving you shit," Thomas said. "No, really, you're stealing a horse and you're riding by moonlight. Van Gogh should've painted this one, Victor. Van Gogh should've painted you."

*   *   *

It was a cold, cold night. I had crawled through the brush for hours, moved by inches so the Others would not hear me. I wanted one of their ponies. I needed one of their ponies. I needed to be a hero and earn my name.

I crawl close enough to their camp to hear voices, to hear an old man sucking the last bit of meat off a bone. I can see the pony I want. He is black, twenty hands high. I can feel him shiver because he knows that I have come for him in the middle of the night.

Crawling more quickly now, I make my way to the corral, right between the legs of a young boy asleep on his feet. He was supposed to keep watch for men like me. I barely touch his bare leg and he swipes at it, thinking it is a mosquito. If I stood and kissed the young boy full on the mouth, he would only think he was dreaming of the girl who smiled at him earlier in the day.

When I finally come close to the beautiful black pony, I stand up staight and touch his nose, his mane.

I have come for you, I tell the horse, and he moves against me, knows it is true. I mount him and ride silently through the camp, right in front of a blind man who smells us pass by and thinks we are just a pleasant memory. When he finds out the next day who we really were, he will remain haunted and crowded the rest of his life.

I am riding that pony across the open plain, in moonlight that makes everything a shadow.

What's your name? I ask the horse, and he rears back on his hind legs. He pulls air deep into his lungs and rises above the ground.

Flight, he tells me, *my name is Flight.*

"That's what I see," Thomas said. "I see you on that horse."

Junior looked at Thomas in the rearview mirror, looked at me, looked at the road in front of him.

"Victor," Junior said. "Give me some of that stuff."

"But you're driving," I said.

"That'll make it even better," he said, and I had to agree with him.

"Tell us what you see," Thomas said and leaned forward.

"Nothing yet," Junior said.

"Am I still on that horse?" I asked Thomas.

"Oh, yeah."

We came up on the turnoff to Benjamin Lake, and Junior made it into a screaming corner. Just another Indian boy engaged in some rough play.

"Oh, shit," Junior said. "I can see Thomas dancing."

"I don't dance," Thomas said.

"You're dancing and you ain't wearing nothing. You're dancing naked around a fire."

"No, I'm not."

"Shit, you're not. I can see you, you're tall and dark and fucking huge, cousin."

They're all gone, my tribe is gone. Those blankets they gave us, infected with smallpox, have killed us. I'm the last, the very last, and I'm sick, too. So very sick. Hot. My fever burning so hot.

I have to take off my clothes, feel the cold air, splash the water across my bare skin. And dance. I'll dance a Ghost Dance. I'll bring them back. Can you hear the drums? I can hear them, and it's my grandfather and my grandmother singing. Can you hear them?

I dance one step and my sister rises from the ash. I dance another and a buffalo crashes down from the sky onto a log cabin in Nebraska. With every step, an Indian rises. With every other step, a buffalo falls.

I'm growing, too. My blisters heal, my muscles stretch, expand. My tribe dances behind me. At first they are no bigger than children. Then they begin to grow, larger than me, larger than the trees around us. The buffalo come to join us and their hooves shake the earth, knock all the white people from their beds, send their plates crashing to the floor.

We dance in circles growing larger and larger until we are standing on the shore, watching all the ships returning to Europe. All the white hands are waving good-bye and we continue to dance, dance until the ships fall off the horizon, dance until we are so tall and strong that the sun is nearly jealous. *We dance that way.*

"Junior," I yelled. "Slow down, slow down."

Junior had the car spinning in circles, doing donuts across empty fields, coming too close to fences and lonely trees.

"Thomas," Junior yelled. "You're dancing, dancing hard."

I leaned over and slammed on the brakes. Junior jumped out of the car and ran across the field. I turned the car off and followed him. We'd gotten about a mile down the road toward Benjamin Lake when Thomas came driving by.

"Stop the car," I yelled, and Thomas did just that.

"Where were you going?" I asked him.

"I was chasing you and your horse, cousin."

"Jesus, this shit is powerful," I said and swallowed some. Instantly I saw and heard Junior singing. He stood on a stage in a ribbon shirt and blue jeans. With a guitar.

Indians make the best cowboys. I can tell you that. I've been singing at the Plantation since I was ten years old and have always drawn big crowds. All the white folks come to hear my songs, my little pieces of Indian wisdom, although they have to sit in the back of the theater because all the Indians get the best tickets for my shows. It's not racism. The Indians just camp out all night to buy tickets. Even the President of the United States, Mr. Edgar Crazy Horse himself, came to hear me once. I played a song I wrote for his great-grandfather, the famous Lakota warrior who helped us win the war against the whites:

> *Crazy Horse, what have you done?*
> *Crazy Horse, what have you done?*
> *It took four hundred years*
> *and four hundred thousand guns*
> *but the Indians finally won.*
> *Ya-hey, the Indians finally won.*

> *Crazy Horse, are you still singing?*
> *Crazy Horse, are you still singing?*
> *I honor your old songs*
> *and all they keep on bringing*
> *because the Indians keep winning.*
> *Ya-hey, the Indians keep winning.*

Believe me, I'm the best guitar player who ever lived. I can make my guitar sound like a drum. More than that, I can make any drum sound like a guitar. I can take a single hair from the braids of an Indian woman and make it sound like a promise come true. *Like a thousand promises come true.*

"Junior," I asked. "Where'd you learn to sing?"

"I don't know how to sing," he said.

We made our way down the road to Benjamin Lake and stood by the water and laughed softly. Junior sat on the hood of his car, and I danced around them both.

After a little bit, I tired out and sat on the hood of the car with Junior. The drug was beginning to wear off. All I could see in my vision of Junior was his guitar. Junior pulled out a can of warm Diet Pepsi and we passed it back and forth and watched Thomas talking to himself.

"He's telling himself stories," Junior said.

"Well," I said. "Ain't nobody else going to listen."

"Why's he like that?" Junior asked. "Why's he always talking about strange shit? Hell, he don't even need drugs."

"Some people say he got dropped on his head when he was little. Some of the old people think he's magic."

"What do you think?"

"I think he got dropped on his head and I think he's magic."

We laughed, and Thomas looked up from the water, from his stories, and smiled at us.

"Hey," he said. "You two want to hear a story?"

Junior and I looked at each other, looked back at Thomas, and decided that it would be all right. Thomas closed his eyes and told his story.

It is now. Three Indian boys are drinking Diet Pepsi and talking out by Benjamin Lake. They are wearing only loincloths and braids. Although it is the twentieth century and planes are passing overhead, the Indian boys have decided to be real Indians tonight.

They all want to have their vision, to receive their true names, their adult names. That is the problem with Indians these days. They have the same names all their lives. Indians wear their names like a pair of bad shoes.

So they decided to build a fire and breathe in that sweet smoke. They have not eaten for days so they know their visions should arrive soon. Maybe they'll see it in the flames or in the wood. Maybe the smoke will talk in Spokane or English. Maybe the cinders and ash will rise up.

The boys sit by the fire and breathe, their visions arrive. They are all carried away to the past, to the moment before any of them took their first drink of alcohol.

The boy Thomas throws the beer he is offered into the garbage. The boy Junior throws his whiskey through a window. The boy Victor spills his vodka down the drain.

Then the boys sing. They sing and dance and drum. They steal horses. I can see them. *They steal horses.*

*   *   *

"You don't really believe that shit?" I asked Thomas.

"Don't need to believe anything. It just is."

Thomas stood up and walked away. He wouldn't even try to tell us any stories again for a few years. We had never been very good to him, even as boys, but he had always been kind to us. When he stopped even looking at me, I was hurt. How do you explain that?

Before he left for good, though, he turned back to Junior and me and yelled at us. I couldn't really understand what he was saying, but Junior swore he told us not to slow dance with our skeletons.

"What the hell does that mean?" I asked.

"I don't know," Junior said.

There are things you should learn. Your past is a skeleton walking one step behind you, and your future is a skeleton walking one step in front of you. Maybe you don't wear a watch, but your skeletons do, and they always know what time it is. Now, these skeletons are made of memories, dreams, and voices. And they can trap you in the in-between, between touching and becoming. But they're not necessarily evil, unless you let them be.

What you have to do is keep moving, keep moving, keep walking, in step with your skeletons. They ain't ever going to leave you, so you don't have to worry about that. Your past ain't going to fall behind, and your future won't get too far ahead. Sometimes, though, your skeletons will talk to you, tell you to sit down and take a rest, breathe a little. Maybe they'll make you promises, tell you all the things you want to hear.

Sometimes your skeletons will dress up as beautiful Indian women and ask you to slow dance. Sometimes your skeletons will dress up as your best friend and offer you a drink, one more for the road. Sometimes your skeletons will look exactly like your parents and offer you gifts.

But, no matter what they do, keep walking, keep moving. And don't wear a watch. Hell, Indians never need to wear a watch because your skeletons will always remind you about the time. See, it is always now. That's what Indian time is. The past, the future, all of it is wrapped up in the now. That's how it is. *We are trapped in the now.*

Junior and I sat out by Benjamin Lake until dawn. We heard voices now and again, saw lights in the trees. After I saw my grandmother walking across the water toward me, I threw away the rest of my new drug and hid in the backseat of Junior's car.

Later that day we were parked in front of the Trading Post, gossiping and laughing, talking stories when Big Mom walked up to the car. Big Mom was the spiritual leader of the Spokane Tribe. She had so much good medicine I think she may have been the one who created the earth.

"I know what you saw," Big Mom said.

"We didn't see nothing," I said, but we all knew that I was lying.

Big Mom smiled at me, shook her head a little, and handed me a little drum. It looked like it was about a hundred years old, maybe older. It was so small it could fit in the palm of my hand.

"You keep that," she said. "Just in case."

"Just in case of what?" I asked.

"That's my pager. Just give it a tap and I'll be right over," she said and laughed as she walked away.

Now, I'll tell you that I haven't used the thing. In fact, Big Mom died a couple years back and I'm not sure she'd come even if the thing did work. But I keep it really close to me, like Big Mom said, just in case. I guess you could call it the only religion I have, one drum that can fit in my hand, but I think if I played it a little, it might fill up the whole world.

1993

BIOGRAPHICAL NOTES

SHERMAN ALEXIE is a Spokane / Coeur d'Alene Indian. He is the author of numerous books, including *The Toughest Indian in the World*, a national bestseller, and *The Lone Ranger and Tonto Fistfight in Heaven*, which he adapted into a screenplay for the movie *Smoke Signals*.

TONI CADE BAMBARA is the author of the short-story collections *Gorilla, My Love* and *The Sea Birds Are Still Alive*, and the novel *The Salt Eaters*. She died of cancer in 1995 at the age of fifty-six. In her obituary, the *New York Times* called Bambara "a major contributor to the emerging genre of black women's literature."

RICHARD BAUSCH is the author of *Hello to the Cannibals*; *Good Evening Mr. & Mrs. America, and All the Ships at Sea*; *Rebel Powers*; *Violence*; and *The Last Good Time*. He is recipient of the Lila Wallace–Reader's Digest Writer's Award and the Award in Literature from the American Academy of Arts and Letters.

MARITA BONNER was born in 1899 in Boston and became one of the most versatile of early twentieth-century writers. Her book, *Frye Street & Environs*, is a collection of essays, plays, and short stories set in Chicago, where she lived and worked for forty-one years until her death in 1971 from injuries suffered in a fire.

NASH CANDELARIA, a native of New Mexico, is the author of an acclaimed series of historical novels about the Southwest. His novel, *Not by the Sword*, received an American Book Award in 1983. His most recent book is *Uncivil Rights and Other Stories*.

SANDRA CISNEROS was born in Chicago in 1954. She has been the recipient of many awards for her fiction, including the Lannan Literary

Award and the American Book Award, and of fellowships from the National Endowment for the Arts and the MacArthur Foundation. Cisneros is the author of numerous books, including *The House on Mango Street, Woman Hollering Creek,* and *Hairs / Pelitos,* a children's book.

MICHELLE CLIFF is the author of the novels *Abeng* and *No Telephone to Heaven,* and the short story collections *Bodies of Water* and *The Story of a Million Items.*

EDWIDGE DANTICAT was born in Haiti in 1969 and came to the United States when she was twelve years old. She is the author of six books, including *Breath, Eyes, Memory; Krik? Krak!;* and *After the Dance: A Walk Through Carnival in Jacmel, Haiti.* She is also the editor of *The Butterfly's Way: Voices from the Haitian Dyaspora in the United States* and *The Beacon Best of 2000: Great Writing by Women and Men of All Colors and Cultures.*

JUNOT DÍAZ was born in Santo Domingo, Dominican Republic. He is a graduate of Rutgers University and received his Master of Fine Arts degree from Cornell University. Recipient of a Guggenheim Fellowship, he has published fiction in *Story, The New Yorker, The Paris Review, Best American Short Stories 1996,* and elsewhere. His debut collection of short fiction, *Drown,* was a national bestseller.

CHITRA DIVAKARUNI is the author of the bestselling novels *The Mistress of Spices* and *Sister of My Heart,* the prizewinning story collections *Arranged Marriage* and *The Unknown Errors of Our Lives,* and four volumes of poetry. Her work has appeared in *The New Yorker, The Atlantic Monthly, Ms., Zoetrope: All Story, Good Housekeeping, O: The Oprah Magazine,* and the *New York Times.*

LOUISE ERDRICH was born in 1954 in North Dakota, the daughter of an Ojibwa-French mother and a German-American father. She is the author of two books of poetry, a collection of nonfiction, and many novels, including *Love Medicine,* which won the National Book Critics Circle Award and the *Los Angeles Times* Award, and *The Last Report on the Miracles at Little No Horse.*

MEI MEI EVANS is Assistant Professor of English and Director of the Master of Arts degree program at Alaska Pacific University. A published fiction writer and longtime activist, she recently co-edited the anthology *The Environmental Justice Reader: Politics, Poetics, and Pedagogy.*

JEWELLE GOMEZ has published seven books, including three collections of poetry, a book of personal essays, and her black vampire novel, *The Gilda Stories.* A contributor to *Best American Poetry 1996* (Robert Haas, editor), she is the Director of the Cultural Equity Grants Program for the San Francisco Arts Commission.

JESSICA HAGEDORN was born in the Philippines in 1949 and immigrated to the United States when she was thirteen. Her numerous books of poetry and fiction, including the novels *Dogeaters* and *The Gangster of Love,* are largely concerned with Filipino and Filipino American culture. She is editor of the anthology *Charlie Chan Is Dead: An Anthology of Contemporary Asian American Fiction.*

OSCAR HIJUELOS was born of Cuban parentage in New York City in 1951. He is a recipient of the Rome Prize, the Pulitzer Prize, and grants from the National Endowment for the Arts and the Guggenheim Foundation, among others. His novels have been translated into twenty-five languages and include *Our House in the Last World, The Mambo Kings Play Songs of Love,* and *A Simple Habana Melody (From When the World Was Good).*

GISH JEN was born in New York City in 1955 and grew up in Scarsdale, New York. Her work has appeared in *The New Yorker, The Atlantic Monthly,* and *The Best American Short Stories of the Century.* She is the author of two novels, *Typical American* and *Mona in the Promised Land,* and a collection of stories, *Who's Irish?.*

LEROI JONES/AMIRI BARAKA is author of the internationally acclaimed and Obie-winning play, *Dutchman,* as well as numerous works of poetry, nonfiction, and fiction. A Whitney and Guggenheim fellow, he is Professor and Chair of African American Studies at the State University of New York, Stony Brook.

KIM YONG IK was born in Korea in 1920 and came to the United States in 1948. His stories have appeared in numerous periodicals, and he is the author of a collection of stories; three novels, including *Love in Winter*; and two children's books.

THOMAS KING is of Cherokee and Greek descent. His first novel, *Medicine River*, was a finalist for the Commonwealth Writers Prize; his second, *Green Grass, Running Water*, was shortlisted for the Governor General's Award and won the Canadian Authors Award for fiction. He has written two children's books, *A Coyote Columbus Story* and *Coyote Sings to the Moon*. His short story collection, *One Good Story, That One*, is a Canadian bestseller.

MONFOON LEONG was born in San Diego in 1916. He taught at the University of California at Berkeley. He is the author of one collection of stories, *Number One Son*. He was not published until after his death in an automobile accident during a trip to Yugoslavia in 1964.

BERNARD MALAMUD's short stories and novels have earned him an honored place in American letters. His collection of stories, *The Magic Barrel*, received the National Book Award, as did his novel, *The Fixer*, which also won the Pulitzer Prize. He died in 1986.

PAULE MARSHALL was born in Barbados and grew up in Brooklyn, New York. She is the author of two collections of short stories and three novels, including *Brown Girl, Brown Stones* and, most recently, *Daughters*.

NICHOLASA MOHR was born in New York City's El Barrio in 1935, after her parents emigrated from Puerto Rico. She is the author of thirteen books, including *In Nueva York* and *El Bronx Remembered: A Novella and Stories*.

TOSHIO MORI was born in Oakland in 1910. His work has been published in numerous periodicals, and he is the author of two collections of stories, *Yokohama, California* and *The Chauvinist and Other Stories*, and a novel, *Woman from Hiroshima*, During the Second World War, Mori was camp historian at the Topaz relocation center in Utah. He died in 1980.

BRUCE MORROW is the co-editor of *Shade: An Anthology of Fiction by Gay Men of African Descent* and an associate editor of *Callaloo: A Journal of African American, African and African Diaspora Arts and Letters.* His work has appeared in numerous publications, including *The New York Times* and *aRUDE Magazine.* A recipient of the 1995 Frederick Douglass Creative Arts Center Fellowship for Young African-American Fiction Writers, he is Associate Director of Teachers and Writers Collaborative in New York City.

BHARATI MUKHERJEE is the author of five novels, two works of non-fiction, and a collection of short stories, *The Middleman and Other Stories,* which won the 1998 National Book Critics Circle Award.

MIKHAIL NAIMY was born in Lebanon in 1889 and came to the United States in 1911. Many of his stories were published in the untranslated *Kana Ma Kan (Once Upon a Time)* and are inspired by the Syrian community where Naimy lived in New York City. He died in 1988.

TAHIRA NAQVI was born in Pakistan. She is the author of two collections of short stories, *Attar of Roses and Other Stories of Pakistan* and *Dying in a Strange Country,* and the translator of a number of books from Urdu into English.

GREGORY ORFALEA is a descendant of the first documented immigrant Arab family to the United States (1878). He is the author of several books, including *Messengers of the Lost Battalion: The Heroic 551st and the Turning of the Tide at the Battle of the Bulge* and *Before the Flames: A Quest for the History of Arab Americans.* He has taught at several institutions of higher learning, including in a gifted students writing program at Stanford University. Orfalea has published several memoir pieces about growing up in southern California in the *Los Angeles Times Magazine.*

GRACE PALEY is a writer, teacher, feminist, and activist. Long recognized as a master of the short story, she was a finalist for the National Book Award for *Collected Stories.*

AGNES ROSSI is the author of *The Quick,* the 1992 story collection that was named a *New York Times* Notable Book of the Year, and the 1994 novel *Split Skirt.* She was a finalist for *Granta's* Best of Young Novelists Award in 1996.

JEANNE SCHINTO was born in Connecticut and is the author of a novel and a story collection, and the editor of *Show Me a Hero: Great Contemporary Stories about Sports* and *Virtually Now: Stories of Science, Technology, and the Future.*

LESLIE MARMON SILKO was born in New Mexico of Laguana parentage. She is the author of numerous books of fiction, nonfiction, and poetry, including *Ceremony*, a novel, and *The Story Teller*, a collection of short stories.

MICHAEL STEPHENS has published several books of fiction and non-fiction, including a novel, *Season at Coole*, a memoir, *Lost in Seoul*, and a play, *Our Father.*

SUI SIN FAR was born Edith Maud Eaton in Macclesfield, England, in 1865 to a Chinese mother and an English father. She was the first Asian American writer of fiction to be published in the United States. Her collection of stories, *Mrs. Spring Fragrance*, was published in 1912. She died in Montreal in 1914.

ALICE WALKER won the Pulitzer Prize and the American Book Award for her novel *The Color Purple*. Other bestselling novels include *By the Light of My Father's Smile, Possessing the Secret of Joy*, and *The Temple of My Familiar*. She is also the author of two collections of short stories, three collections of essays, six volumes of poetry, and several children's books. Her books have been translated into more than two dozen languages.

DAVID WONG LOUIE is the author of a story collection, *Pangs of Love*, which won the *Los Angeles Times* Book Prize for First Fiction in 1991, and *The Barbarians Are Coming*, a novel. He teaches at the University of California at Los Angeles.

HISAYE YAMAMOTO was born in Redondo Beach, California, in 1921. From 1942 to 1945 she was interned in a relocation camp in Poston, Arizona. She has been publishing stories since 1948. In 1988, a collection of short fiction, *Seventeen Syllables and Other Stories*, was published; in that same year, Yamamoto received the Award for Literature from the Association for Asian American Studies.

Grateful acknowledgment is made to the following authors, publishers, and literary agencies for permission to reprint stories in this collection:

Sherman Alexie: "A Drug Called Tradition," from *The Lone Ranger and Tonto Fistfight in Heaven* by Sherman Alexie. Copyright © 1993 by Sherman Alexie. Reprinted by permission of Grove/Atlantic, Inc.

Toni Cade Bambara: "The Lesson," copyright © 1972 by Toni Cade Bambara, from *Gorilla, My Love* by Toni Cade Bambara. Reprinted by permission of Random House, Inc.

Richard Bausch: "Old West," from *The Fireman's Wife and Other Stories* by Richard Bausch. Copyright © 1990 by Richard Bausch. Reprinted by permission of Harriet Wasserman Literary Agency, Inc.

Marita Bonner: "The Whipping," from *Frye Street & Environs: The Collected Works of Marita Bonner*, edited by Joyce Flynn and Joyce Stricklin. Copyright © 1987 by Joyce Flynn and Joyce Stricklin. Reprinted by permission of Beacon Press, Boston.

Nash Candelaria: "El Patrón," from *The Day the Cisco Kid Shot John Wayne*. Copyright © 1988. Reprinted by permission of Bilingual Press/Editorial Bilingüe.

Sandra Cisneros: "Barbie-Q," copyright © 1991 by Sandra Cisneros, from *Woman Hollering Creek* (Random House, New York, 1991). Reprinted by permission of Susan Bergholz Literary Services.

Michelle Cliff: "Election Day, 1984" is from the collection of short stories, *Bodies of Water* by Michelle Cliff, published by Dutton/Penguin. Copyright © 1990. Reprinted by permission of the Faith Childs Literary Agency, Inc.

Edwidge Danticat: "Children of the Sea," from *Krik? Krak!* by Edwidge Danticat. Copyright © 1995. Reprinted by permission of Soho Press (New York).

Junot Díaz: "How to Date a Browngirl, Blackgirl, Whitegirl, or Halfie," from *Drown* by Junot Díaz, copyright © 1996 by Junot Díaz. Reprinted by permission of Riverhead Books, a division of Penguin Putnam, Inc.

Chitra Divakaruni: "Silver Pavements, Golden Roofs," from *Arranged Marriage* by Chitra Divakaruni, copyright © 1995 by Chitra Divakaruni. Reprinted by permission of Doubleday, a division of Random House, Inc.